The sword speaks...

The Gairden C

Book One

DAVID L. CRADDOCK

Heritage

TYCHE BOOKS LTD.

The Swan speaks...

David L. Craddock

Heritage

Heritage: Book 1 of the Gairden Chronicles

Published by Tyche Books Ltd.
www.TycheBooks.com

First Tyche Books Ltd Edition 2014

Print ISBN: 978-1-928025-01-6
Ebook ISBN: 978-1-928025-04-7

Cover Art by Lili Ibrahim
Cover Layout by Lucia Starkey
Interior Layout by Skyla Dawn Cameron
Editorial by M. L. D. Curelas

Table of Contents

For Margaret Curelas, editor and friend.

For Mom and Dad.

Last but never least, for Amie Christine.

Chapter 1

The Great Day

AIDAN GAIRDEN OPENED HIS eyes to see the first rays of the Lady's light creeping through the thick layer of frost over his bay window. He rolled over and nuzzled his pillow, granting himself a royal decree to spend the day burrowed beneath his blankets. His eyelids grew heavy. Just before they closed he caught a glimpse of the day's outfit laid out for him on the table across the room. His eyes snapped open.

No royal decree could save him. Today was the great day.

Aidan groaned and threw his bedding over his head. *The great day*, he thought with more than a hint of sourness. That was what his mother and everyone else in Sunfall called it, and in the most aggravatingly cheery tones. As if reciting it in tones as sweet as birdsong would make him believe it.

A knock sounded at his door. Aidan peeked out from his covers. Maybe whoever it was—his mother, probably—would take pity on him and let him sleep a few minutes longer. Then the door opened and a troop of attendants bustled in.

"Happy sixteenth birthday, Prince Aidan," they said in perfect unison. Aidan gave one last groan that rivaled the most enthusiastic of his mother's *great days*. Then they swarmed him, yanking off his bedcovers and hoisting him to his feet. He gasped, shocked at the cold of the stone floor. The attendants gave him no time to recover. One propped his arms out to either side while another slipped on the white shirt his mother had set out and began doing up the buttons. Others smoothed out wrinkles and straightened his collar.

"I still—" Aidan began, but cut off with a yelp when their pack leader, a bald man of medium height, stood on tiptoe and ran a comb through his curly brown hair.

"Need to trim that," he muttered, combing none too gently.

Aidan shook free and flapped his hands at the lot of them. "I still know how to dress myself!"

"Still?" one of the women murmured. Two of the other girls broke into a fit of giggling.

Aidan glowered. "That will be all."

"Very well, Prince Aidan," the bald man—Gilton; that was his name—said, bowing low. "When can we tell your mother you'll be ready? Ten minutes? Perhaps five?"

"Fifteen. Perhaps twenty."

Aidan waited until they left, then finished buttoning his shirt and crossed to the dresser to scrutinize the day's other garments. White pants, white boots, and a cape. A *cape.* He rolled his eyes. At least it was white, too. He could blend in with the snow and sneak away.

He finished dressing and cracked open his door. Sounds of chatter made their way up from the corridor to the left, the one that led into the heart of the palace. Aidan went right. His footsteps echoed through Sunfall's empty corridors, galleries, and parlors. Gray light lit the tall, frosted windows that ran the length of each corridor as he wound his way along. He drank in the quiet. It was likely the last stretch of solitude he would ever enjoy.

Aidan rounded one last turn and saw Helda, his mother's head cook, standing in the doorway to the kitchen, hands on her hips and a wooden spoon tapping against a leg as thick as a ham. Filling the doorway was more like it. Helda always said that one didn't become head cook in the royal kitchens by skipping meals.

"Up with the Lady, I see," Helda boomed, spotting him. "Never thought I'd see the day."

Before Aidan could reply she put hands as large as dinner plates on his shoulders and steered him into the kitchen. All around him, cooks clattered pots and pans, stoked roaring fires, and carried trays containing freshly baked bread, steaming platters of meat, and desserts. Aidan absently reached for a cookie. Helda rapped his fingers with her spoon just as absently and steered him on. She planted him at a small table in the corner where a jug of juice and a plate of poached eggs, fried potatoes, and three strips of bacon crispy as a twig sat waiting.

Aidan brightened. Helda never forgot his favorite meal and had made it every year on his birthday. He used one of his bacon strips as a shovel to break ground in his yolk, spilling golden goop over the pile of potatoes. Feeling quite like an artist, he dipped his bacon into the egg and painted streaks over his potatoes while Helda fussed at his hair and straightened his collar.

"Your mother says to swallow without chewing and make your way to the south gate," Helda said, stepping back to admire her handiwork.

Grumbling, Aidan began shoveling his last meal down his gullet.

Her fists returned to her hips as she came around to face him. Aidan wondered if she had been born that way.

"Won't you be needing a coat? You'll catch your death out there. Wouldn't want your guests to remember the great day *that* way, would you?"

Aidan chewed on the idea while his mouth chewed on a greasy strip of bacon. Dropping dead from the sniffles wasn't exactly a demise worthy of the heroes from the stories, but it would be memorable.

"You'll fetch a coat, then?"

He shook his head and waved a stick of bacon in an elaborate gesture.

Helda harrumphed. "No coat warmer than the Lady's light, I guess."

Aidan munched leisurely until Helda began tapping her foot. He took the hint, slurping up the last of his eggs and chasing them with swigs of juice.

"Your mother says to use the east path down to the city," Helda called after him as he hustled to the door. "People are already gathering in the south courtyard. Tyrnen will meet you outside in... Well, at this rate, he's probably there *now.*"

Aidan turned on his heel and slipped down a side hallway that deposited him in the east hall. Tall arched windows frosted over with ice ran down either wall, stamping the floor with light. Below each one, Wardsmen in white mail stood straight and still, backs against the wall and a spear standing point-up in one hand. They moved their eyes, caught sight of the prince, and relaxed, breaking their statue-like postures.

"Are you ready, Prince Aidan?" one called. His name was Thomas, Aidan recalled. He was only a few years older than the prince.

Aidan pasted on a grin. "Do I have a choice?"

The Wardsmen shared nods of understanding. They knew what it was to lead lives of duty. The two stationed at the door that opened onto the courtyard gripped either handle. "Leaving this way?" one asked. Through them, Aidan could hear muffled laughter and shouts. Flutters in his stomach churned his breakfast like a plunger churned butter.

It's happening. This is really happening.

"I'm to take the east trail," Aidan said, stretching his grin as far as it could go and gesturing at the door. "The women are already lined up out that way. Can't have them getting a look too early, now can we?"

The younger Wardsmen crowed and banged the butt of their spears on the floor while the older ones chuckled and shook their heads.

Aidan headed down another side passage and entered the east courtyard. Walking paths and stone benches hibernated beneath a blanket of white; a curtain of snow as thick as fog stitched new layers over top it. Over the icy walls, the babble of the gathered assemblage doubled in volume. This time Aidan ignored it. The cold was a bigger concern. Forcing himself to relax, he let a sliver of daylight flow into his skin while he whispered a prayer to the Lady of Dawn, spoken in the Language of Light, from between chattering teeth.

Kindling, men called the process. Men who wrote stuffy textbooks that were even older than Tyrnen. Aidan preferred to think of it as *playing with fire*, but his grumpy old teacher discouraged the term. As his lips closed over the last word of the prayer, warmth settled over him like Darinian fur. He crossed the courtyard to the wrought iron gate at the far end. Snow peeled away and ice melted to watery trails as he went.

He took his time picking his way down the twisty, rocky path from Sunfall's mountaintop perch to Calewind's backstreets. The tumult rose with every step. People had gathered in the city, too; he could see them below, a shifting mass of heads, furs, ribbons, and banners flapping in the wind. His feet grew heavier. He had to drag himself up to the gate that opened into the city. The four Wardsmen standing guard clapped him on the shoulder in greeting. Two of them broke away and walked him along the predetermined route through empty side streets. Bodies clogged the alleyways that fed into Calewind's main thoroughfare. Wardsmen stood at each opening like dams built from steel and flesh.

At last he reached the south wall and banged his fist on the door to the guard tower. The door opened and a Wardsman waved him in. Another hurried to unlock the far door while the others crowded around Aidan, talking idly of the turnout for the *great day* and holding up their hands to him as if he were a hearth. Then the door swung open, the Wardsmen wished him luck, he stepped out, and the door clicked shut behind him.

The heat bubble surrounding him cut a path through the ankle-deep snow as he walked a mile outside the city, toward the white expanse of rolling hills and skeletal woods. All at once a great roar rose up from Calewind's four walls. Aidan paced back and forth, now quite positive his heart would break free from his chest at any moment and go tearing across the hills.

Aidan would have watched its flight with the utmost envy.

Unbidden, his gaze rose up from Calewind's high walls to where Sunfall sat on the lowest peak of the Ihlkin range. From here, the palace was a gleaming mass of spires, arched bridges, and stained-glass windows.

He resumed pacing. He didn't *have* to go back. A few prayers, a little light, and he could be on Leaston's sandy coasts, or hiking along one of Darinia's mountain ranges. He would come back to visit, of course. His mother and father would miss him dearly. He would explain his reasons to them later. Right now he needed to get moving. If he left now, he—

Aidan felt his skin grow warm. He looked around, alert. Someone had kindled, or was in the process of kindling. A wave of snow slapped against his cape and pants. Aidan spun—and immediately felt his shoulders loosen. Moments ago, the north had been an unbroken quilt of white. Now an old man in fine blue robes and a long, white beard stood behind him. Together, they gazed out at Calewind's high walls.

"You can't run, you know," the old man said pleasantly, coming up beside the prince. Aidan's skin warmed as the old man kindled again. Heat radiated from him, drying the patches of snow clinging to his clothes and the braids dangling from his long white beard and peeling a hole in the snowy quilt beneath his feet.

"Do you read minds, too, Tyrnen?" Aidan said. His heat bubble had already dried the patches of wetness on his back and legs that Tyrnen's sudden appearance had kicked up.

Tyrnen's bushy brow rose. "I've spent the last thirteen years watching you stare daydreaming out of windows. I don't need to read your mind to know what you're thinking." He paused. "Although I do dabble in telepathy from time to time."

Curious, Aidan forgot all about the terrible fate about to be thrust upon him. "Could you teach me?"

"It involves reading. You wouldn't be interested."

"What a hurtful thing to say," Aidan said, pouting. "You're my oldest friend, Tyrnen."

"Really?" Tyrnen said, sounding touched.

"Yes. You are *so* old."

The old man scowled and opened his mouth to deliver a scathing riposte. Another cheer rose up from Calewind. Aidan's anxiousness came flooding back.

"Is it time?" he asked.

Tyrnen consulted the Lady's position, squinting up through the falling snow. "Hard to say with all this cloud cover." He eyed Aidan. "I suspect we can wait a few minutes longer."

Aidan shifted his weight from foot to foot, fidgeting with his cape.

"Stop fussing," Tyrnen said.

Aidan sighed and let his arms dangle. *No one can tell me to stop fussing once I'm on that rock of a chair. Why can't we just get this over with? I—* He noticed Tyrnen picking at his robes and muttering a string of curses under his breath.

"Stop fussing," Aidan said, and laughed when Tyrnen glared at him.

The old man flailed around before gathering his composure with an effort and folding his arms behind him. "I'm practically swimming in this... this *tarp* your mother asked me to wear."

Aidan's laughter caught in his throat at the sound of bells clanging from inside the city. The cheers amplified, swelling over the walls. Calewind's southern gate split down the center; both halves swung slowly inward, revealing roads bordered by throngs of onlookers.

Tyrnen placed a gnarled hand on Aidan's shoulder. "Let's get this over with. Then, after things quiet down, we'll see about your first telepathy lesson. How would that be?"

Aidan felt some of his tension trickle away like the snow at his feet. "Really? Tonight?"

"I was thinking tomorrow morning, but, yes, all right. If you don't mind keeping an old man up far past his bedtime."

"I don't. Why am I only hearing about this now?"

"It's not a skill I use often, although I've been known to pluck out a thought from time to time," Tyrnen said airily. "Not from your head, of course." He smiled and gave Aidan's shoulder a squeeze. "Are you ready, boy?"

"Of course," Aidan lied.

Tyrnen took a step forward, then sighed. "I had almost forgotten. The fountain in the square, correct?"

Aidan broke into a sly smile. He *had* forgotten about his plan for this part of the ceremony: a harmless little display he had concocted all on his own.

"Correct. Race you there?"

"Very well," Tyrnen said. "On your mark."

"One, two, thr—"

Tyrnen kindled and vanished, kicking up another flurry of snow.

"Cheater," Aidan muttered. Then he let his body relax, opening himself to the Lady's light. Not that there was much for the taking. A few faint rays seeped through the gray clouds overhead. The paltry warmth bled through his skin like water soaking through a sponge. As quickly as he'd opened himself up, Aidan closed himself off, no longer a sponge but a rock that rejected water that lapped against it.

The scant amount of heat he'd drawn ran through him like hot cider racing down his throat to warm his belly. For almost any other Touched, shifting was much more complex than forming a heat bubble. Aidan had only taken in a dewdrop's worth of heat, but he had never needed much. He pictured the ornate fountain in the center of the Calewind, directing his will at it. Then he closed his eyes, spoke a prayer to the Lady of Dawn in the Language of Light, and the dewdrop propelled him forward.

The shifting was over and done in an instant. One moment he was a mile outside Calewind. The next, the roar of shouts and cheers crashed into him, as if he'd been listening to a conversation from outside a closed door that had been thrown open. He stepped down from the fountain's rim, gawking. People were everywhere; leaning from windows, packed into alleyways, pointing down at him from rooftops. Wardsmen, red-faced from the effort of holding back the tides that surged forward at the sight of him.

He looked around the fountain and saw Tyrnen moving toward him, wincing against the deafening roar. Cringing himself, he kindled again, feeling the Lady's light warm him as his prayer was swept away in the commotion. A soft touch like fingers in silk gloves settled into his ears. All at once the whistles, shouts, and screams cut off, leaving him in blissful silence. The people still strained for him, their mouths opening and closing without sound.

Now that he could actually form a thought, Aidan studied the crowd. Hundreds—no, it had to be thousands—had journeyed from all across Crotaria's three realms to see him. They deserved a fitting way to remember the day they had traveled an absurd number of miles to see a man wave around a sword and sit in a big chair.

With a flourish Aidan threw back his cape and began his long march up the center road toward Sunfall. Occasionally he pointed at mounds of snow, kindled, and prayed in the Language. The snow rose upward in a dazzling coil that sprayed out in every direction, and the crowds lining the street burst into applause and cries of delight.

Aidan's skin warmed again. Suddenly a torrent of snow arced over his head and froze in place, glittering like a rainbow caught in ice. Up ahead, snow on either side of the road leaped high into the air and collided, freezing to form another arch. Another arch appeared, and then another and another, crowning the road with ribs of ice. Aidan looked over at Tyrnen to see the old man's eyes sparkling as his lips and fingers waggled.

The prince broke out in a grin, his first genuine smile of the day. *A challenge, old man?*

Aidan drew in more light and directed it all across the snow shoveled to either side of the street. Clumps of snow spun together to form miniature snowmen who scrambled up Tyrnen's arches and capered about, spinning and bowing and leaping and tumbling. He turned to Tyrnen and gave him a bored look.

"Showoff," Tyrnen mouthed, then flicked a hand. The ribs popped one by one, raining flecks of ice over the onlookers. Aidan's snowmen fared less well. With their platforms destroyed they twirled through the air magnificently—he wouldn't let Tyrnen have the last word—until they plopped to the street, splattering to piles of slush.

As if on cue, Aidan and Tyrnen turned to opposite sides of the road and bowed. Aidan couldn't hear them, but the renewed enthusiasm of the crowd as they surged against the lines of Wardsmen and strained to touch him made him smile.

Word of the duo's antics appeared to have spread to the throngs bordering the shallow mountain trail leading up to Sunfall. At every turn, people watched with pleading eyes and waved their hands in gestures that only the magically un-gifted believed had anything to do with conjuring up the fantastic. Aidan obliged them, juggling balls of fire that zoomed in and out of tendrils of snow that Tyrnen spun with a finger.

Aidan was in the middle of a particularly deep and graceful bow when he felt a tug on his sleeve. Looking up, he saw Tyrnen pointing. He had been so busy bowing and showboating that he only just realized they had reached the southern courtyard. The doors to Sunfall stood open ahead, revealing a great hall filled with columns and banners. The fun part of *the great day* was over. Grudgingly, his feet suddenly weighing as much as a Darinian blacksmith's anvil—or, indeed, most Darinian blacksmiths—he marched over a scorched patch of stone toward the maw of the palace, opting to meet fate with his head held low.

As he crossed the threshold, one pair of eyes seemed to settle more heavily on Aidan than all the rest. He stopped and turned back, fixing on the wall to one side. A young woman of about his age, dark hair spilling over her shoulders, stood calmly amid the tumult, moving only when others jostled her. She watched him with her almond eyes, and when he finally noticed her, she gave him a lopsided smile. She was Sallnerian, he realized, perhaps the only southerner who had dared make the journey north to witness his ceremony. And she was the most beautiful woman Aidan had ever seen in his life.

He stared, transfixed. She noticed him noticing and smiled, and his heart once again took off at a gallop. Then Tyrnen pulled him inside the palace and the doors boomed closed behind them, cutting the woman off from view.

Chapter 2

Choice and Destiny

AIDAN STARED THROUGH THE doors at the spot where he'd seen the Sallnerian girl until he felt a tap on his shoulder. He turned to see Tyrnen mouthing words and gesturing wildly. With regret, Aidan dissipated the swabs of air in his ears. Sound rushed back in: bustling footsteps, shouting, the creak of armor worn by the Wardsmen ringing the room, and Tyrnen's reproving tone.

"—showing off like that. Honestly, Aidan, you need to learn to act—"

"—my age," Aidan cut in dryly. "You're right. I should act my age. Even better, I should act *your* age. Or was there another Touched in the crowd building bridges from ice?"

Tyrnen snorted. "Thirteen years of lessons, all so you can create dancing snow people."

"You're just upset because you were outdone," Aidan said, adopting an imperious pose. "On this day, the student became the teacher."

"I bow to your superiority in the art of foolishness."

"Ah, don't sell yourself short. You made your master proud."

"And shifting instead of walking? What a flair for the dramatic, and a superfluous use of the Lady's light."

"It was a much more impressive entrance than strolling through the gates," Aidan said. "People came from leagues away to see their beloved Prince Aidan—"

"*Beloved*?"

"—so I gave them something special to remember."

"Special? I've seen you shift across a room to pick up a book."

"I've never done that!"

Tyrnen scratched at his chin. "You're right. What would you do with a book?"

"Actually," Aidan said, his thoughts returning to the woman outside the door. "There was a girl outside the door, just in the courtyard. Do you think she liked the display? She was Sallnerian, but—"

"No good can come of that," Tyrnen said quickly, steering Aidan from the closed doors. "Best to forget about it, especially when you should be focusing on what is to come."

Tyrnen guided Aidan to the doors of the throne room. Aidan's chest tightened. All thoughts of the beautiful Sallnerian fled from his mind. He felt as if his world had suddenly been carved into two separate realms: the one outside the throne room, and the one within, the one that would change everything.

Tyrnen placed a wizened hand on his shoulder. "It won't be so bad, you know," he said, his voice soft. "Or so different."

Aidan laughed nervously. "I'm beginning to think you really can read minds."

The old man squeezed. "Only yours." He winked. "I enjoy light reading now and again."

Before Aidan could retort, the Wardsmen flanking the doors threw them open. A red carpet divided the marble floor. Merchants, tradesmen, sailors, visiting foreigners from the farthest corners of the realms filled the space on either side, peering over shoulders to catch a glimpse of him. Above, galleries wrapped around and around the room all the way to the ceiling. Colorful banners bearing crests and sigils lolled over the lip of each gallery like tongues. Nobles dressed in flowing golden robes looked down at Aidan from on high, weighing him as if he were a fish at market. Great windows between galleries flooded the room with the Lady's light.

Fighting the urge to bolt, Aidan took one last breath and took a step forward. A tug on his sleeve made him look back. Daniel Shirey stood like all the other Wardsmen: straight and tall, spear held parallel to his body, mail freshly polished, eyes boring a hole through the wall across the room. Aidan swallowed a laugh as he noticed the one flaw in Daniel's image of the perfect Wardsman. Red hair spilled out from beneath Daniel's helmet like sloppily bundled hay.

"Good luck," Daniel mouthed. Aidan nodded back. Tyrnen nudged Aidan forward, well aware of the mischief that seemed to spontaneously occur when Daniel and Aidan were together for longer than a few moments.

Men and women bowed low as Aidan passed, like wind flowing over tall grass. Visitors from the western and eastern realms of Darinia and Leaston inclined their heads. At last he mounted the handful of steps that led to a tall throne, lacquered gold and polished to a shine. The Crown of the North, men called it—both the ornate chair and the Gairden who sat upon it. Beside it sat a smaller companion chair where a Gairden's mate, co-ruler of Torel, sat during court.

A bearded man adorned in ceremonial mail only slightly less silvery than his hair stood between the thrones, one hand gripping the hilt of the sword at his waist. Aidan knelt and waited until he felt the man's gauntleted hand touch his shoulder. Then he rose slowly, digging through his memory to remember just how the customs of *the great day* dictated he greet his father.

Edmund Calderon was known by many names. King. General of Torel's Ward. Many, mostly the Wardsmen and the clansmen of Darinia, referred to him as Edmund the Valorous. Twenty-three years ago, Edmund had been a lieutenant in the Ward when a wave of barbarians from across the Great Sea had stormed through the Ihlkin Mountains and cut down General Lotren Kietel in a surprise attack. Edmund had rallied the beleaguered Wardsmen and pushed the invaders back in a series of clashes through the mountain range's peaks and valleys to sweep them from the cliffs and back into the sea. After the war, Charles Gairden, Aidan's grandfather and then Crown of the North, had bestowed the title Valorous on the Ward's new general. In repayment for his aid and bravery, the best smiths in Darinia fashioned him the sword he wore at his waist. Valor was etched into the flat of the blade.

Before Aidan could speak, the king swept him into a warm embrace. The cloud of worry hanging over Aidan's head vanished in a puff. Torel's people could keep Edmund the Valorous. Aidan had Edmund the Father.

"Happy sixteenth birthday," Edmund said, speaking over cheers of "Valorous!" and "Long live the Ward!"

"I am so proud of the man you are, and the man I know you will become," the king continued.

"Thank you, Father," Aidan said.

Edmund held his son out to arm's length and gave him an amused look. "I trust you left the capering snowmen outside, Prince of Mischief?"

Aidan grinned. Edmund had given him the title when he had caught the eight-year-old prince and his newest playmate, Daniel Shirey, whose family had just moved to Torel from the east, sneaking down to Helda's kitchens in the dead of night in search of sweets. Aidan probably would have pulled off the late-night raid if he hadn't managed to stumble into every suit of armor lining the wide and otherwise empty corridors. Prince of Mischief didn't hold the same weight as Edmund the Valorous, but Aidan did his best to live up to the title. Secretly, he vowed it would be one of many.

His stomach gave a lurch as his father came to stand by his side, giving Aidan a view of the throne. He turned away.

"I left a little something for you in your bedchamber," Edmund said, draping an arm across his shoulder and leaning in close to whisper as the assemblage resettled themselves.

Aidan's eyes brightened. "What is it?"

Now it was Edmund's turn to look mischievous. "You'll have to wait and see."

Aidan's mind, enflamed by curiosity, turned over at least a dozen possibilities as Tyrnen approached the thrones. The old man did not fold himself over, but simply inclined his head to Edmund, who returned the gesture.

"For the past thirteen years," the old man said, his voice magically amplified to reach the far corners of the room, "it has been my privilege to instruct Prince Aidan Gairden in the development of his gift." He paused. "A privilege most of the time, and a trial at others."

Waves of soft laughter swept through the room.

"The opportunity to step aside from the onerous responsibilities involved in leadership and personally instruct a Touched is a privilege for any Eternal Flame," Tyrnen continued, his voice serious. "But the opportunity to instruct a Gairden, a duty never before shared by any outside the royal bloodline, is a true honor." Tyrnen raised his hand dramatically then plunged it into a pocket, withdrawing—nothing. Frowning, he fished through a dozen pockets in his blue *tarp* until he at last revealed a gold ring set with a plum-colored stone. The sight of it made Aidan's mouth go dry.

"I am delighted to say that today is the culmination of my efforts," Tyrnen continued, holding the ring high for all to see. An identical ring adorned his right forefinger. Lowering his arm, Tyrnen held the ring out to Aidan.

"As the bearer of the Lady of Dawn's Eternal Flame," he continued, "I hereby grant Aidan Gairden his Cinder Band, an honor earned, not given."

Extending his quivering right hand, Aidan allowed Tyrnen to slip the Cinder Band on to his right forefinger. Aidan eyed it, stunned. Most Touched did not ascend to Cinder rank until the age of thirty, sometimes even older. Tyrnen had always told him he was the most gifted Touched he had ever taught, evidenced by the first sip of light Aidan had taken at the age of three. But to receive such an honor at sixteen...

The longer he gazed at his Cinder Band, the more his chest

swelled with pride and emotion. *Aidan Gairden, Cinder*, he thought in wonderment. He looked up at his master and tried to speak, but could only nod.

"Congratulations," Tyrnen said, his voice thick with emotion. Then he folded his arms behind him and peered at Aidan over his spectacles. "Have you selected a creed?"

"Soldier," Aidan replied automatically. After earning a Cinder Band, many Touched went on to pursue healing, architecture, engineering. Some joined the crew of a Leastonian ship to navigate the seas by following the stars. Others entered the Temple of Dawn to spread the Lady's light across Crotaria. As a Gairden, Aidan's creed, like everything else in his life, was predetermined. If that meant sacrificing himself for the good of Torel or all of Crotaria, so be it. From this day forward, he was a tool, an instrument of the Lady, not a man. Not a person.

"So you have decided, Aidan Gairden," the old man said formally.

No, I *most certainly didn't*, Aidan thought.

Tyrnen inclined his head to the king and prince again and glided to one side of the thrones.

The next phase of the *great-wonderful-splendid day* brightened Aidan's mood considerably. Visitors lined up along the carpet and approached the throne one by one, each bearing a gift. He accepted medallions, jewels, colorful clothing that would have made him feel right at home aboard a Leastonian ship. Then the merchants' guild, the governing body of the eastern realm, presented him *with* a ship—or rather, the deed to a ship.

Aidan assumed no other gift would trump a ship, but Torelian inventors from the Lion's Den university proved him wrong. The inventors, a cadre of older Touched with singed beards, hands, and clothing, knelt and presented Aidan with a necklace fashioned from a clear, glass-like material. One clear cylinder as long as his forefinger dangled from the loop.

"We call it a lamp, Your Highness," one of the inventors said from bended knee. "We just finished it yesterday."

Aidan frowned. "It holds fire?" he asked.

"After a fashion, Your Highness," one of the inventors said, rising. He swallowed as Tyrnen came around the thrones to stand behind Aidan, eyes alight with curiosity. "Think of it as a water skin for the Lady's light, Your Highness," the inventor continued, voice quivering with excitement. "The lamp collects light simply by exposing it to a light source. It holds the light for up to a full day and can be used when needed, even after the Lady has given way to the Lord of Midnight." He shuddered, a reaction echoed by many throughout the room.

"This is amazing," Aidan said, fastening it around his neck. "Thank you!"

"Does a lamp have to take the form of a necklace?" Tyrnen asked, lifting one of the jewels from Aidan's neck and turning it over in his hand.

"Not at all, Eternal Flame," the inventor said, hands clasped. "We wanted something practical for His Highness, but we are working to construct lamps in other forms."

"We should talk more of this," Tyrnen murmured.

"At your convenience, Eternal Flame," the inventor said breathlessly as he and the others bobbed their heads.

The line of gift-givers continued. Aidan's stack of trinkets, treasures, books—he shot Tyrnen a meaningful glare each time he received one of those, making sure to page through each one with a show of great interest—and medallions grew taller. He found his thoughts drifting to the Sallnerian girl—woman, he corrected—he'd seen in the courtyard. He had gazed at her for what felt like minutes, drinking in her fair skin, her long legs, and her eyes, which had been the color of... He frowned, annoyed. Her features had already begun to fade. He didn't know her, didn't even know her name, but he knew she was bold. A Sallnerian had to be to enter Torel, let alone Leaston or Darinia, so casually. Seeing him must have been important indeed. Maybe he could—

"... all the way from the Plains of Dust to bring word of your betrothed," his father was saying. Aidan blinked at him, then followed Edmund's gaze to see a Wardsmen step out from his place in line and bang his spear against the floor.

"Romen of the Wolf, War Chief of Darinia."

He stepped back to admit a mountain of a man, tall even for a Darinian. Romen's fur vest displayed his muscular chest tanned from life spent roaming Darinia's mountains and deserts. Tattoos snaked up his arms and spread over his chest. Some, like the wolf running up his left arm, symbolic of his clan, were easily understood. Others, like the elaborate string of orbs, triangles, and a series of dashes and swirls that coiled around his right bicep, symbolized significant events in the wearer's life, but Aidan could not interpret them. As a clan chief and the war chief of the west, Romen was especially decorated.

A tiny woman dressed in clothing dyed in blue and gold stepped out from the crowd and slipped her arm through the war chief's. Every head on the floor craned up to take in Romen as he escorted his wife to the thrones. Her arms were adorned in gold and silver rings, and the bracelets looped over her slender arms chimed as she glided forward. A handful of clansmen fanned out behind them, each a head shorter than Romen and bearing a different tattoo: one wore a wolf identical to Romen's, while different animals danced among the symbols that branded the other clansmen.

"Welcome back to Sunfall, Cynthia Alston," Edmund said, kissing her hand.

"It has been too long, King Edmund," she said, smiling.

Romen inclined his head to Edmund. Turning, he greeted Aidan in the custom of Darinians, placing a fist to his left breast. "Steel is stronger than flesh," the big man said.

"Blood stronger than steel," Aidan finished, mirroring the salute.

Romen nodded, pleased. "It is good to see you well, Aidan Gairden," he said, speaking the words slowly as if they were a maze for his tongue to navigate.

"And you, war chief," Aidan said. "Your common is excellent."

"My wife is a fine teacher," he said, glowing as he beheld his Leastonian beauty.

"My husband is a quick learner," Cynthia said, and she smiled up at him.

"How fares Darinia?" Edmund asked.

"We are blessed with fast horses, good hunting, and the Lady's warmth," Romen said.

"And Nichel?" Edmund asked, looking at the clansfolk standing behind and around Romen and Cynthia. "My future daughter-in-law accompanied you today, yes?"

Every thought of the Sallnerian woman from earlier flew from Aidan's head.

"She couldn't be here today," Cynthia said, then cast a worried look at her husband.

Romen also frowned. "Our daughter was not well enough to make the journey. I am afraid your wedding vows will have to wait, Aidan Gairden."

"She'll be all right, won't she?" Aidan asked, genuinely concerned. Nichel was only a year younger than he. They had played together during the infrequent visits his mother made to Darinia during Aidan's boyhood. She might be another chain that shackled him to his throne, but she was his friend.

"Her illness came on suddenly," Cynthia said. "She insisted we be here today without her. We will reschedule the wedding."

Romen nodded. "You will see her when the snows melt, Aidan Gairden."

"I look forward to it," Aidan said, feeling relieved. Nichel would recover, and he had more time to adjust to the idea of starting a family of his own. He'd give back every one of his gifts in exchange for more time to adapt. Most of his gifts. A few.

After exchanging farewells and a promise to unite Aidan and Nichel at the first hint of spring, Romen and Cynthia rejoined the crowd. The clansmen melted into the crowd behind them. Several moments passed. Gradually, eyes swiveled toward the closed doors. As if on cue, they swung open to reveal a solitary figure standing in the center of the doorway, a sword sheathed at her side.

Everyone along the aisle fell to one knee as Annalyn Gairden, Crown of the North, sword-bearer, Guardian Light, flowed down the aisle to her family. The light filtering through the icy stained-glass windows played against the jewels weaved through her hair, which shined almost as brightly as the smile she fixed on her family as she glided toward them. Tyrnen nodded to Annalyn when she approached; she nodded back and fixed all her attention on her husband, who was rising from bended knee. Each swam through the other's eyes, seeming to forget the hundreds of people watching. Edmund lowered his head and kissed his wife's curly brown hair, streaked with blonde as if the Lady's tears had ran down it. A few women cooed softly.

Aidan cleared his throat, and his mother turned her smile on him. When she opened her arms, Aidan stooped and embraced her. Leastonian perfumes made her hair smell like fresh peaches. He breathed deep.

"Dancing snowmen, I understand?" Annalyn murmured in Aidan's ear.

He tensed, then loosened as he felt her shaking with laughter.

"They were quite talented," he said. "I'm sorry you missed them."

She laughed softly. "I do hope you can bring them back for an encore."

"They met a terrible fate, but their kin would love to perform for you, I'm sure."

She squeezed him and turned to face the assemblage. "Today, my heart bursts with love and pride. You have come here today, friends, countrymen, and honored guests, to witness my son's Rite of Heritage, our family's passage to adulthood. Before this hour has passed, you will see the new Crown of the North and sword-bearer before you—and more, besides."

Annalyn raised her hands and spread them far apart, and the windows faded to darkness. A golden flush appeared in the center of the ceiling and inched outward like fog, bathing the room in a golden glow. Folding her arms across her chest, Annalyn flung them up and out. As she did, the golden veil ripped away to reveal a blackened ceiling speckled with stars. The assemblage made low sounds of appreciation before lapsing into silence—the Crown's story had begun.

"Eight hundred years ago, Crotaria was divided into four realms of equal power and territory—Darinia in the west, Torel in the north, Leaston in the east, and Sallner in the south. King Dimitri Thalamahn, ruler of Sallner, became discontent with his borders. He yearned to expand, to conquer, and to own. When Dimitri's grown daughter, Princess Anastasia, became smitten with Ambrose Gairden, Crown of the North, it was hoped that a union between the two kingdoms would quell Sallner's desire to expand. But Dimitri and his bride, Luria Elden, did not desire unity. They desired dominance."

The crowd emitted awed gasps as the stars began to shift and contort, taking the shapes of humans, castles, and sprawling battlefields to accompany Annalyn's words.

"Dimitri, known as the Serpent King across the four realms for his malevolence, gathered his army and stormed Leaston, which was unprepared for invasion. The banner of Sallner flew over the ruined realm. Thus began the Serpent War. With the east conquered, Sallner set its sights on Darinia. Janleah, war chief of the west, united the clans and called upon Torel for aid. King Ambrose Gairden allied with the clans and led the north against Sallner. Anastasia, a supremely gifted Touched, defected from Sallner and joined her beloved at the head of his army.

"It soon became known that Dimitri and Luria Thalamahn were more than just ruthless tyrants—they were disciples of Kahltan, the Lord of Midnight. Calling upon dark magic, Luria and Dimitri corrupted their people, guiding Sallnerians down the wide road of evil, greed, and bloodshed. Luria grew more wicked as the war continued, and became known as the Queen of Terror for her depravity, for the blasphemous acts she committed on those she slaughtered. Combing the battlefields, Luria breathed life into the dead and turned them against the living."

Sharp cries and sounds of revulsion sprang up as corpses made of stars rose from the ground, glowing a deep scarlet, and threw themselves against former allies. Aidan watched the spellbound audience. Most stared at the events unfolding above them, enraptured by the history of his family's bloodline. Lifting his eyes to the galleries, he noticed several nobles watching him, measuring. Aidan felt the weight between his shoulders increase. He could almost hear their thoughts: *How will history remember Aidan Gairden?*

Taking a breath, he looked to his right. A gap of at least two feet separated the last line of tables and the wall. Perhaps if he moved quietly, he could sidle to the door. Daniel would surely let him slip out. After that he could—

"... after so much death and destruction, Ambrose wasted no time. He married Anastasia in the southern courtyard of Torel Fortress, and guests from Leaston and Darinia flooded to act as witnesses. As the ceremony drew to a close, legends say the clouds parted and a crone descended from the Lady's light. She had come, she said, on behalf of her goddess to bless the marriage. Each Gairden would produce only a single heir, and the blood of Anastasia and Ambrose would flow through their line, but forked like a river. Along one fork flowed the blood of Anastasia, the most exceptional Touched of her time. Along the other, a finely balanced savagery and skill in combat inherited from Ambrose Gairden, considered by many to be the greatest warrior who ever lived.

"On the battlefield, the Darinians had stood in awe of the strength of Ambrose and Anastasia. They called Ambrose *Ordine'kel*, or the Guardian Blade; Anastasia was *Ordine'cin*, the Guardian Light. As a show of respect toward their allies in the west, the Gairdens named the gift *Ordine*, and their strength of the Guardian would guard Crotaria until the end of time."

Aidan stole a glance at his father. Whether Edmund the Valorous could have equaled or bested the Gairden patriarch was the subject of many boisterous tavern debates. Aidan had spent hours watching his father spar in the training yard, wondering what it would be like to move so gracefully. He would never know. He had inherited *Ordine'cin*, and could wield a sword about as effectively as he could wield a log. That was fine by Aidan. Being born with *Ordine'cin* did not make a Gairden a Cinder the first time they kindled, or make those born with *'kel* equal to Ambrose Gairden the first time they picked up a blade. Aidan had studied hard—most of the time—the same as any Touched outside his bloodline had to do. He fingered the gold loop around his right forefinger, admiring it. He had earned it.

He blinked and redirected his attention to his mother as she concluded the tale.

"The crone bestowed one final gift to Ambrose Gairden:

Heritage, a blade crafted from the Lady of Dawn's light and passed from generation to generation. She departed, and the Darinian builders worked with the Gairdens to rebuild Torel Fortress. They renamed it Sunfall, named in honor of the disciple's appearance. With the Serpent War ended, Ambrose and Anastasia took Heritage into Sallner and carried out the realm's punishment for succumbing to sin."

Overhead, the stars that made up the southern realm of Crotaria winked out, one by one. Abruptly the other lights vanished, leaving the room blanketed in darkness. Nervous muttering broke out. A sharp hiss rang through the room as Annalyn pulled her sword from her sheath and raised it high. Cords of fire shot across the room, lighting torches hanging from either side of each balcony. The windows remained dark, as if looking out on a black, blank sky. No one noticed. All eyes, Aidan's included, were on Heritage.

The double-edged blade was unblemished. Legends said Heritage was made from magically reinforced steel, and could not be chipped, dented, or broken. Engravings of lightning bolts curled down its length. The hilt was wrapped in leather to provide a surer grip. In the center of the guard that joined hilt and blade was the Eye of Heritage, an egg-shaped ruby. At Annalyn's touch, the Eye glowed a warm scarlet.

"There is but one criterion that must be met for a Gairden to become sword-bearer," Annalyn said as she faced Aidan. "Heritage must be willingly accepted. By so doing, it is not only the blade that is accepted, but the responsibility it carries."

Annalyn ran her free hand across Aidan's cheek, then dropped her arm and donned a sober expression as she lowered herself to one knee and held Heritage hilt-first to her only child.

"I extend Heritage to my son, Aidan Gairden. Aidan, do you accept Heritage, knowing that doing so names you Crown of the North and sword-bearer, guardian of the four realms? Do you swear to lay down your life before harm comes to friend or kin, to people or land?"

Aidan looked at his mother. Her smiling face spoke of confidence, pride, and love. He looked at his father. Edmund's left hand gripped the hilt of Valor as he nodded to his son. Then Aidan sought Tyrnen's eyes. The Eternal Flame stood rigid, his hands lost within the many folds of his robe. He gave a small nod.

Aidan took a deep breath and raised his eyes to take in the faces gathered all around him. A baby's cry cut through the room's absolute stillness, followed by a mother's soothing voice as she rocked the child to stillness. The torches above fell into low muttering, and the throne room itself seemed to hold its breath.

This was it. This was what all the people had journeyed hundreds of miles to see. He would take Heritage, hold it over his head. The crowd would cheer, they would all sit down to Helda's feast, and then he could go back to bed, claiming the excitement of *the great day* had caught up with him. All he had to do was hold a sword.

He reached for Heritage.

—Destiny is never a choice, Aidan Gairden, a voice whispered.

A chill swept through him. Looking around, he heard only smothered coughs. He stared at his mother. She was looking at him, smiling, nodding. She must have been the one who had spoken. She was always going on about destiny and making choices.

He took another deep breath, and, with as much confidence as he could muster, he reached out to the sword.

Heritage wrenched from Annalyn's grip and tumbled to the floor. Crimson sparks shot from the Eye, crawling along the floor toward Aidan. He leaped back with a cry. Spitting sparks, the sword convulsed on the floor as the Eye bathed the room in red light.

Heritage gave a final shudder and went still. The Eye went dark, and light flooded through the windows. A nervous muttering broke out as Annalyn lunged forward to scoop up the sword, staring at it with large, intent eyes.

"What happened?" Aidan whispered.

She was silent.

"Mother?" he asked, reaching out to touch her shoulder. She jumped and looked up at him as if just realizing he was there.

"I'm sorry, Aidan," she said. "Heritage does not accept you."

Chapter 3

Under Shadow

CYNTHIA ALSTON THREADED BETWEEN clansmen and horses until she found her husband in Sunfall's stables. Romen of the Wolf, war chief of the west and a man chiseled from stone, looked like a mountain bowed from the wind. He brushed his stallion absently, stroking the same patch of hair over and over. Wolf Runner snorted his displeasure at the lack of attention, but Romen ignored him. His eyes were clouded with worry.

Cynthia placed her hand over his until it came to rest.

"Aidan will be fine," she said to him in the Darinian tongue.

He looked at her but said nothing.

"Are you certain you wish to leave?" she asked, taking the brush from his hands and running it along her mare's fine coat. Narra leaned into Cynthia's strokes, her tail swishing. The horse had been a wedding gift from Annalyn and Edmund and seemed to take as much pleasure in her appearance as Cynthia took in beautifying her.

"Nichel needs us," Romen said, cupping his wife's chin in one rough hand. "And you need to be with her."

"I do," Cynthia admitted. "But you're worried about our friends, as am I."

Romen's hand fell away. He was silent for several moments. "It was as if the sword slapped his hand away. I have never heard of an object able to do such a thing."

"The Gairdens are a mysterious people," she said. "Annalyn can consult her ancestors. Surely they can solve this matter." She hesitated. "Unless you think we should stay?"

Romen turned her words over. "No. What happened is a family matter, and as you say, the Crown of the North will know what to do. And..." He gave her that small, almost sheepish smile he reserved only for her, as soft as the man who wore it was hard. "And I am worried about our daughter. It will do my heart good to see that she has recovered fully."

His smile faded as he looked up at the sky and glared at the clouds as if they were enemies boiling over his mountains. Cynthia followed his gaze and shivered, pulling her cloak tighter around her shoulders. The snowfall had stopped during Aidan's Rite of Heritage, but the Lady bled into the sky. Soon, this half of the world would belong to the Lord of Midnight. Torches lined the path leading out of the stables and down the mountain to the city. Shadows danced over the snow. The world seemed a different place under shadow.

"Are you sure we should leave tonight?" she asked, truly torn. As much as she wanted to see with her own eyes that Nichel was on her feet again, the thought of the Lord of Midnight's gaze on her as they traveled made her skin crawl.

He began to speak, caught her gaze, hesitated. "If you would rather..."

She forced herself to stand straighter and spared a quick glance around. The clansmen were preoccupied with their horses, preparing them for the journey home. That was good. Her husband's clan respected her, but she knew many of them saw her as soft. As the daughter of one of Leaston's wealthiest merchants—and one of the most influential members of the merchants' guild besides—she had grown up swaddled in the most expensive fabrics, not the rough, sand-scoured hides of animals stalked and killed across the sand-swept plateaus and fiery mountains of the west. Draping those fabrics over her body felt like wrapping herself in the softest clouds, a dalliance in decadence her husband encouraged. Unlike so many clan chiefs, he did not want his mate to give up who she was after taking his clan's sign. Still, she wanted to be worthy of him as he was worthy of her.

Besides, Kahltan's shadows held nothing her husband could not swat away. Romen would protect her, protect all of them. They would ride their horses south to the Avivian River and board a ship that would carry them into Darinia. She yearned to feel a deck bobbing under her feet and the sight of water around her, even if it didn't carry the scent of the sea.

More than anything, she yearned for her daughter.

She touched Romen's arm. "Let's go home."

He beamed at her, and the pride on his face warmed her like the Lady's noontime touch. He scooped her up and set her in her saddle. She giggled, unable to help herself. The first time Romen had scooped her into his arms had been immediately following their marriage ceremony. He had made a habit of settling her into her saddle every ride since. It was courteous of him, certainly, but it was also one of their little traditions, an excuse for them to touch during an otherwise innocuous action, and she loved it.

After handing her the reins, Romen climbed onto Wolf Runner, gave the word, and the clansmen set off down the mountain. They rode at a canter down the shallow trail into Calewind and through the city gates. Romen set an easy pace as the night grew darker, trotting over rolling hills and across open plains to avoid crippling the horses in the deep snow. Clansmen fanned out around the war chief and his wife, lanterns dangling from poles. Occasionally they passed cities and villages. The buildings within their walls seemed to huddle together, waiting for the Lady of Dawn to rise. All around her, trees stripped bare of leaves reached for the sky with twisted, frozen limbs.

Cynthia hitched her cloak tighter and resisted the urge to flick Narra's reins. The Leastonians had a saying: *the Lord of Midnight keeps secrets*. A realm filled with traders and seafarers knew all about secrets, but only the Lady of Dawn could reveal those hidden under shadow.

She shook her head, naming herself a fool. Her husband was near, and so she was safe. She guided Narra closer to his mount, and he gave her another smile, this one free of worry.

Snow returned a few hours later. It fell in a thick curtain, forming a hazy screen in the night. Romen slowed the horses to a walk. The wind picked up, throwing icy darts that stung their faces. The clansmen pulled thicker furs from their packs. Narra whickered, head bent against the wind and snow while Cynthia dug in her pack and withdrew a heavier cloak. She almost lost it; the wind snatched at it and howled when she successfully shrugged inside of it. The howls grew louder, drowning out the sound of Narra's hooves crunching through snow.

Cynthia bowed her head, tried to take a breath, gasped when the wind stole it from her. She lifted her cloak over her face, breathing deeply, whispering to herself that the storm would soon pass. And if it didn't, there were high walls all across Torel. Romen would call for them to take shelter. He would build a fire to throw back the shadows and hold her close until the snow died down. Or until the Lady awakened. That sounded even better.

She reached for him, wanting him to take her hand. When she didn't feel his calloused fingers lace through hers, she looked over at him.

He was gone.

Cynthia looked up, back, all around. They were all gone, her husband and the clansmen, swallowed up by the shadows. Panic welled up in her.

"Romen?" she called, but the night swallowed that up, too.

Panting, eyes darting around, she pulled Narra to a stop and twisted around in her saddle. What was she to do? Should she keep moving? Should she stay here? She couldn't stay still. The cold bit through her fur, piercing her like a careless inksmith's needle.

She choked back a sob—then gasped. Forms appeared out of the night, tall and powerfully built. The clansmen. They must be. *Had* to be.

Relief made her sag in her saddle. What a sight she must be to her husband, who faced wild boar and invaders along the spiny ridge of the Ihlkin range without fear. She was unworthy of him—but she didn't care. She was just glad he was back.

As the forms moved in closer, a thought struck her. Where were their horses? Romen would put himself in mortal danger before he let anything happen to Wolf Runner. Then the forms came close enough for her to make them out through the snow, and terror cold as ice enveloped her like the sea crashing over a fishing boat.

They were Wardsmen, or had been once, all snow-white armor that jingled with every step. The men—the things—stalking toward her did not have eyes but empty sockets where eyes had once been. Their heads were skulls, spotted with clumps of hair and rotten skin, teeth clicking and clacking with harsh, guttural laughter.

Cynthia screamed as they descended on her, and then the shadows swallowed her, too.

Chapter 4

Lost

THE BUZZ OF CONVERSATION, the *thunk* of goblets smacking tabletops, and the clatter of forks scraping against plates faded as Aidan strode deeper into Sunfall. The scent of Helda's feast—roast duck, hams, chicken, buttered rolls, pies, and every last vegetable from Torel's and Leaston's crops from the fall—dogged him, triggering rumbles from deep in his belly. He ignored it, just as everyone had chosen to ignore him.

The only Gairden in our long and storied bloodline to be turned away by Heritage, yet we mustn't miss dinner.

His path wound through great halls and narrow passages decorated with expensive rugs and tiled floor carved by Darinia's finest builders until at last he rounded a corner and paused. Night gave the windows dark, blank faces. Bracketed torches hung between each one like sentries, crackling and filling the corridor with warmth and light. The row of torches to his right was broken by a large gap of bare wall. *Heritage* was carved there in broad, ornate letters. Raising his hand to the "H", Aidan caressed it. As he went along from letter to letter, a thin line ran down the center of the stone like a tear leaving a trail. He looped his finger through the final "e" and the stone split in half. The slabs rumbled to either side as he stormed through, then boomed closed after he passed.

Only in Sunfall did a traitorous sword warrant as fine a bedroom as the crown prince's quarters. The sword chamber was wide and circular. Stained-glass windows adorned the walls, each raised a bit higher than the last and spiraling upward. Colors pulsed behind each pane, illuminating the faces of every Crown of the North since Ambrose Gairden and throwing colored squares along the walls and floors. His mother's window gazed down from on high. Above and to one side of her window was a blank space.

Aidan mounted the handful of stairs that ringed a dais in the center of the room. Heritage hung suspended, point down, rotating slowly, its tip dangling just above the blue carpeting that unfurled over the stairs. Dust motes sprinkled down, and the sword coaxed them into its lazy waltz. Aidan glared at the Eye of Heritage. When he'd entered, the ruby had sat dark. Now it flared red, boiling like a storm over a far horizon.

They were watching him now, he knew. All of them. Within the Eye was Sanctuary, a spirit realm where Gairden souls rested for eternity after their bodies expired. From within Sanctuary, the Gairdens of the past guided sword-bearers in a multitude of ways—ways he would have come to understand upon becoming sword-bearer.

The Eye flashed again, continuing to watch him. Just as they had watched earlier when the sword had rejected him. Just as the entire northern kingdom had watched. Propped against the wall behind the sword was a pane of stained-glass depicting Aidan at his Prince-of-Mischief best: wide grin, raised brow, bright eyes. With a wordless cry he shot forward and drove his fist through the window. It shattered gloriously as a spider web of blood broke out across the back of his hand.

Quick footsteps outside the chamber slowed, then paused. A hand slapped the stone in a knock. Breathing through clenched teeth and gripping his bloody hand, Aidan went to the entrance and touched it. The stone slid open to reveal Edmund the Valorous. The king entered and swept his gaze over the room, taking in Aidan's hand, the shards of glass. His face became expressionless as the doors slid closed.

"If smashing windows makes you feel better, by all means, bloody your other hand," Edmund said, waving to the glass visages of Ambrose and Anastasia Gairden.

Ignoring his father, Aidan focused on the blood running down his hand. The crisscrossing cuts weren't deep, but would continue to ooze without healing. Aidan looked around. The Lady, whose bountiful light was like a bottomless well of the clearest water, had set over the horizon hours ago. Man-made heat would do, but the sword chamber contained not even a single candle flame to kindle from. Then he remembered the lamp fastened around his neck. It was half empty and glowed with a soft light.

He kindled just a fraction of the light, wanting to leave a little in case he decided to break something else, and prayed for healing as heat trickled through him. Small pieces of glass popped out of his flesh and clinked to the floor. The abrasions sewed themselves shut, leaving only drying trails of blood as evidence of his temper.

"You see, Father?" he said, flexing his hand. "I still have my uses." He began to pace before the sword. "I might be the only Gairden ever rejected by Heritage, but I can still heal cuts and scrapes. Do you think it's too late to change my creed? I should become a healer. Helda could sure use me in the kitchens. Her cooks are always suffering minor burns and cuts."

"We will get to the bottom of this, son," Edmund said. Aidan continued pacing. Edmund caught his arm. "What happened earlier is not important. You—"

"Not important?" Aidan echoed. "I was humiliated in front of all Crotaria!"

"That is easily—"

"And Romen!" Aidan scrubbed a hand over his eyes. "I'm supposed to marry his daughter. He thought he was getting a king for a son-in-law."

"The clans are our friends, Aidan. They will not think less of—"

"Mother," Aidan whispered. He stared through his father with large, unseeing eyes. "Dawn's ghost, what she must think of me."

"She's on her way. We have something we must discuss with you."

"Trying to decide what to do with your failure of a son?"

Edmund grabbed Aidan's shoulders and shook him. "Enough!"

Aidan gaped.

"You're huffing about like a child sent to bed without dinner. You're sixteen, now. A grown man, if not a sword-bearer. This behavior is unacceptable."

The prince swallowed. His father was right. "What would you have me do?"

"You don't know why Heritage rebuffed you," Edmund said, his tone lighter. "Nor does your mother, but she's working to find out. This is not the end. There might be a way to try again."

"Try again? I didn't want to do any of this in the first place."

"But you did. You tried, and if possible, you will try again."

"Will I?"

"Yes. You will. You will accompany me at the Lady's first light during my inspection of the barracks, just as we planned. You will oversee drills and patrol changes, just as we planned. What you will *not* do is admit defeat. You can't simply give up when you fall off the horse, son. You've got to get back on and try again."

Annoyance and rebellion boiled up in Aidan. Already they were making plans for him, once again without his consent.

"What if I no longer wish to learn military tactics?" he asked. "If I no longer wish for you to teach me, or to learn statecraft from Mother. What then?"

"What else would you do?"

Aidan folded his arms. He knew his anger wasn't rational or fair, but he couldn't help it. "Maybe I'll travel to Ironsail and pick up my ship. Ride the open waters, see the world, probably become a pirate. Do whatever *I* want for a change."

Edmund faced his son in silence.

The chamber door slid open and Annalyn stepped through. "What have we here?" she asked, one hand on the doorway.

"Our sixteen-year-old son," Edmund said, "is in the throes of a tantrum." He spun on his heel and marched from the room. Annalyn stared after him for a long time. Finally she swept toward Aidan.

"Why are you in here?" she asked.

"I didn't want to see anyone."

"Everyone knows where you are, Aidan. Your cursing rang through the halls like bells during Dawn worship."

He felt his face warm. "Hope you ate your fill."

"I see you've smashed a window. That's very productive. Do you care to explain yourself?"

"No."

"Very well. But you will explain what happened between you and your father."

"Father was trying to convince me that everything will be just fine."

"Do you disagree?"

"The sword told me what I knew all along. I'm not worthy of it."

"I don't think that is the message Heritage was trying to send, Aidan."

"Then why was I rejected?"

"I don't know, yet."

He shrugged. "I should be grateful. It saved me quite a bit of inconvenience."

"Oh, stop with the theatrics, Aidan. This is a bit much, even for you."

Shame cut through his anger. "I'm sorry for disappointing you," he said, looking down at the floor.

She walked toward him, wrapping him in a hug. "You have never disappointed me, nor could you ever." The tightness in his body loosened as he sagged against her.

"This is a setback, dear, nothing more," she went on. "We will find out why this has happened, and we will fix it."

"Why do I even *want* to fix it?" he muttered.

Pulling back, she gave him an inquisitive look.

"I did everything I was supposed to. I didn't want the responsibility, but I was prepared to accept it. For you, for our people, for Father, for Tyrnen." He spread his hands. "And yet after all that, after everything I was prepared to sacrifice, *it* rejected *me*."

"I don't understand it either, dear. But we will solve this problem."

"We?"

She nodded. "The two of us, along with your father and Tyrnen."

"What do you have in mind?" he asked.

"Tyrnen has invited us to come away with him for a little while. He has volunteered his office at the Lion's Den, where we can research our little problem and perhaps even solve it, all out of the public eye."

Aidan bit his lip. The Lion's Den was the most prestigious school for Touched in all of Crotaria, and the headquarters of the Eternal Flame. The customary headquarters. Tyrnen visited the Lion's Den often but made his home in a tower on the Sunfall grounds in order to remain close to his pupil—a pupil who had not delivered on the potential the leader of all Touched had seen in him. Aidan had not spoken to Tyrnen since before the ceremony. *The first Touched outside of Gairden blood to help train a Gairden blessed with* Ordine'cin, *and I failed him.*

"What about Grandfather Charles?" he asked. "Or one of our other ancestors? Surely they have some insight."

Annalyn hesitated, glancing behind him at Heritage. The Eye continued to flicker.

"They don't understand it either, I'm afraid."

Aidan felt his chest grow cold.

Annalyn stepped forward to cup his face in her hands. "Come away with us. It will give us some distance. More importantly, it will give our family some time together, and time to figure this out."

"But, who will stay behind to—"

"Your father stomped off to speak with the colonel to see to things here while we're gone, I'm sure."

Aidan nodded, warming to the idea of a retreat. He didn't *want* to take up Heritage, but it was what he had been born to do. He hadn't planned for failure. Misery, yes. But not failure. He felt like a Leastonian merchant at sea without a compass. And the weeks leading up to *the great day* had been stressful, filled with constant reminders of the heavy responsibility he would wear at his hip. Some time away would give him time to clear his head, and maybe, just maybe, come to terms with what fate had in store for him.

"A retreat sounds nice," he said, smiling a little.

"I think so, too," she said, reaching up to smooth his hair. "Now then, I'm going to go confer with Tyrnen. He'll be pleased to hear that you're coming along, and then we'll—"

Aidan's breath caught. "What?"

"I'm sure Tyrnen won't mind that you're coming along. You two are so close, it will give him someone to talk to while your father and I—"

Renewed anger pumped through him. "Tyrnen didn't invite me?"

"Not in so many words, dear, but he won't mind if—"

"I'm not going."

Annalyn sighed. "Of course you're going."

"No. If Tyrnen doesn't want me to come along, then I don't want to spoil his fun."

"What are you talking about?"

"Don't you understand, Mother? I've failed him. That's why he didn't invite me to go in the first place."

"You're talking nonsense, dear."

"His revered pupil, failing to become the sword-bearer." Then, so quickly he didn't have even a second to clamp his mouth shut: "Kahltan take me, I wish I wasn't a Gairden."

She stiffened. The true name of the Lord of Midnight was not spoken lightly, especially not in Sunfall. "You don't mean that."

"I do. And I am not going."

Annalyn's face turned red. "You are behaving like a spoiled child."

"Are you disappointed yet, Mother?"

"I am beginning to be."

There was a long silence.

"You will stay behind, then," his mother said at last, her tone soft. "I will make certain that your father asks Brendon to see to things until our return."

"You don't trust me to see to things while you're away?"

"Not at the moment, no."

"Fine. I've been proven unworthy to do so, anyway."

"Goodbye, Aidan."

He remained quiet until he heard the door close behind her. Then he strode from the sword chamber, marched down the corridor to his bedchamber, threw open the door, and smashed his fist against the top of his dresser, sending his candle into spasms that spit wax on the polished surface. Groaning, Aidan cradled his hand. As he held his fist, candlelight glinted from his Cinder Band. The plum amethyst winked at him. He tore the Band from his finger and hurled it across the room. The ring clanged against something near the door then clicked along the floor. Frowning, Aidan picked up the candle and went to investigate.

Hanging from the wardrobe was a suit of light armor. Alabaster steel gauntlets matched beautiful hauberk. He ran his hand along the left breast, letting his fingers trail along a small, steel patch he knew would be set there. The letters “EC” had been engraved. Edmund Calderon, who had been a Darinian blacksmith’s apprentice before enlisting in Torel’s Ward and rising to the rank of general, had crafted the armor himself. This must be what his father had whispered to him about before the ceremony had begun.

A small piece of parchment was tucked into the opening of the right gauntlet. Aidan withdrew it and held the candlelight up close.

To my son on his most special of days. I am proud of you.

Earlier that very day, the words would have filled him with pride. Now they only made him feel worse. He held the parchment to the candle’s flame and dropped it, smoking, to the floor. It curled inward as the flame fed, reducing it to blackened scraps.

Aidan replaced the candle on the dresser and collapsed on his bed. Anger, confusion, and rejection raged through him, sprouting tears in his eyes. He refused to wipe them away. After a time his eyes began to feel heavy, each blink becoming a struggle.

—It was not your time, Aidan Gairden, a grandmotherly voice whispered in his mind.

“Hmm?” he mumbled, his breathing already beginning to even.

—Sleep now. Your time will come.

Chapter 5

Nichel's Gift

JONATHAN HILLSTREAM, TOUCHED AND adviser to Romen of the Wolf, smiled as his charge appeared in the doorway. "It is good to see you out of bed at last, wolf daughter." His smile wavered. "You look... much better."

Nichel shuffled into the council room of Janleah Keep. One hand ran through her head of dark, wavy hair damp with sweat. The other was splayed across her belly, and her eyes shied away from the Mother's light blazing through the windows.

"How are you feeling?" Jonathan asked, concern creasing his handsome face.

Nichel opened her mouth, snapped it shut, swallowed. "Better," she managed.

"Your attendants will be pleased to hear that," Jonathan said lightly, offering an arm. "They've only recently declared it safe to change their clothing."

"Dinner did not agree with me, it seems," Nichel said.

"Dinner, wolf daughter?" Jonathan guided her to her mother's seat, a chair carved from stone that jutted out of the far wall.

"Yes," Nichel said as she sank into the cushioned seat. Her mother had never quite adapted to the idea of sitting on solid rock. Nichel, too, preferred a bit of padding to support her curved frame, though she never used it when her father was around. His throne jutted from the wall next to her mother's seat, and was even craggier.

"I thought the meat tasted a bit off, but no matter," she said. "I assume my parents left for Torel last night as planned. I'll be ready to set off after them shortly."

"Your parents have been away for a fortnight, wolf daughter."

Nichel blinked. "A fortnight? No, that's not possible. We were going to leave for Sunfall to attend my wedding, and Aidan's Rite of Heritage."

"Aidan Gairden's Rite of Heritage took place days ago, actually."

"Days?" Nichel repeated weakly.

"That's correct. You've been bedridden since just before their departure. I imagine your parents will bring word of how the new Crown of the North has handled his responsibilities thus far."

Nichel's mouth worked silently. "How is it that I slept for so long?"

"You were delirious most of the time, barely able to keep anything down." He paused. "You do not remember any of this?"

She shook her head slowly. "Could it have been the food I ate the night we were supposed to depart?"

"That is my guess, yes."

"Did either of my parents fall ill?"

"Not to my knowledge."

Nichel nodded absently. "They left as planned?"

"Yes, though I do not expect them to return for several days. I expect the weather in the north has made travel difficult."

Nichel ran a finger along the designs carved into the arms of the throne. "And they didn't... that is, did they come to see me?"

"Of course, wolf daughter," Jonathan said, patting her hand. "They refused to leave your bedside that entire first night."

Nichel bowed her head to hide the tears welling in her eyes. Her father would frown at the display, but her father wasn't here, was he? "What made them decide to go to Torel without me?"

"It was only food poisoning. I assured them you were in no real danger, and you never were, I promise you—just as I promised them."

"But, wouldn't they have wanted to—"

"—see Aidan Gairden take up the sword? Of course, and so they did. It was only after I worked on you that the war chief consented to leave your side for a short time. I had a bit of healing instruction when I studied at the Lion's Den, though it wasn't my primary area of expertise." He smiled. "I wouldn't fret too much. A spring wedding would be much more beautiful than one where icicles were used as a substitute for a chandelier."

Nichel managed a smile. Aidan. Her betrothed. It had been too long since she'd last seen him. *He's probably as handsome as he ever was—even more so.* Nichel had gone to great lengths to select just the right shade of blue for her gown, giggling over fabrics with her mother, who knew all the best colors and materials for every season. It had been fun to indulge in the Leastonian half of her blood, and to listen to her mother cooing over how much Aidan would fancy her in this or that color. *Aidan.* He was the Crown of the North, now. In just a few months, she would be his queen.

"If you feel up to it, wolf daughter, I have reports to convey," Jonathan said.

"Very well," Nichel said, and her roiling stomach permitted a sigh to escape her lips.

Jonathan's voice faded to a dull buzz as Nichel sank into her mother's chair. Making sure to keep her gaze fixed on Jonathan, and to nod at all the right parts, she swept her eyes around the cavernous, brightly lit hall. Janleah Keep had been built eight hundred years ago and named in honor of her ancestor, Janleah of the Wolf. The Serpent King and his undead army had razed Leaston first before marching into the west and overwhelming several clans with their superior numbers and dark magic. Janleah had gathered the surviving clans and united them under his banner, making him the first war chief. He had gone on to forge an alliance with Torel, and it had taken their combined might to drive the Serpent King back into the south. Back into the kingdom that had become his grave.

After the war, the clans disbanded, but they paid respect to Janleah for the courage he had displayed in battle and the wisdom he had shown in bringing them together by building a fortress worthy of the war chief, a title they would honor only in times of greatest need. The builders had cut and smoothed sandstone and marble using the Mother's light, and raised Janleah's Keep beside the largest oasis in the west.

Pride filled her. She had been raised on the hot, dusty plains of Darinia, her dark hands calloused from wielding tools, hunting spears she'd sharpened herself, and from scaling her ancestral home. She was as hard as any Darinian, and she would bring that hardness and honor to her marriage. Her thoughts returned to her betrothed, and she blushed. She was also a girl—a woman at fifteen—and had as much right as any Torelian or Leastonian woman to fantasize about her wedding.

Her gown. That was the problem. She'd wanted blue, but blue just wasn't appropriate for a spring wedding. She would ask Mother to make her a new one. Still, Aidan did love blue. His parents made him wear white, but she wondered if maybe—

"... should be in your chambers, wolf daughter."

She raised her head. "I'm sorry, Jonathan. I..." She blushed. "I'm still quite tired. I'm afraid I faded out."

He gave her a warm, sympathetic smile. It occurred to her that, if not for her betrothal to Aidan, she would let Jonathan court her.

"Certainly," he said. "Earlier this morning, a messenger

arrived bearing a gift from your parents. No doubt they intended for it to reach you before they returned home."

A thrill of excitement swept through her. "Where is it?"

"I requested it delivered to your chambers."

Nichel squealed with glee. Jonathan raised an eyebrow, and Nichel composed herself.

"Thank you, Jonathan. You've been most helpful. I'll make sure my father knows of your diligence."

She crossed the room in what began as a youthful stride but ended in careful lurches, and almost reached the entryway before Jonathan cleared his throat.

"Was there something else?" Nichel asked.

"Much more, I'm afraid."

Nichel sighed. "Follow me."

They walked through passages that twisted and turned. Nichel nodded where appropriate as Jonathan rambled on and on. Through an open window, she caught the scent of roasted meshia. To her surprise, her stomach growled instead of cowered. The hide of the horned beast was thick—she had broken enough spear points to know—but became deliciously tender after hours cooking over an open flame. She slowed, tempted. More than tempted. She was contemplating crawling through the aperture and tearing the beast from the spit with her teeth. But, no. Gifts first, food second.

When she arrived at the closed door of her chambers, she gave Jonathan a flat look as he attempted to enter alongside her. He stepped back, raising a fist to his chest in salute as he moved to stand beside the door. Closing the door behind her, Nichel's face broke into a grin. A large silver package sat waiting atop the tangled mess of sheets and blankets.

She moved as fast as she dared, not wanting to break the peace treaty her stomach had signed with movement of any kind. A tiny piece of parchment was attached to the lid. Nichel plucked it off and prepared to read it, but her eyes drifted back to the package as if caught on a fishing line. She let the note drop to the floor.

As had been her custom since she was old enough to understand what gift-wrapped boxes meant, she gave the present a delicate shake. The contents thudded against the side of the box, causing the princess to wobble as she steadied herself. *Nice and heavy!* She tore the paper off in a gleeful frenzy, threw away the lid, and screamed.

Inside the container, leaving gory trails where they had rolled around during their long journey, were the decapitated heads of Romen of the Wolf and Cynthia Alston.

On the floor, the crumpled parchment slowly unfurled like a blooming flower. In the center was a design—the letter 'H', the blade of Crotaria's most well-known sword sheathed in the letter's center bar. Below it, written in the blood:

Long Live the Crown of the North

Chapter 6

Bad Dreams

AIDAN OPENED HIS EYES with a start, deeply afraid and confused over why. Blinking, he looked around. Galleries cascaded upward around the walls. Torches flickered in between each gallery. The floor beneath him was cold, hard. Stone. Raising his head, he saw the Crown of the North and its companion throne across the room. They looked small from where he lay, like toy chairs meant for dolls.

I'm in the throne room. Another thought: *Why?* The last thing he remembered was dozing off in bed after a long day riding the hills outside Calewind. Had he walked here in his sleep?

Shadows writhed along the walls. No light stretched beyond the flickering pools of orange cast by the torches. A chill hung in the air, as if the windows—all clamped shut—had been left open. Aidan shivered. He could sense... something, a vague presence that was not welcome. It smelled dirty and rotten.

He attempted to rise when he noticed movement at the edge of his vision. Turning, he stared around in confusion, wondering what had caught his attention—then drew a sharp breath. The torches mounted around the walls flickered, but the shadows they made had gone still. As he watched, they stirred as if awakening from sleep then oozed toward the center of the ceiling, a confluence of streams of tar.

Aidan's breath caught. Low laughter drifted into his ears as the shadowy bulk, twice as wide as his bed coverings, seeped down the wall. The fiery heads of torches shied away. Suddenly the dark mass pounced, snuffing out the flames. The room grew dimmer. The shadow continued downward, gaining speed. Again it slowed near a line of torches, and again it flowed over them, wrapping around the room and extinguishing the lights with a hiss. Smoke curled up from each bald torch, its dying breath. The raspy laughter grew stronger, the shadow spilling down now, choking all the light from the room until Aidan was left lying in darkness.

Unable to move, barely able to breathe, Aidan shivered,

waiting. An icy vapor ran up his legs; he felt as if he were slowly sinking into a lake in the grip of winter. The coldness slid forward, spreading over him. The laughter was all he could hear now, drowning the pounding of his heart and his clacking teeth.

The darkness reared, considering him, laughing. Then it lunged, streaming into his mouth and down his throat, gagging him. He tried to raise a hand to pry it away. He couldn't budge it. The shadow was light as air, solid as steel. It pinned his arms to the ground and surged into his nose. He was choking, suffocating...

And then it was gone. His chest heaved, pulling air into his lungs in sharp gasps. His eyes watered, his throat and nostrils burned, and the sweat covering him chilled his bones. His clothes were drenched, leaving him a sopping, shuddering mess. But he was alive.

Footsteps nearby, hard boots biting into the stone, bouncing echoes off the walls. As the footfalls drew to a halt, his father appeared, standing over him, somehow perfectly visible in the darkness as if the Lady illuminated him and only him. Edmund cocked his head, considering his prone son, and the relief Aidan had felt at the other man's appearance leaked away.

Edmund's face was contorting, skin warping like shifting sand and bones snapping like dry twigs until the face became plain and expressionless. His eyes, flat and lifeless, rolled back and sank into his skull. The king grinned; dirt and grime caked gaps where teeth should have been. Vertical strips of flesh ran from his top lip to his bottom, like fleshy cell bars.

"You are a failure to me," he said, voice thick with earth. The fleshy strips vibrated like taut strings as he spoke, and clumps of dirt spilled from his lips like crumbs. "Your mother and I gave you opportunity, provided you with everything a man could need, everything he could want. But it wasn't enough for you. You are not fit to lead Torel's Ward, Aidan. You are not fit to take your mother's throne."

The terrible face leaned in closer, its rotting mouth hovering inches from Aidan's ear. He spoke in a whisper, but the words boomed through the room like thunder.

"I disown you. You are not my son."

Edmund vanished. Annalyn stepped forward. Aidan stared up at her, tears streaming down his face.

"Mother," he said, struggling to control his voice. "Mother, I'm sorry. I didn't mean to fail. I did everything I could! But Heritage—it did not accept me. It wasn't my fault!"

Annalyn leered down at him. Like her husband's, her eyes

were dead and glassy. Emotionless, as if she felt nothing. Nothing for him.

"You," she began, then shook her head. "What did I do, Aidan?"

"What do you mean?"

"It has to be something I did. Did I not love you enough? Did I not teach you faith? Or pride in our family?"

"No!" he said, reaching for her hand. She reared back as if he were a snake.

"Mother, please. You did everything right. It... It was me. I just wasn't ready."

"I know that now, Aidan. There was nothing I could have done differently." Her eyes sank back into her head. Four vertical bars of flesh appeared, sewing lip to lip. "I did everything a mother should. I tried to raise you with a sense of honor and responsibility. I tried to show you the pride of being born a Gairden.

"None of it was good enough for you, was it, Aidan? Be silent!" she screamed at him when he opened his mouth. "Do not speak to me." A worm wriggled from one of her empty sockets and through the other, vanishing inside her skull.

"Do not ever speak to me again, Aidan. You are nothing but a disappointment." She leaned in closer still, just as his father had, but she did not whisper as he had.

"You are weak, Aidan. You are not a Gairden. You are *not my son!*"

She disappeared then, leaving him in darkness and with the echo of words that pierced him deeper than the shadowy cold that had almost drowned him.

A failure. A disappointment.

Why? Why did this have to happen to me?

He closed his eyes, letting pity overtake him.

A soft hum echoed above him. He opened his eyes to see Heritage suspended in midair, floating point down and twirling like a carefree girl. Rising to his feet, he lunged at the sword. The sword floated out of reach. Aidan went for it again.

"You! You did this. You made them hate me, made them turn away from me! Made me a *failure!*" He leaped for it, but every time the sword slid through the air, always just out of reach. Aidan fell to his knees, too drained to continue. Cautiously, the sword drifted close. The Eye churned, fixing him in its gaze. Then, to his utter amazement, it spoke.

—You must have courage, Aidan.

His head snapped up.

—Your hardships have just begun. Will you face them, or hide in your bed?

Aidan shook his head slowly. "That voice," he whispered. *Where have I heard that voice before? Destiny...*

—Awaken!

The Eye flashed. A storm rumbled within the stone.

— I can hold him at bay, but not for long. AWAKEN!

Aidan sat upright in his bed like an uncoiled spring. His bare chest and wrinkled trousers were soaked with sweat. A trail of tears laced his cheeks. He closed his eyes and rubbed at them, wishing he could scrub away the nightmare that replayed itself against his eyelids.

A gust of wind blew past him, upsetting his hair and snuffing the candle he kept near his bed. He opened his eyes to see his door slam shut, sending a weaker gust of air over him. The loud crash stunned Aidan for the briefest of moments before he shot out of bed. Thoughts came to him in a rush, broken and disorganized. How long had he slept? Days and nights had blended together since his parents had left.

Shaking his head to clear away sleepiness that clung to his mind like cobwebs, he bounded to the door and threw it open. The Lord of Midnight held court; all the torches lining the corridor had been extinguished.

Puzzled, he closed the door. *How...? The wind I felt.* He blinked. He glanced at his window. It was sealed shut, and he'd had no reason to open it. He could draw heat through the glass, which was a mercy during the coldest winter months.

I know I closed my door before falling asleep. So the wind would have to have come from... inside *the room. But how?* He rubbed at his arm absently, then frowned and studied it. His skin was warm to the touch, even though the stone floor felt as cold as a sheet of ice. His eyes widened. Someone had kindled. Someone had been here, or nearby, and had shifted away as he awakened. How, though? Wards set by Gairdens hundreds of years in the grave prevented anyone from shifting into or out of Sunfall.

Muffled footsteps reached his ears, scattering his thoughts. Aidan opened his door and looked into the corridor. A familiar form appeared in the darkness, hustling toward him. One hand clutched a torch, its light flickering along the walls.

"Hello, Daniel."

His childhood friend, one year older than he, made an elaborate bow and straightened, grinning, leaning in the doorway.

“Good evening, Prince of Mischief.” Daniel cleared his throat and scratched at his head. “I’m, ah, supposed to bring you to the south courtyard.”

“At this hour? What’s the matter?”

“Your parents. They’re back.”

Chapter 7

Prince of Tears

AIDAN PULLED HIS DOOR closed and stepped out into the corridor. The windows glowed faintly with the Lord of Midnight's sickly light. Shadows hunkered along the walls, bunched and ready to pounce. He shivered, remembering the shadowy creatures from his dream.

"Are you ready?" he asked Daniel, who stood picking at the wall nearby.

"Hmm? Oh, yes," Daniel said. He started forward, stopped, and turned back, looking as if he wanted to say something. "Colder than Kahltan's backside down here," he grumbled. Then they set off, walking in silence through the passages that led to the southern courtyard, the firelight from Daniel's torch leading the way.

Aidan inspected the suits of armor lining the halls, the tapestries purchased from Leastonian merchants who spent their lives coming and going from faraway lands. That made him think of pirates, rogue Leastonians who combed the Great Sea in search of treasure. The merchants' guild denied any such rumor, but Daniel said his father knew of many pirate ships that sailed free because of the profits fetched from the obscure trinkets they *found* in their travels. Other rumors claimed the Leastonians ran a network of thieves that lived beneath the surface, but Daniel had laughed that off as pure hearsay. That, or he didn't really know. He had only been eight when he and his family had moved to Calewind. Aidan wondered what it would be like, living underground.

They walked along. Aidan pointedly avoided looking ahead, his mind grasping at any subject except what awaited him when he saw his parents. He reviewed complicated spells, gave serious consideration to claiming his ship from Ironsail and becoming a pirate, thought back on his adventures galloping through the hills every day since his parents had left, and—

There it was. The subject he most wanted to avoid. He had treated his parents horribly before their departure. Were they still upset with him? Undoubtedly. And Tyrnen hadn't even come to check on him after his failed Rite of Heritage. The old man was probably furious, and disappointed. Aidan's stomach started doing flips. Would his failure reflect on Tyrnen's status as Eternal Flame?

What was he supposed to say to them? What *could* he say?

"Aidan?" Daniel said

"Yes?" Aidan responded, drawing to a stop. Not because he wanted to avoid meeting his parents. It was just hard to walk and talk, that was all.

Daniel passed his torch to his free hand and cleared his throat. "I don't understand what happened on your birthday, and I don't really care, either. You're my friend, and I won't judge you. Whatever happened, happened, and that's that. I'm sure your parents and Tyrnen will fix everything—but I'd like to help in any way I can. We're friends, and we've been friends a long time. So if you need anything, you can count on me." He took a breath.

"Thank," the prince said, warmed more by his friend's words than by the torch in his hand. "That means a lot."

Daniel nodded, looking much more at ease. They resumed their walk. All too soon they crossed the antechamber leading out to the courtyard. Snow drizzled down, coating the grounds in a layer of sparkling white. Throngs of Wardsmen and nobles in Darinian furs lined the space, talking softly or standing at attention. His parents were nowhere in sight.

Conversation faded away as Aidan appeared. He stood beside Daniel, eyes locked straight ahead, waiting for the gate to open or for the palace walls to collapse in on him. Anything to remove stares that dug in like hooks.

A trumpet call from the pass leading to Calewind diverted the crowd's attention. Daniel passed Aidan the torch and shot him a confident look, then joined a line of Wardsmen fanning out around the gate. Aidan kindled from the torch and wrapped himself in a heat bubble. He dipped the torch, its flame smaller, in the snow. It extinguished with a hiss. He shivered despite his warmth, remembering that same steamy *hsss* the shadow creature in his dream had made each time it had feasted on fire.

The gate cranked open, loud in the still night. He heard the beat of hooves moments before half a dozen horses rounded the last bend in the mountain trail. His father rode at his mother's side and at the center of the line, their mounts snorting and trotting. An escort of three Wardsmen rode in front of and behind the royal couple.

Aidan frowned. His father had always insisted on Wardsmen

riding at least one hundred paces away when they traveled, saying that it was his responsibility to protect his family. Annalyn had echoed her husband's sentiments. Why did the escort travel so closely tonight?

Stares prickled his skin once again, drifting between him and his parents. He looked straight ahead. *Everything will be fine. They'll have come up with an idea, and I'll be able to...*

He squinted. *Where is Tyrnen?* Other than his parents and the escort, no other figures had appeared. *Perhaps he doesn't want to see me.*

Kneeling, he felt his worry melt away like the slush around his feet. They were home now; that was all that mattered. *Things will return to normal.*

Edmund and Annalyn drew to a halt and dismounted. Attendants took the reins of their animals and led them off to the stables. Aidan rose and stepped forward.

"Welcome home, Father," he said, smiling. Then he shrank back. His father was travel-stained, which was understandable. But his eyes were expressionless, vacant.

Edmund looked Aidan up and down with his flat, dull eyes. "I trust you've helped look after affairs in our absence."

The last vestige of Aidan's smile fell away. "I... actually, no. I've been resting so I could better assist you upon your retu—"

"Assist me with what?" the king snapped, and Aidan's mouth clamped shut. "Crying into your pillow for weeks on end will have sapped all your strength, I expect. Your behavior brings shames to your family. Aidan Gairden, Prince of Tears. That is what we should call you."

Aidan licked his lips and dropped his gaze.

"Look at me, boy."

Aidan complied. The crowd was silent.

"You can speak, can't you?" Edmund asked.

"Yes."

"Then answer my question. Assist me with what?"

"I wish to continue as your apprentice, so that I may learn to command the Ward."

Edmund studied him. "Good. I will soon have need of you," he said. He brushed past Aidan and strode into Sunfall, not looking back. Two Wardsmen stepped out of formation and flanked him.

Aidan watched him go. *This isn't supposed to happen. It's not supposed to be like this.*

"Tyrnen has already returned to his tower," Annalyn said softly from beside him.

"I'm sorry, Mother," he blurted out.

Annalyn was silent. Her eyes were flat, as his father's had been.

"I just wasn't ready," he continued. "But I will be. I just need help."

"How am I supposed to believe a word you say," she said at last, her voice calm, "when instead of taking charge while your father and I were away, you wallowed in pity like a child?"

She stepped toward him, her gaze making the night air seem as warm as a spring breeze.

"I am very disappointed in you, Aidan."

She too brushed passed him, another pair of Wardsmen surrounding the Crown of the North.

The crowd slowly dispersed. Aidan felt his hope freezing over in the unforgiving winter cold.

He heard footsteps crunch into the snow behind him.

"Aidan—" Daniel said.

"Leave me," he said without turning. Several moments passed before he heard Daniel turn and walk away.

Snow and ice dripped from Aidan's boots in a watery trail as he strode into the throne room. A cluster of nobles buzzed around the thrones. Most were the richly dressed Hands of the Crown, emissaries hand-picked by the Crown of the North to govern far-off towns and cities that the Crown could not visit frequently. A tall, bald man in light armor stood between the thrones, arms crossed over his chest, watching each petitioner as if he expected them to draw steel at any moment. Brendon Greagor, Colonel of Torel's Ward, spared him a quick glance, just long enough to take him in as a part of his assessment of the room.

"I wish to speak with my parents," Aidan said over the drone of conversation. The Hands turned to him, silence settling over the room. "Alone."

Edmund considered his son before nodding. "Leave us."

The assemblage scattered. Brendon stepped down as the last bunch of nobles made their way out of the room. Annalyn reached out to touch his arm.

He turned. "Yes, Crown?"

She gestured toward her husband. Brendon knelt and Edmund cupped his hand and whispered into Brendon's ear. The other man's eyes widened for half an instant, which for Brendon indicated a revelation shocking enough to make a normal man faint. He nodded once before rising, bowed, and glided out of the room, offering a bow and the flicker of a smile to Aidan. The doors closed behind him.

Edmund sat with an arm propped on his armrest and his chin in his palm. Annalyn tapped a nail against her crossed legs, her lips pursed.

"I want to apologize," Aidan said. "I have replayed the events of my birthday over and over in my mind. You both know I didn't want any part of what the Rite of Heritage entailed, but you also know—you *should* know—that I was ready to take the sword and do what needed to be done. But it rejected me.

"I failed you, and I failed our people as well. I don't know how to fix that, but I will do whatever I must to try. I want to continue my training under Tyrnen. He graduated me to Cinder, but I know he has more to teach. I want to continue learning everything I can from you, Father, and from you as well, Mother, so that when all this is finally settled and I take the sword, I will be the best ruler I can be."

Falling to one knee, Aidan continued. "Tell me what I must do, and I will do it."

Then he waited. The silence seemed crushing, but he had said all he could say.

He heard his mother's riding dress rustle and his father's armor clank. To his surprise and immense relief, his mother extended a small hand. He took it.

"We're so proud of you, Aidan," Annalyn said, holding him by the arms. She was smiling. They both were. But their smiles did not touch their cold eyes. "I am sorry to have been so harsh. I've been scared, too."

"Did you discover anything?" he asked tentatively. "About my Rite of Heritage, I mean?"

She shook her head, frustration bordering on anger twisting her beautiful features. "But we will solve this. I promise."

Edmund put a hand on his shoulder. "It's good to have you back, son."

"Thank you, Father," Aidan said. "I only want to live up to what you said to me on my birthday, before..." *Before I let you both down.*

Edmund frowned, obviously confused. Aidan felt a pang of hurt. Obviously Edmund's words about his son growing into a young man he could be proud of meant more to Aidan than they had to his father. Edmund nodded slowly. "Oh. Yes. I remember now. My apologies, Aidan. It was a long journey."

"Of course," Aidan said in a chipper voice.

Edmund put a hand on his shoulder. "What happened that day is in the past, son. We're moving forward. Speaking of which, I've got a very important meeting with Brendon at the Lady's first light. Care to join me?"

"I do," Aidan said, and he meant it.

Edmund watched him, and suddenly his eyes did not seem tired at all. "You meant what you said, of course. That you would do anything to fix this... situation."

A twinge of shame wormed back in. "I meant it," Aidan said.

"Then that's all we need to say on the subject." He paused. "We love you, son."

Annalyn stretched to the tune of a deep yawn. "My, it was a long journey, wasn't it. Shall we turn in, dear?"

Edmund yawned even wider. "That sounds wonderful. Not many hours left before..." He glanced at Aidan. "Well. We'll discuss it in the morning. Goodnight, son."

Curious but plenty tired himself, Aidan bowed and made his way out of the throne room. His hands clenched and unclenched as he practically skipped to his chambers. They were just tired. Of course they were.

Everything is going to be fine. I knew it would be. I may not want the sword, but if it means proving myself to them, I'll do it.

He slowed when he neared the sword chamber. Something tickled the back of his mind. The sword had spoken to him in the dream, and that wasn't so odd. He'd sprouted wings and flown to Darinia and back in dreams. In the world of dreams, swords could talk and men could fly. No, it wasn't that the sword had spoken, precisely. It was...

His eyes grew round as the answer came charging up on him. He remembered Annalyn kneeling to him on his birthday, extending the sword while half of Crotaria leaned in so close he had almost felt their breath on his neck. A voice had whispered in his ear. He had thought it was his mother, but it had sounded older. Firm, but still older.

Heritage spoke in that same voice in my dream, he thought. Was that it? Had the sword spoken to him on the day it had set him up for failure? He raised a hand to the "H" on the door, but let it drop. *What am I going to do? Interrogate a sword?*

Aidan stifled a yawn with his fist. It didn't matter. He would tell his parents about his theory. Maybe it would help them figure out why Heritage had rejected him. Everything would work out.

—Destiny still waits to call your name, Aidan Gairden.

He snapped his jaw shut. There it was again—old but firm.

Grandmotherly. Aidan ran his finger over the *Heritage* inscription and shoved through the sliding stone doors. There was the sword, blade twirling, Eye flickering without a care.

"You mentioned my destiny the night of my ceremony, and yet this destiny you speak of obviously has little to do with you," he said, standing before Heritage with clenched fists. "So what is it, then? Share my fate with me if you know so much about it."

Heritage spun lazily, remaining silent. Then it went still. The Eye flashed, a red wink.

—Leave this place, the voice said. *Wait around the corner.*

"Why should I—"

—Go. Quickly.

Aidan bit back a retort and hurried out into the hall. He slipped into his bedroom and left the door ajar, peering out. Several moments passed. His mother appeared and halted before the chamber. He watched her trace the inscription. The doors opened, she stepped through, the doors closed. Almost immediately she emerged, Heritage in hand, and vanished the way she had come.

Aidan rose slowly from his hiding spot. *Was that all it wanted me to see?* he thought. *My mother is the sword-bearer. She comes and goes from the sword chamber at all hours of the day. What significance could that possibly—*

—Great significance. The signs of deception are obvious, yet you allow self-pity to blind you.

Aidan's eyes had slowly widened during the sword's response. Had the sword read his mind? He swallowed; then, hesitantly: *What do you mean?* he thought, projecting his words at the sword.

—Have you asked yourself why your mother would leave me behind when I've always been at her side? it responded.

Aidan almost yelped with surprise. The sword had heard his thought as clearly as if he had shouted, and had responded! Then he focused on its question. "Of course she took..."

But she hadn't. Heritage had been in the chamber, and he did not recall seeing the sword at his mother's side upon her return. Had she returned it to the chamber between returning to the palace and meeting with the Hands? Probably not, he decided. Not much time had passed between their confrontation in the courtyard and their meeting at the throne.

He shook his head. *It was a short retreat. Why would she have taken you? She wasn't going into battle.*

—A retreat intended to help her son plan his future. A future you seem content to have others decide for you.

What's your point?

—My point, Aidan Gairden, is this. Through Heritage, a sword-bearer can communicate with generations of Gairdens. Suppose one of them holds the information necessary to deciphering the mystery behind your rejection. Why would your mother leave such a valuable tool behind?

Aidan ran his hand through his hair. "I'm too tired to continue this discussion. If you won't just *tell* me—"

—Soon, Aidan Gairden. All too soon.

Chapter 8

Voices

AIDAN RAPPED THE BRONZE KNOCKER against the door. Several moments later, the door swung inward. His master stood in the doorway, hair and robes disheveled, bushy eyebrows raised in surprise.

"Aidan? I'm surprised to see you here so late."

"I figured I'd come say hello, since it didn't seem you'd be stopping by anytime soon." He dropped into a soft armchair in front of the hearth. Heat flooded from the logs roasting in the hearth, blanketing the tower room and mixing with the musty aroma of books and yellowed parchment. More books covered Tyrnen's desk in stacks that rose up like shoddily-built turrets. Aidan was convinced that simply sticking one's head through the door and breathing the scent of all the musty scrolls, books, and strange artifacts Tyrnen had accumulated over the years could make one grow smarter. Sadly, his parents and mentor disagreed.

He had spent months of his life in this room, reading ancient texts, reciting spells, dates, names, figures. At the end of lessons—and in the middle of them, when he managed to divert the old man's train of thought—Aidan would perch on the edge of this very chair, mugs of tea or hot cocoa—a sweet delicacy his parents always purchased from Leastonian traders who passed through—growing cold as he listened to Tyrnen spin tales of brave heroes, terrible monsters, and princesses in need of rescue and a good cuddle.

When Tyrnen told his stories, his tower seemed to lift off and soar into the sky. Now Aidan sat quietly, watching the flames. His eyelids drooped. Each time he forced them back up, finally straightening to resist the chair's tempting cushiness. He was so tired he felt sick, but he would not fall asleep. Not even here, a place where he always felt safe, more so than even the sword chamber where only Gairdens could enter.

He had gone back to bed after talking with Heritage, unanswered questions tumbling around his head. The nightmares had returned the moment he drifted off, pouncing like a beast rewarded for stalking wary prey that had finally lowered its head to drink. He had seen his parents again, their bodies deformed and rotten as they screamed at him, telling him they knew he would fail them again. Heritage took its turn, rambling about destiny, lies, and deception. None of the dreams had felt as dire, as *real* as the first, but they were horrifying all the same.

Aidan caught the scent of warm milk and creamy cocoa. Tyrnen lowered himself into a chair beside Aidan, placing two steaming cups of cocoa on the table between them. Mumbling thanks, Aidan took one and sipped at it. The warm sweetness melted through the chill of his nightmares. None had felt quite so real as the first, but they had still left him afraid to close his eyes.

"Where is your ring?" the old man asked, gesturing at Aidan's bare right hand.

Aidan shrugged. "Wherever it landed after I threw it."

"You threw your Cinder Band?"

"I haven't felt like recognizing my few accomplishments as of late."

"You *must* wear it always, Aidan."

Setting his cocoa on the table, Aidan propped his feet on a cushioned stool. "You're not disappointed in me, are you?" he asked, trying to sound indifferent.

"Disappointed?"

"Because of what happened—or didn't happen—on my birthday."

Tyrnen folded his hands. "No, I am not disappointed. I was certainly surprised, but disappointment never crossed my mind."

"Mother and Father seemed to be."

"They said as much during our brief retreat, yes."

Aidan winced. "Why didn't you invite me to go along?"

"I didn't think you were in the mood for company. Your mother's account of your reaction when she extended an invitation confirmed my assumption."

Aidan ignored that. "Why weren't you with them when they returned?"

"I had gone ahead to my tower. There were matters that needed—"

"They came to talk to me after the ceremony. They at least pretended to care. Where were you?"

"I chose not to disturb your pouting session."

"I was not—"

"You were. You acted like a petulant child. I was on my way to speak with you when I bumped into your father. He told me what happened during his visit, and I decided I had better things to do then visit a whiny brat."

Aidan took a gulp of cocoa to hide his embarrassment. He *had* acted foolish—then, and now. The cocoa scalded his throat all the way down.

Tyrnen leaned forward. "Your parents love you, my boy. So do I. We just want what's best for you."

Aidan nursed his drink and stared into the flames.

"Have you spoken to them about your feelings?" Tyrnen asked.

Aidan nodded. "Earlier tonight after they returned."

"And what did they say?"

The cup clinked as Aidan lowered it onto his plate. "At first, they looked at me as if they'd never seen me before. The way they treated me, you'd have thought I'd slaughtered all the children in Torel."

For a moment, Tyrnen wore a sympathetic smile. Then his face abruptly clouded over and his voice became harsh. "Can you blame them?"

Aidan sat back, momentarily stunned. Then anger flushed his cheeks.

"Yes, actually, I can. I was the one rejected by Heritage. I was the one humiliated in front of my people, and visitors from Leaston and Darinia besides. And what did I do? I did what duty required, and I was punished for it. And I'm *still* being punished for it. They didn't have to be so harsh, and neither do you. Do you think I know what's happening or *why* it's happening? Well, I don't, so give me some time to prepare myself before it happens all over again, would you?"

Tyrnen pursed his lips but said nothing.

Aidan sighed and ran his hands over his face. "I'm sorry for snapping. I'd simply appreciate it if you all remembered that I haven't any clue why this is happening."

"They were caught off-guard, you know," Tyrnen said quietly. "Perhaps even more than you were. It is not every day that a Gairden is rejected by his bloodline."

Aidan felt his cheeks warm, though not from anger this time. He hadn't really thought about it like that. It was easy to think of Heritage as just a sword—a magical sword, true, but still an object. And he knew that his ancestors had *seen* what happened during his ceremony. It was something else entirely to know that they had voted to keep him out of their inner circle. Aidan's jaw tightened. His Grandfather Charles, who had been as close to him growing up as Tyrnen was, had been a part of the decision. Ambrose, Anastasia... They all had.

"I am sorry, my boy," Tyrnen said. "Your attitude perturbed me. I should have thought more about everything you've gone through."

Aidan lifted his cup to his lips, then lowered it. "I told Mother and Father I was sorry for disappointing them, and that I would do anything to prove that I am still worthy of their... trust." *Of their love*, he'd wanted to say before catching himself. Of course they still loved him.

"They know that," Tyrnen said. "You simply need to work hard to show them you'll do what is necessary to fix this..." The old man spread his hands and looked at the ceiling, as if the word he needed was hidden in the stonework. "This unprecedented occurrence."

Aidan cringed again. He knew Tyrnen hadn't meant anything by his words. What had happened *was* unprecedented. He didn't need reminding, though. Then he thought of something.

"The sword is speaking to me," Aidan said in a low voice.

"The sword is... speaking to you?" Tyrnen said, blinking.

Aidan stiffened. "Don't use that tone with me, Tyrnen."

"I didn't mean to imply anything." The old man scratched at his chin. "What do you mean the sword is speaking to you?"

"There aren't a lot of ways to interpret that," Aidan snapped. He took a calming breath. "I'm sorry. I just don't understand what's happening."

"Start at the beginning," Tyrnen said in a soothing tone. After drawing a deep breath, Aidan launched into his story. When he finished, he sat back in his chair, took a long drink of cocoa, and closed his eyes, feeling more relaxed since... Well, since before his birthday. It felt good to unburden himself, especially to Tyrnen. He'd never judged Aidan when the prince did something foolish, instead saying that all experiences, no matter how terrible, offered some sort of lesson. Learn that lesson, the old man always said, and remember it.

Tyrnen sat back, tapping his fingertips together. "I believe you."

"You do?" Aidan said, relieved. "You don't think I'm mad?"

"Given what you *have* heard, it does seem as if Heritage is communicating with you. But instead of inspecting the *how* of the matter, I feel we should examine the *why*."

The Eternal Flame began pacing around the tower. After two circuits, he stopped near the hearth and regarded Aidan intently.

"The sword denied you during your ceremony. Yet according

to your family's history, only the sword-bearer is able to communicate with the sword. No records have ever been kept as to how this communication takes place, at least none that I've seen. This must be one of the sword's many secrets known only to Gairdens."

Aidan nodded in agreement. He'd read his family's historical account several times. The volume detailing the lives of his predecessors had been required reading material during his mother's lessons, but Annalyn had told him that many secrets had been left intentionally undocumented. They were to be revealed to a sword-bearer over time, or during the Rite of Heritage.

"But since you are not the sword-bearer," Tyrnen continued, "why would Heritage reach out to you? Could it be preparing you for a second chance? A rebuff by the sword is an unparalleled event, so there's no way of knowing for certain, unless... Have you asked the sword why it's been speaking to you?"

"Not in so many words."

Tyrnen cocked his head.

"I, ah, I yelled at Heritage, as I recall."

"You *yelled* at a sword?"

"It made me angry."

"Even so, Aidan. Yelling at a sword..."

"It finally went quiet, which made me happy."

Tyrnen resumed pacing, mumbling to himself. The old man sighed after several long minutes, throwing up his hands. "The only reasonable explanation is the sword might give you a second chance. But without any precedents to study..." He shrugged. "I've got nothing to go on, though I'll continue to investigate. If there's a second chance to become the sword-bearer, I'd say it warrants our full attention, wouldn't you?"

Aidan said nothing.

"Is that what you want?" Tyrnen asked.

"I don't know."

Tyrnen nodded, saying nothing more. Aidan could have hugged him. He loved his parents, but giving such a vague, indecisive answer to either of them would have brought on a lecture about responsibility and duty. Tyrnen understood him, could read him like one of his books written in a language that time had forgotten.

"What should we do?" Aidan asked. Tyrnen didn't answer. He was leaning against the mantle, scrubbing his hands over his face.

Aidan squinted at his friend. "Are you well, Tyrnen?" He felt like a callous fool. He'd been so wrapped up in his own problems that he hadn't noticed Tyrnen's pallid complexion.

The old man snorted. "It's nothing, lad, nothing at all. Just tired."

Aidan nodded, clearing his throat. "I'm sorry for my earlier outburst."

"Think nothing of it," the Eternal Flame said, sinking back into his chair. "I cannot begin to imagine everything that's going on in your head. Even with your, ah, unpleasant demeanor, I must say you've handled all of this better than I would have."

The old man reached for his mug of cocoa and gave it a dainty sip. His face twisted and he swallowed in one large, gulp. "Bloody thing's gone cold on me," he grumbled, drawing a grin from Aidan.

Tyrnen returned his mug to the table, then stared hard at his pupil. "Your parents love you. You must know that."

Aidan's grin slipped a bit. "I do. I just don't want to let them down again."

"Then don't. They'll need you more than ever, I'm afraid."

"Why? Has something happened?"

"Yes, my boy, something terrible. While we were away—"

A gong went off in the distance, startling both men. Aidan shot from his chair and moved to join Tyrnen at the tower's window, drawing heat from the fire and placing his hand to the frost to clear it away. The Lady's first rays peeked shyly through the clouds. Below, Wardsmen adorned in full plate mail were pouring across the courtyard.

"It's happening, then," Tyrnen said quietly.

"What do you mean? What's happening?"

But Tyrnen was already moving. Aidan caught up to his mentor as they ran down the steps of the tower, falling in with the Wardsmen crossing the grounds. They cut their way through the throng and slipped into Sunfall through a side door. Inside, Aidan saw Daniel hustling through the corridor. He pushed his way across and reached out to snag the Wardsman by the arm.

"What're you...?" Daniel said, then gave an apologetic glance. "Sorry," he said, his voice raw. "Everything's happening so fast."

"*What* is happening?" Aidan said.

Daniel swallowed. "War."

Chapter 9

War

ROWS OF WARDSMEN COVERED head to toe in gleaming mail thundered through Sunfall's south gate, boots rising and falling in perfect step. Daniel, Aidan, and Tyrnen cut ahead of the first lines flowing toward the throne room and ducked behind the open doors.

"They haven't told us much," Daniel said as he removed a gauntlet and wiped a line of sweat from his brow. "Brendon came into the barracks not less than fifteen minutes ago, shouting to don full armor and march to the throne room. I was just on my way in here for my shift when he gave the order."

Aidan ran a hand through his hair. *Full armor*, he thought, dazed. "You said something about war."

"I've told you all I know. I suspect we'll learn details shortly." Bowing to both, he replaced his gauntlet and took his place to one side of the doorway.

Still reeling, Aidan turned to see his parents sitting on their thrones. Brendon knelt between the royal couple; the three had their heads together, exchanging furtive whispers. Hands of the Crown dressed in brocaded robes climbed the spiral staircases and took seats in the galleries.

"What's going on?" Aidan said to Tyrnen. "Before we rushed down here, you said something is happening."

"You will find out soon enough," the old man said. "I'm only sorry I didn't get a chance to explain things earlier." He led Aidan to his place by the Crown of the North, then moved to stand beside Edmund's throne. Folding his arms, Aidan watched columns of Wardsmen flow into the room, splitting as they crossed the threshold to line both walls with white steel.

Then a flock of men and women wearing emerald-colored robes entered, like leaves mixing with the snow-white mail of the Wardsmen.

"Torel's Dawn," he breathed.

Commissioned by the Gairden family from the Eternal Flame

for use in Torel's Ward, the realm's most elite battle mages—five men, five women—wore forest-colored robes that flowed down over their boots, giving the impression that they floated across the floor. Crimson sashes stretched from their right shoulders down to a red sash around the mid-section. In the center of the waistband was a patch depicting a sword set against a golden orb.

Aidan blinked. Torel's Dawn was made up of ten Touched, yet he counted only eight.

At last the room was lined with Wardsmen. Every man fell to one knee. Daniel and another Wardsman rose first, moving in unison to swing the doors closed.

Annalyn, stunning in cream-colored robes and sapphire earrings, stood and stepped forward.

"We have all been fortunate to enjoy one of the longest stretches of peace in recorded history—a stretch that, several days ago, came to an abrupt and violent end." She paused, letting her words sink in. Wardsmen, trained to stare forward even if fire tickled at their toes, exchanged frowns. The galleries broke out in nervous mutters. Aidan swallowed. War, Daniel had said. He'd read about them, studied them. But wars had been words in history books, names and dates he had been forced to recite.

"The morning after my son's birthday, my husband and I decided to depart with Eternal Flame Tyrnen Symorne on a brief retreat," Annalyn continued. "We had much to discuss, the most important matter being a way to assist Prince Aidan in dealing with his..." She turned to regard the prince, who lowered his eyes to the floor. "With his unforeseen circumstances." Finally the assemblage hushed, waiting for her to go on.

"We decided to make camp in the vast expanse of forest that surrounds Lake Carrean, where we intended to discuss Aidan's... unique situation."

Aidan flushed—then blinked. Hadn't his parents told him that they would be staying at the Lion's Den? That was in Sharem, the largest trade city in Crotaria divided equally between the three realms and what little remained of Sallner. Why had they instead journeyed to Lake Carrean, which was further east? His mother's next words blasted away his thoughts.

"In the forest, we came upon the carcasses of the mounts that carried Romen of the Wolf and his beloved, lying near a cluster of rocks at the lake's shore."

Buzzing again sounded from above. Aidan felt an icy block of fear settle in his stomach. He stepped forward, intending to ask after his friends, when he saw movement out of the corner of his eye. A Darinian leaped from his seat and gripped the rail. Aidan recognized him as Cotak of the Spirits, clan chief of the spirit clan, a people known for their stealth in battle. Aidan had heard stories of spirit clansmen approaching fortresses locked tighter than a Leastonian's purse—guards at every entrance, walls lined with spikes, cauldrons of bubbling pitch ready to rain down at the first sign of a ladder. According to the stories, a handful of spirit clansmen could enter such holds and leave minutes later, leaving no evidence of their passing but corpses stuffed in alcoves and pantries, all traps undisturbed.

Cotak spoke hastily in the Darinian tongue before composing himself. "Was the war chief unharmed?" he said, speaking in halting common.

Annalyn's reaction to the clan chief's question chilled Aidan to the bone. "Your war chief and his wife emerged from the trees behind us. As we moved to greet them, the clansmen who had accompanied them to my son's celebration came forth. They drew steel as they advanced, and to our horror, Romen did the same."

Everyone in the room was silent. Aidan's mouth hung open in shock; his was not the only one unhinged. Above, Cotak seemed oblivious to the stares peppering him like arrows. All the color had drained from his face.

"The battle did not last long." Annalyn's mouth quivered as if she were about to weep, but her eyes remained neutral, almost bored. "Only Romen and Cynthia remained. They said their ambush would pale in comparison to the battles they would wage to claim Torel for themselves. I tried to reason with them. But in the end, they would not be persuaded. They left us no choice. We executed them."

Shocked and confused cries rang out from above. The Wardsmen remained composed, though many had gone ashen.

"You killed them?" Aidan said, his voice barely a whisper.

"I'm sorry, son," Edmund replied, though he did not sound it. His visage was ice covering stone. "It was our lives or theirs."

"And you didn't think," Aidan began softly, "that after all these centuries of peace, after all these years of friendship, after there never once being *any* indication of malice toward Torel, that this matter was serious enough to require at least some investigation?"

Everyone in the room had gone still as Aidan's voice had risen. Staring at his son, Edmund remained silent. Aidan's breathing echoed around the room as he clenched clammy fists.

"It doesn't make any sense. Why would Romen attack you—a Gairden, the Eternal Flame, and the general of Torel's Ward—with only twelve men? War chief or not, he couldn't—"

"Those men were expertly trained," Edmund said. "Surely you can understand—"

"They could have attacked you with dozens of men and you, *you alone,* could have handled them easily."

The prince's tone drew gasps from above. Struggling to control his tone, Aidan drew a deep breath.

"There has to be more to it than that. How did they know you two would be traveling with Tyrnen?"

"We informed the war chief and his pack of our travel plans before they departed," Edmund said.

Aidan considered that. "But if they were going to organize an ambush, don't you think it would have been in their best interest to make sure none of you came back alive? They would have needed more men. If Romen truly wanted to rule Torel, killing you and Mother would have been the best way to get things started. With you three out of the way, that would've left the kingdom vulnerable because—" He cut off, swallowing. *Because I was moping around here without any idea what was happening.*

"The thought of the Prince of Tears weeping into his pillows like a child is not an image I will soon forget," Edmund said coldly.

Aidan stiffened. "That's my point. They could've taken Torel before I even knew what was going on. Don't you see? It just doesn't make any sense."

Edmund looked up to Cotak. "Why don't we ask our friend?"

All eyes locked on to the spirit chief. Cotak's arms trembled, making the ghostly apparitions that trailed up his biceps and chest shudder. He shook his head slowly.

"Your son raises many points, Edmund the Valorous," he said at last, working through the words carefully.

Edmund's fists clenched at his side. "You will address me as king, wildlander."

The room went absolutely still. Aidan could barely breathe. Darinians wandered their deserts, carved cities from rock and abandoned them just as quickly when the urge to wander took hold. Most of the great cities of the north and east had been built by Darinian hands. To call a Darinian a savage was more than untrue. It was almost as grievous an insult as murdering his kin in cold blood.

Cotak had gone still. He gripped the rail in white knuckles. "You would insult my honor, king?" he said, biting into the last word.

Edmund tore off his right gauntlet and raised his arm,

revealing a long gash. "Your war chief's blade tasted my blood. I thought him a man of honor. I was mistaken."

Cotak looked less sure of himself. "I know nothing of that. I—"

"Lies," Edmund said, his mouth twisted. "Romen would not make such a bold play without first calling the clans together. Darinia's deception goes deeper than an attempt on the Crown of the North's life." His face darkened. "You are in Calewind to conduct trades for supplies. Or so you say. How do we know you are not here to finish what your war chief started?"

Cotak had been shaking his head all through Edmund's words. "I told you, I do not—"

"I'm afraid evidence mounts against you, clan chief," Tyrnen said, stepping forward. "Perhaps I can help you all understand what transpired, as well as what is no doubt happening as we speak. I am sorry to say that the deceitful machinations of the clans have been in motion for quite some time. Following the attack, more news reached me by way of students enrolled in the Lion's Den."

Tyrnen paused, gathering a deep breath. "The wolf daughter has taken Sharem."

Pandemonium erupted above. Nobles took to their feet, shaking their fists and shouting. Cotak's eyes darted around, his shoulders hunched as if anticipating a blade buried up to the hilt. Below, the Wardsmen broke rank, turning to speak to those around them. Brendon barked commands that were lost in the din. Tyrnen raised his hands and the crowd gradually fell silent.

"The city was taken with swift and violent force by a small contingent of clansmen. The coup transpired on the day of Aidan's ceremony, which I believe to be proof that Romen's plot has been in motion for some time, now. As far as I can tell, the war chief's visit to witness Prince Aidan's Rite of Heritage was a ruse designed to steal our attention away from their actions at the border—actions orchestrated in part, no doubt, by their daughter."

More shouting rang out from. Aidan shook his head. *It can't be true. I've known Romen and Cynthia. Nichel wouldn't... Would she?* He hadn't seen her in years. If she hadn't fallen ill, she would be on his arm right now as his wife. Or had she fallen ill? Was that part of the ruse—if there was a ruse?

His thoughts trailed off as his mother resumed speaking.

"... all saddened by the actions we are forced to take. As of this moment forward, Torel makes a formal declaration of war against Darinia."

Aidan fought to keep himself upright. *War.*

Edmund stepped forward and pointed at Cotak, who was reaching for the blade at his back. Wardsmen burst through the door to the gallery. Nobles shied away from them as the Wardsmen fell on Cotak, shoving him to the floor and sending his blade skittering away. He struggled, roaring and flailing. Wardsmen flew from him, crashing against the walls. One man almost tipped over the rail before another Wardsman grabbed him and pulled him to safety. More Wardsmen stormed the gallery and fell on the clan chief.

"Throw him in the depths," Edmund shouted. "He'll find his kin waiting to keep him company."

The Wardsmen—first five, now ten strong—pulled the clan chief, still shouting in Darinian, from the gallery. His shouts and the sounds of struggle faded away as the Wardsmen dragged their prisoner below Sunfall to dungeons that hadn't been used in decades.

Annalyn rose from her throne, looking cool and composed. "What we are about to enter into will tear Crotaria apart, but I believe it is for the best. A temporary rift that, once healed, will make the realms stronger. Eternal Flame," she continued, turning to Tyrnen, "where do the Touched stand?"

Tyrnen frowned, his hands lost inside his robes. Aidan sent him a silent plea. The old man's gaze flickered toward him.

"I am a Torelian," he said, holding Aidan's gaze, "but the Eternal Flame does not belong to any one realm." He looked away and faced Annalyn. "Yet given what I have witnessed and the other evidence made known to me, the Touched stand with Torel in this grave matter."

The Crown of the North nodded, obviously expecting the response. "Our first objective is to free Sharem." She turned to her son. "Prince Aidan, you will lead two hundred Wardsmen to drive the Darinians out of the city. Take it swiftly and quietly, if you can. Word cannot reach Nichel of our plans."

Aidan felt his stomach lurch as he digested the command. All eyes in the room fell upon him, crushing him like thousands of rocks poured over him. He knew what Edmund and Annalyn wanted. They were waiting for him to make good on his promise. *Tell me what I must do, and I will do it.*

Something about this felt wrong. And yet, he had seen the wound on his father's arm, one that had not been there before. If the Darinians were guilty, then he wouldn't be killing innocent men; he would be enacting justice.

It must be done, he thought, feeling his shoulders bow under the weight of the stares. *For our people. For Mother and Father.*

He took a breath.

—*You know this is not right*, Heritage cut in.

His mouth snapped shut. "What?"

Confused whispers broke out above him. Some of the Wardsmen eyed him warily.

Edmund stepped forward. "Your mother gave you a royal command."

—*This is not right. You know it. Will you be responsible for more death and destruction? Will you kill just because you have been ordered to do so?*

"No."

Edmund stepped closer, fixing him with blank eyes. "What did you say?"

Aidan felt sweat break out over his body. His heart hammered against his ribs, but he kept his gaze level. "I won't do it." His voice shook, but only a little.

Now Annalyn came slowly toward him, boxing him in. "You... won't?"

"Mother, please, I beg you to look further into this matter. I believe something else is going on here. This is not right. If we take the time to ask more questions, perhaps talk to Nichel, we can—"

"You are content to sit around and look for answers we have already given you," Edmund interrupted, "when Torelian lives could be lost by the second?"

"Even more lives will be lost if this war continues," Aidan said.

"The time for talk and negotiation has passed," Edmund snapped.

"But you haven't even tried to—"

"This is the time for action boy. You gave us your word that you would do what must be done to repair the dishonor you have done to your mother's line. The time has come to prove your worth."

Aidan's mouth worked soundlessly. What was he to do? They were asking him to kill, to take the lives of men he did not yet believe were guilty. Perhaps they were. Perhaps his mother and father were right.

—*You know they are not.*

The sword's words were soft, barely a whisper, but Aidan grabbed hold of them as if they were a rope tossed to save him from drowning. He met his father's stare. "I do not believe in this war. I refuse to take part in it."

The room shuddered as a loud ringing noise filled his ears. He raised a hand to his cheek, mouth open in astonishment. His mother lowered her hand, her palm red.

She hit me. She hit me.

"You failed me when that sword rejected you, when the entire Gairden line rejected you," she said, her tone cold and sharp. "If you refuse this offer, you are refusing *me*, and you are proving that my only son, the only child I will ever bear, is not strong enough. Not good enough. Am I so unimportant to you, Aidan? Is it so easy for you to shirk the future of our people?"

Aidan felt his resolve slough off like melting snow. He was tired of fighting: tired of trying to decide what he wanted and what he did not; tired of being told he was a failure, a disappointment.

"I'll do it."

He whirled, hand still cupped to his face as he strode toward the closed doors.

"Aidan," Daniel whispered as the prince reached him.

"Open the doors."

"Maybe you shouldn't—"

"Open. The doors."

They began to swing open. Aidan shouldered through, his mother's stare digging into his back like a knife.

Chapter 10

Stains

AIDAN ABSENTLY FINGERED HIS Cinder Band—the gold loop once again hugged his right forefinger, at Tyrnen's insistence—and trotted his horse to the head of the regiment. He creaked as he moved. He wore the mail his father had fashioned for him—heavy enough to turn back all but the strongest blows, yet light enough that he could move almost as easily as if he wore wool. Today, it felt heavy and tight.

The Lady peeked over the horizon, faint beams breaking through the slate-gray sky to caress the lamp once again fastened around Aidan's neck. The clear vial stirred at her touch, emitting a faint luminescence. Aidan had immediately kindled upon setting foot outside Sunfall, but not even a heat bubble could melt away the chill he felt in his bones.

I'm only doing this because they forced me. I don't want *to do it.*

Aidan turned his mount to face his charge. The Wardsmen ceased fidgeting with mounts, saddlebags, weapons, and armor, and looked up at him, waiting. The words he had stayed up all night preparing for their departure, for this moment, died on his tongue.

Why am I doing this? How did we even get here?

—Interesting questions, Aidan Gairden, the grandmotherly voice broke in. *Why* are *you doing this, if you believe it to be wrong?*

His jaw tightened. Annalyn had chosen to stay behind. Naturally, the sword-bearer kept Heritage by her side, or tucked away in the sword chamber, or any of a dozen other places within the palace and away from Aidan. Unfortunately for him, Heritage didn't seem to care much about proximity. The voice had poked holes in his thoughts repeatedly since the disastrous conclusion to yesterday's disastrous announcement, pestering him with the same question: Why?

"Stay out of my head," he muttered.

—Someone needs to do the thinking in this relationship, and

it obviously won't be you.

I have a plan.

—Oh? Care to share?

No.

Shoving the sword from his mind—literally, he hoped—Aidan took a deep breath and gave up trying to recall his speech. It so happened that he *did* have a plan, and the grandiose words he'd prepared by candlelight did not fit with what he intended to attempt at Sharem. He settled for speaking from his heart.

"It is never easy," he began, steadying his voice before continuing, "to do what it is we set out to do. Remember that you fight for Torel so that we can cultivate her land and work her metals into instruments of productivity instead of war. You fight so your children can grow up in a realm free of danger and strife, and as full of opportunity as limitless as the Lady's light."

He swept his gaze over the men. "I give you my word that I will do everything in my power to bring you back to this very spot." He clapped his left fist to his chest. Two hundred fists echoed the salute, gauntleted fists ringing against chests coated in steel mail. "For Torel!"

"For Torel!" the Wardsmen returned.

"For Torel," a lone voice at the back of the columns called out.

Aidan watched his father gallop past the lines, slowing as he drew up to the prince. They faced each other in silence, the heat from yesterday's bitter exchange hanging over them like a thunderhead ready to burst. Then Edmund dismounted and dropped to one knee. Stunned, Aidan's mouth worked to form words.

"This is what you've trained for, son," Edmund said, looking up. "What you march toward this day is the culmination of everything I have taught you."

Aidan said nothing.

"I remember the day when you first asked to accompany me on a tour of the training grounds," Edmund said, his voice trembling with pride. "I will never be able to teach my son how to wield a blade. That is not your gift. The Lady blessed you with *Ordine'cin*, and you are as extraordinary a Touched as has ever walked Crotaria, as your mother and Tyrnen say."

Edmund rose. "But you have another gift, Aidan. You have an incredible mind, and you have used that mind to absorb the lessons I have taught you—lessons of leadership, discipline, and strategy. Those gifts will lead these men to victory. And I would like to be by your side to witness that victory, if you will have me."

"If *I* will have *you*?" Aidan repeated. "You are General of Torel's Ward."

Edmund shrugged. "This is your campaign. The command is yours."

Aidan regarded his father for a long time. "You may join me."

Edmund bowed. "I predict this glory will be the first of many for you, son," he said as he hoisted himself into his saddle.

"I don't seek glory," Aidan snapped. He turned and shouted a command. The gate began to crank open, and Aidan guided his horse down the mountain pass and into Calewind.

The march lasted eight days and seven nights. Each day, when the Lady tucked herself away for slumber, Aidan called a rest. Edmund grumbled about haste, but Aidan reasoned that the Wardsmen needed to conserve energy for the battle that awaited them.

"The people of Sharem are being held captive by an enemy," Edmund said to Aidan the first night. They stood in his father's tent. A table littered with maps stood between them. Edmund leaned forward over the table, fists planted against its surface. "Your pace is leisurely, as if we go to pay a visit to friends. Imposing a forced march could place two hundred men outside Sharem's walls in four days, maybe three. Give the order."

"No."

Edmund slowly straightened. "Why?"

"This is *my* campaign, Father," Aidan said, his voice calmer than he felt. "*My* men need to be rested. We halt at dusk and break camp every morning at dawn."

"Very well," Edmund said. "I don't agree with your methods, but I will defer to you."

Aidan searched his face but saw no sign of contradiction. Nodding, he joined Edmund at the table to go over the maps. Sharem sat in the heart of Crotaria where all four realms met, dividing up the trade city like a pie. The Temple of Dawn, a towering monument made from sparkling marble, sat in the very center of the city so that each corner of the temple touched one of the four realms. The Lion's Den was located in Torel's district amid dozens of laboratories, observatories, schools, and shops that dealt primarily in foods and academic supplies. Darinia's district hosted smiths proficient in crafting all sorts of materials, mostly iron and steel. In the eastern district, Leaston's wealthiest merchants kept a steady flow of goods coming in and heading out, contributing a great deal of the coin that flowed through Sharem like a dog chasing its tail until they spread out into the realms beyond.

All but one. Like the rest of the southern realm, Sallner's district was a slum. Efforts had been made over the centuries to bring the district up to modern standards, but few, save patrols of Wardsmen charged with monitoring the south's activities, set foot there. Most Sallnerians lived in communities on the Territory Bridge, anyway, a strip of land bordered by the Great Sea and connecting the main body of Crotaria to the southern realm. What *remained* of the southern realm.

"What reconnaissance do we have?" Aidan asked, studying a map of the city.

"Tyrnen's student contact inside Sharem estimates the force within the city to be thirty strong. If we—"

"How did such a small force take one of our key cities from us so easily?"

Edmund gaped at him as if the answer should be obvious. "We believed Darinia to be our friends, Aidan. The Wardsmen in Torel District would not have been prepared for an attack orchestrated by former allies."

"What about the Leaston and Sallner Districts?" Aidan asked. "Are they under Darinia's control?"

"We should assume as much. Tyrnen's sources said that the gates have not opened since the Darinians took the city—no one in, no one out. They could smuggle clansmen across the border into each district until they're ready for a large-scale attack."

"Dawn's light," Aidan cursed. "We only brought two hundred men. You're telling me we could be marching into battle against all the clans?"

Edmund shook his head. "Unlikely. Romen's death has thrown the clans into turmoil. The chiefs are probably fighting amongst themselves to determine who will ascend to war chief. Nichel is the most likely candidate, but she has not yet come of age. That's why we need to strike now, while the wildlanders sort themselves out."

Aidan flinched. The slur stung like a blow. Until the day his mother had declared war on the west, he had only heard the term muttered by drunken tavern dwellers, and they had been promptly booted from the establishment. Hearing it twice in the span of as many days was a sharp reminder of just how quickly his life had spun out of control.

"There is still time to reconsider this," he said. "We could—"

Edmund yawned and covered his mouth with a fist. "I'm quite tired. You can show yourself out."

At mid-morning of the eighth day, when Sharem was three leagues away, snow began to fall. Aidan called for a final stop and looked at his father's tent. A soft ball of light glowed within. He set his shoulders and trudged forward. Deep snow encouraged his reluctance. He nodded to the guards out front and went through the flap. Edmund stood poring over his maps. A squat lamp sat in one corner of the table.

"What is our plan?" Edmund asked as Aidan joined him.

Aidan hesitated. *That depends on which plan you mean.* "I'll strike here," he said, pointing to Sharem's northern wall. "I don't want to march up to the front gates, no matter how small the attack party inside the walls is rumored to be. I will not squander lives." *From either side,* he wanted to add.

He took a breath and rushed on. "Once the wall falls, the Wardsmen will enter the city, and I will give the Darinians a chance to surrender peacefully."

Edmund's face tightened. "Aidan—"

"Bloodshed should be a last resort," the prince cut in, keeping his eyes fixed on the map. "You taught me that. The clans have been allies for hundreds of years. If I can find a way to resolve this conflict here, today, I will take it."

He looked up to meet Edmund's gaze, refusing to drop his eyes. To his surprise, Edmund shrugged.

"What you suggest might work to our advantage."

Aidan frowned, surprised and more than a little cautious. "How so?"

"We need to hold the city until your mother arrives with all of Torel's Ward. From there, we—"

"What do you mean? Why is she leading the army here?" But Aidan thought he knew.

Edmund gave a low, rumbling growl. Aidan realized it was supposed to be a laugh.

"Sharem is the perfect staging ground for the war. Our troops will have access to all the food, water, shelter, and supplies they could ever need." He looked up at his son's shocked face and smiled. His eyes remained devoid of humor, of light. "This *is* a war effort, Aidan. Sharem is but one phase of that war. Negotiation, bloodshed... Use any approach you like to take Sharem. Just don't fail."

Aidan turned back to the maps. "What about the Leastonians?"

"They're probably captives, too. Freeing them all but assures the merchant guild's cooperation. And if not..." He shrugged.

Aidan's eyes widened. "You want to fight them, too?"

"I didn't *want* to fight the clans, yet here we are. What we do is for the good of all Crotaria. Adding the Leastonian navy to our effort protects their realm from the wildlanders, too. If they can't see that, then we must consider them an enemy, as reviled as the snakes in the south."

"What is wrong with you?" Aidan said, voice trembling. He could feel his emotions boiling over, but he couldn't stop them. Either his father had gone mad, or he'd never awoken from his first nightmare. He suppressed a shudder and forced the visions of his parents—staring at him with eyeless sockets, their mouths open in unending screams—from his mind. "The friendship we shared with Darinia was prosperous for both realms, for all of Crotaria! War will deplete our resources—money *and* lives. There must be a way to fix this without more violence. Please, let me find a way."

"What's done is done." Edmund's tone left no room for argument. He turned away. "You have a battle to prepare for, son. I suggest you get ready."

In a daze, Aidan went to the tent flap.

"Aidan."

He hesitated, glanced over his shoulder.

"What?"

Edmund's eyes burned with intensity brighter than the lantern on the desk. "Will you be able to go through with this? This is only the first strike in a war we must win. You gave your word, son. I must be certain of your cooperation."

"I will do what I have to do only because I have to do it."

"Your kingdom needs you, Aidan. The outcome of this battle is crucial."

Aidan stormed out of the tent.

Snow leaked from the clouds as the Lady continued her slow flight through the sky. The Wardsmen stood waiting, nine rows of twenty men, at the top of a hill that overlooked Sharem's northern wall. The hill flowed down to a flat stretch of white earth that ended at the north wall of the trade city, bordered on one side by a thick forest buried under a glistening canopy of snow and ice.

The silence was interrupted by a single trebuchet lumbering forward, creaking as twenty Wardsmen Aidan had plucked from his force rolled it to the top of the hill. The long arm of the trebuchet was cocked back; the large sling at the far end was empty and dangled over the ground. The men grunted into the stillness of the afternoon as they stopped and lifted a boulder into the sling. Ten knotted ropes dangled from the short end of the cocked arm, brushing polished helmets. After dropping the boulder into the sling, the Wardsmen hurried under the trebuchet and took hold of the ropes, two men to each rope. Then they turned and looked at Aidan, waiting.

Stroking his mount's neck nervously, Aidan breathed in the crisp air and looked at his father, beside him atop his own steed. His gaze was pleading. *Give me a chance. Let me talk to her.* Edmund was studying Sharem, pointedly avoiding his son. Sighing, Aidan signaled to a lieutenant several rows up. The man nodded and shouted at the Wardsmen operating the catapult. As one, the twenty Wardsmen heaved on their ropes. The long end of the arm shot upward and the boulder flew down toward the city.

The boulder slammed into the center of the wall, shattering heavy stone. Seconds after the echoes of the first strike faded, another boulder rocketed downward and slammed home with a thunderous crash. Broken stone fell away from the wall. Through the gap, Aidan could see people scrambling away, screaming as they fled. He raised his hand to signal a halt to the barrage and considered his next move as the twenty Wardsmen abandoned their post and fell into place at the rear of his force. He could do it. He could ride forward now, enter the city, find Nichel or whoever had led the attack, and—

One of his scouts sounded a note of alarm. Below, a group of perhaps forty clansmen stormed through the eastern gate and curved to the north. Plated mail covered the tattoos that decorated the clansmen's bodies. The helms they wore—steel fashioned in the form of wolf, bear, and ram heads, fiendish masks capped with horns and fangs and painted in streaks of colors—made them look like half-human beasts.

Cursing inwardly, ignoring his father's smirk, Aidan raised his right hand. The back two rows of Wardsmen drew their longbows. Lieutenants shouted trajectories. Forty bowstrings went taut. The front lines hefted swords and spears in one hand, raised shields in the other.

Aidan's right hand dropped. The Wardsmen let fly; arrows whistled as they took flight. They fell in a hail. Screams rang out as half a dozen clansmen fell. The rear line of Darinians responded with a volley of their own while the rest charged forward, racing across the flat ground and hefting axes as tall as stalks of corn in fists the size of a small man's head. Aidan shouted an order. Every Wardsmen not holding a bow dropped to one knee and raised their shields, forming a wall of wood and steel. Missiles thudded and snapped against the wall like hail on a rooftop.

His archers dipped their hands smoothly into quivers, nocked a fresh round of arrows, and loosed. A third round leaped from bowstrings while the second was still in flight. The Darinians returned fire. Arrows filled the sky like flocks of crows streaking at one another. Several of the projectiles collided and plummeted in jumbles of splinters and sharpened heads. Below, the clansmen surged forward like a single arrow intent on flying up the hill and shattering Aidan's men.

"Forward!" Aidan bellowed.

Aidan's men charged down the hill. Halfway down, they split like a stream breaking around a rock. The unbroken mass of men had become a pincer designed to crush the Darinians. Meanwhile, the archers split, flanking the divided infantry, and continued their storm of arrows. The Darinian bowmen responded in turn, dividing into two groups and spitting arrows at Aidan's divided force. This time the Wardsmen continued running as they raised their shields. Not every man raised his in time.

Aidan kindled and wove a flat, invisible barrier that hung over the heads of his infantry and archers. It was as if someone had lowered a dome of thick, polished glass over their heads. Arrows snapped and slid harmlessly to the ground. Still sprinting, the Wardsmen lowered their shields just slightly, holding them in front. The two forces collided in a thunderous crash.

"All goes well," Edmund said from where he and Aidan watched at the top of the hill. Steel rang against steel. Shouts turned to shrill cries as blade bit through armor and tasted flesh.

Aidan chose not to reply. *Well* was not how he would have defined the battle. The Darinians, proficient fighters though they were, could not beat the numbers game. The Wardsmen cleaved through them, spilling their blood across the snow. For every Wardsman who fell, three Darinians crumpled. But fighting was still his least desirable course of action. He hadn't been given even a moment to enter the city without bloodshed. The clansmen had stormed out almost immediately.

Aidan narrowed his eyes. *As if they had been waiting for an attack.*

He turned the thought over and decided it wasn't too far-fetched. Any party that took a city by force would expect resistance eventually. Still...

A horn sounded from within Sharem. Aidan turned to his father, confused. Edmund wore a flat, emotionless expression. A roar erupted from the forest to the east of Sharem. Hordes of clansmen burst through the trees and poured forth, a swarm of pagan faces, steel, and a mail hide crafted using techniques known only by Darinia's finest blacksmiths—form-fitting, yet as strong as plate mail—and mounted atop armored horses.

Aidan's mouth hung open as clansmen continued pouring from the trees like wasps from an upset hive. Less than half a mile separated his men from the horde rushing toward them, a wave of steel that would sweep away everything in its path.

"They'll all die," Aidan whispered. His men had turned to brace themselves against the surprise charge, but Aidan knew it would not be enough. Many from the smaller attack force that had charged out from Sharem—a decoy, he understood now—were still alive and rallying, sending ululating war cries at the scores of brethren rumbling to their aid.

"You can save them, Aidan," Edmund said.

"You said this wasn't possible," Aidan said, as if he hadn't heard. "You said a force this size couldn't possibly—"

"I was mistaken. You can save them."

Aidan looked at him, face ashen.

"You haven't lifted a finger in this conflict, Aidan," Edmund said. "You've been content to simply issue orders, convincing yourself that you were only doing what had to be done, that the blood of your enemies would stain the hands of your Wardsmen instead of your own. Prove your worth, boy. Your gift is more than enough to prevent this slaughter."

A line of sweat oozed down Aidan's forehead. He didn't want his men to be killed, of course he didn't. But if he acted, he would spill the blood of a people he believed to be innocent. Raising his palms, Aidan quickly replayed the tale his mother had told the day the war had been announced. It still did not ring true. His hands lowered.

"The enemy outnumbers us at least four to one, Aidan," Edmund said, his voice tight.

He didn't know what to do. He couldn't leave his people to die—and they surely would; clansmen continued to rush from the forest. The Wardsmen would make a stand, but it would not last long. But Aidan could not convince himself of the Darinians' guilt. He wished he could just sit down and let his father figure everything out.

—The time is now, Aidan. Make your choice.

He had never been so thankful to hear from Heritage. *Tell me what to do! Please!*

But the sword had gone silent.

"The lives of our people, Aidan. What will you do?" his father said.

Breathing heavily, Aidan swept his eyes across the battle below. The clansmen—there had to be close to a thousand, their masks and armor making them appear like wild animals —would cross the road and wash over his men in seconds.

—*What will you do, Aidan?* Heritage asked.

"Make your choice, boy! Now!" his father said.

Aidan swore and drank in the light, raised clenched fists, shouted a prayer. The spell his confused and terrified mind latched onto was a difficult one and required a large amount of light. But the Lady heard his plea, and the results were suitably devastating.

The road in front of the approaching Darinian force exploded. Masses of rock, ice, and gravel rained down on the clansmen, crushing heads and bodies. The gash ripped through the roadway as Aidan kindled again. A pallid fire shot from his left palm and sparked through the first line of trees in the forest. The magical inferno melted through ice and snow to light wet branches as if they were dry. The remaining lines of trees followed suit, bursting into fiery existence one after the other. The forest became a funeral pyre. Tortured screams and terrified whinnies emanated from the blaze as flesh melted from bone and bone withered to ashes.

Aidan kindled a third time, gorging on the Lady's light until he felt drunk, and spit out a third prayer. A bolt of lightning pierced the ground, shattering Darinians. Blood and limbs sprayed across the battlefield like sparks from a fire. More bolts stabbed down. Crackling energy spread outward like ripples from a pebble cast into a pond, shredding earth, flesh, and bone. The earth heaved like the deck of a ship caught in a storm, scattering what remained of the clansmen's resistance.

Aidan slipped from his horse and fell to his knees, tears streaming down his cheeks. He kindled one last time. The fire chewing through the forest dissipated, leaving piles of ash and bloody slop. Silence resumed its hold on the day, broken only by the moans of the wounded and dying from below and Aidan's deep, full-body retches. Snow drifted down, knitting a blanket to hide the gore smeared over the muddy ground.

Edmund stood over Aidan, oblivious to the scent of roasted flesh carried on the afternoon breeze. "You did what you had to do. You saved your men, Aidan. They would have died had you not acted." Edmund raised his eyes to the smoldering, torn battlefield. "I'm proud of you," he added, as if in afterthought. He galloped down the hill to round up the Wardsmen.

Aidan didn't look up. He looked instead at the snow falling onto his hands. Hands that were stained with blood only he could see. Blood that could never wash away.

Edmund approached the guards outside his tent and gave orders not to be disturbed under any circumstances. He strode to the table and whispered a word, low and guttural, into the lantern. The flame went low for a moment. A pair of eyes appeared.

"Is it done?" a voice asked.

"Yes, master," Edmund said. "The boy passed the test, though not without a great deal of hesitation. Almost a pity, actually. I would have happily killed him right there."

"If he passed, then he is still useful to us."

"He used pure-fire, my lord," Edmund said, his voice quivering with excitement. "It was magnificent. You should have heard the screams. And the lightning ripples... the blood..." Edmund shivered in ecstasy. He forced himself to take a calming breath. "What of the sword?"

"The tests continue to prove too dangerous, but there is still a chance the blade will accept Aidan. It is still useful to us."

The flame flared as if in anger, causing Edmund to shrink back.

"Annalyn returned it to the chamber at no small risk," the voice continued. "Her injuries were too grievous to go unnoticed. I discarded the body and replaced it. I fear the sword would react poorly to you as it did to her. It will remain in the chamber until the boy has use for it."

"And if he uses it against us?"

"Aidan will either be tamed, or..." The voice trailed away for a moment. "Or he will die before he has the chance to raise Heritage," it went on. Edmund blinked. It sounded conflicted. It continued, firm once more. "Should that come to pass, the sword must be destroyed. We—"

Edmund raised a hand as he heard the guards outside raising their voices in anger. Abruptly they fell silent.

Aidan strode into the tent, livid. "Protection, Father? Even from me?"

Edmund turned to his son. "What is it you need?" He kept glancing at the lantern.

"Your men outside will be fine. I'll tell them you were concerned."

"I asked what I can do for you."

Aidan blinked in surprise. Edmund didn't seem to care whether the guards lived or died. He shook his head before continuing. "I'm done."

"What do you mean?"

"I don't believe in this war, Father. I don't believe the Darinians to be guilty. You have not even made an attempt to negotiate with Nichel, or with Cotak, or the other clan chiefs. You taught me that war is nothing to be entered into lightly. You have been nothing but eager to engage Darinia, a people that have been friends and allies for decades."

Aidan took a breath before plunging onward. "I don't believe in this war. I am through."

Edmund's cold smile dipped into a dark frown. "You cannot walk away from this, Prince of Tears," he said softly, stalking forward. "You don't get to quit this like you have everything else. If you do, you will be a disappointment to me, and a failure to your line."

Shock filled Aidan's throat like a gag. "Why are you treating me like this? You and mother both, you've never—"

Edmund's hand shot up, lightning fast, and slapped Aidan's mouth. The prince staggered, more from surprise than pain, and raised a shaking hand to his lips. Edmund reeled back for another blow, but Aidan grabbed his father's hand, grunting as his father's arm shook, straining to reach him.

"Stop," Aidan said, sounding weak and pleading. He didn't care.

"I will not," Edmund said, straining against his son. "This appears to be the only language you understand." He swung his other fist, but the blow never came. Aidan raised his hand and kindled. A ball of air collided against his father's chest, sending him sailing over the table and crashing into the snow.

Edmund scrabbled back to his feet, snarling. "This is your last chance, Aidan. I will forgive what you just did. We will pretend this never happened, and that is something you should want very, very much. But if you turn away, it's over for you, boy. Do you understand? You will be dead to me, and to your mother. This is your last chance."

The words cut Aidan like a knife. He began to tremble, but his jaw tightened. "I am sorry, Father. I will not take another life that I believe to be innocent."

Edmund's smile held no mirth. "Guards!"

Several Wardsmen burst into the tent. "General," one said, "the men outside your tent are—" He cut off, looking slowly between Edmund and Aidan.

"Arrest my son. The charge is... Stop him!"

The Wardsmen ran forward, but Aidan did not even notice them. He had closed his eyes and begun murmuring. The Wardsmen lunged for him as he disappeared in a burst of wind, scattering maps from the table and leaving only a soft imprint in the snow where he had stood.

Chapter 11

Acceptance

THE LAST LIGHT OF DAY winked through the tent flap before the Lady sunk into the west horizon, handing Crotaria over to the Lord of Midnight. By itself, that last glimmer of light wasn't enough for Aidan to escape the madman that wore his father's face. Topped off with the glowing jewels around his neck, it was just enough.

Aidan lunged at the light, combining it with his lamp while his father shouted for guards. In his mind he pictured his safe place, maybe the safest place in Crotaria. The light he needed to complete the kindling was far greater than the prayer he had used to shift into Calewind on his birthday. That only stood to reason; he had been less than two miles outside the city then. The Language of Light passed through his lips in a whisper—he couldn't let his father catch on to what he was doing—and suddenly wind rushed through the tent, spiriting him leagues and leagues to the north. A blink, not even a heartbeat later, and Aidan was slumped against Tyrnen's tower door.

Fever pounced on him, settling over him like heat that hung over Darinia's deserts. Sweat broke out all over his body, dampening his hair and clothes. The arm he lifted to the knocker shook uncontrollably. Just before his fingers could grip the icy bronze knocker, the door flew open and Tyrnen was there, his expression flashing from surprise to concern.

"My word," the old man said, taking in Aidan's disheveled form and bloodied lip. "You're supposed to be in Sharem."

Aidan didn't seem to hear him. He stared through Tyrnen with glazed eyes. "He hit me."

"Who hit you?"

"My father. I killed them all, and then he hit me."

Aidan slumped forward, unable to stay upright on his quivering legs. Tyrnen caught him, throwing an arm over his shoulder and steering Aidan inside out of the cold. The Eternal Flame eased Aidan into his favorite chair in front of the fire. Aidan waved at the heat. He tried to stand but Tyrnen placed a firm hand on his shoulder until he settled back down.

Aidan didn't struggle long. He couldn't. The spells he had used at Sharem had already left him weak and roasted, as if Helda had cooked him in one of her pans. The lamp clinked against his armor, empty save for a few drops of light that pulsed weakly. Even the thread of light he'd used to supplement the lamp's full vials to shift back to Sunfall had almost been enough to burn his gift from his blood. To a Touched, losing the Lady's gift of light magic was as crippling as losing both arms. Aidan would have given his gift *and* his arms if it meant escaping his father's tent. He saw the king's face again, his features twisted in rage and disgust, and... And other emotions he preferred not to think about.

"How did you get here?" Tyrnen asked from where he rummaged around in his desk.

"Shifted."

"From *Sharem*?"

Aidan lifted the lamp from his neck. His hand shook, rattling the chain against his armor.

"Incredible," Tyrnen murmured, eyeing the invention. Then he carried over two mugs of tea and extended one to Aidan. He shied away from it, but Tyrnen's hand followed.

"Drink," the old man said. "The light you drew heated your blood, stealing energy your body needs. You need sleep to dispel the fever, but you also need to keep warm. Drink," he said more firmly, pushing the mug at Aidan.

Aidan took it and raised it to his lips, pulling in sips.

"Now, tell me what happened," the old man said as he settled into his chair.

Aidan smiled at Tyrnen over the rim of his cup. No matter what happened, the Eternal Flame was his friend, someone he could always count on. *I thought I could count on my father.* He frowned into his cup.

"I killed them, Tyrnen."

"Killed who, Aidan?"

"The clansmen at Sharem. The attack party stationed at Sharem was small. We had them, Tyrnen. My force was larger, and everything seemed to be happening as I expected. But the Darinians in the city were a decoy. A much larger force emerged from the forest after the attack began." He shook his head. "I had to act quickly. If I didn't, they would have killed my regiment to the last man. But I hesitated. I didn't believe the Darinians were guilty."

He looked over at his friend. Tyrnen sat quietly, legs crossed, hands folded in his lap.

"I killed them all," Aidan finished in a whisper. "Not a single Darinian was left standing after what I did."

"You did it to save your people, Aidan. You had no choice."

"I *know* that. If there was any other way, don't you think I would have—"

"I was trying to make a point, which you have just reiterated: you did it because you had to. I know your heart, lad. You would not have killed for any reason other than need."

"I've never killed a man before. Today, I killed hundreds. A few words, and—" Aidan snapped his fingers "—gone. Just like that. They... they *exploded*, Tyrnen. There was so much blood. And I did that. I caused all that death."

"You did the only thing you could have done. And what's more, I believe it was the *right* thing to do."

Aidan was horrified. "How can you say that?"

"Do you believe the clansmen would have spared a single man from your regiment? You? Your father?"

"No, but—"

"Do you regret saving the lives of your people?"

"No!"

"Then whether or not you believe in your actions, you did the only thing you could have. You protected your people from a threat—and they *were* a threat, whether you regard them as an enemy or not."

Aidan stared into the cold hearth for a long time. "I know I saved the lives of my men by what I did. I don't regret that part. But I don't believe in what I had to do to accomplish that goal. I don't believe in this war."

He took a deep breath. "Tyrnen, you know my family's history, so you know what *Ordine'kel* and *Ordine'cin* mean. They're not just gifts. I *am* the Guardian Light." He made a sound of frustration. "Or at least, I was supposed to be. My point is, the Gairdens are responsible not just for Torel, but all of Crotaria. As long as I am involved in this war, every act I commit will feel wrong to me. What I did tonight feels like murder. I am not convinced of Darinia's wrongdoing. And until I am—*if* I am—I will not fight them. I can't."

Watching him, Tyrnen chuckled.

"What's so funny?" Aidan asked.

"You, boy. Speaking of responsibility and duty." He chuckled again, but his face was warm. He leaned forward and patted Aidan's leg. "Don't look now, boy, but I think you're growing up."

"It snuck up on me," Aidan said quickly, but he was also smiling.

Tyrnen set aside his cup and gave Aidan a serious look. "But what if you're right?"

"Right about what?"

"There is nothing you can do to change what you did. You can lament your actions, and I understand that. You have a noble and kind heart, just like your mother. But lamenting what happened will not bring men back from the dead."

"I know. Just as I know I will never do again what I did today."

"All right. What now?"

The question caught Aidan off-guard. What *would* he do now? *Maybe I should talk to... No. They don't understand. My confrontation with Father proved as much.* At that, Aidan's lip throbbed with fresh pain.

"Your father did that?" Tyrnen asked, gesturing at his face.

"Yes. He's never raised a hand to me, Tyrnen. Never. It's not just that, though. It was the way he looked at me. He didn't look angry, or upset, or disappointed, even. His eyes, they were... Blank. There was nothing there. Mother is the same way. They have been so cold since returning from the retreat with you to Lake Carrean. You saw mother strike me in the throne room when I refused to lead the Wardsmen to Sharem. She'd never raised a hand to me before that day. And Father—just before I left Sharem, he was going to have me arrested. Me! His own son!"

"And did you share with your father what you've just told me?"

"Yes. I told him I couldn't continue with the war until I was convinced of—"

"Those are treasonous words, Aidan." The old man raised his hands when Aidan looked at him sharply. "You may have led the attack on Sharem, but your mother is still Crown of the North. I fear your failure to follow your parents' orders could cost you more than the crown. Think on that."

Aidan's shoulders sagged. *Is all of this worth it? Tyrnen is right. Feeling sorry won't bring back the men I killed.*

Heritage barreled into his thoughts.

—Killing in defense is not intrinsically wrong, Aidan Gairden. You did save the lives of your men. But to save them, you went against something you believed to be true. Your struggle to stand up for yourself and for your beliefs was minimal. Instead, you gave in. You lashed out. You will hear the screams of the men you murdered for the rest of your life. They will follow you everywhere, even in your dreams. If you continue with this war,

you will fight again, and you will kill again. Is that what you want? Can you do again, over and over, what you did today?

"No," Aidan said, resolved. "No. I won't do it. I can't. It isn't right."

Tyrnen nodded after several quiet moments. Both men turned at the sound of boots pounding up the tower stairs.

"Wardsmen," Tyrnen said, rising.

Aidan shot to his feet. "What? How?"

"Your mother gave your father a magical means of communication so he could tell her of your progress at Sharem. He must have told her about your confrontation."

A fist pounded on Tyrnen's door. Aidan looked wildly between Tyrnen and the door.

"Aidan, you must—"

But he was already gone.

Aidan fell to his knees outside his bedchamber. Fingers scrabbling at the doorframe, he panted heavily and tried to pull himself upright. At last he succeeded, but his legs buckled as he took a step forward. He reached out with both hands, framed in the doorway like a scarecrow. He grabbed at the lamp around his neck, hoping he could drain its last ounce of light for a burst of energy that would keep him standing and awake, and whimpered. The vial was empty. He'd lapped up the last sip of the Lady's light shifting to the base of Tyrnen's tower. From there, he had dashed across the courtyard and through the side entrance.

Aidan stumbled into his room and dropped down on his bed, too tired and frightened to move again. Like the lamp, his courage had dried up. Everything had seemed so clear a few minutes ago. He had felt proud of his decision. The sound of the Wardsmen rushing up the winding stairs of Tyrnen's tower had boosted his adrenaline, masking the exhaustion caused by his long shift home. Now he was winded and teetering on the edge of consciousness. Even the short skip from the tower left him feeling like he'd sprinted all the way from Sharem to Sunfall. The candle on his dresser, its tiny flame an island of light in the sea of darkness, had more strength than he.

He was spent—physically, mentally, emotionally. Perhaps if he just stayed here and waited for someone to find him, they would be lenient. He could explain that he'd come home to think, to talk with his mother about—

—You must be brave, Aidan Gairden. If you give in, you admit that what you did at Sharem was right. Is that what you

believe? If it is, by all means, take a nap. Otherwise, pull yourself together.

His body shook with fatigue. "What can I do?"

—Leave Sunfall.

Aidan went utterly still. Leave his home? Could he do that? He had known taking a stand would anger his parents—they seemed so quick to anger these days, especially where he was concerned—but he had thought... Well, what had he thought, exactly? That he would be allowed to stay in his room and ponder the world's mysteries while war raged around him?

—It's not forever, Aidan. Just temporary. Please trust me.

Where will I go? I'm a Gairden. I can't just disappear.

—I will guide you. As I said before: trust me.

Reluctantly, Aidan shambled to his closet and pulled out a thick cloak. As he threw it around his shoulders, a fist rapped against his door. Aidan froze, then crept over to the door. Tyrnen had said his parents had some way of communicating. Word of his treachery must have spread all through the palace. Perhaps if he waited just a few moments, the guard would leave.

The door flew open and slammed into Aidan's head, knocking him flat. Two Wardsmen barged in and stalked toward him as he struggled to regain his senses. One of the men closed the door while the other yanked him to his feet and drove a fist into his stomach. Aidan doubled over, gasping for breath. The hand around his throat tightened and hoisted him into the air. Aidan beat at the arm—*Dawn, but he's strong!*—that held him, but that only made the fingers dig deeper into his throat. Spots danced in front of his eyes.

"Keep watch," the Wardsman said to his companion. The other man nodded and stood in the doorway.

"Unfortunately, Aidan Gairden," the Wardsman holding him said, "your usefulness has expired." His lips tugged upward, a failed attempt at a smile. His eyes were flat and hadn't changed—hadn't even blinked—since he'd lifted Aidan from the ground. As the prince watched, the man's free hand dug into his lower throat and *peeled the skin away*, tearing upward as if pulling off a mask. The flesh stripped back with a thick tearing sound until it snapped off and hung limply between the Wardsman's fingers. In its place was a grinning skull covered in blood and dirt.

Tossing the face away, the man—the man-*thing*—inhaled deeply and let out a slow, contented sigh. "Much better than hiding behind that suffocating layer of human hide." It pulled Aidan close. Its breath stank of meat left to rot under the Lady's searing gaze.

"Soon there will be no further need to hide. Our freedom begins with your death."

Terror pierced exhaustion like a bubble. Aidan drew the candle's light, plunging the room into darkness. The man-thing growled; Aidan felt its fist tighten. Pointing a finger, Aidan kindled, firing a blast of air from his fingertip like an arrow. Aidan dropped to the floor as his captor flew back and crashed into the wall. Blood pumping, he threw himself into the outline of the Wardsman stalking in from the doorway. They tumbled into the corridor, a tangled mass of limbs.

Aidan kicked free and pulled himself up, chest heaving as he looked around desperately. Torches crackled along the corridor, but there was no way he could kindle again. Spots danced in front of his eyes and his vision swayed. He could hear the creatures, growling in the dark room behind him.

—The sword chamber, Heritage said. *Quickly!*

Spinning, Aidan slammed his door closed and took off down the hall. A crash sounded behind him. He glanced over his shoulder to see chunks of his door scattered across the hall. The two man-things burst through the doorway and turned toward him, shouting and pointing. The one that had removed its mask had attempted to replace it, but had apparently given up; it drooped like clothes over a line, half covering the skull. Aidan choked back a yell and staggered on.

A sharp cramp pinched his gut as he fell against the stone door. He ran his fingers along the *Heritage* inscription. They shook and were slippery with sweat, streaking the door with moisture. He looked down at them, willing them to focus on their task. Just as he finished tracing the "a", bony fingers clamped down on his shoulder. His chest tightened as he looked down. The flesh from the fingers had split open, the bony digit protruding like the tip of a banana still in its skin. He fought to keep his breathing steady as he traced the final letter of the word. The door began to rumble open.

Aidan shot his outstretched arm backward, driving his elbow into the face of the creature that held him. He dived into the room and rolled into the small set of stairs leading up to Heritage. The slabs began grinding shut behind him, but not before his pursuers lunged through. They spread out to either side as he struggled to his feet. He turned and eyed Heritage. In the hands of a Gairden without *Ordine'kel*, swinging any sword felt as natural as swinging a door.

At least it's something.

Backing up the stairs, Aidan fumbled behind him until his fingers brushed the hilt of Heritage. He wrapped his hand around the leather, keeping his eyes on his attackers as they stalked up the stairs, flanking him. At his touch, Heritage hummed, sending shivers up his arm.

—Do you accept us?

"What?"

—You have run all your life, Aidan Gairden. Now you can run no further. Accept us, or die.

He shook his head, trying to let the meaning of the words sink in as his tormentors drew closer. He tightened cold, shaking fists around the hilt and took a wild swing, cleaving through the air and almost spilling down the stairs. One of the creatures let out a raspy laugh and continued stalking forward.

—Do not be afraid.

Abruptly Aidan stopped shaking. The voice had a point. Where had running brought him? Right here, trapped in a room with creatures born of nightmare and blood on his hands.

He lowered Heritage and looked directly into the Eye.

"I accept."

Something burst free within him, a slight pressure that swelled until it crushed the breath from his lungs. The world went white.

Chapter 12

Questions and Answers

INCESSANT RINGING IN HIS ears coaxed Aidan back to consciousness. He sat up slowly, groaning. Pounding like a Darinian hammer shaping steel rang through his skull.

—... finally awakened, Aidan Gairden.

Gingerly he massaged his head and pulled himself to his feet, shielding his eyes. Even the low pulse of the magical light that illuminated the portrait windows that wound up the room jabbed at his vision like splinters.

—You must leave quickly. You are no longer safe here.

"Mmm." He opened his eyes slowly, first blinking than going bug-eyed as he took in the room. The two creatures that had pursued him into the sword chamber lay at his feet. Green gore oozed from their chests; more was splattered across the walls and floor. Near their fallen forms were two decapitated heads. The fleshy human mask of the one that had exposed its true form lay nearby like a discarded rag.

As his hands tightened, he became aware of Heritage clutched in one fist. The sword had never left his grip. Green blood clung to the blade—and Aidan gasped as the liquid faded, leaving the sword as clean as if it had just been cleaned and polished.

"What happened? Why did I lose consciousness?"

—There is no time for questions. We must escape this place.

"The last thing I remember is you asking me to accept you. Was that what saved me?"

—Everything will be explained in due time. But we must make our way from this place.

Nodding, he took a step forward, then stopped. He was doing it again. Leaping to obey even though he didn't want to, even though doubts buzzed through his mind like gnats.

"No."

—This is not the time for—

"This is the perfect time. Everyone is always telling me what to do, and I do it, even when I don't want to. Well, I'm done."

—Aidan, we can talk later. You need to—

"Let me tell you about my day, as if you don't already know. I killed hundreds of men. My father hit me and tried to have me arrested for treason. Now here, in my own home, these... these *things* try to kill me. I did what you told me. I accepted you, and I did that because *I decided* to. And you know what? It felt good. Fantastic, actually. So the way I see it, why stop now? If I'd had the courage to make a decision and stand by it days ago, I might not be in this mess."

The sword was quiet for a long moment. *—Fair enough. What do you propose?*

Aidan thought about that. "Only those of Gairden blood can open the sword chamber. The only reason those creatures managed to follow was because the door didn't close in time. So, we're safe, and I'm not leaving until I get some answers."

The Eye of Heritage glowed softly. *—May I suggest a compromise? You may ask three questions. I promise to answer them, though due to the danger that apparently only I am concerned with, my answers will be succinct. However, I promise to expound as soon as we are a suitable distance away from the palace.*

Nodding, Aidan stared into the Eye. "Fair enough. I wish to know..."

What *did* he want to know first? He had so many questions, and most of those questions carried still other questions. His eyes returned to the corpses littering the floor.

"What are those... those things?"

—Corpses risen from the grave and manipulated like puppets using a powerful artifact wrought from dark magic. Men called them vagrants in millennia past. These bodies belonged to Sallnerians, likely those corrupted during the Serpent War eight centuries ago.

The sword's tone was detached and matter-of-fact, but the words left Aidan's head spinning. Dark magic, the essence of the Lord of Midnight and a forbidden art to all who walked in the Lady's light. That magic had, apparently, breathed life into the eight-hundred-year-old history lessons lying dead at his feet. More disturbing was that their actions were not their own. Someone, or some*thing*, had sent them after him. To kill him.

—We're running out of time.

Aidan shuddered and focused on plucking a new question from his tangled thoughts. "How was I able to defend myself with you?" he asked. "What I mean is, I have *Ordine'cin*. I don't remember how I killed the... the vagrants, but I really didn't expect to, at least not with a normal weapon."

—I understand the question, Aidan Gairden.

"Please stop calling me that," he mumbled. "Just 'Aidan' will do."

—Very well... Aidan. You have Ordine'kel.

The answer hit him like a splash of icy water. "That's impossible," he breathed. "I was born with *Ordine'cin*. No Gairden can have both halves of *Ordine*."

—Of course it's possible. *It simply had never occurred until now. When you accepted Heritage, you laid claim to the other half of the Lady's blessing. It has always been inside your bloodline, locked away until needed. For lack of a better term, you unlocked the dormant half of the full* Ordine *gift.*

"That's how it felt," he said, his voice awed. "Like I'd been given the key to a door I was never allowed to open."

—You have one question remaining.

He grimaced. There was so much he still wanted to know. *Why was I born with the full gift? Why did everything turn white before I lost consciousness? And why have you been...?*

He looked straight into the Eye. "Why have you been communicating with me?"

—Because you are the sword-bearer.

He expected to feel shock, surprise. He didn't. He was angry. He had been humiliated during his Rite of Heritage, his parents had treated him like their greatest failure since returning from their retreat, and he had committed an atrocity at Sharem—all as a result of a rejection to a birthright he was due to receive a bit later on.

"Why?" he growled. "Why have you done this to me?"

—I have not done anything to you. Now, I have upheld my end of our agreement. You must do the same.

"No."

—You gave your word, Aidan.

"I want you to understand something. My life hasn't been the same since you rejected me. I need to know why I was turned away if I was to become the sword-bearer in the first place."

—I will happily answer that question after *we have left this place.*

"This is important to me. I want to understand, and I am not leaving until I do."

The grandmotherly voice sighed. *—I will grant you this final answer, but you must promise to make good on your part of our* *bargain once I do.*

"I will."

—Truly?

"Yes."

—I did not accept you because you were not ready to accept me. You did not want to become sword-bearer, nor were you prepared for the responsibility.

Aidan considered the response. Perhaps the sacred blade had noticed his reluctance to take his mother's position. A thought struck him.

"What about my mother? She was the sword-bearer before me. Why is the position no longer hers?"

The sword had gone silent.

With a vexed sound he bent down and removed a sword sheath from one of the vagrants, fastened it to his belt and tucked Heritage away. He trailed his thumb along the pommel. Before, even the thought of Heritage, of holding it and of what it meant, had terrified him. Now the weight of it at his side, the smoothness of the leather grip over the hilt—it felt good. Moreover, it felt right.

"Where am I supposed to go?" he said quietly.

—South.

"South? What's in the south?" But he knew. The bodies leaking all over the floor told the story. Sallner. A realm razed and left to rot after the Serpent War, those who were not corrupted by Dimitri and Luria Thalamahn relocated to camps along the Territory Bridge. No one had set foot in the main body of Sallner for over eight centuries. He nudged one of the corpses at his feet. No one except these delightful fellows and whoever had raised them.

You said this place is dangerous, and you want me to enter Sallner? Are you mad?

—I have answered your allotted questions, Aidan. Stay true to your word. We must leave.

"Fine. But more answers later."

—Yes. Now, I suggest leaving by one of the side entrances. Speak to no one. Once outside, you should—

The doors slid open, and Annalyn entered. She blinked when she saw her son, then smoothed her features. "Aidan. I am surprised to see you here."

Relief flooded through him. "Mother. Thank the Lady!" He took a step toward her.

—Don't trust her.

Aidan paused, confused. *It's Mother.*

"Have your Wardsmen returned with you?" Annalyn asked. "Can I assume a victory for Torel?"

Aidan felt a rush of exultation. *She hasn't spoken to Father, yet. I can still explain!* "No. Well, yes, we were victorious, but..." He shook his head. "Mother, something has happened."

"Obviously," she said, looking around at the carnage that decorated the room. Not even two corpses and walls painted in green blood could ruffle Annalyn Gairden.

Aidan laughed humorlessly. "You'll never believe it." He took a breath. "Apparently I am the sword-bearer."

Annalyn took a step back. "How do you know this?"

"The sword has been speaking with me ever since my ceremony. Then, during the proclamation of war... well, just now when the vagrants—the bodies over there—they..." He shook his head, overwhelmed.

Annalyn smiled and held out her arms. "You're upset. Come. We'll get it sorted out."

Relief and gratitude washed through him. He took a step toward her.

—Do not go with her. The sword's voice cracked like a whip.

Aidan frowned. "What are you about?"

"Pardon?" Annalyn said.

"Oh, not you, Mother. It's Heritage. It—"

—Grip me tightly. Blink.

What?

"Aidan?" Annalyn's voice was tense. "Come here, please."

—Do it.

Aidan blinked. Opening his eyes, he gasped. Whiteness lay atop his vision, as if the entire room had been buried in snow. Details such as the outlines of his hands and clothing, the sword, the cracks in the wall and floor, the green blood—they were black, like charcoal on white canvas.

Panicked, Aidan turned to Annalyn. He screamed. Standing in his mother's place was an aberration. Her clothing was white and outlined in black, like his, but the rest of her was in full, horrible color. Her skin was putrid and saggy. Her eyes were empty pits, and her mouth gaped in a silent scream. Bands of flesh stretched from one lip to the other. The strips quivered as she spoke.

"What's the matter, boy? Living a bad dream?" She raised her arms and hooked her fingers into claws.

"Come willingly. You are to be kept alive, but I've no qualms with—"

Before he knew what was happening he lunged at her as if compelled by some force that had assumed control of his body. The creature's cavernous sockets widened for an instant before Heritage severed head from shoulders in one clean blow.

He turned, blinked again, and looked down at the floor. He no longer saw a creature from his nightmares spun into flesh. He saw his mother's head.

Chapter 13

What Friends Do

AIDAN DROPPED TO ALL FOURS and retched.

—Get up.

He barely heard the old woman's stern voice. He ran his arm over his mouth and looked into his mother's face—mouth open in surprise and terror. That was how she had spent her last moments. Terrified of her son. Green blood gushed from her head and torn neck. Aidan recoiled with a scream.

—You must leave. Now.

Teetering on unsteady legs, Aidan watched blood seep along the floor like honey oozing from an upturned jar. His stomach gave another nasty lurch.

—Aidan, please listen. That was not your mother. It is not natural.

He turned from the body and concentrated on breathing. In and out. Slowly, naturally. *Then what in Kahltan's name is it?*

—A vagrant, and more will come. They will not be caught unawares like this one.

Cautiously, Aidan turned and fixed his gaze on a high point on the wall across the chamber, keeping his latest kill below his line of sight. He stepped over the body, cringing as one boot squelched in the spreading pile of emerald blood.

—Don't think. Keep moving.

It's not her?

—No. I promise. Now go.

Where?

—Out the side entrance on the east side. Go, and be on the lookout. More will come.

Wiping his boot along the floor, Aidan touched the door and peeked out. The corridor was empty. He started off in a crouch, moving as quietly as he could, avoiding the revealing light of torches when he was able, inching his way closer to the east wing.

Memories of the past month crept into his thoughts as he picked his way from shadow to shadow. He saw the faces of the clansmen at Sharem, wide eyes and open mouths pleading with him to extinguish the pure-fire that burned the flesh from their bodies, the lightning that shattered bodies like an axe shattered a log. His lips throbbed as he recalled his father striking him. Unbidden, his mother's severed head floated into his vision. Aidan gritted his teeth against the image. *That wasn't her.*

Footsteps reached his ears. At least three pairs, all in step and growing closer. He ducked into an alcove and waited until a trio of Wardsmen marched by and around a bend. Slinking out, he set off again.

"Since I'm doing what you asked," he whispered as he crept along, "would you tell me what it is we seek in the south?"

—Not what; whom.

"All right," Aidan whispered with forced patience. "Whom?"

—The Prophet.

"Who is the Prophet?"

But the sword had gone silent yet again. *Even more stubborn than I am,* he thought.

He finally made his way to a side door and eased it open, slipping into the night. Clouds scudded across the sky but added no snow to the ankle-deep carpet. The torches adorning the courtyard were unlit. Aidan paused, frowning. The Lord of Midnight made all men and women nervous, but the Touched especially so. Wardsmen patrolled Sunfall's grounds all night long as much to keep torches lit as to fend off intruders. So why were these lamps unattended?

A ball of light came into view. A Wardsman emerged from the shadows, one hand holding the lantern in front of him while the other gripped the sword at his waist. Aidan squirmed, undecided. The Wardsman was probably on his way to light the lamps along the stone path that meandered through the courtyard. That would make his escape more difficult. *But what has been easy as of late?*

Quietly, he started forward, sidling along the wall so the shadows covered him like a cloak. The crunch of his boots as they settled into packed snow topped with brittle ice sounded deafening in the quiet night, but he didn't slow. Glancing at the Wardsman—he strode past him without slowing—a terrible thought struck him.

Can only Sallnerians be vagrants?

—Dark magic can raise any dead, but I suspect most do come from Dimitri Thalamahn's reign eight hundred years past.

Could he be back, too? The Serpent King?

The sword hesitated. *—No.* It went silent.

Finally he rounded the corner and settled into the bend in the wall. He expelled his breath in a steamy puff, drinking in gulps of sweet, crisp air. He looked around to determine where to move next—and stared into the eyes of a Wardsman. The other man grinned, a humorless expression that did not fit with his soulless, dead eyes.

Eyes like his mother's.

The vagrant issued a loud guttural sound into the night sky and raised its short double-headed axe. Aidan glanced to his right and saw the fiery light of the first Wardsman's torch bobbing closer. No. No human would answer that call. He thought about stealing the torch's light, but even as he did he felt his body cry out in protest. He was exhausted. Kindling so much as a spark seemed as daunting as lifting a mountain.

—You do not need magic for this.

"What do you mean?" he whispered.

Heritage rattled in its scabbard.

—Hold me and blink.

Pulling the sword free, Aidan's hands shook as much from the effort of holding Heritage as from fear. Then he blinked. The world was awash in bright white light, the vagrants sketched in obsidian outlines. He felt his feet shift and looked down. His stance had changed, balancing his weight. He didn't remember moving, but the stance felt natural, appropriate. The Wardsman now looked anything but natural. Their human faces had vanished, replaced by leering skulls dotted with flesh and dirt.

—Aim for their heads. No other blow can stop them.

The vagrants dropped into defensive stances of their own and split, each moving to flank him. The one on his right lunged in. Aidan parried its attack almost offhandedly, swatting it aside and keeping his focus on the second one that continued to circle. How he had anticipated the move, he couldn't say. Spinning Heritage, Aidan drove his shoulder into the creature's stomach. The blow sent it stumbling back as he whirled and slashed at the neck of the other vagrant. Heritage cleaved through rotten skin as if it were water. The head tumbled to the ground, settling a short distance away. The body crumpled soundlessly.

He turned to advance on the vagrant he had forced back. The creature swung its axe down. Aidan darted to one side, preparing to lunge back in.

—Behind you!

He felt a boot plant itself in his lower back. He toppled over, Heritage disappearing in a bank of snow. Instantly his vision returned to normal. A third Wardsman stepped from the shadows as Aidan lay groaning.

"Tell the master we have him," one said. Its partner nodded, turned away, and stiffened. A spear burst through the back of its skull. The shaft tore free and the vagrant dropped, dead again.

Aidan didn't know who had come to his rescue, and he didn't care. He grabbed Heritage from where it had fallen beside him and blinked, barely aware of his vision returning to onyx outlines against a white field. Rising smoothly to his feet, he brought Heritage slicing across the neck of the last vagrant. It jerked, went limp, and fell.

He watched with wonder as the white glow receded, returning the world to its natural color. Exhaustion traded places with the vigor that took hold of him when he wielded the sword—which suddenly weighed as much as four blades.

Daniel stood in front of him, staring in shock at the vagrant he'd slain. The lower half of his spear, splintered in the center where it had snapped off in the vagrant's skull, trembled in his grip. Daniel dropped it but didn't seem to notice.

Aidan sheathed Heritage before reaching for Daniel's shoulder. At his touch the Wardsman yelped and leaped back.

"It's just me," Aidan said, raising his hands.

Daniel relaxed. "Aidan," he croaked, toeing the lopsided face of the first one he had killed. The human mask had torn free and hung loosely like molted skin. "What are those things?"

"Sallnerians. Well, they're called vagrants, but..." He shook his head, too tired to explain.

Daniel nodded as if the answer made complete sense. His eyes widened when he saw the sword at Aidan's side. "I saw you fight, Aidan. Some of those maneuvers would have made your father envious. But—and no offense—I've seen blind men swing more steadily than you."

"I..." Aidan paused. He could see himself wielding the sword, weaving in and out of the reach of the vagrants' weapons, but it was as though he'd *watched* the battle rather than participated in it. He could see the movements, but he didn't understand how he had performed them. "I guess I just swung and hoped for the best."

How in the Lady's name did I do all that?

—Not now. Also, watch your language.

Aidan laughed helplessly.

"Are you all right?" Daniel asked, looking at him warily.

Aidan got control of himself. "Yes. Just thankful to be alive, I guess."

"Same here."

"Thank you, Daniel," Aidan said, his tone serious.

"Any time," Daniel said, forcing a grin onto his face.

Nodding, Aidan turned to leave.

"Where are you going?"

"I have to go away."

"Your mother just issued orders that you are to be arrested on sight. Patrols are looking for you everywhere. And now these things..." He trailed off, gesturing at the vagrants. "What's going on, Aidan?"

"My mother? How long ago did you see her?"

Daniel shrugged. "Not long ago. Have you seen her?"

"Sort of," Aidan said absently. *What does he mean, do you think? My real mother, or another vagrant?*

—Your real mother wouldn't order you arrested. It's likely that another creature already impersonates her and is looking for you. Say nothing of this to Daniel. Act natural.

Aidan didn't see how that was possible at this point. "Did my mother explain to you why I'm to be arrested?"

"She told the search party that you assaulted your father," Daniel said. "I volunteered to search, hoping I could find you before anyone else did."

Aidan said nothing.

Daniel cleared his throat. "I've known you a long time, Aidan. I'd like to think I know you better than anyone. And I know that whatever happened to bring you to this place, right here and right now—well, you must've had a good reason. Wherever you have to go, and whatever you have to do, I'm with you."

"You can't come with me."

"Why not?"

"I'm in trouble, Daniel. I—"

Daniel shrugged. "I've been in trouble before."

"My own parents want me arrested for treason. If you come with me, you'll be hunted, too. I can't let that happen."

His friend shrugged again. "I don't care."

Aidan sighed. "I appreciate—"

Daniel raised a hand. "You're my friend. Whatever is happening to you, you need help. You can't do this alone. I'm going with you."

Chewing his lip, Aidan said, "Give me a moment." *What should I do?* he sent to the sword.

—What you said was the truth: he will be in danger with you.

Aidan nodded. "I can't let you come with me."

"Funny," Daniel said with a small smile. "I don't remember

asking for your permission. You need my help, O Mighty Prince. I'm going with you, and that's that."

Aidan looked at the sword, back to Daniel, and shrugged. Privately, he was thrilled. The idea of leaving everything he had ever known behind with only a talking sword for company had not exactly filled him with confidence. He started toward the gate leading down the east pass.

"We'll probably encounter more of them along the trail," Aidan said.

"That's why we're not taking the trail."

Aidan started to ask what Daniel meant then yawned, his jaw cracking. Daniel motioned for him to follow. At the far side of the courtyard, Daniel bent over a stone bench.

"Help me with this, would you?"

Aidan's arms felt as wobbly as his legs, but together they pushed the bench to one side. Daniel knelt, brushed away snow to reveal a slab of stone that made up part of the path that meandered through the courtyard, then, grunting, lifted it and set it to one side, revealing a square-shaped hole.

"What is that?" Aidan asked, crouching beside his friend.

"Just a tunnel I found once," Daniel said casually.

"Where does it lead?"

"Into Calewind, right near the south gate. We might have our hands full when we get there, but I'd rather crawl on my belly like a worm than go down that pass. Nowhere to hide along the trail, right?"

"Right."

Daniel eased himself into the hole feet-first. "Come on, then," he called softly. Aidan went in and blinked in the dim light that Kahltan sent from high overhead. Ahead, Daniel moved in a crouch. Aidan followed. A few minutes later Daniel stopped and rapped against the rough wall to the left. Dirt and dust fell away as the wall slid to one side. They emerged in an alley near the south gate, just as Daniel had said. Aidan hid while Daniel approached the pylon looking out over the city, and the open country on the other side of the wall. A Wardsman opened the door, looked around, then waved him in. Silence for a few moments, then grunts followed by heavy thuds. Daniel peeked out the door and waved Aidan forward.

Aidan stepped over the bodies carefully. Then he recognized the men who had led him out of the city on his birthday. "Did you...?" He swallowed, unable to continue.

Daniel shook his head. "They'll be fine." He led them outside.

"Where are we headed?"

"South." Aidan thought about explaining, but Daniel was already walking.

"Then to the south we go."

Aidan stepped forward. A moment later, blackness overtook him, and he felt an icy sting spread over his face.

"Are you all right?" Daniel asked, hauling Aidan up from a pile of snow.

"What happened?" Aidan asked, brushing ice and slush from his face.

"You fell over," Daniel said. "Are you ill?"

"Tired," he mumbled.

Daniel hoisted Aidan's arm around his shoulder. "We've got to get moving." Lips thinning, he studied the thick clouds hanging above them. As a Leastonian, Daniel could read the sky as easily as Torelian scholars drank in books. "We need to get moving. Can you walk?"

Aidan wobbled slightly, but gestured that he would be fine.

"All right," Daniel said. "Let's go."

Chapter 14

Fire and Fishing Lines

SNOW BEGAN SPRINKLING DOWN less than an hour later. At first, Aidan and Daniel ignored it. They had decided to keep clear of the North Road, huffing and puffing between hilltops and picking through stretches of woods. When they crested a hilltop that overlooked the village of Gotik, Daniel asked Aidan if he wanted to stop. He proposed sneaking into the city and taking shelter in a stable, just for the night.

Aidan, bent over and wheezing, did want to stop. He wanted nothing more than to curl up right there on the hilltop and sleep. But they didn't. Gotik was too close to Calewind. Aidan would almost certainly be recognized there. Daniel cast a nervous glance at the clouds and nodded. They steered clear of Gotik's walls and ran on.

Within another hour, Aidan severely regretted his decision. The wind picked up, howling and stinging their ears. The curtain of snowflakes turned into a blinding torrent of stinging darts. Squinting against the onslaught, Aidan slogged forward. Ahead of him, Daniel bent into the wind, his cloak streaming out behind him like a cape.

Stopping, Aidan shouted at Daniel to halt, but the wind smothered him, stealing words and breath. He turned his head and gasped in air, wishing he had a smidgen of light to draw so he could wrap his friend and himself in heat bubbles. He looked this way and that in search of shelter, but the snow hid everything beyond arm's length. For all he knew he was standing right in front of a copse of trees or a village.

He started forward again, calling to Daniel that he hadn't seen anything yet. He waited for a reply, but none came. Peering about frantically, Aidan felt his chest grow even colder. Daniel was nowhere in sight.

"Daniel? Daniel!"

The wind's shrill cry drowned out each call. He turned this way and that, but everywhere he looked revealed only blinding, numbing whiteness. Perhaps Daniel was looking for him. He stopped, pivoting about so he would be sure to see Daniel when he came into view. If he came into view.

I'm never going to find him. We'll both die out here, and it's my fault.

—Look behind you.

Whipping around, Aidan saw nothing but a swirling, stinging wall of white.

"Where?"

—Walk forward.

When Aidan hesitated, Heritage hummed at his waist.

—The Eye of Heritage can see clearly, even in this storm. Do not fear, Aidan.

Raising an arm to shield his face, he trekked forward.

—Turn left.

He changed directions at once. As he walked forward, he made out a dim shape in the distance. At first, he thought it might be nothing more than a tree, but as he moved closer he realized the unlikely odds of a tree being able to call his name.

Daniel spotted him and ran forward. The friends grasped arms and loosed triumphant and grateful shouts that were instantly spirited away.

Daniel jutted his finger at a point in the distance and beckoned for Aidan to follow. They broke into a slow, trudging run, practically hopping through knee-high snow. Daniel stumbled and fell, stamping the snowy ground with a man-shaped imprint. Aidan hauled him up and they continued forward.

A cave slowly materialized in the distance. Its maw was short but wide. They had to crawl through the opening. The walls fell back and the ceiling rose gradually as the passage sloped downward. They emerged in a grotto as dark as a starless sky. Aidan was aware of Daniel's presence only by the scuffs of his boots against stones.

Heritage rattled at his side. Looking down, he was delighted to see a red glow from the eye that peeled back the darkness. Raising the sword above his head, he saw walls slick with ice and a rough, uneven floor. A strange design, like a V set inside another V, was scratched into the wall near the opening they had crawled through. Aidan gave it a glance then ignored it, diverting his attention to a more interesting and crucial discovery. A few paces ahead lay a pile of sticks. A tinderbox rested nearby.

Daniel scooped up the box and fumbled at it. Cold made his fingers shaky and stiff. Aidan crouched beside him and held the sword out like a torch. Daniel turned to the fire and struck flint to steel over and over. Cursing, he tossed them aside and hugged his arms over his body.

"Won't light," he chattered.

Aidan nodded, wondering why his own teeth weren't chattering.

"Can you make fire?" Daniel asked.

"I don't think so," he said. "I'm so tired."

"Try?" Daniel pleaded.

With a slow, heavy nod, Aidan understood why he didn't feel the cold as keenly as before. Exhaustion was settling over him like a blanket, warm and inviting. He shook his head roughly. If he fell asleep now, they would both freeze to death.

"I need light," he said. He raised the lamp from his neck but the vial was still empty. "There's no light," he said, panic creeping in.

"It's all right," Daniel said, trying to smile. He picked up the flint and steel with trembling hands, struck them together feebly, cursed, and tossed them aside before picking up two twigs.

"A spark? Can you work with a spark?" Daniel asked.

"That should be plenty," Aidan said.

Pressing his lips together in concentration, Daniel ground the sticks together. The minutes stretched on like hours without so much as a hint of smoke.

Aidan closed his eyes. *We're going to die in here. Kahltan take me, I shouldn't have let Daniel come along.*

—If you need fire, Aidan, all you need to do is ask.

Aidan blinked dumbly at the sword. *You can do that?*

—Not me. Not exactly. Others. Have Daniel replace the twigs, then raise the sword and make your request.

Aidan relayed the sword's request. Lifting Heritage, Aidan thought, *Fire. Um... please.*

All at once the strangest sensation settled over him. A breeze caressed his hand, but it was not soft. It was rough, like a hand calloused from hard labor. The scent of sawdust, fresh earth, and pine tickled his nose. A streak of flame as thin as a rod burst from the Eye of Heritage, striking the wood and setting it aflame. Daniel shouted and leaped away but recovered quickly, whooping with joy and scooting close to warm his hands over the roaring bonfire.

As quickly as it had occurred, the sensation faded. The Eye went dark. The scent of the outdoors, like a dish made of nature's finest ingredients, faded away, surrendering to the cave's natural aroma of earth and ice.

—*Better?* the sword asked.

Aidan didn't say anything. The smell of dirt and sawdust, the touch of a rough hand guiding his... It was as if his Grandfather Charles had settled behind him, one hand on his shoulder, the other lifting his tired arm to help and support. History painted Charles a stern king, but a fair one, and beloved by his people. Aidan couldn't attest to any of that. Charles had passed Heritage to Annalyn long before Aidan was born. He had only known his grandfather as a happy man quick to booming laughter and an avid outdoorsman. Charles had often smuggled Aidan away from lessons—and, later on, Daniel with him—for a day spent tromping through woods, splashing through streams, casting fishing lines, and carving toys and trinkets in his woodshop.

Once, Charles had packed a rucksack and taken Aidan on an extended camping trip. For three nights, they had camped out under Kahltan's cold, pale gaze. Aidan had not been afraid. Not *very* afraid, anyway. Every night, Charles had made a fire and kept his grandson up telling stories: stories of Ambrose and his skill and bravery in battle against Dimitri Thalamahn; tales of Marvin, Ambrose's grandson and a wild and scatterbrained inventor who had once blown a hole the size of an apple cart in one of Sunfall's walls after an experiment involving barrels of Darinian ale and lots of fire; and plenty of stories that were not about anyone real at all. Those had been Aidan's favorites. He had often wondered what it would have been like to sit in on a story told by both Tyrnen and his grandfather.

Charles had passed away when Aidan was twelve. Tyrnen, as much a part of Aidan's life as his grandfather, had helped fill that void, but only to a small degree. Despite his gruff demeanor during studies, Tyrnen loved a good bout of fun as much as Charles. But he did not appreciate the smell of a crisp winter morning the way most people appreciated the aroma of a fine meal, nor could he carve toy wagons for Aidan, Daniel, and himself to race up and down Sunfall's long corridors, laughing while attendants scurried out of their way. He loved Tyrnen, but Tyrnen was not his grandfather.

Aidan came to the fire, sitting opposite Daniel. He felt warm again, and that was wonderful. But he also felt deeply sad. For the briefest of instants, he had been back home—not the home he had known these past terrible weeks. The Sunfall from before everything in his life had gone horribly wrong. The Sunfall where he had felt safe, wanted, and loved.

"How did you do that?" Daniel said. "I thought you were

spent."

Aidan only shrugged.

"Well, I guess we don't have to figure it out this instant, do we?" Daniel said as he flexed his fingers in front of the flames.

"I guess not," Aidan said, though he couldn't help looking at the sword. The Eye's red glow had vanished, dwarfed by the bonfire.

How did *I do that?* Aidan thought to the weapon.

—You *didn't.*

Care to explain that?

—Certainly. But not now. You'd better warm yourself and get some sleep. We'll talk later.

The blade went silent. Peeling off his gloves, Aidan flexed his hands near the flames. Beside him, Daniel blinked heavily, teetering on his knees.

"Why don't you get some sleep?" Aidan suggested.

Daniel's eyes shot open before slowly closing again. "I'm not that tired."

Aidan's brow rose. "So you weren't about to pitch forward into the fire? I didn't make it to roast you for dinner."

Yawning, Daniel nodded and stretched out beside the fire, first wrapping himself in his cloak then tossing the soaked garment aside with a curse. Aidan drew light, whispered a prayer, and wrapped a heat bubble around his friend. Daniel stirred and sighed.

"So that's what that feels like," Daniel said dreamily.

"Wonderful, isn't it?"

"Best spell in the world," Daniel mumbled. A few moments later, he began to snore.

Aidan spread out and set Heritage to one side, just within reach. He tucked his head against an outstretched arm and studied the Eye, wondering. Then he drifted off, dreaming of lakes and fishing lines and toy wagons.

Chapter 15

The Siblings

TYRNEN STASHED THE ARTIFACT away and folded his hands on his desk. "Enter."

The Sallnerian entered the tower first. Christine was even more beautiful than the day she had entered the Lion's Den years before—medium height; slanted, hazel-colored eyes; a riding skirt and knee-high boots that showed off long, shapely legs. Her skin was fair, unlike like that of pure-blooded Sallnerians. Her schooling had been sporadic given the girl's need for independence from her father, but Christine had far surpassed her fellow Touched—all but Aidan—and had earned the honor he was prepared to bestow. She carried herself with confidence, even in the presence of the Eternal Flame of Crotaria. He liked that. A bit of confidence was allowed, so long as it did not give way to arrogance.

Her brother, Garrett, followed, closing the door behind him. Tyrnen's smile wavered. That one was not Touched by the Lady's light, nor did he have his sister's Sallnerian features. Those came from their mother's side. This one resembled his father: tall, blonde hair tied back in a ponytail, and blue eyes that glittered as they roamed the tower room, soaking up the treasures Tyrnen had sprinkled around.

Christine came up to his desk and bowed. "It is an honor, Eternal Flame," she said, tucking a lock of silky black hair behind her ear as she straightened. She looked at her brother and made a sound of annoyance. Garrett glided over and bowed even deeper than his sister had.

"An honor, Eternal Flame," he said.

Standing, Tyrnen extended his hand to Christine. "You know why you are here," he said as she kissed the Eternal Band.

"Because I have achieved Cinder rank," she said.

"Correct. It is standard practice for the Eternal Flame to visit the university when a student graduates so he or she may receive the Band in person. But, in this case"—he reached into his robe, withdrew a Cinder Band, slipped it onto her right forefinger—"I felt an exception was in order."

She withdrew her hand and bowed again. "Thank you, Eternal Flame."

"The honor is mine. I assume you intend to choose the soldier creed?"

She hesitated. "I don't know yet, actually."

"Take some time to think about it," he said, smiling warmly. Gesturing to the chairs near his fireplace, he moved out from behind his desk. "Sit, sit. We have much to discuss." He lowered himself into a seat. "I trust your journey did not take too long."

"A handful of shifts," she replied, shrugging.

He blinked. "From Sharem?" he asked, unable to keep the surprise from his voice. On Crotaria, there were Touched, and then there were Gairdens born with *Ordine'cin*. The difference between the two was like a candle next to a roaring inferno. Christine Lorden had held enormous potential since childhood. The fact that she was graduating before twenty years of age testified to her abilities. Even so, if Christine was telling the truth, Tyrnen had vastly underestimated her. Her untapped talent burned like a Gairden funeral pyre.

"Yes," she replied.

"How do you feel?"

"A bit light-headed," Christine admitted. "I have never felt the fever, though. I am careful."

—Show her, a voice purred in his thoughts.

Mistress? he sent back, heart hammering.

—Show her. Now.

Jealousy swept through him, hot and rancid. *She is not that powerful, mistress. Surely—*

Suddenly a wave of affection for his mistress washed over him. Desire to please and obey overrode all thought. Rising, he smiled at his guests.

"I find myself struck with a sudden urge for a drink," he said. "Would either of you care for warm cider? I held a jug back from the last Leastonian import of the season."

"Cider sounds excellent," Garrett said. His sister nodded.

Moving to his desk, Tyrnen conjured a steaming pitcher and three wooden cups. With a wave of his hand he sent them drifting toward his guests. Garrett took the pitcher and poured the drinks, then released his grip on its handle. The pitcher floated in place, ready when needed. Waiting until his guests buried their faces in their cups, Tyrnen tapped on the surface of his desk three times.

On the third tap, his hand sank through the desk. He withdrew a golden scepter decorated with gems.

Returning to his chair, he held the weapon out to Christine. When she looked at it, her eyes glazed over.

"What is—" the man started to ask. Tyrnen kindled—only a word of prayer to the Lady, but that one word tasted like ashes. The man's chin drooped to his chest. He began to snore.

Tyrnen placed the scepter in his lap and watched the woman, waiting. Her cup tumbled from her hand and spilled on the stone floor as she slowly reached forward. Her fingers hovered over the scepter. Abruptly she blinked and sat back.

—Her will is too great, his mistress said.

Feeling a surge of triumph, Tyrnen tucked the scepter under his chair and snapped his fingers at the siblings, who looked around sleepily.

"What...?" Christine began.

"We were talking about you shifting all the way from Sharem. It appears you do seem rather tired. Not surprising."

She frowned. "I suppose I should rest." She saw her spilled cup on the floor and gasped. "Oh! I'm sorry, I... I don't even remember..."

Tyrnen spun another cup out of thin air and handed it to her. "Not at all. Now then, how would you feel about joining the ranks of Torel's Dawn?"

The cup froze halfway to her lips. "Truly?" she whispered.

Tyrnen nodded.

"I am honored, Eternal Flame," she said, then hesitated.

"Your university attendance is not a factor, here," he said. "Talent is all that matters. Yours is a strength I have not seen since my last pupil."

Her eyes widened further. "Aidan Gairden?"

Tyrnen nodded once.

"I cannot thank you enough for what you have given me, Eternal Flame," Christine said a trifle breathlessly. "I will not fail—"

He raised a finger. "I haven't given you the position yet. There is one task you must complete."

"Name it," she said.

Tyrnen suppressed a smile. "The prince has fled Sunfall. It seems the battle at Sharem proved too much for him. In this trying time of war, acts of treason cannot be ignored. I need you to find him."

"How am I to find him? He could be anywhere."

"I will give you the means to track him."

"If you can do that, why must I?" She flushed. "I am sorry, Eternal Flame. It's just that..." She spread her hands. "If you are able to find him, why ask me?"

"These are hard times, my dear. The Crown of the North is busy preparing for the next stage of the conflict against Darinia, and she needs me by her side. There is also the matter of preparing the Touched to go to war. I don't have the time to chase Aidan."

She hesitated.

"The rewards will be great," he said. He watched her brother lean forward. "Your position will be secured in Torel's Dawn, and as for monetary compensation... Well. You won't want for anything ever again, I assure you."

Her eyes searched her lap. "I think—"

"Sister," Garrett interrupted. "If I may have a word?"

She glared at him before nodding. "You'll pardon us for a moment, Eternal Flame?"

Tyrnen smiled. "Of course."

Garrett draped an arm across Christine's shoulders and led her to the tower door. "We must do this."

Her face was tight. "Don't you realize what will happen to Aidan if we bring him back here?"

"*Prince* Aidan, dear sister. And no, I do not, because the old man didn't say."

"An act of treason. Aidan might be executed."

"What concern is that of mine?"

Her gaze was hard. "You'll do anything for a few coins, won't you?"

"Torelian coin, especially." He laughed at her look of disgust and gripped her shoulders. "He said we will never want for *anything*. No more traveling the world performing for a meal and a room each night. This is an opportunity I cannot pass up."

"*You* cannot?"

"I am a bounty hunter, Christine. Work has been slow, but to capture a fugitive prince..." He shrugged. "How can I refuse?"

"The offer was not made to you."

"No, it was not. It was made to you, and your reward includes a place in Torel's Dawn." He reached out and tucked a lock of silky hair behind her air. "The Dawn, Christine. It's what you've always dreamed of."

"I know. It's just..."

Garrett assumed his most sympathetic smile. "You can tell

me."

"When we saw Aidan, and when he crossed the courtyard, he smiled at me, and I felt..."

He snorted. "He did not smile at *you*. He smiled at everyone. He was showing off, just as he has every time you've forced us to attend one of his public appearances." He smirked. "Honestly, I half expected you to throw yourself at him like—"

Her eyes glittered dangerously. "You are not helping your case."

He raised his hands. "I'm sorry. Sister, the Eternal Flame favors you. He could have awarded you a Cinder Band at the Lion's Den, as he does for every graduating class. But he didn't. He gave it to you personally."

The woman bit her lip.

"Maybe you could suggest that Tyrnen ask for leniency on the prince's behalf," her brother continued.

"Do you think he would?"

He shrugged. "Tyrnen trained the prince himself, and I doubt the Crown of the North really wants to execute her own son. Besides, if we don't find him first, someone else might. At least if we bring him back, he'll have a chance."

"That is true."

"Are we in agreement, then?"

Shrugging, she folded her arms and went back to her seat.

Watching the siblings converse, Tyrnen's thoughts turned to Aidan. He hoped the boy was all right. He hoped—

An inundation of love for his mistress so intoxicating it bordered on fixation passed through him. Tyrnen scowled. *Fool boy. He deserves all that befalls him. If he hadn't run, I could have offered him everything.*

Tyrnen smiled as the siblings resumed their seats. "Is everything settled, then?"

"It is," Christine said. "When do I begin?"

"Immediately."

"You said you knew how to track him?"

Nodding, Tyrnen gestured for her to extend her right hand. He placed a finger on the amethyst in her Cinder Band and kindled. She gasped, and turned to look south.

"I feel him." She began to stroke the amethyst in her Band.

"That sense will grow stronger as you draw closer to him," Tyrnen said. "You should know that the standard rules of shifting apply. You must know his exact location in order to shift to him.

Nevertheless, what you feel acts as a compass that will inevitably lead you to him. When that happens, you are to alert me at once."

Silence filled the room for a few long minutes. Christine stood. "With your permission, Eternal Flame, we will depart."

"You may," he said, also standing. "There are always tests to pass if one wishes to join the ranks of Torel's Dawn, my dear. Accomplish this task, and the position is yours."

Nodding, she strode to the door. Her brother started after her. Tyrnen caught his arm.

"Lead me to him," the old man whispered, staring into Garrett's eyes. Tyrnen extended a closed fist to the man and turned it so his palm faced the ceiling. He opened it. In his hand were at least two dozen Torelian coins, each bearing the "H" with Heritage sheathed through the center bar. Garrett found himself unable to look away.

"This is just the beginning of the fortune I will bestow upon you," Tyrnen said. He handed Garrett the coins. They disappeared into his purse as if sucked up.

When the Eternal Flame released his arm, Garrett blinked and frowned, momentarily confused. His eyes again focused on Tyrnen, and he smiled.

"It will be done."

After the door closed behind them, Tyrnen retrieved the scepter from beneath his chair and gazed at it adoringly. "Are you pleased, mistress?"

—For now.

Chapter 16

Rabbits on the Run

AIDAN SAT BOLT UPRIGHT, panting. Vagrants had slashed into dreams of home and chased him awake. As he looked around, his breathing slowed. Other than the crackling of the fire, Daniel's ripping snores, and satisfying creaks and pops as he arched his back, the cave was quiet, empty. He moved closer to the fire.

—Oh good, you're awake.

He pulled his cloak tighter and screwed his eyes shut.

—I'm in your head, you know. You can't ignore me forever.

Aidan gave a horse-like snort and propped himself on an elbow to face Heritage. The Eye glowed faintly, winking at him.

"I'm still tired."

—Twenty-four hours of sleep should be enough for anyone, don't you think?

His mouth snapped shut, stifling another yawn. "I slept for a day?"

—I suggest we carry on our conversation through thought. We wouldn't want to wake Daniel.

Aidan turned to regard his friend. Daniel lay curled up across from him. His chest rose and fell evenly, his breathing disturbed only by an occasional cough.

—You're actually quite lucky, Heritage said. *Your body was begging for sleep. Any longer and you would have collapsed. Given the weather, that would not have ended well.*

He put a hand to his forehead. He felt warm, and not only from the fire.

I needed the rest.

—You pushed yourself near to burnout, Aidan. You should sleep for a week, at least, but you don't have that much time.

Things would have been much worse without your help.

—I didn't do anything.

Of course you did. If you hadn't led me to Daniel, that storm would have swallowed me whole. Thank you.

—Oh, that. You're welcome. It's one of many ways Heritage

can help a sword-bearer.

Like creating fire without drawing light?

—Ah, that. I didn't do that.

Aidan frowned. *Well, I certainly didn't.*

—Correct. You asked for help, and your family answered.

Aidan remembered how strongly he had felt his grandfather's presence. *What does that mean? Did my grandfather...?*

—It's complicated. It has to do with the connection a sword-bearer has to his or her predecessors.

I don't know much about that, yet, Aidan confessed.

—No. You would have learned more during the rest of your Rite of Heritage.

He grunted. *Thank you for reminding me. The first to be rejected by Heritage, the first to have the full* Ordine *gift—I'm setting all sorts of precedents. Speaking of which, are you ready to tell me why I've been granted the full gift?*

Heritage offered no response. Aidan rolled his eyes. He hated the sword's annoying tendency to only answer questions that appealed to it. He drummed his fingers absently along his leg, yawning again.

—You did exert yourself, didn't you? Get some more rest. You have a long journey ahead.

All right. But first, I have one other question, and I'd like you to answer it.

—We'll see.

Will you please explain to me how I became the sword-bearer?

— You know how. You had to accept me. Once you did, the position became yours.

What I mean is, if I'm the sword-bearer, that would have to mean that my mother isn't. Swallowing, he thought back to the creature that had worn his mother's face. *You said you offer a connection to previous sword-bearers. What happened to my mother? Where is she?*

The Eye went dark, and Heritage fell silent.

The heavy silence of the cave awakened Aidan several hours later. He sat up and looked around. He was alone. He scrambled to his feet and crawled through the shaft to the surface. When he emerged outside, he shielded his eyes. The spread of snow was like a mirror that stabbed the Lady's light in his eyes. Daniel was nowhere in sight.

His ears cocked as they picked up a faint sound to one side.

Daniel appeared, jogging from a copse of bare trees. He shouted as he noticed Aidan, then doubled over in a fit of coughing. Clutched in his right hand by their ears were two lifeless rabbits; in the other hand were two long branches.

"Are you all right?" Aidan asked as Daniel drew nearer. The heat bubble Aidan had weaved last night still surrounded his friend, but Daniel's eyes were glazed and red-rimmed.

"Never better," Daniel said, then turned his head and broke into another fit of coughing. "I got breakfast," he said finally, motioning for Aidan to follow him into the cave as he ducked into the opening.

"How did you find this place?" Aidan asked as they crawled. "I couldn't see a thing in that storm."

"Just lucky, I guess," Daniel said over his shoulder.

They spilled into the cave, hunger making them clumsy. Daniel handed Aidan a small knife from his belt and a rabbit, then began to skin and gut his rabbit with another blade. After they'd finished, Daniel sharpened the ends of the branches he'd found and handed one to Aidan. Impaling the animals on the spits, they held them over the flames.

"Are you as hungry as I am?" Daniel asked as he turned his rabbit.

"Hungrier," Aidan replied. The fever left a Touched ravenous, as if recovering from an illness. Once the meat darkened, they tore into their meal.

After Daniel finished, he smacked his lips and leaned back against the wall. "How are you feeling?"

"Better than you look," Aidan said through a mouthful of meat.

Daniel shrugged. "It's the weather. Your mother moved me from the throne room to the courtyard just after you left for Sharem. Then there was that storm the night we left. Anyway, I didn't want to wake you. I could tell you needed to sleep. Almost a solid day—your parents would think you a lazy oaf! Not that they'd be wrong."

Aidan's chewing slowed. He hadn't thought much of home since his conversation with Heritage earlier that morning. "I suppose they would," he said softly.

Clearing his throat, Daniel looked down at his lap. "Do you know where we're headed?"

Aidan shook his head, swallowing his last bite before he answered. "Just south."

"What's in the south?"

"I'm not really sure. All I know is that I'm looking for someone called the Prophet."

"The Prophet? Who's that?"

Aidan hesitated, not certain how much information he should divulge.

"Did you learn about him in one of those history books you were always reading?" Daniel asked, picking scraps of meat off the bones of his catch.

Aidan chewed thoughtfully. He and Daniel had been through a lot recently, but even Aidan was having trouble believing everything that was happening. Of course, Daniel had seen a vagrant with his own eyes. After something like that, what wouldn't he believe?

He took a breath. "Since my ceremony, I've been hearing a voice in my head. At first I thought maybe I was just hearing things. A couple of weeks ago, I found the source of the voice." He reached beside him to grip the sword, pulled it from its sheath, and held it before him.

Daniel let out a low whistle. "I saw Heritage last night, but we had more pressing concerns so I didn't bring it up." He looked at Aidan with wide eyes. "Why do you have it?"

"Because according to Heritage, I am the sword-bearer."

Daniel's mouth dropped open. "But that's impossible. I saw what happened the day of your ceremony. The sword rejected you."

Irritation clawed at Aidan. "I know. I was there, remember?"

"And your mother is the sword-bearer," Daniel continued, oblivious to his friend's reaction. "Shouldn't the sword be with her?"

"I don't know why she—"

"And why would—"

"I don't know!" Aidan shouted.

Daniel coughed again and looked away, scratching at his cheek.

"I don't know what's happening or why," Aidan said in a whisper, looking into the flames. "I only know that the sword told me to travel south and find someone called the Prophet. And since I have no home and nowhere else to go, I'm going to do as it says."

Silence stretched out between them.

"I'm sorry," Daniel said. "I didn't mean to upset you. I'm just surprised, is all. Everything's happening so fast."

"For you and me both," Aidan snapped. Daniel drew back, looking hurt.

—He didn't deserve that, Heritage said.

Aidan felt shame and embarrassment boil up. He started to apologize when Daniel froze.

"Did you hear that?"

"What?" Aidan said. Then he did hear something, a muffled crunch from above. Another crunch, louder this time, then again and again in a steady cadence. Footsteps.

Aidan kindled and the fire shrank to a small flame. A faint shaft of light filtered down through the entrance. He crawled over and pressed his back to one side of the mouth. It was wet and slippery; the fire had melted the ice coating the wall. Daniel crouched opposite him, one hand clenched around his dagger, the other corked over his mouth to bottle another cough.

The footsteps paused outside the entrance. Keeping still, Aidan held his breath. After several moments, the footsteps moved slowly away.

A cough erupted from Daniel. Muffling a curse, the Wardsman ducked his head into his arm and continued hacking. The footsteps rushed back, then paused. A long moment stretched out. Then scratching noises and deep breathing reached his ears, coming closer and closer down the shaft.

Aidan glanced at Daniel. The Wardsman's face was tight. Aidan raised three fingers. "On three," he mouthed. "One. Two—"

A skull head popped out of the opening. Roaring, Aidan brought Heritage crashing down, shattering the skull. The vagrant crumpled. Aidan's momentum carried him forward. He stumbled on the body and almost crashed on top of it. A hand pulled him upright.

"We need to get out of here," Daniel said hoarsely.

"Hold on," Aidan said. Closing his eyes, he pictured the thicket where Daniel had emerged with their food, and kindled from the tiny flame. Wind rushed around him. He opened his eyes just as Daniel whispered a curse and pulled him to the ground behind a tree. Peering around, Aidan saw several other Wardsmen moving through the woods. Each grunted like an animal scrounging for dinner as they stomped around, heads whipping this way and that to peer around trees. Their eyes were blank and cloudy. Vagrants.

Focusing on the farthest point north of their location that he could see, Aidan clasped Daniel's wrist and shifted again. Dizziness swarmed over him.

—*You need to take it easy*, the grandmotherly voice reminded him.

"Come on," he said, rising and breaking into a run. "Let's keep moving."

Daniel followed, coughing every step of the way.

Chapter 17

Whites of His Eyes

BY DAY, THEY TRAVELED, keeping off the main road and sticking to tree cover when possible. The bare trees provided little protection against the cold; Aidan cast heat bubbles for both men and made small fires for meals. Save for the crunch of their footsteps through the snow, Aidan and Daniel were as silent as the land was still. Aidan realized his outburst in the cave had been unfair to Daniel, and that he should be the one to break the silence first. But the longer he allowed the silence to stretch, the less sure he was how to broach it. He wasn't angry with Daniel at all, really. He wasn't even frustrated with him. He was frustrated with Heritage. The sword instructed them to journey south, but where were they going *exactly*? When did they need to get there? And why did the sword only see fit to answer one or two questions at a time when they had hours upon hours with nothing to do but run, hide, and talk?

Daniel hunted game whenever they stopped, but the meals were always eaten in silence. Three times each day, Aidan awkwardly took hold of Daniel's arm and shifted—first using the light stored up in the lamp, twice drawing from the Lady. They devoured ground, skipping over several miles with each jump. Even so, Aidan grumbled. He wanted to jump further, but he could feel the fever ebb overnight then trickle back in, stronger after each shift.

By night, they camped wherever they found shelter, taking turns holding watch while the other slept for a few hours. Aidan slept first, making sure to keep his body rested so he was ready for the next day's shifts. He tried apologizing when Daniel woke him for his turn at watch, but Daniel immediately curled up in his cloak and turned away. The only words they exchanged were directed not at each other, but at the sky. "The Lady rises and burns away the night," they said by rote at first light each morning. Then they packed what little supplies they had brought and resumed their silent march.

On the evening of the sixth day after they'd fled the cave,

Aidan stopped in the middle of picking his way down a slippery hill and took Daniel's arm.

"I'm sorry."

—There. That wasn't so hard, was it?

Daniel doubled over coughing, waving him away. "Forget about it," he said, turning to spit. He gave Aidan a wan grin. "I shouldn't have asked so many questions."

"I really didn't mind," Aidan said, smiling back. Apologizing had left him feeling better, lighter, than any amount of sleep. "I just don't know the answers, either," he went on, throttling the sword hilt.

—Ouch, Heritage said, sounding bored.

Oh, shut up.

"We'll figure everything out," Daniel said. "For now, let's just find a place to sleep."

"Preferably someplace indoors," Aidan said, frowning at his friend. "You look terrible. No offense."

Daniel started to insist that he was fine but stepped forward a bit too quickly, lost his balance, tumbled into Aidan, and sent them both rolling down the hill in a flurry of shouts and snow. As he rose and dusted himself off, Aidan let out a great laugh, his first in weeks, and pulled his friend to his feet. Daniel let out a gruff "Thanks" and trudged forward.

They continued on for three more days, using the long poles for support as they hiked up and down an endless spread of rolling hills. At twilight on the ninth day, just as they were making their way up another small hill, Daniel stopped and turned, looking back the way they had come.

"What is it?" Aidan asked.

Chewing his lip, Daniel scanned the land behind them. "I feel like we're being watched."

Aidan looked around nervously, hand going to his sword hilt. Daniel jabbed his rabbit-roaster-turned-walking-staff into the ground thoughtfully before resuming their trek.

The wind gained speed over the next few hours, whipping at their cloaks and snatching away breath. By evening, small flurries of flakes leaked from the darkening sky.

"We're going to want to find cover soon," Daniel said.

Aidan pointed ahead. "I think I see a village."

Daniel frowned. "If we're going to be ambushed by walking corpses again, I'd rather be hiding among trees than caught inside," he said hoarsely.

"We're staying indoors tonight," Aidan said firmly.

Daniel started to protest before breaking down in a fit of coughing. "I don't want to slow us down."

"You think I'm worried about you?" Aidan said, and tried to laugh off his concern. "Staying in an inn means lanterns, candles, hearths—plenty of light I can use should anything happen."

Daniel nodded weakly. Less than an hour later they entered the village. Quaint houses spread out in neat rows, their roofs thick and sloped to dump snow to the ground. Not that much covered the ground. In every Torelian city, a handful of Touched, usually first-year Learners at the Lion's Den and other universities, encased themselves in heat bubbles and walked up and down the streets, melting the snow to keep the lanes clear. Soft lantern light glowed through frosted windows. They came to a stop in front of a large brick building. A wooden board with *Hornet's Nest* carved into it hung above the entrance. After examining the board for a moment, Daniel pointed to one corner of the sign and turned to his friend, one eyebrow lifted. Aidan leaned in closer then recoiled. The mark showed a snake coiled around a dagger. The Sallnerian serpent.

Not all Sallnerians stayed in their assigned Territory Bridge communities. Many southerners settled in Torel, Leaston, or Darinia—a rare occurrence, given the west's hundreds of miles of deserts—but were required to show the mark on their homes and establishment to reveal their nationality. Aidan remembered reading about an outbreak of disease some four hundred years ago in the east. Torelian healers had etched a skull on the door of every home where the infected lay dead or dying. Uninfected would cross the street at the first sign of the skull, afraid that even touching the door would strike them down. Spotting the Sallnerian serpent had a similar effect.

Aidan looked from the sign to Daniel's pale face. "It's the only inn we've seen so far."

Daniel nodded and turned the knob before glancing again at Aidan. "Better cover your face. I can't imagine you'd be popular with the clientele."

Aidan donned his hood and they ducked inside.

A tiny, unlit hearth left the room nearly as cold as the outdoors. A few large men—Sallnerians all, marked by their brown skin and almond-shaped eyes—sat at the bar staring into dirty mugs. The walls were scuffed and discolored with dried splotches of booze, likely scars from where mugs had shattered during tavern brawls. A pungent miasma of pipe weed hung over pockmarked benches and tables. In the corner near the hearth, a group of boys with dirt-smudged faces and wearing ratty clothes threw a pair of dice against the wall.

The innkeeper, a scrawny fellow whose oily skin shone in the room's dim lighting, was bent over wiping stains from the counter as they approached. Glancing up, his frown stretched into a lopsided grin when he noticed the jewel-encrusted hilt of Aidan's sword.

"Welcome to the Nest," he said, rubbing his hands together. "Help you?"

"We're looking for a room," Daniel said.

"You Wardsmen?" the skinny man asked, nodding to Daniel's partially concealed armor. The "H" across his chest was just viewable.

Daniel shrugged open his cloak. "We are. You'd do well to show proper respect to Crown's men."

The innkeeper absently batted at a wisp of greasy hair. "You got coin?"

Daniel drew three gold coins marked with the serpent from his pouch and tossed them onto the counter. The innkeeper snatched them up before they could clink twice against the counter and held them up to a lantern. His face drooped in a pout. "Southern coin?"

"That's more than enough, I'm sure," Daniel said, then motioned for Aidan to follow him as he made his way to the back of the common room.

Daniel signaled to the serving girl as they sat on opposite sides of a table. Aidan kept his head down as he peered about the room, hoping no one had taken special interest during their exchange with the innkeeper. He didn't need anyone getting ideas about slitting their throats and robbing them while they slept. After a quick look around, he let himself breathe easier. None of the men at the bar had looked up, the innkeeper had gone back to polishing dirt, and the boys in the corner whispered among themselves and threw their dice, the cubes rattling against the wall and floor.

"Would you like to get some food, or...?" Aidan asked. Daniel wasn't paying attention. He was watching the youths thoughtfully. Aidan tapped the table. His friend jumped, startled.

"Hmm?" Daniel said. "Food? No, that's all right." He turned back to the dice game. Another throw sent the cubes rattling against the walls and floor. One of the boys looked over and flashed his hands at his friends. The boys glanced their way but continued throwing their dice. "Unless you're hungry," Daniel went on absently. "I'm more thirsty."

"All right. I'll see about—"

The door banged open, letting in a gust of snow and a shrill howl of wind. A man and a woman bundled up in cloaks entered. They were silent as they crossed the room to sit at a table directly opposite the two friends. The woman shrugged out of her cloak to reveal a head of long, silky black hair. She inclined her head to her companion as he took her cloak, then slid onto a bench with her back to Aidan and crossed her legs. Her companion, his hair blonde and pulled back in a ponytail, hung their belongings on a peg and sat, leaning in to hear what she was saying.

Aidan frowned. Something about the woman tickled the back of his mind.

"Hey, did you notice...?" He looked up but Daniel was gone, striding across the room and kneeling to talk with the boys. To Aidan's astonishment, Daniel peeled off his gloves, dug into his purse, and held up a coin—a *square* coin. One of the boys took the coin, turned it over, bit it, and handed it back, nodding to the others. Daniel tucked it away and made a series of gestures, his hands a blur. The boys glanced at each other and gestured back. While Daniel's fingers waggled, one of the boys stood, slipped behind the bar unnoticed, and crept back with parchment, an inkpot, and a quill.

A waitress stepped up to the table, blocking Aidan's view. He looked up and into the dimpled smile of a dark-haired woman.

"What would you like?" she asked, leaning in and giving him a bold stare.

Aidan felt his face catch fire. "Uh... I, we would... uh..."

"Two mugs of swamp water," Daniel said, sliding onto his seat and tucking something into a pocket. The waitress turned right to him and fixed him with the same look. Daniel leaned in to talk to Aidan then noticed the woman noticing him. He blushed and repeated the order.

"Anything for you, handsome," she said, and glided toward the bar, swiveling her hips as she went.

"Rather forward, isn't she?" Daniel asked, but Aidan wasn't paying attention. His eyes were on the woman across the room. She had been staring at him over her shoulder but quickly looked away. Aidan rubbed at his nose absently. There was something familiar about her. The woman laughed at something her companion whispered.

Daniel fell into another coughing fit, pulling Aidan's attention away.

"We need to find you a healer," he said.

Daniel took a deep, shuddering breath, wiped his mouth. "I'm actually feeling a bit better. The heat bubble has helped. It just failed to melt the cold already building in my chest." He began tracing random patterns on the tabletop. "I've been thinking. We're taking too long, even with the shifts."

Aidan propped his elbow on the table and cupped his face with one hand, more to hide his profile than out of tiredness. "I agree. I thought about taking a ship, but they're slow. I'd also rather not be on the water. The vagrants could sink us."

"That would be bad," Daniel said, nodding.

"So, what other option is there?"

Daniel glanced at the boys throwing the dice, folded his arms and leaned forward. "Did I ever tell you why my family moved to Torel?" he said quietly.

"No," Aidan said, interested.

"I... got in some trouble back east."

Now Aidan leaned forward. "What kind of trouble?"

"Have you heard of the sneaks?"

Aidan frowned, then his eyes bulged. "The thieves' guild? They're *real*?"

Daniel lifted his hand and shook it in a *sort of* gesture. "My father was always out at sea, and my mom was busy around the farm. I got bored and sort of fell in with them when I was seven. I had a friend who knew where to find them, and they brought me in." He squirmed. "The sneaks caught a tough break. They're known as the thieves of the east, yes. That's what got me into trouble. No need to get into that right now," he said in a rush. "But they're also the eyes and ears of the merchants' guild. There's nothing that goes on in Crotaria that they don't know about. Plenty of places beyond this rock, too.

"Anyway, the sneaks like to... well, they sneak around, obviously. But not above ground. Not unless they have to. They use a series of underground tunnels. These tunnels are like strands in a spider web. They're all over Crotaria. We—I should say, they—have passages into every city and village in Torel, Leaston, the Ihlkin mountains through Darinia. Even down in Sallner, though I hear most of those tunnels have been blocked off."

"You hear? From who?"

Daniel nodded at the boys in the corner.

"They're sneaks?" Aidan asked, stunned.

"The guild prefers to recruit young. It's easy to teach kids how to creep around. They're small, quiet. Adults bumble and fumble about like... well, like princes trying to pinch sweets in the dead of night." He flashed Aidan a grin, then grimaced. "Or like men in armor." He shifted, and his mail rattled. "I never have gotten used to wearing all this."

Aidan chuckled. "So, what about these tunnels? Could we use them?"

"We already have, actually. Do you remember the passage I used to get us off the Sunfall grounds?"

"And the cave you happened across during the storm?" Aidan said, letting out a low whistle. "I can't believe you found it."

"The storm made things difficult," Daniel admitted. "But I knew about where we were. Well, there's a tunnel nearby, and I got the key." He took a piece of parchment out of his pocket and unfolded it. Sketched in the middle was an "X" with a wiggly line through each side. "I showed them my sneak coin—everybody gets one of those; show it to the right person, give a password or twelve using the sign language"—his fingers flickered then dropped back to the table, so fast Aidan was almost convinced his friend hadn't even moved—"and there's nothing they won't give you. So they gave me this key and told me where to find the tunnel."

"How do we use the key?"

"All the sneak tunnels are connected, like I said. Once you're underground, you come to what they call waypoints, large caverns with a bunch of passages. Just look for your key next to the passage and follow it."

Aidan nodded, remembering the V-in-a-V he'd noticed scratched in the stone back in the cave. "I agree that moving underground will feel safer, but will it really be any faster?"

"Much," Daniel said, and he shifted in his seat, looking uncomfortable. "The tunnels are magic."

"Incredible!" Aidan said. "I doubt even Tyrnen knows about these tunnels." The thought of Tyrnen's mouth dropping to the floor as he, Aidan, lectured his teacher—pacing back and forth and waggling a finger, of course—on these century-old passageways made him smile. *You cannot learn everything from dusty papers older than you are, old man.* His delight sharpened into a pang of homesickness. "How do they work?" he asked, pushing the feelings away.

Daniel took a breath. "Dark magic."

Aidan's breath caught in his throat.

Noticing Aidan's look, Daniel shook his head hard and fast. "I don't use it. I don't have a magical bone in my body. The architects who built the tunnels, thousands of years ago—maybe more—they used it. Running the tunnels is like... It's like riding shadows, they've said. Like waves of darkness that carry you forward."

"Dark magic is..." Aidan glanced around and lowered his voice. "It's forbidden, Daniel. Dark magic is what dug up those vagrants from the ground and sent them after me."

Daniel sat back, looking troubled. "Can it really be all bad? I've seen friends of mine feed on dark magic so they could slip away before getting arrested for stealing food they needed to survive."

"Stealing is still wrong."

"As wrong as forcing dead bodies to hunt us down?" Daniel shook his head. "This is why I didn't mention the tunnels earlier. Look, I don't claim to know much about dark magic, or light magic, or mid-afternoon magic, or any other type of magic you can think of. I'm just saying a sword can spill any man's blood, not just the ones who deserve it."

Aidan went quiet at that.

Daniel cleared his throat and continued. "Anyway, we won't have vagrants stalking us, and you won't need to worry about anyone recognizing you. We just follow this key"—he tapped the paper—"and take the tunnels straight into Sallner." He shrugged. "I just figured moving underground would—"

"It's a good plan," Aidan said, not looking up.

Daniel nodded, coughed into a fist. "Do you want to talk about it?"

"Talk about what?"

"What happened at Sharem?"

Aidan looked up. "What have you heard?"

"Not much. Only that... Well, that you assaulted your father after the battle. He sent word back to Sunfall, believing that you had shifted there, and..."

Aidan leaned back, no longer hearing Daniel as a horrific thought took root. His father had also undergone a drastic personality change since returning from the retreat. And his eyes, like his mother's impersonator, had been lifeless, devoid of emotion.

The creature that impersonated my mother... could my father have a doppelganger as well?

—I would assume so, yes.

Where are they? Where are my parents?

—That is not a question I can answer now.

If you can't help me, I need to know who—

—The Prophet will help you.

Aidan grimaced. *That's what you keep saying.*

—Do you trust me?

Do I have a choice?

Silence. It was then that Aidan noticed Daniel waving his hand in front of Aidan's face. "Are you all right?" Daniel asked, his face creased in worry.

"I'm fine," Aidan said, hoping he sounded it. "Just tired."

Daniel slowly sat back. "You're sure?"

"Yes. I was, ah, conferring with the sword."

"I didn't hear anything."

Aidan tapped his head.

Daniel's eyes widened. "Oh," he breathed.

Aidan nodded and cleared his throat. "What were you saying about my father?"

"The colonel told us that Tyrnen and your father communicated while you two were at Sharem, and that the old man told your mother that you'd come to see him."

"Oh," Aidan said slowly. *Why would Tyrnen turn me in?* He pursed his lips. *He probably didn't have much choice. If he would have tried to cover for me, he might have made himself an enemy of Torel. Or maybe he doesn't know about my parents, about what they are.* Despair washed over him. *Maybe the vagrants got to him, too.*

"We don't have to talk about Sharem if you don't want to," Daniel said. "I just wondered, because of everything that's happened since you got back, that maybe something there triggered... I don't know... all of this." He gestured expansively.

"Trouble did start at Sharem, yes." Aidan stared levelly at Daniel. "The Darinians had a force hidden in the forest across from the city. The regiment I led was nothing compared to the number of clansmen stashed away in those trees." He paused. "I butchered every last one."

Daniel let out a slow whoosh of breath. The waitress returned, bending to offer them a generous view as she set their drinks in front of them. Aidan was too involved in his examination of the table to notice, and Daniel was staring straight ahead. She shot them both a sulky frown and went back to the bar.

"You did what you had to do," Daniel said. "They would've killed our men."

"I know. But I don't believe in the war, Daniel. The way I see it, I was forced to choose between lives. If I wouldn't have acted, Wardsmen would've been killed. But because I got involved, clansmen were killed. I'm not certain of Darinia's guilt, so what I did doesn't feel right."

He shook his head. "Something doesn't fit. Think about it.

Romen, Cynthia, and a few clansmen make the trip to my Rite of Heritage. No hostile words—at least none that I know of—are exchanged between them or my parents. Then suddenly we're at war? A party of seven Darinians ambushes the Crown of the North, the Eternal Flame, and Edmund the Valorous, one of the greatest Torelian generals since my great-great-great-great... Ah, since Ambrose Gairden? Why? That was suicide! Romen and the clansmen are great warriors, but to attack those three... It just doesn't make sense."

Daniel tapped his finger against his cup. "Tyrnen said he believed they'd probably been plotting against Torel for a long time. You don't believe them?"

Aidan started to reply when a sudden realization struck him. It was after his parents had returned from their retreat that their behavior had so drastically changed—but their behavior had changed because *they* had changed. His parents hadn't entered into a war; the creatures *impersonating them* had done that.

Which meant his parents had never returned from Sharem, or Lake Carrean, or wherever they had really gone.

"We've got to return to Sunfall," Aidan said tensely.

"What? We just ran away!"

"I'll explain on the way," Aidan said, starting to rise.

—Home is not safe, Aidan.

I'm not listening to you anymore. You haven't told me anything about my parents, and I—

Slow, heavy footsteps cut him off, and both men looked up to see a large, Sallnerian man standing to the side of their table. He was tall, powerfully built, and dirty.

"This is my table," the man growled. "I want it back."

"Odd," Daniel said. "I remember you sitting at the bar when we came in."

Glancing over his shoulder, Aidan noticed the innkeeper whispering with two other large men from where they watched events unfold at the bar.

The man popped his knuckles as he stared at Daniel. "Know what I think? I think you two are the only Wardsmen around tonight. I think I'd watch your tongue if I were you, Torelian. I might have to rip it out."

"It will get easier," Daniel said.

The man narrowed his eyes. "What's that?"

"Thinking. It always hurts the first time."

The burly fellow snarled and yanked Daniel out of his seat. Gripping Heritage, Aidan blinked. His vision went black-on-white.

He slid out from behind the table and went behind the man in one smooth motion.

"Let him go," Aidan said. The man whirled to face him. His scowl receded into a pale, thin-mouthed stare. He released Daniel and raised his hands in surrender, but his eyes kept darting from Aidan to something past him.

Stools scraped and clattered to the floor behind him. Aidan spun to meet the other men as they rushed forward. They halted as they looked into his eyes, stopping so fast they almost tumbled forward.

—Behind you.

Pivoting, Aidan swung Heritage around and severed the first man's fist from his arm. The disconnected hand plopped to the floor. Blood pooled around it. Aidan continued to spin, coming back around to face the three men he had been staring at a moment before. The wounded thug howled and stumbled out of the bar clutching his gushing stump. Pushing past each other, his friends hastily followed.

Aidan blinked and his vision returned to normal. He looked at Daniel, who wore a look of shock.

"It seems I'm the only Gairden blessed with both sides of *Ordine*," Aidan explained in a low voice, then noticed Daniel shaking his head. "What's wrong?"

"Aidan—your eyes were glowing white."

Startled, Aidan looked at Heritage. *Why did my eyes glow?*

—The change your vision undergoes when you wield me in battle is reflected outwardly as well.

But why does that happen?

—All of your questions will be answered, but only if you continue south to the Prophet.

I already told you, I need to get home to—

—Home is dangerous, Aidan. You have seen that. Also, your family is not there. Please. For now, I ask that you trust me.

Aidan thought for a moment. *Will you answer more of my questions?*

—The Prophet will answer—

Rage and desperation, blacker than the despair he'd felt when he'd lost control at Sharem, swept through him. *No. You've had me waiting and running for days. I'm exhausted, I'm angry, and... and I'm afraid. Give me answers or I turn around and go home.*

—Very well. But not now.

When?

—Later tonight. I promise.

Aidan focused on Daniel. "It has something to do with wielding Heritage."

"Oh," Daniel said faintly. "I suppose that's fine, then."

Adjusting his hood, Aidan strode to the innkeeper. The bony man had turned a pale shade of gray. Aidan leaned in close to the cowering man. "I trust that while we sleep tonight, none of your large friends will mistakenly enter the wrong room."

"N-no, sir. I'll m-make sure of it."

"Good," Aidan replied. Then he had an idea. He bowed his head, gripped Heritage, blinked, and slowly raised his eyes. The innkeeper took one look at his eyes and let out a terrified shriek, dashing through the doorway behind the bar.

—Oh, that was fun, the grandmotherly voice said.

With a grim smile, Aidan motioned for Daniel to follow him. They bounded up the stairs.

Down in the empty common room, the Torelian man and Sallnerian woman sat forgotten. They shared a look, then the man reached down to kiss his companion's hand and made his way up the stairs. The woman continued to sit, studying the severed hand, and thinking.

Chapter 18

Whispers in the Night

AIDAN TOSSED AND TURNED a few more times before sitting up. He looked across the room. In another narrow bed, Daniel mumbled in his sleep and coughed softly. Swinging his legs to the floor, Aidan dressed and took Heritage from beneath his pillow. Pulling his hood down over his eyes, Aidan tip-toed to the door, cringing with every creaky step, eased it open, and closed it gently behind him.

Wind shook the Hornet Nest's thin walls as he made his way down the stairs. The common room was dark but for lanterns that cast flickering pools of light on every other tabletop. Aidan grabbed a lantern and made his way to a booth against the far wall with a perfect view of the front door, the stairs, and the door behind the bar. He sat down, tugged away his hood, and placed Heritage and the lamp on his table.

I didn't wake you, did I? he asked.

—Not at all. I don't need to sleep.

Good. You said we would talk more later if I chose not to leave. It's later.

—So it is. You can speak aloud if you like. We are quite alone.

Aidan winced. "I feel funny talking to you out loud."

—I'm hurt.

"You know what I mean."

—I suppose I do, though I don't understand why it bothers you so much. You are partaking in one of the most intriguing traditions of your family. I would think your embarrassment would be dampened by your fascination.

"Are you one of my ancestors, then?"

—No.

"Then who are you?"

—That question will be answered in due time. What others do you have?

Aidan sifted through his many inquiries. "Why do my eyes glow when I wield you? And my vision change—does all of that have to do with *Ordine'kel?*"

—Actually, no. Gairdens who were gifted with only one half of Ordine *did not experience what you have. It is, as with so many things of late, unique to you.*

"Why?"

—I will answer the 'why' regarding the vision shift you experience, but as for why so many unique events are happening to you, that is better left for another conversion.

"Fair enough."

—In short, when you combine 'cin *and* 'kel, *you are tapping the full potential of the Lady of Dawn herself.*

He expelled his breath in a slow whoosh. "Do you mean to tell me that I can channel the power of a goddess?"

Heritage was silent for a moment.

—I mean you are the most powerful human *to have ever existed. You were strong before; you are even more so, now. Your vision changes because...* The sword paused. *Because the Sight, as I call it, is perfect, allowing you to see what is truly there.*

Aidan was speechless. He thought back to his confrontation with the vagrant posing as his mother. When he'd embraced *Ordine'kel,* its true face had been revealed as if its mask did not exist.

—You are rightfully impressed.

"Why me?"

—As I said, we will discuss that in due time. There is one other significant facet to the full Ordine *gift. Because you did not tap into* Ordine'kel *before accepting Heritage, your access to* 'kel *is dependent upon holding Heritage.*

"And *Ordine'cin* is always available to me because I was born with it."

—Correct.

He pondered what he had learned over the past several days. "The way you and I talk. Is that how sword-bearers communicate with our ancestors?"

—Primarily. There is another method, but that, too, is best saved for another chat.

"What about when a Gairden undergoes the Rite of Heritage, accepting the position of sword-bearer from a Gairden who is still alive? Does the previous sword-bearer lose communication with the sword?"

—Yes... in a manner of speaking.

"So my mother can no longer communicate with her ancestors?"

Heritage did not respond.

Aidan banged his fist on the table, sending Heritage and the lantern ratting against the wood. "Why won't you answer?"

—Because it is a very complicated matter. We'll discuss it soon.

"Why not now?"

—You are not ready.

"I am tired of everyone telling me what I *am* and am *not* ready for."

—I thought you preferred to have all your affairs handled for you. Minimal effort, minimal responsibility. Isn't that your way of life?

Aidan closed his eyes, seeing the shocked faces of the clansmen at Sharem, heard their screams as they were burned alive and ripped apart. He remembered the odor of burning flesh, their blackened hands outstretched in unanswered pleas for mercy.

"Not anymore."

—I am happy to hear that, Aidan.

They were silent for a few moments.

"So," he said, steeling himself, "if I'm the sword-bearer, then my mother is not." He thought back to the corpse that had worn his mother's face in the sword chamber. "Something has happened to her. Why was she demoted? Where is she?"

Silence.

Aidan's eyes stung as hot tears rolled down his cheeks. "It's my fault. Whatever's happened to her is my fault."

—You have told me what you find tiring. Would you like to know what I find tiring?

He didn't answer.

—Your constant desire to make everything about you.

"You don't understand. This *is* my fault. I—"

—No, Aidan, it is not *your fault. Everything always has to be about you, doesn't it? Good things, bad things—they* must *have something to do with you. Stop wallowing in self-pity, child. It is past time you grew up.*

Aidan stared open-mouthed.

—I am proud that you have decided to think for yourself and take matters into your own hands. But this is not only about you, Aidan. Do not presume to make it so.

"I just want to understand."

—You will, in due time. But for now, will you swear to never forget what I'm about to tell you?

Aidan nodded.

—Your parents love you dearly. They always have, and they always will. Never forget that.

He nodded again, not trusting himself to speak.

—I believe that's enough for tonight. Get some rest for the journey ahead.

Suddenly flooded with weariness, Aidan pushed himself from the table and gathered Heritage. There were other questions to ask, but they could wait. Replacing Heritage at his side, he began to cross the common room when he heard footsteps coming down the stairs. The dark-haired woman from earlier that night entered, then stopped when she saw him, startled.

"I guess I'm not the only one having trouble sleeping tonight," she said, smiling. Her hair bobbed against her shoulders as she strode toward him. Her wool tunic and trousers were simple, clothes meant more for riding than time spent in palace courts, yet the plainness of her garments was offset by rings adorning each finger that glittered in the room's dim lighting. A golden bracelet, which Aidan recognized as the unmatched craftsmanship of the Darinian smiths of Zellibar, jangled on her wrist.

Aidan smiled and nodded, preparing to move around her toward the stairs, when she reached out and placed her hand on his wrist.

"Would you mind keeping me company? My brother is asleep, and I'm a bit restless."

"I'm rather tired," he began.

"I'll only keep you for a short while," she promised, flashing another dazzling smile. It was beautiful—but there was something familiar about it as well, he noted. The soft touch of her fingers decided for him. He sat down at the nearest table, carefully setting Heritage on the bench beside him after he was settled.

"Thanks," she said as she sat across from him. "I'm Christine." She extended her hand.

Taking her hand, Aidan began to voice his own name before instead saying, "Thomas." It came out awkwardly, as if it was a word he'd just learned and was having difficulty pronouncing.

She held his gaze and his hand for a few long moments then retracted her arm to fold her hands on the table. "Nice to meet you. Thomas."

Aidan felt a moment of panic when he realized his face was not concealed. His hand twitched, wanting to pull down the hood of his cloak, but he resisted. It would seem too suspicious now, and she didn't seem to recognize him, covered as he was in dirt and muck picked up from travel.

"I'm surprised you want to talk with me," he said.

"Why wouldn't I?"

Because you're Sallnerian, and I'm Torelian, and civil conversation just won't do, he thought. "After what happened earlier tonight, people seem eager to stay as far away as possible," he said instead.

"Except for your friend," she noted.

"He wouldn't be a friend, otherwise."

"Good point. I assume it was magic you were using?"

"Yes."

"I am also one of the Touched." She held out her right hand. Among the ornately crafted rings inset with different jewels was the gold loop and purple stone of a Cinder Band, which occupied her forefinger.

"Where did you train?" he asked her.

"At the Lion's Den in Sharem."

"Ah," Aidan replied, eager to steer the conversation away from that particular city. To his delight she seemed to pick up on his discomfort.

"Where are you from?" she asked. "You look Torelian."

Aidan hesitated. She seemed nice enough, but the less anyone knew about him, the better. "From Torel, yes. Now I'm a vagabond." It was true to a degree. "I have no home."

She made a sound of understanding. "My brother and I have traveled the world since childhood. I paid for my education as I earned a living: spent time learning, then spent time working, and so forth. It took a long time, but I did it."

He nodded. "If I may ask, weren't your parents able to help with your education?"

She lowered her eyes. "My mother died when I was very young."

"I'm sorry."

"You didn't know," she said, unperturbed. "Garrett and I stayed with our father for a year or so, but we don't really get along with him."

Aidan nodded. *The man with her in the common room.* He felt oddly relieved. He opened his mouth to say something, but yawned instead. "Sorry. I'm afraid my travels are catching up to me."

"Not a problem," Christine said, again flashing that enchanting smile. "Thanks for entertaining me for a bit."

"It was my pleasure." He lifted Heritage from the bench and

rose. "Goodnight, Christine." He got about halfway across the room before she spoke again.

"Thomas," she called, and it took him a moment to realize she was talking to him. He turned. Rising from the table, she sauntered toward him with a lopsided smile.

"Since we're both travelers, I wonder..." She paused, and a slight blush spread over her cheeks. Aidan was surprised; blushing didn't seem like the sort of reaction she had very often. He found himself smiling. She wore the blush well.

"Would you and your friend like to travel with Garrett and me?" she continued.

"That's a nice offer, Christine, but—"

"We travel all over, like I told you," she said in a rush. "We perform a small magic show in every city and village we come to. We have our own group, just the two of us, called Spectacle. We'd be happy to have you both." She winced. "I apologize for rambling, I'm not used to... never mind." The blush spread further.

Aidan gave her an easy smile. "I do appreciate the offer, Christine. But I'm afraid I can't accept. I have somewhere I have to be."

"Oh. All right," she said, giving him a bright smile.

"It's not that I don't want to. But my friend and I have plans that cannot be broken."

"I understand."

"Maybe we will meet again," he said, and he hoped it was true. "Now just isn't a good time. It was nice to meet you, Christine."

The crash and yell from downstairs brought Aidan and Daniel awake with a start. Raising a finger to his lips, Aidan grabbed Heritage, dashed into the hall, and peered down the stairs. The inn door lay in pieces across the floor. Howling wind vomited snow through the doorway. There were Wardsmen in the room, five of them that Aidan could see, each looking around with flat, dead eyes. Aidan grabbed the hilt and tapped into *'kel*. The Sight stripped the human faces from the vagrants. Aidan cursed under his breath. How did they *always* manage to find him?

One turned to look up the stairs. Aidan darted behind the wall and slunk back to his room. Behind him, heavy footfalls sounded on the stairs.

"Vagrants," he whispered to Daniel as he shut and locked the door behind him. Daniel leaped from his bed and hastily dressed. Aidan dressed just as hastily, hopping around as he struggled with one boot.

"Where can we escape?" Daniel croaked.

Aidan pulled hard on the window, but it wouldn't budge. Footsteps reached their door and halted. Aidan stepped back and swung Heritage at the window, shattering it. Snow gusted in, stinging his face. He used the sword to wipe away loose fragments of glass as he motioned for Daniel to crawl through. From outside the door came a deep bellow, and a moment later, the door shuddered with a heavy thud.

Aidan crawled through the window and scrambled down the icy slanted roof to the ground, moving to follow Daniel's running form into the night. He heard their door shatter with a loud crash. He looked back and saw one of the creatures lean out of the window, its skull twisting at unnatural angles as it searched for them. It spotted the escaping duo and roared. The wind howled in reply.

"Where are we going?" Aidan shouted.

Daniel pointed straight ahead at a large expanse of trees barely visible in the blinding snowfall. They staggered into the forest and stopped to catch their breath. Aidan drew a few deep gulps of air and looked back at the inn. "I don't see anything," he gasped.

"Maybe we lost them," Daniel wheezed.

Straightening, Aidan looked around warily. Shadows, bent and twisted like the trees they belonged to, seemed to seep forward. Soft laughter whispered through the branches, audible even over the wind. Aidan drew Heritage as his eyes darted about. Something moved against a thick trunk several paces away. The shadows *were* sliding toward them. They detached from the trees and glided along the ground, inching closer to their trapped prey. The laughter grew louder, dwarfing the howl of the wind, as the shadows drew closer.

Daniel whipped his dagger out of its sheath and stood beside Aidan.

Aidan gasped as the creatures continued to close in. "I've seen these shadows before."

"Where?"

Aidan swallowed. He remembered them crawling on top of him when he was unable to move, pouring down his throat and nostrils, suffocating him, choking him...

"In a nightmare."

Daniel gritted his teeth. "Dream shadows? At this point, I'm willing to believe anything. How did you kill them?"

"I couldn't."

The shadows banded together, knitting into one enormous spread. The soft laughter rose in pitch as the bulk flowed around the trees like water, surrounding them. Daniel shouted and flipped a dagger into the amorphous mass. A tendril shot out and snatched the knife in mid-flight and sucked it into its core.

"Try magic!" Daniel shouted hoarsely.

"No light!" Aidan shouted back.

The shadow was almost touching their feet. Soon, neither would have any room to move at all. Suddenly the shadow beast let out an ear-splitting shriek. It slithered back a few paces, its wispy tendrils twisting like ebony serpents as plumes of smoke rose from its mass.

"What did you do?" Daniel asked.

Another bolt of pure-fire whizzed through the branches and lanced the creature. It gave a hoarse, rumbling moan as a third bolt streaked toward it. It stiffened, absorbing the attack, then continued to move toward them.

"It fears fire!" came a shout from their left, and Aidan saw Christine and her brother charge into sight on horseback, each holding a torch. Instantly recalling how the shadows had attacked first in his nightmare like dogs attacking a slab of meat, Aidan began to kindle from Christine's torch. Then he heard his lamp clink against his armor, cursed himself for a fool, and kindled from the lamp instead and shot his own bursts of pure-fire at the branches all around him. Magical flames cut through the wetness of the snow and ice to set wood aflame. Christine shifted her focus as well, aiming high at the trees to spread the fire. The shadow creature drew in on itself as if trying to avoid notice, but the fire was spreading rapidly. It shrieked as flames licked its fringes and streaked through its form.

Aidan advanced, hurling ball after ball of pure-fire. It howled one last time and vanished, leaving behind curling wisps of darkness. As one, Aidan and Christine cut off their spells. Daniel and Aidan burst through the trees and looked around frantically for their rescuers.

"Thomas!" Christine shouted as she galloped toward them.

Daniel turned a confused look on Aidan.

"Just go with it," he said.

The siblings came to a halt beside them, their horses pawing at the ground and throwing their heads at the scent of smoke.

"Hey, stranger," Christine said as Aidan scrabbled up behind her. "Going my way?"

Chapter 19

Shelter from the Storm

AIDAN CRANED HIS NECK over his shoulder as the horses pounded through the night, expecting to see vagrants or shadows rushing toward them like a flood of darkness, but the snowstorm shrouded the road.

"What are you looking for?" Christine shouted over the wind.

"Before you found us, a pack of creatures tried to ambush us at the inn," he shouted in reply.

"What kind of creatures?"

"You probably wouldn't believe me if I told you."

She laughed. "I think you owe me more credit."

"True enough. What was that shadow creature?"

"I'll explain soon," she shouted. "Right now we need to find shelter."

Garrett's horse caught up and galloped beside them. Aidan glanced at Daniel. He swayed on the saddle behind Garrett, his hands loosely wrapped around the other man's waist. His eyes weren't open.

"I don't suppose you know of anywhere close?" Aidan asked.

As Christine started to reply, Daniel toppled from his saddle.

"Stop!" Aidan cried.

Christine reined in her horse, kicking up snow. Garrett had already wheeled around. Aidan looked around frantically.

—Behind you and to your left.

Aidan looked and saw Daniel lying face down. Snowflakes swarmed over him like flies to meat. Aidan scrambled from his saddle and ran to his friend. Garrett appeared and helped Aidan hoist Daniel back onto his horse, then climbed up behind him and covered Daniel's front with his cloak while Aidan drew light from the torches and wrapped Daniel in a heat bubble.

"He's sick," Aidan shouted, climbing behind Christine. "We need to get him to shelter."

Shielding his eyes, Garrett pointed north with his free hand. "Tarion should be about a league from here."

"Let's go," Aidan said.

They rode as hard as the storm would allow. The snow was growing deeper. Their horses slowed and picked their way up and down hills. Aidan watched Daniel worriedly as they moved. He was slumped forward; only Garrett's hand wrapped around his middle kept him from spilling to the ground again. As they rode, the sky began to lighten.

As they crested one rise, Aidan saw faint squares of light spread out below. Tarion, the second largest city in Torel. They hurried down and approached the city's gate. In a tower above the gate, two Wardsmen glanced down before ducking away. The gate opened.

"Our friend is ill," Garrett explained as the Wardsmen greeted them. Aidan clutched his hood to hold it in place against the wind.

"The Fisherman's Pond has vacancy," a Wardsman shouted. He pointed and started to give directions.

"We know the place," Garrett said. "Thank you."

The Wardsmen nodded and hurried to close the gate and return to the warmth of the gatehouse.

Christine dug her boots into her horse's flanks and set off after Garrett, who was already trotting through the gate. Aidan looked around. Thick layers of ice and snow coated tiled rooftops. Their horses kicked up snow as they went along, revealing patches of smooth, paved road that the snow buried almost as soon as they passed. The buildings were made of wood and stone, evidence of stout Darinian craftsmanship. Riding close to one, Aidan glanced at a parchment flapping in the wind and drew his hood tighter. The parchment showed his face, mouth curled in a snarl and eyebrows drawn down. Below the menacing portrait was a very large number.

Rewards, he thought. *They're looking for me.* Heritage did not respond.

They came to a stable set next to a wide, brightly lit building. Even before the party had dismounted, two stable hands came running up. Aidan and Garrett carefully lifted Daniel from the saddle, each slinging one of his arms over their shoulders. Garrett tipped the workers and led the party through the door of the Fisherman's Pond.

Aidan found the atmosphere far more promising than the Hornet's Nest. A broad, white-washed stone fireplace was carved into the tanned granite wall at the end of the common room. Snapping flames emitted a warm glow. Chairs adorned the spacious room. A portly woman with gray hair pulled into a tight bun polished mugs behind the bar as they approached.

"Welcome to the Fisherman's..." She blinked and leaned forward, squinting, then set down the glass and beamed. "The Lady hold me close, is that you, Christine?" She rushed out from behind the counter.

"Hello, Martha," Christine said. The last syllable was a grunt; the larger woman had wrapped meaty arms around her in a bear hug. Aidan instantly took a liking to her. Her voice boomed but was motherly at the same time. That, as well as her bear-like size, reminded him of Helda.

"So sorry, dear," Martha said before turning to crush Garrett. "It's been ages, you two." Noticing Daniel, her cheery smile abruptly vanished. "The Lord of Midnight's got his claws in that one. We've four rooms upstairs. Get him up there. I'll send after a healer."

—You will tend to him.

Aidan blinked. *Me? I don't know anything about healing.* That was not entirely true, he amended, thinking back to the night he had broken the stained-glass window. Tyrnen and his mother had taught him the basics, just enough to heal minor wounds on the battlefield should a healer not be present. Daniel's sickness was much worse than a cut. His face was ashen, and he shivered almost hard enough to pull Aidan and Garrett to the floor.

—I will guide you, Heritage said. *Call off the healer.*

All right...

"We won't need a healer," Aidan said.

Christine, Martha, and Garrett looked at him in surprise. Keeping his head low, Aidan continued, "I can look after him."

"Are you a Touched, then?" Martha asked, trying rather obviously to peer beneath his hood.

"How much do we owe you?" Garrett asked, grabbing Martha's attention.

"Nothing at all," the innkeeper said, and waved off the siblings' protests. "I won't hear another word about it. Now get your friend upstairs."

They guided Daniel into a room and eased him onto a bed. Aidan sat beside Daniel while Christine and Garrett watched from behind him.

What do I do first?

—Ask them to leave. They might see the sword. You will need it.

Clearing his throat, he turned to the siblings. "Would you give me a few minutes?"

Garrett glanced at Christine, but his sister nodded. "We'll be right outside," she said. The door closed behind them.

—Grip the hilt of the sword and touch Daniel with your other hand.

He complied.

—You'll need all the light stored up in that necklace of yours.

Aidan pulled the lamp out from underneath his shirt.

—Kindle the light, but keep a grip on it.

He did as she asked then sat waiting. Several moments passed.

—Good. Now, one hand on the sword, one on your friend.

Again, he did as he asked. "What now?" he asked—and gasped as a surge of energy flooded through him and poured from his hand and into the Eye, which bloomed a fiery pink like the Lady's first light. Once again he was overwhelmed by a presence, but not his grandfather's. The hand that guided his was soft, small, and smelled of freshly cut flowers. Under his hand, he felt Daniel's skin grow cool. He watched in amazement as Daniel's breathing evened out and lost its grating hoarseness.

The energy cut off. Gasping, he rocked on his heels. The sensation had been incredible. At first, it had been like wielding *Ordine'kel:* techniques he had never even known or thought of were suddenly as simple as breathing. But unlike after releasing *'kel,* he held a glimmer of understanding after the fact. He had drawn light, passed it to Heritage, and *the sword* had kindled. More astonishing was that he mostly understood what it had done. He didn't think he could do it again without another lesson—maybe two—but the basics were clear.

—Through Heritage, the sword-bearer has access to the knowledge of his or her ancestors, the sword explained in answer to his unspoken question. *Those with* 'cin *have access to centuries of arcane knowledge, much of which is unknown outside of your bloodline. The same is true for* 'kel, *which, as we have discussed, is how you are able to wield it.*

For several moments, Aidan reeled at the staggering amount of magic available to him. *Summoning fire from the sword back in the cave felt different, though.*

—It was. Simple spells, such as a bit of fire, can pass through the Eye. It was crafted from the Lady's light, after all. More complex spells, like the one used just now, require the sword-bearer to kindle and pass the light to the sword. One of your ancestors knowledgeable in the necessary spell took the reins from there.

Aidan grew curious. *Who?* Then: *Let me guess. Not yet?*

—I knew you'd catch on eventually.

Aidan studied Daniel. *When will he awaken?*

—Like herbs and tonics, healing requires lots of rest to do its work.

Biting his lip, he looked out the frosted window. Dim rays from the Lady glinted against ice and glass. The wind continued to howl. *There's no way he can go back out in this.*

—Nor can you afford to expose yourself to the elements. One cannot heal oneself, Aidan. Though we haven't time to spare, Daniel should rest at least until this evening, as should you.

But the vagrants are probably still following me.

—Most likely, yet this is a large city. It will not be so easy to track you down as it was in the village. Rest here while you can, but be prepared to move on tonight.

The door cracked open. Garrett stuck his head in. "How is he?"

"He will recover," Aidan said with a small smile. He blinked as weariness weighted his eyelids.

"You look as if you could do with some rest yourself," Garrett said. "But first, we should talk."

Aidan pulled the blankets up to Daniel's chin and followed Garrett to another room. Christine smiled at Aidan as he entered and took a seat on the bed beside her.

"Before we discuss anything," Aidan said, "thank you for saving our lives."

"Not at all," Garrett said, leaning back against the wall. "Christine came bounding into my room with a shout, saying she had just seen a young man she'd met earlier running straight for the forest as though Kahltan himself was after him."

Aidan wanted to ask why the siblings had been watching them in the common room, but decided against it. They had, after all, proved to be worthwhile companions. "We were being pursued," he explained. "The creatures that were after us..." He hesitated. "They're called vagrants."

"Vagrants?" Christine said with a frown.

"Yes. They're..." He hesitated, then decided to tell the siblings what he knew. They had risked their lives to help him. It was only fair that they know what they were up against. "Well, as I understand it, they're corpses of Sallnerians from the Serpent War. They want to kill me." He barked a laugh and shook his head. "I know it must sound strange, but it's true."

"We believe you," Garrett said. "After some of the things we've seen..." He shivered. "Why are they after you?"

"I don't know," Aidan said, straight-faced. He didn't want to lie to his new friends, but the fewer people who knew who he was, the better. "What were those shadow creatures?"

"Whispers," Christine answered, and it was her turn to shudder. "Shadows given life from dark magic. They make your worst nightmare seem a fond, peaceful dream."

Unless they inhabit your dreams, Aidan thought. "How did you know their weakness?"

"A few years ago," she began, "Garrett and I were performing at a small tavern about ten leagues from here. Near the end of our show, a man came tearing through the door, shouting and carrying on about shadows that had stalked him through the streets. He babbled something about how the shadows seemed to fear fire, but that he had dropped his torch in his haste to escape."

She shook her head. "A few of the men bought him a drink and tried to calm him down, but he wouldn't have any of it. He was hysterical. The innkeeper managed to slip a bit of powder into his drink, just enough to calm him, and when he realized why he was feeling so tired he really threw a fit. The men dragged him upstairs to an empty room. We kept hearing him shout down the stairs for a torch, a candle, anything he could use to 'keep the whispers away,' as he said. One of the men couldn't take the yelling any longer and gave the poor man a candle to keep by his bedside. After a while he quieted down, and we all assumed he had finally drifted off to sleep.

"We were awakened by shouts in the middle of the night. The innkeeper was pounding on doors, yelling that there was a fire. We ran outside, and everyone was accounted for except the man who had come in earlier. As we looked up at his window, the glass smashed, and he peered out with a mad grin on his face. We begged him to get out of the building, insisting that the flames would eat him alive, but he refused."

Christine swallowed. "Before he disappeared back into the blaze he leaned out and yelled, 'The fire keeps the whispers away'."

Her tale quieted the room for a time.

"You look exhausted," Garrett said, breaking the silence. "Feel free to sleep as long as you like. There won't be much happening with this storm going on."

Aidan nodded, his head heavy as he rose from the bed. "That sounds wonderful. Thank you again," he said, and shambled to his room. He could barely keep his eyes open as he stumbled around undressing, but a question nagged at him.

"Have you ever seen a whisper before?"

—I have not. It is fortunate your new friends were familiar with them. What do you think of Garrett and Christine, by the way?

Aidan considered. "They saved our lives."

—Christine seems especially friendly, don't you think?

"She does indeed." A lopsided smile curved his lips. *Especially for a Sallnerian.* Instantly he felt ashamed. Christine had been nothing but kind to him. *Dawn burn me, she saved my life. I shouldn't think of her like—*

A soft knock sounded on his door, and before he could answer, Christine stepped into the room. The silk nightgown clinging to her body was almost entirely translucent, leaving little to Aidan's suddenly active imagination. A silver chain wrapped around her waist slid along her curves as she sauntered toward him. Her bare feet padded softly against the wooden floor. The corners of her mouth twitched slightly, and her eyes twinkled with amusement.

—You might want to cover up.

Aidan scrunched his face at the suggestion, too transfixed to immediately comprehend.

—Look down, 'Thomas'.

He managed to tear his eyes away from Christine long enough to glance at his lap. His undergarments stared back at him. Flushing, he clawed at the sheets and hastily covered his lower body. Christine came to rest in front of him.

"I hope I'm not disturbing you," she said softly.

"Oh, no, you—that is, I wasn't, uh... It's nothing."

Her eyes sparkled as she gave him a small smile. "I heard you talking from outside."

"I was just, ah—I was talking to myself."

"Oh?"

"Yes." He cleared his throat. "Just repeating your story to myself. That poor man."

She sighed as she sat down next to him. "I'll never forget that," she said. "We lost sight of you after we ran out of the inn, and when I looked toward the woods, I saw nothing but darkness, darkness that seemed to be moving inward. I heard your cries, and..."

Shrugging, she slowly crossed her legs. The bottom hem of her nightdress slowly retreated up her leg, revealing skin as white as snow as she leaned back on her palms. "If I ever had any doubts about that story, they were dispelled when I looked into those woods tonight. I somehow knew that the darkness I saw was what that man had described."

Aidan concentrated on looking her in the eyes. His gaze kept wanting to slip downward. Giggling, Christine uncrossed her legs and rose from the bed to make her way back to the hall. As she pulled the door closed, she let her upper torso hang out of the partially open portal. The nightgown drooped forward to reveal shapely pale skin.

"I'd better let you get some rest," she said, and the dazzling smile was set back in its place.

Barely able to swallow, Aidan nodded.

"Sleep well," she whispered. The door clicked shut behind her.

—Subtle, that one.

Aidan sank back into the mattress. For this first time since leaving home, he let his thoughts meander down softer, much more pleasant trails than danger and death.

—Sleep for now, Heritage broke in. *Our journey should resume tonight.*

Chapter 20

Fork in the Road

AIDAN SHUFFLED INTO THE inn's private dining room shortly after noontime.

"Awake at last," Garrett said.

"Guess I was more tired than I thought," Aidan said, smiling at Christine as she pulled out the chair next to her. He had enjoyed a sleep free of dreams. The fever was almost gone. He felt better than he had in days, and had actually woken up an hour earlier to scrub and polish the armor his father had given him before going to find his friends.

Across from his sister, Garrett tipped his chair back to prop against the wall, hands laced behind his head. Daniel sat next to him, his red hair ruffled as if he'd rolled out of bed at the first scent of the platters of roasted bird, freshly baked rolls slick with butter, steaming vegetables, and pumpkin cake that covered the tabletop. Aidan wouldn't have been surprised; that same glorious mixture of food had snared him like a fish on a hook and reeled him downstairs.

Heavy wind buffeted the windowpanes on either side wall, rattling the glass. Flames in the hearth at the end of the room rose higher as if in defiance of the cold.

"I was beginning to think I'd have to eat your share," Daniel said with a small smile. His voice was fuller than it had been, though his eyes drooped and his face was still pale.

"Good thing I got here in time," Aidan said. He picked up his plate and looked around at the dishes, unsure where to start. His stomach whined impatiently, but he hesitated.

"I can't pay you for our rooms, or this meal. I can't possibly accept this."

Daniel looked across at him with a guilty expression as a chunk of steaming carrot dropped from his chin onto his empty plate.

Garrett waved a hand dismissively. "Think nothing of it. Christine and I wanted to treat our new friends to a fine meal." He gestured to the food. "I insist."

"Far be it for me to refuse such a kind gesture," Aidan said, grinning. He leaned over the table and scooped up heaps of anything and everything. Stabbing a piece of bird, he took a bite and sighed as he chewed.

"This meal is just an appetizer compared to what Martha's crew is preparing for dinner," Garrett went on. "Christine and I insisted on performing tonight in exchange for the free room and board. My sister has told you about Spectacle, yes? I think you'll both enjoy what we have planned."

Christine gave her brother a level stare that Aidan did not notice.

"I don't mean to be rude," he said, "but we'll be leaving tonight."

The room went quiet. Christine picked at her food, and Daniel set down his fork before glancing at Aidan.

Garrett cleared his throat. "You might want to think about staying here."

"Why is that?" Daniel asked.

Garrett gestured to the windows. "The storm doesn't show any sign of letting up, and you, my friend, are in no condition to brave it."

Just as Aidan was preparing to decline, Heritage wriggled into his thoughts.

—I suggest staying through dinner. Your friend is right: Daniel could use a bit more rest. Besides, the storm might diminish over the next few hours.

A strong desire to put as much distance between him and the vagrants made Aidan shove down rising anxiety. "I'll give the storm a few hours," he said, forcing a smile.

Daniel blinked at him in surprise. Aidan shook his head slightly.

"It's settled, then!" Garrett said. He raised his cup. "If I may propose a toast?" His three companions raised their drinks. "To friendship."

"To friendship," they echoed, bringing the wooden cups together with a clack.

Aidan raised the cup to his lips and held it there. *I want to keep moving tonight, storm or not.*

—Agreed.

What about Daniel?

—Advise him to rest. You may have to continue on without him. He will be safe here.

Continue to where? Predictably, Heritage did not respond.

Aidan took a hearty swallow and lowered his cup. “You should get some more sleep,” he said to Daniel. “I’d like to leave early this evening if possible.”

The siblings shared a glance. Garrett stood and stretched. “I’m going to go pay my compliments to Martha, and then I do believe I’ll take a nap. Perfect weather for a doze.”

“I’m going to change into something warmer,” Christine said, rising. “Will you be down here when I return, Thomas? Perhaps we could talk.”

“I’d like that,” Aidan said, then felt his face flush at the enthusiasm in his voice. He *did* need to be moving on, but a little extra time with Christine wasn’t anything to complain about.

Christine bounded into her room and sifted through her travel trunk. Her outfit should be practical, yet pleasing to the eye... to *Thomas’s* eye, especially. Deciding on a tan blouse and skirt, Christine changed. She brushed at her blouse, straightening it so it rested just so against her body—then stopped when she caught sight of her Cinder Band in the mirror’s reflection.

Examining the brilliant sheen of the amethyst sent her mind wandering to a conversation she’d had with her employer. She had done what he’d asked. All she needed to do was contact him. The Eternal Flame would reward her services with an induction into Torel’s Dawn, something she’d been surprised to discover she wanted very much.

Her smile became a sneer. *What would you think of that, Father?* She shook her head, scattering thoughts and sending her black hair tumbling over her shoulders.

But what would become of Aidan? She couldn’t imagine any parents executing their own child, but the possibility made her blood run cold. She cared for Aidan. She’d cared about him for years. Tyrnen had trained Aidan with his mother. Surely the prince’s mentor could be convinced that leniency should be shown for...

The amethyst within her Band pulsed with a low, plum-colored glow. Swallowing, Christine pressed a finger to it, and the old man’s voice entered her thoughts.

—Have you found him?

Christine remained silent in voice and thoughts for a long moment.

“Not yet.”

She adjusted her blouse and left the room.

A door opened down the hall, and Garrett Lorden peered out. Clutched in a white-knuckled grip was one of the Torelian marks the old man had given him. It pulsed with a low, crimson light. A voice entered his mind. He nodded once, smiled, and disappeared behind his door.

Aidan arched an eyebrow as Christine stepped into the private dining room. "That's warmer?"

She smiled and gave a little twirl, sending her skirts into a flutter.

"It serves its purposes," she replied. Pouring herself a cup of warm cider, she sipped at her drink and sat in the chair beside him. For a time they sat staring at the flames, the silence broken only by the fire's pleasant crackling and the creak of the inn as wind threw itself at the walls. Every so often, Aidan glanced over. Every so often, he caught her looking at him.

Aidan cleared his throat. "May I ask you something?

"Of course."

"I felt a powerful vibe from the magic you used to defeat the whispers last night. All that training, especially with a guild as prestigious as the Den, and achieving Cinder rank... You don't look old. Er, sorry, I mean—"

She giggled. "I'm one year your senior, young man. You'd better not think I look old."

He laughed back. "I only meant that you're obviously talented. Most Touched don't achieve Cinder rank until well into their thirties. Did you ever want to do anything with magic besides simple tricks?"

Her grip on the mug's handle tightened. "What is that supposed to mean?"

"Nothing," he said hastily. "I just wondered what would make you go through all that education if you didn't want to choose a creed. Truth be told, I wish I could do what you do."

She nodded, and he relaxed. "After Garrett and I lost our mother, we decided we didn't want to stay with our father. So, we needed to earn a living. I didn't particularly want to stay in school, but it was something Garrett insisted I do. Garrett is not a Touched. He's always been adept at tricks showcasing the sleight of hand."

Her voice hardened. "Sallnerians, even mutts, have to scrape and claw for everything in this world. We came up with an idea to combine our talents and Spectacle was born. We've made a decent living from it, and we're proud of it."

"I'm looking forward to see you perform."

She smiled. "Thank you. What about you?"

"What do you mean?"

"It was more than just my pure-fire that saved us. Where did you learn?"

"I trained in Calewind," he said simply. *That's true enough.*

She was silent for a few moments. Then she set her cup on the hearth and turned to him. "What are you running from, Aidan?"

He started to answer, then stiffened. "I told you, my name is—"

"I know who you are. I recognized you the instant I saw you at the Hornet's Nest. Don't worry," she said as he started to rise, his eyes darting frantically. "Your secret is safe with me. You obviously don't want to be noticed. Given who you are, that must be difficult, and I appreciate your desire to remain anonymous. That's why we asked for this dining room; no one comes back here without Martha's permission.

"To be honest, I wouldn't have given you more than a second glance—you were quite dirty and travel worn—except that..." She picked at her skirt. "I've been an admirer of yours for quite some time. I've been to many of your appearances, even your Rite of Heritage. I was—"

"Outside Sunfall," he said suddenly, the memory of the Sallnerian girl outside the southern entrance to the palace on his birthday rushing back to him. *Dawn take me, how did I ever forget that face!*

She smiled, pleased. "You noticed me."

"Of course. You're beautiful." His throat instantly felt parched. *Did I just say that?*

"I am glad you think so." She hesitated. "Forgive me for being forward, but I find you beautiful as well." She laughed. "Handsome, I mean. I've watched you for years. From afar, of course. A Sallnerian can't exactly walk up to the Prince of Torel and curtsy. But I have watched."

She covered her face. "I can't believe I'm saying this."

"I'm glad you did."

She lowered her hands cautiously. "Really?"

"Yes. Talking with you is easy. It's hard to find that in a companion."

"A companion?"

"A friend, I mean."

"Oh, so I am your friend, am I?" she said teasingly.

"Well, yes, but..." He shook his head. "I believe you're doing this on purpose, my lady."

"You believe correctly. It amuses me to see such a prominent and handsome man so utterly tongue-tied."

It was his turn to laugh, but he cut off abruptly as a thought came to him. "Does Garrett know who I am?"

"Yes. But he won't tell."

"There are posters of me hanging just outside this inn that give him many, many reasons to tell." Aidan regretted the words as soon as he said them. Christine and Garrett had saved his life, and Daniel's.

Christine didn't seem to mind the slight. "Garrett loves his gold, but we make plenty. Your secret is safe."

He relaxed. "Thank you."

She nodded. "Aidan?"

"Yes?"

"I know what happened at Sharem. Is that what you're running from? The war?"

He didn't answer.

She reached out and took his hand, lacing her fingers through his. Aidan's heart danced a wild beat.

"I'd like to help, if you'll let me."

For a time Aidan sat, enjoying the feel of her touch. "I'm sorry, Christine. I don't really want to talk about it. Just... things weren't going well, and I had to get away."

They sat in silence for a time. "I would like to come with you," she said at last. Her stare was direct. "If you'll have me."

His smile vanished as quickly as it had appeared. Why did she have to want this now, when so many difficult and confusing things were happening in his life? He was interested in her. How could he not be? She was beautiful, independent, intelligent, and she liked him. But the timing just wasn't right. Maybe someday, when he'd made things right with his family and his kingdom. *And Darinia.*

"I'm sorry, Christine," he said again. "You're a beautiful woman, but now is just not a good time." Thoughts of the horrors of the past weeks bombarded him, crowding over his eyes, her smile, the touch of her clammy palm. "I'm very sorry," he said again.

She considered him for a moment, then rose and sat on his lap. "I am a patient woman, Aidan," she said, taking his hand again. "I can wait."

The scent of the bath salts she must have used that morning filled him. Her closeness stole his breath. Not a good time, he'd said. The words struck him as ludicrous. War brewed around him.

Nightmares stalked him, ready to drag him into darkness. Would there be a good time? Maybe not. Maybe now was all the time he had.

He leaned forward and kissed her, and she kissed him back, looping her arms over his neck. They held each other, snug and cozy in front of the flames.

"Stay one more day," she said softly, her arms tightening around him.

"All right," he said without pause. *Daniel needs rest, after all.*

They sat that way for a time, letting the storm blow and shake the walls around them.

Chapter 21

Tide

WHEN THE DOOR CLICKED open some hours later, Aidan tried to scramble to his feet, but Christine didn't budge. Garrett and Daniel crossed over and stood, grinning first at them then at each other.

"Enjoy your afternoon, Thomas?" Garrett said.

"I—" Aidan began.

"He most certainly did," Christine said, glaring around defiantly. "And it's all right, Garrett. He knows we know his name."

For a moment, no one spoke. Then Daniel coughed and nudged Garrett with his elbow.

"Back home, we called him the Prince of Passion," Daniel confided to Garrett. They doubled over in howls of laughter.

"They did not!" Aidan said, reddening.

"Now, now," Christine said, stroking Aidan's cheek. "Don't let them bother you. Jealousy is such an ugly emotion, don't you think?"

"We were just talking," Aidan said hastily.

"My apologies for interrupting your *conversation*," Garrett said, "but my sister and I must prepare for this evening's events. I do hope you'll reconsider staying a little longer, Aidan. We have so many surprises planned for tonight."

"Actually," Aidan began, "I've decided to stay through the morning." He ignored Daniel's sound of surprise.

"Excellent," Garret said, beaming. "We have a pleasant evening in store."

Abruptly Christine uncrossed her legs and stood up to face her brother, her cheeks pink. "I don't know that I can go through with this."

Aidan frowned in confusion, but Garrett seemed unperturbed. "It is expected of us," her brother said. "We will continue with the work as planned."

Christine looked as if she had more to say. Instead she stalked out of the room.

"What's the matter with her?" Daniel asked Aidan, who

shrugged as if it were of no moment to him. But it was a moment—more than one. The most pleasant he had spent in his entire life. The sudden absence of her weight made him feel too light, his lap too cold.

He looked up to see Garrett glaring after his sister. At that moment Martha came bustling into the dining room, exclaiming over how anxious the crowd was for the show to begin. Aidan quickly stood and made a show of examining the hearth, keeping his back to her.

"The common room is practically fit to burst," she said. "Everyone's eager to see your performance after being cooped indoors with nothing to do for so long. We're all waiting on you, dear," she said to Garrett before hustling out of the room.

"All right then," Garrett said. "Wish me luck."

"Good luck," Aidan said, and moved to follow. Daniel placed a hand on his arm, then crossed to the door and locked it.

"I found our tunnel," he said in a low voice, looking mistrustfully at the window and moving over to pull the shade.

Aidan felt his stomach drop. In all the excitement of the past day, he had forgotten all about the sneaks and their sneaky tunnels. Would Christine still want to travel with them if she knew they'd be burrowing around in the dirt?

—She should stay behind, Aidan, Heritage said. *You need to continue on alone from here.*

Disappointment welled up, but he swallowed it. The sword was right. He had already put her in danger. He would just come back for her. Maybe, when all of this was over with...

"You still want to use the tunnels, right?" Daniel asked.

Aidan squared his shoulders. "I do. How do they work?"

"It turns out there's a tunnel entrance down in the cellar, behind a shelf of wine. We'll go down, follow the trail to the waypoint, and you'll take us to our destination."

"And where is that, exactly?"

Daniel shrugged. "The sneak I talked to back at the Hornet's Nest wasn't very specific, but that's because *I* wasn't very specific. You don't know exactly where we're going, other than into Sallner, so that's all I could tell him. We'll just pop up in the south, I guess."

"So a pack of vagrants can lop off our heads like overgrown flowers as soon as we peek aboveground?"

"I doubt it. Most tunnel entrances are well hidden. The sneaks don't want just anyone stumbling into the underground. People get lost down there."

"That makes sense, I guess," Aidan said. "All right. We'll plan to leave tomorrow morning after breakfast and run the tunnels."

Daniel handed Aidan the parchment. "No, *you'll* be running them. I'll be holding on to you for dear life."

Aidan blinked. "Me? I thought you said anyone can use the tunnels."

"Anyone can walk through a cave, sure. But only the Touched can use the..." He bobbed his head from side to side, thinking. "The quick method, I guess you could call it."

"Riding the shadows like a wave," Aidan said, recalling Daniel's words from the night before.

"That's right."

Now it was Aidan's turn to lower his voice. "Daniel, I don't know dark magic. You can't tell me anything?"

Daniel spread his hands. "My humblest and sincerest apologies, Most Passionate of Princes—"

"I wish you'd cut that out," Aidan muttered.

"—but I'm about as magical as a stick," Daniel continued. "All I know is every sneak who rode the shadows was a Touched. I saw them juggle fire and everything else you, Tyrnen, and your mother can do." He grinned. "Never saw anyone make dancing snowmen before, though."

"I *knew* people would enjoy that."

"You do know your public, O Passionate Prince of Kisses—"

Aidan fled the room.

A few minutes later, Aidan stood, hood back in place, Heritage at his side and hidden beneath his cloak, shoulder to shoulder against Daniel and the other onlookers who had packed the common room. Garrett and Christine stood at the hearth across the room. Conversation buzzed excitedly around them, and Aidan suddenly realized something quite pleasant. Christine's oval face and dark, slanted eyes gave away the Sallnerian half of her ethnicity, but no one seemed to care. She was their girl, homegrown talent. They were just excited to see a show, no matter the ethnicity of the performer.

Christine looked around, spotted him, and smiled, actually blushing. Aidan couldn't help smiling back. A shy Christine was an especially pretty Christine.

"Good evening," Martha said.

The crowd responded, though they were decidedly less merry.

"These are tense times, I know. To many of us, war is nothing but tales told by old men—tales that are quickly becoming reality. Yet tonight, I ask that you leave your worries at home. Friends, I give you Christine and Garrett Lorden—the Spectacle!"

The assemblage had already burst into cheers, drowning out the duo's last name. The shouts grew louder as Garrett stepped forward. He crossed his arms behind him then slowly withdrew one fist. He opened it, and when the crowd saw it was empty, they made sounds of disappointment. Then Garrett smiled and pointed to the other hand still held behind him. He drew forth a single red ball and began to juggle it with ease. The assemblage called for more. Garrett glanced at his sister, his face a question: *Should I?* She began to clap her hands in short bursts. The crowd joined in.

One of Garrett's hands darted behind his back to produce a bright blue ball which joined the spinning ranks of the first. The crowd continued to cheer him on, and on every third rotation the balls made in the air he would produce another from behind his back, until he had a dozen spinning in the air.

Garrett turned to face his sister before tossing a single ball in her direction. She pointed at it and let her finger drift toward the audience. The ball changed course, zooming out over the crowd where its mistress pointed. At the apex of its flight it *popped* open, sending colored ribbons streaming over the room. Adults laughed and cheered and children squealed with delight.

One by one Garrett tossed the balls at his sister, slowly at first then faster and faster. She sent each one sailing in a different direction, and the audience was soon covered in sparkles and strands of colored paper. The crowd roared with glee as the siblings took a bow. Straightening, Christine found Aidan's eyes. A smile stretched across her face. He smiled back, and she returned to her work.

—Sorry to interrupt your fun, but there's trouble. Look toward the main entrance.

Looking up, Aidan saw three muscular men in coats and trousers enter the inn.

So?

—Use the Sight.

He gripped Heritage and blinked. Sight's white canvas draped over his vision; charcoal outlines appeared around the people filling the room. He looked toward the doorway then quickly cursed and looked away. The human heads of the three men had disappeared, replaced instead with skulls of vagrants. He blinked and removed his hand from the sword, returning his vision to normal.

—We must leave immediately.

He nodded his assent as he raised his arm to get Daniel's

attention.

—No, Aidan. I said earlier that you must go alone, and I meant it. No one can follow you.

I won't leave without my friends.

—They are no longer safe with you.

He stood up slowly, blinked, and glanced again toward the front door. As expected the Sallnerians appeared fully human, comfortable in their duplicitous disguises. He peered sideways at Daniel, but his friend was too enchanted with the show to see what Aidan was doing.

—Get down to the cellar. We'll use the tunnels.

Crouching, Aidan weaved through the crowd to the back door and slipped out.

From the front of the room, Christine watched Aidan duck out of the room. Never dropping her too-wide performer's smile, she entertained the notion of informing Garrett that Aidan had escaped. But she did not.

The cellar was dim and dusty, like every cellar, even the ones back in the palace. Women like Helda and Martha weren't afraid of a few cobwebs. Picking up a lantern set on a crate by the stairs, Aidan drew light from his lamp. Fire bloomed in the glass, spreading a flickering orange pool at his feet. He raised the lantern and looked around. Shelves of wine lined the stone walls.

"How do I know which one blocks the tunnel?"

—Use Sight again.

Aidan swept white eyes over the room. "Ah," he said. An outline like a doorway stood behind one of the shelves on the left.

Sight is quite useful, he thought.

—I think so, too.

He set the lantern aside and wrestled the shelf out from the wall, grunting into the musty stillness. Brushing his hands on his shirt, he retrieved his light and held it out to see a set of rough, wet stairs leading down into darkness. The sweet scent of wine hung in the air, clinging to the steps and walls of the passageway.

"Care to finally reveal exactly *where* we're going, specifically?" he asked, his voice rather unsteady as he took his first step down, not expecting an answer.

—The Duskwood, Heritage replied.

Inside the Fisherman's Pond, the Lordens mingled with their guests. All raved that tonight's performance was the most amazing exhibition they had ever seen. The siblings thanked them, made small talk, shook hands, and after a while the patrons sauntered over to the bar and tables where Martha and her servers uncorked ales and wines from all across Torel.

Seeing no sign of their friends, Christine and Garrett clomped their way up the stairs and knocked softly on their doors. Daniel burst from Aidan's room in mid-knock, his face flushed.

"There you are," Garrett said with a grin. "Did you enjoy—?"

"Have you seen Aidan?"

Garrett's grin melted into a scowl. "He's not with you?"

"No," Daniel said slowly.

Garrett turned to his sister. "What did you say to him?" he asked her.

"I didn't say anything," she said, her face smooth.

Garrett shoved past her down the stairs.

"What's with him?" Daniel asked. She gave him a sad look.

Garrett bounded back up the stairs and into the room to join Daniel. Daniel was about to ask if he had found anything when three large men—Darinians by the size of them, though they wore clothes and hoods to cover their tattoos—entered behind him, ducking through the doorway.

"These are some friends of mine," Garrett said. "They believe Aidan left during our little show, and they've offered to help us find him."

Daniel rose from the bed, his face uncertain. "I don't think we need—"

"What you think isn't important."

Daniel's eyebrow rose, but before he could reply, Christine stepped between them.

"You don't need to talk to him like that."

"Be quiet, sister," Garrett said. He pulled her close. "He must be here. We—"

Daniel stepped forward and shoved the other man away. "Do not touch her like that again," he said.

Smiling crookedly, Garrett signaled to his three burly friends. They came at Daniel in a blur, knocking him to the ground and pounding at him with their huge fists.

"Garrett, *stop it!*" Christine said. Her brother paid her no heed. His smile grew at every dull thud that came from Daniel's body. To Christine, they sounded like a hammer whacking meat.

She raised open palms toward the attackers. "I said—"

A terrible pain gripped her stomach. She clutched her middle and gasped for air that would not come. The grip on her insides tightened, rending and squeezing. Tears poured from her eyes. She crumpled to the floor, still clutching her stomach as the pain increased. Her heart was beating furiously. Her vision darkened, and—

—the pain vanished, like a too-tight belt that snapped in two and fell away. Her heartbeat slowed. She climbed to her feet slowly, pitching forward a few times before she finally stood upright, still clutching her stomach. She could still sense something inside of her, something that had been there before but had been... changed. Raising shaking hands in front of her, she readied herself to pull in light and unleash it in a torrent on the three men standing over Daniel's limp form.

Nothing happened. She could feel the light responding to her call, rushing toward her—then colliding like water against rock. Her eyes darted around the room in panic. She focused again, reaching within herself to heat the blood of the Touched that coursed through her veins. But she could not. Holding a fistful of air was easier.

A rustling came from behind her. She turned and saw a hooded figure standing in the doorway. Gnarled hands reached up to lower the shroud.

Tyrnen pursed his lips. "You were about to slaughter my servants. Surely you can understand why I would think you might be dangerous." Another man, his face lost in the shadows of his hood, entered behind him, arms folded.

Christine glanced over at Daniel. His chest hitched and shuddered.

"Gather him up," Tyrnen said to the three large men, gesturing to Daniel. "We leave immediately." He turned back to Christine. "You will lead us to Aidan."

Her eyebrows rose. "What makes you think I would tell you where...?" She stopped, considering. If he was dependent upon her to find Aidan, perhaps she could buy her friend some time. She lowered her eyes to the floor and allowed her shoulders to sag. "Very well."

"Excellent. Now, where is he?"

She peered about the room as if searching. "He goes..." She pointed. "East. The prince travels to the east."

Tyrnen sighed. "Are you certain?" He sounded bored.

"Yes. He is—"

She flew backward and slammed against the wall. Her feet dangled several inches above the ground. Invisible bonds held her tight. Tyrnen walked slowly toward her, folding his hands inside his robe.

"You're lying," he whispered.

"No," she gasped. "I swear it! He travels east!"

"I can feel him, Christine. Just as you can. And I know that he does not travel to the east."

She gritted her teeth. "I won't—"

She cut off in a silent gasp as the bonds began to press her into the wall. She felt as if she were caught in between two walls of solid rock that were slowly coming together. At last, the pain stopped.

"South," she panted. "South, and fast."

Tyrnen nodded, muttering something under his breath. Christine thought it sounded like "Using the tunnels." He looked up at her.

"I keep giving you opportunities, and you keep disappointing me. Sadly, the patience of the Eternal Flame only burns for so long." His face twisted, and for a moment he appeared conflicted, his eyes darting back and forth as if watching an argument between two parties. Then his visage smoothed. "Free will is a privilege, girl. Do not lose yours."

The bonds disappeared. She crumpled to the floor on her hands and knees. "I won't let you hurt Aidan," she panted. "I will warn him, tell him that—"

"And do you think," Tyrnen said, "that he will believe you once he learns how big a help you have been to me?"

She paled. "He doesn't have to know."

"Oh, but he does. What do you think he'll say when I tell him that you and your brother were paid—very, very well—to keep him busy for me until I could come for him?"

Christine was speechless. Wringing his hands, Garrett shuffled to the old man's side. Tyrnen smiled as he placed a hand on her brother's shoulder. Garrett looked adoringly at the old man. Christine was reminded of a dog who had performed some trick and knew it deserved a treat.

"You've done well, Garrett," Tyrnen said. He reached his free hand into his robes. A clinking noise sounded from his fist as he pressed his hand into Garrett's. The room's faint torchlight glinted off globular jewels as the young man stared at them, mesmerized.

Christine could not believe what she was seeing. "Traitor!"

Garrett looked at her, confused. "I'm doing the job we were paid to do, sister." He stuffed the jewels into his pouch and tied it closed.

"Partly," Tyrnen said.

Garrett paled. "I will not fail again. Please give me another chance."

Tyrnen scrutinized Garrett, as if weighing the value of his life on a scale. At last he pointed to the group of large men. “Carry that one”—he flicked a hand at Daniel—“and the girl to the cellar.” He turned to Garrett. “Lead the way. No one must see us.” Garrett’s color returned as he smiled and nodded eagerly.

One of the big men scooped up Christine and slung her over his shoulder. A calloused hand clamped over her mouth. She bit down and immediately spit. His hand tasted like rotten meat. She looked up, ready to give him her frostiest glare, and immediately looked away. His eyes were flat and dead.

They wound their way down to the cellar. Tyrnen led the group to a wine rack pulled out from the wall. Behind it was a doorway with stairs that stank of spilled wine. He turned to Christine.

“Make any noise, any at all, and I kill Daniel.”

Without another word he descended the passageway into darkness.

Chapter 22

Riding the Darkness

AIDAN DIDN'T HEAR THE whispers right away. He was too preoccupied feeling terrified.

The stairs ended in a narrow path that snaked between dry, rough walls. The scent of earth was cloying. His breath fogged the air in front of him as he crept along the winding trail. One hand held a lantern that peeled away the darkness ahead; the other strangled his sword hilt.

A strand of inky darkness appeared on the left wall. It ran ahead of him, flowing along the wall like blood through a vein. He rounded another bend and the trail ended at an entrance way. Beyond, purple light flickered, like lightning in a midnight sky. Counting to three, Aidan jumped through, brandishing lantern and sword. His arms dropped to his side as his apprehension for what might lay beyond the next bend gave way to wonder.

He was in a great hall where the tips of stalactites and stalagmites touched to form great columns. Shrieks and the flutter of wings came from the shadows far overhead. Inky trails like the one he had followed ran along the walls and ground like creepers. They glowed faintly in the darkness. Each thread wound its way up, down, around, and over other threads and vanished into arched tunnels like the one from which he had emerged.

This must be a waypoint.

Sheathing Heritage, Aidan turned to trace his finger along the wall, interested in where the tunnel beneath the Fisherman's Pond's cellar might take him. Next to the entrance way he noticed a square carved into the wall. Inside the square were three circles connected by lines to form a triangle. A key.

Excited, he dug Daniel's parchment out of his pocket and examined his sign—an "X" with a squiggly line through the middle. He walked around the waypoint, walking from tunnel to tunnel. Crossing the chamber, he came to a table in the center of the hall. Tyrnen would have blanched at the organization of the surface. Charts, notes in a language he didn't recognize, and supplies such as tinderboxes, parchment, quills, inkpots, bottles of water, and wrapped rations sat neatly arranged. Aidan peeled open a ration and chuckled. Chocolate bars, the ideal meal for a band of adolescents with easy access to Leastonian warehouses cargo holds. His mother would be appalled at the idea of youths wandering through the underground, swiping any goods not nailed down while devouring sweets.

Aidan pocketed three.

He found his mark on the far side of the waypoint, though it was slightly different than the one the sneak had scribbled down for Daniel. Eight sets of four vertical bars were carved into the wall next to the key; another line ran diagonally through each set of four bars, as if keeping count of something.

Shrugging, he stepped through.

The trail unwound in front of him like a ball of string. He followed it around bends, up inclines, and down rough steps. After about another hour he stepped into another waypoint. Threads of darkness unraveled, spooling out to establish links between tunnels that lined the walls from top to bottom like honeycombs. A thick net divided into small squares covered the wall like webbing. Footholds, Aidan presumed, for travelers to use to climb up to their tunnel of choice.

Aidan felt his stomach drop as he followed his vein of darkness up, up, up to a tunnel that lay just below the layer of shadows that hid the ceiling—or dozens more tunnels, for all Aidan knew—from view. Carefully looping his arm through the lantern's handle, he began to climb. The netting was made of coarse rope arranged in wide loops, perfect for finding footholds but a burden on soft hands. Several minutes later he crawled through his opening, sweaty and panting, his fingers red and throbbing. Climbing to his feet, he peered around the side of the chamber to study the sets of vertical bars crossed with diagonal lines etched near the symbol. Then he groaned.

There were thirty-nine marks, one down from the forty count. He caught his breath and trudged on, following a gentle slope and walking in what felt like a circle. His thoughts wandered as the minutes wore on. After what felt like hours he entered a third waypoint even more cavernous than the last. He knuckled his back, sighing as he bones popped, and studied his trail. Again it went up the wall, even higher than before.

Aidan ground his teeth. *There's got to be a faster way*. He set the lantern down and looked around the room, thinking. Daniel had said anyone could walk through the tunnels the old-fashioned way: walking, blisters, lots of sweat. Only those who practiced dark magic could ride the tunnels, as he'd said. How exactly did one do that? Daniel had said that the Touched could use dark magic, but he hadn't said *how* the Touched bit into that forbidden fruit.

That was another thing. Even if Aidan *could* use dark magic, did he *want* to? Should he? All accounts described practitioners of dark magic as corrupt and twisted, like Dimitri Thalamahn. How did that happen? Did years spent dabbling in Midnight rot one's soul like a piece of fruit? Or did the first dalliance invite evil to settle in?

Faint whispers tickled his ears. *What did you say?* he asked the sword.

—I didn't say anything.

Aidan strained his ears and froze. Whispers, lots of them, coming from all around. He couldn't make out the words, but their low and guttural tone made him reach for his sword and move to the center of the room. Shadows danced along the wall. His heart took off at a gallop. Not just whispers, but *whispers*, the shadow creatures that had haunted him awake and asleep. He drew from the lantern and hurled fire at a cluster of darkness against the far wall. The flames clung to the rock, but the whispers were unfazed. There was no shriek of agony, no loss of mass.

Because there were no whispers. These shadows were just shadows.

Then what's making that noise?

An idea came to him. He set the lantern down, held Heritage tight, and blinked. Sight settled over him, painting the walls white but leaving the trails the deepest shade of midnight. He stood listening, but the words remained indecipherable. There was no magical Hearing to go along with Sight, it seemed. He blinked, returning the waypoint to its normal palette of blues and blacks, and stared up at the key that marked the next tunnel he needed to take, wondering what to do next. Just as he was about to slip his foot into the netting and start up, one voice cut through the whispers and spoke a clear, unmistakable phrase.

—Touch and spirit me away, Lord of Midnight.

The voice was low and hoarse, and the words were not common, nor Darinian, nor any other tongue that passed through most lips. It was the Language of Light, the ancient language the Touched used to pray to the Lady of Dawn to complete a kindling. But these words formed a prayer. To the Lord of Midnight, not the Lady of Dawn.

A shiver ran through Aidan. Praying to Kahltan using the

Lady's beautiful language was like filtering spring water through dirt, blood, and ash. Could he do it? He didn't even know what the prayer meant. Touch? Touch what?

—The key, perhaps? Heritage suggested.

Aidan frowned. *Are you encouraging me to try this? To use dark magic?* The suggestion baffled him, and left him wary. Heritage was an instrument forged using the Lady's light. To receive such a notion from so divine an object was as startling as the Lady of Dawn and Lord of Midnight sitting down to dinner.

Heritage didn't respond. Hesitantly, Aidan climbed up the netting, panting by the time he pulled himself through the tunnel entrance and flopped onto his back. Weariness ebbed away, but his mounting nervousness did not. Time was growing short. He didn't know how he knew—the sword hadn't said as much—but he knew all the same. He could feel it, like a low rumble beneath the feet before the earth shook. Daniel had said it best back at the Hornet's Nest. They were moving too slow. Walking and running, even his shifts, just weren't fast enough.

The trail of darkness fed through the key mark just inside the tunnel and continued on. Aidan raised his hand to the key, stopped just short of touching it, then let his fingers settle. The grooves of the "X" and squiggly line felt rough, like they had been carved with a knife. He took a deep breath, kindled from the lantern at his feet, spoke the prayer in the Language—*Touch and spirit me away, Lord of Midnight*—and squeezed his eyes shut, bracing himself as if anticipating a hand made from shadows and nightmares to burst from the wall and drag him into the rock.

Nothing happened.

He opened his eyes to squint and looked around. The light remained in him, coursing through his veins, heating his blood. Through his veins. His eyes widened as he studied the trails of darkness flowing through the wall. Like blood through veins. Light wouldn't work. He wasn't praying to the Lady. He was praying to Kahltan. To darkness. The whispers fluttered around him then, intoning the prayer over and over.

Aidan released the light, letting it drain out of him. Then he reached out to draw from the black veins. As his fingertips sank into the goo, he sucked in a breath through clenched teeth. It was thick, jelly-like, and cold as ice. Colder. He pulled in darkness until his fingers went numb, then yanked them away. Inky goop rushed over the impressions his fingertips had made and flowed onward. Aidan imagined some huge, dark heart buried deep within the tunnels, pumping blood through the passageways and beating in slow, low measures. Wiping his hand on his pants, he extended a trembling hand to the key and prayed in the Language.

The cold rushed out of him and the floor, the walls, the world fell away. Then it reappeared. But it was different. He no longer stood at the mouth of a tunnel dozens of feet from the ground. He stood at the mouth of a tunnel *on* the ground, staring out at another waypoint.

Staring around in amazement, he groped at his feet for the lantern but couldn't find it. It was gone; he had not been touching it when he had... what had he done? It wasn't kindling. Kindling involved warmth and light and a slight warming of the skin. What Aidan had done was cold and dark, and stank of ash in a cold hearth. Darkening.

He stepped out into the waypoint and immediately forgot about the lantern. He did not think it would do him any good here, anyway. This waypoint was similar to the first. Smaller, fewer tunnels leading off every which way. He picked out his thread easily and followed it to another opening. Only the key was displayed on the wall. No marks. He had traveled miles, probably leagues, in a heartbeat. He thought back to how Daniel had described it: *like riding a wave*. Close, but not quite right. It was like shifting with his eyes closed—not nearly as fatiguing as his desperate leap from Sharem back to Sunfall, but somewhat draining, still.

In fact, other than a slight chill and a bit of tiredness, he felt fine. He patted his hair, his face, body, legs. No darkness growing on him like fungus, no urge to raise bodies from their graves and send them on a hunt across Crotaria. He had used dark magic and lived to tell the tale.

Not that he would. Dark magic was forbidden. He let out a laugh, shaky at first, then a full-bellied roar that had him bent over gasping for breath. The living dead pursued him, shadows came to life and tried to eat him, his parents had been replaced by abominations and wanted him arrested for treason. What was one more crime, one more slight, atop his mounting pile of worries?

Aidan got hold of himself and faced the tunnel. One challenge down. Now for the next. Sallner. A kingdom eight hundred years in exile, its people corrupted by their tyrannical rulers, disciples of Kahltan and wielders of the darkest magic—only now, Aidan found himself more curious than revolted. What had Dimitri and Luria Thalamahn done to corrupt themselves and their people, exactly? Such questions were not asked, at least not by those who feared being branded a heretic. It was enough to know that the

Sallnerians had embraced darkness and used it do terrible things.

It *had* been enough. Not anymore. Now he wanted to know. He stepped into the tunnel.

—*Something is coming*, Heritage said, its voice tense.

Footsteps, dozens marching in time along the path before him, like a waterfall heard from far off. The footsteps were growing louder. Aidan ducked into one of the side tunnels and crouched in the shadows to watch. A man in flowing green robes appeared and crossed the chamber. Behind him marched a column of men in a variety of dress—Wardsmen vests, trousers, and mail; Darinian furs; the loose, flowing, colorful garments of Leastonians.

Suspicious, Aidan touched Heritage and summoned Sight. Bile rose up his throat. They were vagrants, every last one, and they surrounded the man near the mouth of the tunnel Aidan had just left. But he was not a man, either. Empty sockets stared around. Fleshy strips ran between his lips like cell bars.

The vagrants milled around him. Half of the group strode on, disappearing into the tunnel. The rest waited. Aidan heard the man who was not a man mutter a phrase—a prayer in the Language of Light—and the rest of the mob disappeared.

Cautiously, Aidan rose and crept back into the waypoint.

They came from Sallner, he thought.

—*And just left for Torel*, Heritage finished.

Not just for Torel. For his friends waiting for him back at the Fisherman's Pond. He fought the urge to race across the chamber and let the darkness spirit him back to Daniel. To Christine.

—*There is little time left, Aidan. You must press on.*

Chapter 23

The Prophet

THE TUNNEL STANK OF death and rot. Aidan gagged and pinched his nose, keeping one hand on his sword hilt in case more vagrants appeared in front of him. Up ahead he saw light filtering through a curtain of vines. He hurried forward, eager to leave the tunnels behind. His first glance at the southern kingdom was almost enough to make him turn right back around.

Sallner was as dead as the vagrants who had chased him across Crotaria. The vines hanging over the cave entrance, which dropped him behind the charred remains of what was probably a shop, were brown and brittle. Aidan brushed them aside and they crumbled and fluttered to the ground in flakes. He took a step forward and tripped, barely catching his balance. The ground at his feet had once been unbroken, smooth, paved stone. Now it was torn by gashes. Some, like the one that had caught him, were as thin as a knife's blade. Others were chasms that stretched far in either direction. Aidan edged carefully around one pit, sending pebbles skittering and clicking down the side.

When the last stone dropped away, a silence Aidan had not noticed before settled back over the land. There was no movement, no breeze, no sound. Sallner sat frozen in time.

—*Keep walking south,* Heritage said.

Aidan barely heard her. Great wonders rose up all around him. There were towers that rose up to the sky; telescopes, instruments crafted by Torelian inventors some five hundred years ago, hung limply from broken windows. Rutted stone steps led up to buildings built from gleaming marble—or at least, the marble had gleamed once. Now it was dull and dirty, smeared with grime.

All the buildings had been gutted. Glass crunched under his boots as he turned in a circle, unable to fix on one spot for too long before another snagged his attention. Spiral staircases, huge chambers, burnt books, colored powders as fine as sand, and a square slab of dirty glass twice the size of a door. It clung to the side of the building like a mirror, tilted back to stare up at the Lady.

Rather, where the Lady *would have* shined her light on its surface if not for the green haze that hung over the sky like a thick forest canopy, covering everything in a twilight haze.

Where am I?

—Illuden, Sallner's greatest city. Many discoveries were made here.

Aidan felt a deep melancholy settle over him. Walking through the remains of these huge structures, spotting marvels every time he swiveled his head, was like walking through the skeletons of some long-dead beast. Walkways that trailed off into nothingness and jagged hunks of wall were its bones, and the discoveries left behind were meat that no one had shaved off to consume.

He passed more buildings, many even larger than the first, all bearing scorch marks like bruises. Empty windows stared like eye sockets. He did not cross through them. He did not want to look. He thought of the mirror hanging from its side, the way it was slanted to catch the Lady's light. It wasn't glass, he knew. He couldn't be sure, but its material reminded him of the lamp hanging from his neck. He thought back to the telescopes drooping out of windows. Torelians had created them five hundred years ago. Sallner had been exiled for eight hundred.

So much squandered potential, he thought.

He came to a rusted iron gate hanging from one hinge. Aidan passed through it, leaving the bones of Sallner's greatest city behind him. He followed a scarred street bordered by rubble that had once been walls, doors, rooftops. Homes. The grass had grown tall before the exile had ceased all growth; it scratched and scraped at Aidan's trousers as he passed by.

After several hours—or perhaps longer; the light never seemed to change in Sallner—the sword spoke up.

—Do you see that shanty over to your left?

Aidan looked. Her term was generous: the shanty was more like a pile of wood and rubble hastily assembled into a square and wedged in between two equally shabby huts.

—We'll be going in there.

Aidan veered off the road and went to the door. He reached for the knob hesitantly, certain the whole place would collapse on him if he so much as sneezed. It creaked open, and Aidan stared into the blackest blackness he had ever seen, like a pit that went to the deepest point of Crotaria.

What is this?

—That is the Duskwood, Heritage said in its grandmotherly

voice. *That is your destination.*

How did it come to be here? How can it grow? And how have I not heard of it before?

—Enter.

A square of light appeared just inside the doorway. Hunched over to keep from hitting his head and inviting spiders to use his hair as a nest, Aidan stepped through and onto the luminescent square. It was narrow; he had to set his heels together to fit within it. Behind him, the door snapped shut, leaving him in still, silent dark. The light from the puddle at his feet did not illuminate his surroundings; it seemed to cower as if afraid or unable to reach beyond its borders. A second puddle of light faded in before him, then a third, all leading deeper into shadows.

—Step forward, Heritage said.

Aidan hastily complied. Turning, he saw the patch where he had been standing fade away. The illuminated ground at his feet was all dirt, roots, and green grass. He continued forward, walking wherever the next spot of light formed. They did not always appear directly in front of him; some winked into existence on either side. More than once he wondered if he was being led in a circle.

What would happen if I stepped off the path?

Heritage did not answer, but something else did. Feet scampered through vegetation. Some footfalls were light and fleeting; others pounded by, their passing sounding like trees being slowly pushed over and cracked beneath too-large feet. Purrs and growls echoed around him. He was reminded of the sounds of prowling nightlife he had heard during his camping trips with his grandfather. Only, Charles was not here to protect him. Aidan wished the lighted spots would appear faster.

What is this place? How can it be so big?

—You will find out soon.

Aidan rolled his eyes. He and Heritage disagreed on the definition of "soon." He walked and walked until finally, no puddle of light materialized beyond the one where he stood. He was preparing to consult the sword when he heard a familiar creaking sound. The door had reappeared, hanging ajar. He stepped through and forgot all about the creatures stomping through the darkness behind him.

He was in a vale, one as vibrant and full of life as Leaston in the springtime. Grass swayed lazily in the light breeze. Wildflowers ran through the grass in strips, painting the ground in rainbow-like swathes of color. Birds chirped and flitted overhead, filling the sweet, earthy, *alive* air with their song. Trees enclosed the space.

Branches from one wove with limbs of another to form screens. Through the cracks, Aidan could see the darkness waiting beyond. In the center of the vale was a plain wooden cabin. Encircling the cabin was a narrow stream of water that bubbled over rocks and pebbles. A narrow wooden bridge led to a simple wooden door. He crossed the stream and knocked on the door without looking, his eyes drawn to the vale's beauty.

—Enter, Heritage said.

The walls were as plain inside as they were out. In the center of the tiny room was a table with two chairs. At the far end was a small stone fireplace. A single burning log emitted a comfortable wave of heat that filled the room. A rocking chair facing the fireplace swayed in a steady, creaky beat. The chair slowed, and the occupant stood and turned to face Aidan. It was an old woman; her skin stretched tight against her bones, and her emaciated form quivered with age as she faced him. Aidan found himself unable to tear his gaze from her eyes. They were brown, and youthful, the eyes of a young woman. When she spoke, it was in a steady tone that defied her ancient features. Aidan's eyes widened as he recognized the voice. He had heard it numerous times before.

"Welcome to the Duskwood Vale, Aidan Gairden."

—I am the Prophet, the sword continued.

"I am the Lady of Dawn," they finished in unison, the sword clattering in its sheath.

The old woman folded her hands in front of her, waiting for something. Aidan pulled Heritage free, looked at it, to the old woman, back to the sword.

"You are the Lady of Dawn."

Her laughter was like the jingle of a wind chime caressed by a breeze. "If I were, I wouldn't appear before you bent like an old tree. No, I am called the Prophet, the foremost Disciple of Dawn, the Lady's liaison to this world. Through me and others before me, the Lady is able to touch the world, and has been doing so for over eight hundred years."

He smirked. "And you are... my sword?"

She laughed; the sound was like wind chimes singing in a breeze. "Don't be silly, Aidan," she said, as if what she had said a few moments ago was not silly enough. "I speak *through* the sword. It is the Lady's creation. Through it, I can communicate with sword-bearers when necessary."

Aidan's smile widened, then dipped into a frown. In the history of Heritage and *Ordine*, an old crone had blessed Ambrose and Anastasia's union. Surely she did not expect him to believe that this woman and the one from the story his mother had shared were one and the same!

"Goodness, Aidan, I am not *that* old." She smiled and took a seat at the table, gesturing for him to join her.

Aidan started. Whoever she was, she had made a habit of reading his thoughts. "Could you explain, then?" he said, sitting across from her. He knew he sounded skeptical, but he couldn't help it.

"It's really quite simple. Disciples of Dawn serve the Lady, as you know—spreading her word, doing her work. That work consists of various tasks, some of which are more laborious than others. I am from a long line of Prophets, a select few plucked from uncountable many, charged with sitting right here, in this cabin."

"Why?"

"We will get to that."

Aidan kept his temper in check. He had not traveled all this way to have her dodge the rest of his questions, especially with more springing up like weeds in springtime.

"Have you spoken to any others of my line?"

"Four, including you."

"Who?"

"You will find out soon enough."

"Typical. Why me, then?"

"Because you're very special. I've been waiting on you for a long time."

"Sorry to have kept you waiting."

Chuckling, she shook her head. "You've come all this way on my word alone. Surely you must believe some of what I'm saying?"

"I came here because I had nowhere else to go."

Two cups of tea appeared out of the air and settled on the table. The old woman took one and sipped.

"Most humans do not believe what they cannot see or feel. The Lady respects that; she gives her light so that we might see." She set her cup on the table and extended her hand toward him. "Would you like to see her?"

"*See* the Lady? You can do that?"

She crooked her fingers at him, beckoning. Aidan hesitated for an instant before obeying. He felt... compelled, as though trusting her was something he wanted to do, *had* to do. She opened her eyes. He looked into them and gasped. They were ageless, eyes that had seen centuries go by as if they were mere seconds, and would see countless more pass just as quickly. They had seen happiness, tragedy, and sadness. Those eyes had seen everything. Triumph and defeat; sorrow and joy; pain and healing; anger and tranquility; madness and sanity; night and day.

Gently she released his hand and her eyes cleared. He withdrew his hand slowly as he sat back. "How...?"

"She sees through my eyes, and on occasion, allows others to see her through me."

"That's incredible," he breathed.

She shrugged and took another sip of tea. "It is a gift, yes. It is also a burden."

"I'm sorry I didn't believe," he continued, but stopped as she shushed him.

"Do not apologize, Aidan. Your recent eagerness to question makes my mistress proud, even if it works against us."

"I still don't understand," he said. "Why have you been waiting for me?"

"Danger swiftly approaches, but you have been waiting for answers, so I will grant as many as I am able," the Prophet said. "When I showed you my mistress, you saw all that she has seen—the good, the bad, the light and the dark. Everything in all of creation comes in pairs, and can be divided into two sides: peace, and destruction."

Aidan swallowed. "You mean the Lady of Dawn and the Lord of Midnight?" The Prophet had not yet commented on his use of dark magic, but she had seen.

To his surprise, she shook her head. "Not exactly like that. Every emotion and state of being has an inverse, like good and evil. But what is not good is not necessarily evil. I know you used dark magic to ride the tunnels, Aidan. You did nothing wrong. You *walked in the shade*, as people say. How did you feel afterwards?"

He thought about the question. "I felt... fine, actually. A little tired..."

"And a tad cold, I'll wager." She continued when he nodded. "Dark magic is the inverse of light magic. Kindle too much light too quickly and you come down with the fever. Draw in too much dark magic, and you... what was the word you used for it?"

"Darken," he said, a little embarrassed.

But the Prophet nodded as if he had given the correct answer to two plus two. "Darken. I like that. Darken beyond your means, or in your case, without giving your body time to fully recover, and you can come down with the sniffles. Or worse. Like kindling, your body needs time to recuperate."

She examined him closely, then leaned back and smiled. "You look fine otherwise, though. No second head. No fangs. You *traveled*, Aidan. You used a tool to reach your destination faster. Others use dark magic to accomplish destructive ends, but the same rules apply to light magic. How did your friend Daniel put it? 'A sword in the wrong hands can spill any man's blood.' The Lady's light can be used to keep peace. It can also be used to destroy. Magic is magic, a sword is a sword. Both are tools. How you choose to use them is what matters."

He looked away. "And what I did at Sharem?"

She patted his hand from across the small table. "What you did was destructive, but that does make you an agent *of* Destruction. We will talk more of that later. Right now you need to understand that peace and destruction are polar opposites. Events big and small continually flip existence from peace to destruction and back again, over and over like a spinning coin. Many battles have been waged between the two sides. Most are skirmishes, but some conflicts are of such magnitude that their outcome affects all living things. These wars are called Points of Fate. A new conflict looms, and you are at the center of it."

Aidan's throat went dry. "The war between Torel and Darinia."

The Prophet nodded. "Both Peace and Destruction have claimed many victories in these struggles," she continued. "The war Luria and Dimitri Thalamahn initiated eight hundred years ago was one such, one that ended in a great victory for peace. But there can be no final victory for either side. Good and evil will always exist. Their struggle is eternal.

"Now a new Champion of Destruction walks the earth, gathering the forces of evil behind him. Sixteen years ago, the forces of peace chose a new champion to lead her people against the coming darkness.

"Aidan Gairden, you are the Champion of Peace."

Chapter 24

Terror and Shadow

TYRNEN STOOD OUTSIDE THE shanty Aidan had entered, mouth unhinged and eyes popping out of his head. He had never seen this hut before, nor had he known to look for it, though he had been looking for *something* over these hundreds of years. That something lay within. He knew it. He could feel it. His mistress could feel it, too. Her will crashed over him like storm waves pounding at a ship.

—*My husband is within,* his mistress said, her words a caress that made him shiver. *Take me to him.*

Thought formed sluggishly; he felt as if he were wandering through a thick fog. *The Lady of Dawn's magic is too powerful, mistress. I cannot enter. I—*

Her voice cut through him. Tyrnen fell to his knees, screaming and clutching his head. *Forgive me, mistress! I simply do not know the way!* His pain ebbed, then vanished. He climbed shakily to his feet.

—*Follow the boy's scent,* his mistress said. *I will protect you.*

Tyrnen dipped a trembling hand into his robe and withdrew the golden scepter. Garrett Lorden appeared at his side and helped him to his feet. Tyrnen brushed him away. Garrett did not really want to help; he only wanted the mistress's praise. Tyrnen thought briefly of killing the other man, but decided against it. His mistress would not be pleased with any more delays. He took a deep breath and raised the scepter high. Slowly, the door doubled over, like a man clutching at his belly. The wood splintered and groaned as it bowed inward. Tyrnen felt his lips curl upward. It was like the sound of bones snapping. Finally the door cracked in two and flew into the darkness within, as if torn free by an invisible hand.

Reverently, Tyrnen gazed at the scepter. "Follow me," he snapped to the party behind him. He stalked through the doorway and disappeared.

Aidan leaned back slowly in his chair, staring at the Prophet, saying nothing. Several minutes passed. Finally he stood and walked to the fireplace.

"Is that why I was born with all of *Ordine*? Because The Lady of Dawn's champion would need to be equally as strong to stand against the champion of Destruction?"

"You are partially correct. In truth, all Gairdens are born with both sides of *Ordine*. When a Gairden child is conceived, only one half is unlocked. The other lies dormant."

"But why? So many lives could have been saved if this power had been available to my ancestors. Dimitri and Luria Thalamahn could have been stopped before corrupting Sallner."

"What if *Ordine* were to be abused? What if a Gairden became obsessed with greed, and with power? It's entirely possible," she said when he shook his head in denial. "The Lady of Dawn took a chance giving your family such power. She had to take precautions in case a Gairden were to choose the wrong path."

"No one in my family would ever do anything like that," he said, his voice hard.

She gave him a soft smile. "What I am about to tell you is known only to the Gairden bloodline, and not until they undergo the Rite of Heritage. Yours was delayed, but the time has come for you to learn your family's true charge, and the reason for the creation of Heritage and *Ordine*.

"Following the end of the Serpent War and the executions of Dimitri and Luria Thalamahn, it became known to Ambrose and Anastasia that the souls of the Thalamahns had been secreted away." She raised a hand at Aidan's sound of surprise. "The details of how this came to be will be made known to you; for now, please just listen.

"You know that Heritage was created by the Lady of Dawn. It has two equals: the Serpent's Fang, a black blade wielded by Dimitri; and Terror's Hand, a scepter carried by Luria. The Thalamahns performed many dark experiments to give them an edge in the Serpent War. Terror's Hand and the Serpent's Fang were the results of two such experiments. Dimitri and Luria imbued their weapons with all manner of magic, but none trumped their primary purpose: to store their souls when they perished. Unfortunately, this magic was known only to the tyrants who used it.

"To walk the world again, Dimitri and Luria would have to find host bodies for their souls. Using a powerful form of coercion, their souls call from within the artifacts to those strong of might and magic, yet weak in will. Those who touch the weapons sacrifice their souls and receive the soul stored within the weapon. Ambrose and Anastasia discovered the Fang and Hand, and were tempted by the souls of the entrapped rulers."

Aidan paled.

"They resisted temptation," the Prophet continued, "but barely. They recognized the malevolent forces that called to them and attempted to destroy the weapons, but not even Heritage proved mighty enough to shatter the two vessels. It was then that your ancestors summoned the Disciples of Light. When their attempts also failed, the disciples conferred with Anastasia. They decided that if they could not destroy the weapons, they should at least mute their calls of temptation. They formed a circle of light, combining their gifts to wrap Terror's Hand and the Serpent's Fang in magical bindings that gagged the fallen king and queen.

"It was decided that two Touched of strong will must dedicate their lives to guarding the artifacts, for if they were found and the bindings removed, Dimitri and Luria would return. Your family insisted that they not be told of the weapons' whereabouts; they feared that they or their descendants would fall to temptation. The Prophet, the first of my line, took the Serpent's Fang and disappeared, telling no one his destination. Terror's Hand was taken away by a holy man named Mathias Emerson. Eight hundred years ago we vanished, seen by no one. Until now."

Aidan needed several moments to digest her words. "You said a Champion of Destruction has emerged, but that I am the first to find you. That means someone else has found..."

She smiled sadly. "Terror's Hand. Luria Thalamahn's soul has subverted a powerful Touched—powerful in magic. His will proved bendable indeed. Now she walks Crotaria again, determined to find a host for Dimitri Thalamahn."

A coldness, piercing and terrible, swept through him. Aidan clasped his hands together to keep them from quivering. "Who is it?" he asked softly. "Who is the Champion of Destruction?"

"Not yet. There is more you should know first."

After several moments of silence, he said, "I appreciate the Lady's faith in me. But I believe it's misplaced."

Her face softened. "I know what you are referring to: your actions at Sharem. What you did was wrong. You thought that by following orders, you would make up for the shame you caused your family. Instead, you shamed yourself. But did you not repent? You did. And you did more than ask for forgiveness. You recognized wrongness and turned your back on it."

"Yes, but only after I—"

"What you did cannot be erased, Aidan," she said. "It will always be with you. But you rejected destruction. You chose to give up everything you knew—your parents, your way of life, even your freedom—if it meant never again complying with that wrongness. Time cannot be reversed and so those events cannot be altered—but in your heart, you are good. You can lead peace against destruction. You must. The battle has already begun."

A shriek, high and otherworldly, echoed from the Duskwood.

"Our time together grows short," she said tightly. "I have told you all I can. The time has come to finish what began on your birthday. Are you ready to complete your Rite of Heritage?"

He let out a breath as he stared at the sword lying on the table. Was he? Even knowing what he now knew, could he do this? Was he worthy, no matter what she said? Then he laughed.

"You've got yourself into trouble asking those sorts of questions," she said.

He nodded. "Plenty. A lifetime's worth."

"We know how you answered then. How do you answer now?"

He took another breath, and shrugged. "I will prove myself worthy. I accept this charge because it is mine, and because my people—all Crotarians—depend on me." He looked her in the eye. "I am ready."

She smiled, then looked at his Cinder Band and drew back with a hiss.

"What is it?" he asked, looking down at his hand in alarm.

"Would you do something for me?"

"Anything."

She held out a wrinkled hand. "Give me your ring."

"My Band? But why—"

"Do you trust me?"

"Of course."

"Then please," she said softly, "hand it to me. When you return, it will be here waiting for you—if you still want it."

He hesitated, then handed her the ring. She placed it on the table in front of her and kindled. The fire in the hearth drained away as she drank from it. Raising a quivering finger, she touched the Band. All at once it grew brighter. The Prophet slumped but shooed Aidan away.

"I'll be fine, and now so you will." She waved off his questioning look and gestured at the sword. "Please raise Heritage and gaze into the Eye."

He picked up the sword and stared into the large stone. The jewel flared, then faded, growing darker. He felt as though he was falling, as though the world around him were receding...

The door exploded, showering the room with splintered wood. Tyrnen barged in, his face a thundercloud, his eyes crimson. Aidan began to look over his shoulder when the Eye flashed. His eyes glazed and his body went slack. Heritage clattered to the table as the Prophet shot to her feet and to his side, moving like a woman in her twenties.

Tyrnen raised one glowing palm. Raised above his head in his other hand was a golden scepter. Lightning uncoiled and sprang at them, bright and thick and terrible—and sailed harmlessly through where the Prophet and Aidan had been standing to blast through the wall.

She reappeared moments later to find him sitting at the table, Aidan's discarded Band in one hand, the scepter in the other, Heritage on the table. Calmly, she took a seat and nodded toward the ring.

"I found the shadow you wove into the ring. We both wondered how you managed to dog him all this way, and through the Duskwood as well. Clever. Not clever enough, but clever."

Face twisted in rage, he flung the Cinder Band away and towered over her. "Where is he?"

"Where are your manners? Hello, Luria," the old woman said.

He smiled. "If it pleases you to think so."

Cocking her head, the Prophet studied him. "Interesting. How did you resist her?"

He began to speak, then clapped his mouth shut. His face darkened. She thought he looked like a child reprimanded by an adult in front of his friends. And she understood.

She looked to the scepter he gripped in a trembling fist. " Eight hundred years of carrying that thing around, struggling. Why, your mind must be in tatters by now, my old friend."

For a moment, Tyrnen's eyes went wide with a silent plea for help, for death. Sweat broke out on his forehead. Then he shook himself as if a cold wind had passed through him. His eyes narrowed at her. Color seeped back into his face.

The Prophet smiled sadly. "Your hold on free will is tenuous at best, Mathias."

"Where is Aidan?"

"He is safe, in a place you cannot reach him. He will come for you, soon."

Tyrnen's complexion paled.

"Are you frightened, Mathias? You should be."

Tyrnen threw the scepter aside and shot to his feet. She didn't flinch. Tyrnen muttered a prayer to the Lord of Midnight, raised his open hand, and squeezed it into a fist. The Prophet gasped as her body went rigid. Thin red marks like deep fingernail imprints appeared on her arms. Blood oozed from each cut.

"I will ask one last time," Tyrnen said, his fingers pulsing with dark red energy. "Where is he?"

A single tear trickled down the old woman's cheek, but she did not speak.

With an angry bellow Tyrnen threw his clenched fists wide. Her body tore in two. Blood sprayed across the room and splattered Tyrnen's robes. Both halves hovered in the air; blood dripped to the floor like water from soaked rags. Tyrnen relaxed his hands; the crimson glow of his fingertips slowly subsided. The fleshy pieces dropped and slapped against the floor.

"Garrett!" Tyrnen bellowed.

Garrett crashed through the entrance. "Yes, master?" he said, wringing his hands. His eyes darted between his master and the ripped carcass on the floor.

Tyrnen handed him Heritage. "Take this. It's yours."

Garrett stared at it. "Don't you want the sword, master?"

Snatching the scepter up and stuffing it in his robes, Tyrnen turned to look at him, and Garrett shrank back.

Tyrnen swept outside, strode up to Christine, and slapped her across the face. She stumbled and fell back. Tears welled in her eyes but she lifted her head and glared at him. Two of the three vagrants stood still, staring passively ahead. The third had not been so quick to step from the cascading pools of light that had appeared on the ground within the Duskwood.

"He will come for the sword," Tyrnen said as Garrett scurried to his side. His eyes were hard as stone. "Delay him."

"Master," Garrett said hesitantly, and again shrank back when Tyrnen turned to glare at him. "Master, Aidan Gairden is very powerful. How can I—?"

"The harbinger will aid you," Tyrnen said as the creature that had helped him tie Christine stepped around the cabin to stand by his side.

—My beloved calls, Luria whispered in Tyrnen's mind. Her voice was unsteady, as if a shiver had worked its way along her body. *Send them away,* she continued. *They must not see our work.*

"Into the cabin," he snapped, not even glancing over his shoulder. He heard Garrett shove Christine toward the structure. The vagrants followed. Moments later, the door slammed closed.

Kneeling, he stroked the grass, which was slowly turning a dead, diseased shade of brown all around the cabin. He kissed his hand and touched it to the grass. Luria was silent for a long time. Tyrnen grew afraid, yet he dared not speak until she was ready. He had made that mistake only once over the past eight centuries.

—*The hag's death has weakened the shielding over this place,* she said. *But she placed stronger bindings over my beloved's blade. It cannot be removed without dire consequences. I would gladly sacrifice you to experimentation, but I have need of you, yet.*

Contentment settled over him. She needed him. He found himself grinning.

—*We will return*, she said after several long moments.

He grew cold. *But mistress, what if the Gairdens—*

—*They will not find the Fang. Bring me a blade.*

"Garrett!" he shouted, scrambling to his feet. The door of the cabin crashed open and the Lorden boy practically tumbled out.

"Yes, master?"

"I need a sword. Not Heritage. Take one from the vagrants. Go!"

Garrett raced back inside. When he returned he handed his sword to Tyrnen. The blade was marked with abrasions and the leather wrapping around the hilt was dark from years of accumulated sweat.

"Leave me," Tyrnen said. Garrett fled.

—*Now listen carefully,* Luria said, *and do exactly as I say.*

Chapter 25

Lake Carrean

THE WORLD FLASHED RED for an instant, then all went dark. Wind battered his face and plastered his clothes to his skin. Aidan opened his eyes and saw his feet planted on a wide stone platform. He walked to the edge and peered over. The platform had no base; it simply hung in the sky like a chandelier. Clouds flowed around him. Some streaked as fast as lightning; others crawled across the blue expanse.

Instinctively—Aidan was surprised at just how quickly the action had become instinct—he reached for Heritage. His fingers brushed his sheath, but... He looked down. Heritage was gone. He shook his head. He would not let worry overtake him. He cleared his mind, trying to focus. The last thing he remembered was staring into the Eye of Heritage. Then he'd felt drowsy, and the Eye had rushed toward him. There had been a flash of red, and then...

Flash.

Aidan was immersed in pitch blackness and hurtled forward yet again, a leaf snapped up by a windstorm. Another *flash*, and he stood before a lake covered with a thick sheet of ice. Snow covered the ground in all directions. Tall oaks, thick and bare of leaves, wore snow and ice like garments. He smiled. *I'm at Lake Carrean.*

Off to the right, tucked into a small pocket of trees, was a small cabin. Lake Carrean was his favorite place to spend time with his parents, just the three of them resting and enjoying one another's company, away from Sunfall and all its demands. Aidan had many fond memories of hot summer days spent swimming with his mother and fishing with his father, fish he cooked *without* magic.

The memories were pleasant, but the sight of his favorite retreat left him confused. *How am I here?*

A torrent of air whipped up along the shore, kicking snow over the ice covering the lake. Tyrnen and his father materialized, and for an instant, Aidan felt confused. Edmund stood with his back to Aidan. His head rested on Tyrnen's shoulder and his arms were around the old man's neck, as if sweeping him up in a hug. His father was affectionate toward his family, but kept a respectful distance from others, as befit the stations of king and general, especially valorous ones.

Suddenly his father stumbled backwards and fell to the ground with a grunt. Tyrnen stood with his arms out, and Aidan realized that the old man had *pushed* his father.

Edmund shot to his feet, his face twisted in rage. “What is the meaning of this, Tyrnen? Where—” His eyes darted around, then narrowed. “Lake Carrean?”

“Bow to me.”

The color drained from Edmund’s face. “What did you say?” Edmund’s voice shook, and not from fear.

“For centuries I have had to kneel before wretches who did not possess even half of the power of which I am capable. Kings, queens, other Touched... No more. Bow,” he said again.

“You forget yourself, Eternal Flame,” Edmund said, his voice deadly quiet. He too stood motionless. “First you grab me and bring me here, without my consent. Now you presume—”

“Perhaps you did not understand my command.” Tyrnen lifted a gnarled finger and pointed behind Edmund. “He will explain it for you.”

Edmund uncoiled in a flash. One minute he was standing before Tyrnen, the next he had ripped Valor from its sheath and spun to parry a blade arcing down to his skull, sending his attacker stumbling. Aidan had watched his father duel. The king never rested; he fought in constant motion, keeping his opponent off-balance. Now Edmund was frozen, his face a mask of confusion and fear. Armor covered his attacker’s body, but its head was a cracked skull peppered with dried blood, its mouth curved in a macabre grin.

“A vagrant,” Aidan whispered hoarsely. He commanded his feet to rush to his father’s side. They wouldn’t listen. He was paralyzed. He tried to call out to Edmund, but his voice caught in his throat. He could do nothing but watch.

Edmund’s initial shock had worn off; his fighter’s senses assumed control of his feet, arms, and mind. Steel rang against steel. Block, chop, dodge, thrust. The vagrant fell, and despite his knowledge of his father’s skill, Aidan felt overwhelming relief. No man could stand toe-to-toe with Edmund the Valorous, but a vagrant was no man. Not anymore.

Two other vagrants appeared.

The creatures rushed him, but he turned their blades aside in one smooth motion and pressed forward, gaining ground against his assailants as they fought to keep pace with his measured attacks. A third vagrant appeared. Then a fourth. A fifth, a sixth. More and more surrounded him, and those he'd cut down rose again and again.

Aim for their heads! Aidan wanted to shout. But he could not.

Valor was a blur of motion, but Edmund was not fast enough. His leather clothing, soft gear meant for riding, not fighting, was torn in a dozen places. Blood covered his face like a crimson mask. His attacks did not slow. He crouched to avoid a whistling chop and brought Valor up in a wide arc. The blade sliced cleanly through the bony neck of a vagrant. Its body dropped to the ground as its head plopped into the snow.

Edmund smiled. Faster and faster he fought, the pile of heads growing on the ground at his feet. Valor spun in a vicious backhand that removed yet another skull from its body until at last he stood alone, his breath coming in long yet controlled pulls. He paused for only an instant then whirled toward Tyrnen, Valor raised for a killing strike. His eyes found a new enemy and he froze.

The opponent grinning at Edmund Calderon, sword extended as he glided forward, was Edmund Calderon. Every feature was identical: black hair tinged with gray, his eyes, his smile. Edmund's face suddenly twisted, astonishment becoming agony. He looked down. A dagger protruded from his side. Grunting, he fumbled at it. His fingers would not close around the hilt.

"Please," the new Edmund said. His teeth bared as his grin widened. "Allow me." He pulled the knife free. Aidan heard his father gasp as blood stained his side like a blooming rose. Valor fell from limp fingers, disappearing in the snow. Edmund dropped to his knees, clutching his side. His doppelganger shoved him face-down and planted a boot in his back. Tyrnen came smoothly forward, gripping Edmund's head like wood caught in a vice.

"I have left you alive," the old man whispered, "so that you can observe what happens next." The Eternal Flame shifted away, kicking up snow. Edmund struggled, grunting into the still winter air. Blood leaked through fingers clamped to his side. The impostor sneered and applied weight to his foot. Edmund cried out, a single sharp cry that bounced off the trees and rode the next breeze away from the shore.

Tyrnen popped back in, and he brought Annalyn with him. Rage and terror consumed Aidan. Bruises dotted his mother's face, and a thin line of blood ran down her lip. Tyrnen shoved her forward and she fell face-first into the snow. Rolling over to sit up, she spit away snow, blinked ice out of her eyes, and saw her husband, tattered and bloody. Rising, the Crown of the North rounded on Tyrnen and raised her hands. Tyrnen watched her. A smile spread over his face as Annalyn's snarl melted into frustration and—evident, to her credit, only by a slight widening of her eyes—fear.

Tyrnen drew a bejeweled golden scepter from his robe. The Lady's light glinted against its stones; Annalyn's eyes sparkled along with it. A voice, soft and purring, entered his thoughts.

—Touch me, Annalyn. Embrace eternal life. Embrace power the likes of which you have never known. With me, you can destroy Tyrnen Symorne. Your kingdom will flourish and prosper, your people will chant your name for eternity. Heritage is nothing compared to—

Abruptly Annalyn shook her head and turned from the scepter, mumbling and whining. She blinked as if awakening from a deep sleep. "What...?"

Nodding as if he had expected just such a reaction, Tyrnen replaced the scepter. He rolled back his sleeves. "Even after what I've put you through, you still have the strength to resist. I have often wondered which of us is stronger. Many have said that you are worthy enough to hold the title of Eternal Flame. Did you know that?"

Tyrnen tapped a finger against his lips. "I have an idea. Why don't we have ourselves a friendly duel? If you win, you and Edmund will be free to go. After all, I'll be dead, and therefore unable to stop you." He gestured toward the impostor that held her wounded husband down to the ground. "You'll have them to deal with, of course."

Annalyn took in the two Edmunds, the blood leaking from her husband's side, in a single glance. Her eyes widened slightly.

"What kind of dark magic...?" She shook her head, her features once again composed. "And if I refuse to fight?"

Tyrnen's smile was frigid. "I will kill your husband, and you will fight me anyway. Now, then. Are you ready?"

"You know I'm not."

Tyrnen slapped his hand against his forehead. "Of course! You've been tied, haven't you?"

She clenched her fists at her sides but said nothing.

He shrugged. "It's just as well. There is one other thing I forgot to tell you. You are familiar with harbingers, are you not?"

Her face paled as she slowly turned back to her false husband. Its mouth curled into a vicious smile. She swallowed and faced Tyrnen. "You are... her?"

Tyrnen ignored the question. "If you try to kill the harbinger, or attempt to free your husband, I will kill him. Do you understand?"

"Annalyn," Edmund said. His voice cracked, fell into a whisper. His face had gone pale, and blood continued to drool from his side. "Don't worry about me. I can—"

"I understand," she said in a harsh whisper to Tyrnen. "When I am through, you will—"

Tyrnen kindled. Hissing, Annalyn clamped one arm around her stomach. In the next instant, the old man raised his arm with a flourish and spit another prayer. A lightning bolt ripped from his palm.

But Annalyn was already gone.

The attack shattered the ground where she'd stood, throwing ice and snow and earth in all directions. Smiling, Tyrnen spun as she reappeared some distance behind him. Fire spewed from her hand before she disappeared again, reappearing in another area to throw lightning. He vanished and materialized just as quickly, hurling an attack of his own.

Aidan watched in awe as shafts of lightning and columns of fire scorched the air and ripped the ground. A bolt shattered a tree near him, but Aidan was too absorbed in what was happening to react. Again and again they shifted, shouting prayers and throwing magic. Aidan's fists tightened. His mother's spells were growing fainter with each successive cast, and her shifts did not take her nearly as far away. She was tiring; the fever crept over her.

Tyrnen's onslaught showed no signs of slowing. Aidan watched the old man in disbelief. How could this be? Didn't Tyrnen possess the same limitations as any other Touched? He had thought only one of Gairden blood was strong enough to—

"Annalyn!"

Aidan turned. The voice was female. He and his mother found its source at the same time, and they both stared in shock at the figure emerging from behind the cabin. It was a woman of medium height. Her brown hair was long and streaked with gold, as if the Lady's tears had stained her hair.

The figure was Annalyn Gairden. Aidan turned to his true mother, and then back to the woman striding from the forest. A sickly smile was stuck on her face, as if she was unsure of the emotion such an expression required.

Aidan looked at Tyrnen, and again wished he could speak, could shout, could at least point. The old man whispered a prayer to the Lady. A streak of lightning smashed into Annalyn's legs, sending chunks of flesh and bone scattering in all directions. She fell to the ground with a wordless scream as crimson mist from twitching stumps sprayed over the white blanket of snow. She stared up, mouth agape, eyes opened wide, her scream trailing off in a hoarse whisper. She flopped around on her back and began to inch backwards, gibbering in fright.

"NO!"

For a moment, Aidan thought he had finally found his voice. Then he saw his father. Edmund struggled to reach his ruined, twitching wife. He raised his bloody hand and reached toward her. Tears spilled down his cheeks, cutting a path through the drying blood on his face. Then he shuddered, gasped, and went still. Nearby, Annalyn gibbered and continued to twitch. She raised herself on shaking arms and tried to scuttle back but fell to the ground, rose, fell again.

Aidan's world rocked. He wanted to vomit, to scream, to close his eyes and let unconsciousness sweep him into its embrace as it had when he had accepted Heritage. But his body would not fall, would not run toward his parents or away from the sight of them. He could only stand and watch.

Tyrnen gestured to the harbinger. "Take him into the woods and bring me his head. Bury the body, and bury it deep. No one must find it."

"No," a small voice gasped.

As one, Tyrnen and Aidan turned to Annalyn Gairden. Through teary eyes, Aidan watched his mother weakly lift a hand and whisper. He could not make out the prayer. Her eyes fluttered open and a small white particle like a snowflake lifted from her head. Another snowy speck lifted from Edmund's still form.

Tyrnen lunged toward her. "She must not—" the old man began. The specks disappeared. Tyrnen ripped an orb from his robe and slammed it to her chest. Annalyn's scream pierced the still winter air.

Abruptly trees, frozen lake, cabin, vagrants, Tyrnen, parents—everything warped and blended together like spilled paints. Aidan found himself once again on the floating stone platform among the clouds, but he barely noticed. He stared straight ahead in stunned, silent disbelief where his mother had fallen.

A hand grabbed him from behind.

Chapter 26

Recall

AIDAN STARED AT HIS Grandfather Charles in shock. Tufts of wispy hair grew around his bald pate. He wore baggy Leastonian clothes, preferring loose-fitting garb to armor and a crown even in death. He smelled of dirt and sawdust, and pine trees. He reached out a leathery hand and pulled his grandson to him, wrapping his arms around Aidan and burying his head in Aidan's shoulder. Aidan held back his own grief until he felt wetness leak from his grandfather's eyes and soak his shoulder. His grandfather's tears shook loose his own like the last leaves of autumn torn from their branches by a breeze.

Minutes later he pulled away. "They're dead?" Aidan asked hollowly.

Charles took a shaky breath and straightened. "Yes. I'm sorry, boy."

Aidan felt heart-wrenching sadness—then a moment of panic.

"Am I dead?"

Charles shook his head. "You are in Sanctuary."

Sanctuary. The spirit realm contained within the Eye of Heritage, where Gairden souls came to rest after stepping off the mortal realm. That did nothing to ease Aidan's rising panic.

"A Gairden comes to Sanctuary at least twice," Charles went on. "Once during the Rite of Heritage, and again upon death. Upon acceptance of Heritage, sword-bearers establish a mental link with the sword. Their consciousness is transferred here so they may learn about—"

"The Thalamahns," Aidan said, catching on. He had known that Gairdens learned many secrets once they inherited the sword. The fact that Dimitri and Luria Thalamahn's souls were hidden across Crotaria was likely the biggest.

Another thought slammed into him. "Where is she? Where is my mother?"

Charles's mouth quivered slightly. "Aidan..."

"Mother should be here. With us. With you."

Charles started to speak, then stopped. He looked up at the clouds streaming fast and slow. The midsummer-blue sky grew sickly, becoming gray. Snow-capped trees surrounded them, bordering Lake Carrean and the cabin where he and his parents had enjoyed one another's company away from the palace. Tyrnen, his face dark and terrible, towered over them like a human inspecting ants crawling along the ground.

Aidan fought the urge to shrink away. "What is this?"

"Recall," Charles said. "It's a spell that saves a memory for future examination. You can then go through it step by step, experiencing every moment, analyzing every nuance, at your leisure." Charles smiled sadly. "Your mother used it once, though she'd had no knowledge of it before asking me to pass her the spell through the sword, as I passed you magic for—"

"The fire in the cave," Aidan finished.

Charles nodded. "Your mother used recall to solve a theft, I believe, a case in which two parties accused each other of the same crime." His smile faded. "Before she died, Annalyn extracted the memory of what happened to her at Lake Carrean, and of what befell your father."

Charles raised a hand and slowly lowered it. Tyrnen began to move toward Annalyn's broken, bleeding form, though sluggishly, as if wading through waist-high snow. With his other hand Charles made a gesture as if he were pushing aside a curtain. To Aidan's amazement the view rotated. Charles let his hands drop, showing them a close view of an object clutched in Tyrnen's hand.

"Look," Charles said, pointing.

Aidan looked. It was a glass orb. A large, storm-gray cloud sat stationary within it. Charles gestured at the orb, and the cloud began to roil.

"What is it?" Aidan asked.

Charles took several moments to answer. "A spirit stone. It holds souls. Whoever holds the stone controls the souls within. Souls can be placed within bodies, and those bodies can be reanimated and reshaped—new faces, statures, colors, but all the memories and abilities of the soul locked within the flesh."

He looked at Aidan. Tears leaked from eyes that had gone stony. "He took your mother's soul, boy. He took my daughter."

"But a Gairden's soul comes to Sanctuary upon death," Aidan said.

Swallowing, Charles shook his head. "Ordinarily, but Tyrnen took her soul with the stone before she died. She is lost to us. As is your father. A Gairden's mate passes on into Sanctuary so that they may remain together always rather than be separated." He paused. "Edmund did not come to us."

Nausea swept through Aidan, making him swoon. Then his grandfather's words took on a different meaning.

"You said my father isn't here. Maybe Tyrnen didn't take his soul. Maybe he's still alive!"

Charles was shaking his head. "No, boy. I'm sorry." He raised a hand and Sanctuary changed again, melting into the image of the vagrants, piles of dead surrounding Edmund, and the Edmund impostor. The impostor stared down at them, face frozen in a sneer. Aidan realized he was looking at the world through Edmund's eyes. A gauntleted hand appeared—Edmund's—reaching, straining toward Annalyn. Then it went limp, and blackness descended. Clouds on blue sky returned a moment later, some speeding by while others swam lazily across the expanse.

"That is where your father's memory ends," Charles said. "They're gone, boy. Tyrnen took them both."

Aidan closed his eyes as more tears spilled down his cheeks.

"I'm truly sorry you had to find out this way, Aidan," Charles said. "I've been watching you since your birthday. I wanted to talk to you, to tell you all that had happened, but the Prophet told us that you needed to find out this way in order to—"

"And you thought that was necessary?"

"Because you had to grow up. Her words, boy, not mine, so you can wipe that look off your face. You weren't ready. That's what she said, and she was right, and you *know* she was right. You had to accept all of this on your own: Heritage, your parents' fate. You had to learn to make your own choices, to act. I didn't agree at first, but the Rite of Heritage is different for every Gairden. There are similarities, of course. We all learn about the Thalamahns and how they cheated death. But for you, the Rite of Heritage was about surviving.

"The Crown of the North and sword-bearer must be strong, and a Champion of Peace even more so. Harsh as it sounds, continuing to go along with Tyrnen's manipulations, or succumbing to the challenges you faced on the road, would have proven your inability to overcome the greater obstacles ahead."

Aidan swallowed and closed his eyes. Tyrnen. Friend, mentor, almost as much a grandfather as Charles. Family, certainly. Tyrnen had murdered his father and his mother. Why? Why had he—

A pair of footsteps interrupted his thoughts. Aidan looked over his grandfather's shoulder and recognized the man and woman crossing the platform. He had seen their visages etched within the first two stained-glass inside the sword chamber countless times. The man was tall, though still a few inches shorter than Aidan. His long dark hair hung loose, but the histories said he tied it into a ponytail for battle. The woman walking beside him, one arm linked through his, was two heads shorter, but her hair was just as long. An indigo gown flowed along behind her, and she smelled of freshly cut flowers.

They halted before him and fell to one knee.

"Well met, Champion," Ambrose and Anastasia Gairden said.

Chapter 27

The Family Gathering

AIDAN'S MOUTH WORKED SOUNDLESSLY. Admiring portraits of Ambrose and Anastasia, the star-crossed lovers who had come together to overthrow King Dimitri Thalamahn and the might of his corrupted army of Sallnerians, was one thing. Standing before them, in the flesh—or however that sort of thing worked in Sanctuary; Aidan was not quite sure—was another.

"You'll have to forgive my grandson," Charles said. "I'm afraid your presence has rendered him speechless—for the first time ever, actually."

Aidan managed to wet his tongue. "You," he said to Anastasia. "You passed me the healing spell that saved my friend's life."

She inclined her head.

"Thank you," Aidan said. He gaped between them, overwhelmed. "It is an honor."

"The honor is ours, Aidan." Ambrose's amused smile disappeared. "That is all the time we have to get acquainted, unfortunately. As you saw, your former mentor has planted seeds of deceit and corruption all across Crotaria."

"Yes," Aidan said slowly. "Tyrnen is using some sort of creatures to impersonate my parents. In my mother's memory, he called them harbingers."

"They are like vagrants, but infinitely more dangerous," Anastasia said. "Harbingers hold the souls of Touched—Cinders, usually—that Tyrnen bested in combat."

"And how is it that they look like my mother and father?" he asked, voice tight.

"A forbidden dark magic known as transfiguration," Anastasia said. "It violates the Lady's edict that no living beast should ever alter its form, as they are created exactly how She intended them to be. Transfiguration is commonly used to mold the undead for purposes of deception. The pain of restructuring flesh and bone is too great for the living to bear. The dead, however, are as clay in the hands of an artisan, able to be reshaped whenever needed."

Aidan digested the information. He thought of the harbinger that looked like his mother that he'd killed before fleeing Sunfall. "So all Tyrnen had to do was transfigure bodies to resemble Mother and Father—"

"—and give them new life via souls stored in his spirit stone, through which he dictates their every action." Ambrose finished. "That was just the start of Tyrnen's deception, however. He had to dress them appropriately, alter their voices..."

"She entered the sword chamber," Aidan interrupted, thinking back to the night the impostors had returned from their retreat with Tyrnen.

"One of those monsters has your mother's soul, boy," Charles said grimly. "With Annalyn's soul, that monstrosity *is* Annalyn. The soul has her memories and abilities. But the harbinger cannot pry secrets from Heritage, nor control the blade—thus far, at least."

"I killed it," Aidan said. "I cut its head off before fleeing Sunfall."

"Destroying a corporal form does not free a soul held by a spirit stone," Anastasia said. "The soul simply returns to the stone." She smiled bleakly. "We watched Tyrnen infuse Annalyn's soul in new vessels time and time again, trying in vain to control Heritage. We took pleasure in destroying those rotten vessels. A pity the old man never tried himself."

"Be careful, Aidan," Charles said. "Because the harbingers, and the vagrants, besides, are undead, their flesh is nothing more than a costume. They are the puppets. With the spirit stone, Tyrnen pulls their strings. Your enemies could be anyone—or anything."

Aidan recalled the vagrant that had peeled away its face the night he had fled Calewind and stifled a shudder. Wardsmen, farmers, innkeepers—anyone could be an enemy.

"Do you remember the nightmare that plagued your sleep several weeks back?" Charles asked suddenly.

Aidan tensed. "How do you know about that?"

"We felt the Prophet soothe you through Heritage."

Now Aidan did shudder. He remembered the whispers that almost suffocated him. Worse were the looks his parents had given him, and the terrible things they said.

"I remember," he said at last.

"Luria Thalamahn was the one who learned how to implant souls in new flesh," Anastasia said. "But her chief weapon was a spell called Night Terror. No one but she knew how to cast it, for it was she who created it. Night Terror transfers a victim's consciousness into a nightmare as real as the waking world, much like how your consciousness resides in Heritage presently, apart from your body. One can die in a Night Terror just as one can perish in reality. You could fall asleep and never awaken, and who could be blamed? Unless the death was a violent one—any wounds received are reflected on the body in the waking world—no one would have reason to suspect foul play."

Aidan swallowed. "And that's what happened to me?"

Ambrose nodded. "You were. The Prophet broke through the spell and intervened."

Aidan sent a prayer of thanks to the Lady for the Prophet's intervention. Then he frowned. "You said Luria created the Night Terror spell, correct?"

"Yes," Anastasia said.

"How does Tyrnen know how to use it?" Then icy shock washed over him as he remembered the golden scepter Tyrnen had held in his mother's memory. "Tyrnen is Luria Thalamahn," he whispered.

"Not quite, it appears," Anastasia said, frowning as she glanced at Ambrose and Charles.

Aidan looked between them. "The Prophet told me that a Thalamahn's soul seizes the body of any who touch their weapons. I saw Tyrnen holding Terror's Hand. Luria must have command of his body."

"We thought so too, at first," Ambrose said. His visage darkened. "Then we saw Tyrnen pay a visit to the Prophet after your consciousness entered Heritage. She too thought Tyrnen had been subverted by Luria, but she was mistaken."

"It is clear that Luria does have some control over Tyrnen, however," Anastasia said. "Tyrnen's will must have been too great to break completely, yet even though he is still in possession of his soul, he is utterly loyal to Luria."

Aidan held up a hand. "Wait. How did Tyrnen even come to possess Terror's Hand? The Prophet told me that you," he gestured to Anastasia, "and the Disciples of Peace shielded the weapons' compulsion to prevent the Thalamahns from attracting hosts."

"We did," Anastasia said. "As the Prophet explained, the weapons were masked and taken far away to a destination known only by the Prophet, who carried the Serpent's Fang, and Mathias Emerson, who carried Terror's Hand. Less than a year after Mathias and the Prophet went their separate ways, we felt Luria reach out to the world from deep within Sallner.

"It would appear Mathias thought to hide the weapon in the

abandoned kingdom. That was poor judgment on his part. Sallner is where Dimitri and Luria practiced their dark craft; as such, their influence was strongest there. We do not know exactly what befell Mathias, but it is obvious that he somehow removed the mask from the weapon and touched it. By the time we came to where Luria had called from, we found only Mathias's body. The scepter was gone."

"Our family has spent the last eight hundred years standing watch for Luria," Charles said. "It was not until Mathias ambushed your parents and tempted Annalyn with Terror's Hand that we realized what had become of it, and of Luria and Mathias."

Aidan raised a hand, confused. "Hold on. You just said he was dead."

The other three shared a look. Anastasia spoke. "Aidan, when Tyrnen entered the cabin and the Prophet saw that the Queen of Terror had not possessed his body, she called him Mathias."

Aidan stared blankly. "Tyrnen and Mathias are one and the same? That would make him over eight hundred years old!"

Anastasia raised a finger. "His *soul* is still alive. We suspect Mathias shed his body because we would have recognized him instantly, whether during our time on Crotaria or from here, within Heritage. My mother knew of a ritual, a dark magic known as sacrifice, that allows the living to inject his or her soul into another living body, whose soul is then terminated."

"The same magic used on the Thalamahns' weapons," Aidan said.

"Correct," Anastasia said. "For eight centuries, Mathias has assumed new bodies and identities, effectively evading the eye of every Gairden who would know him instantly."

"Tyrnen Symorne is Mathias's latest guise," Ambrose said, "one he used to infiltrate Sunfall itself. We presume he did so in order to manipulate Heritage. Using the blade in tandem with artifacts as powerful as the Serpent's Fang and Terror's Hand would make him unstoppable. Of course, to control Heritage, Mathias needed a sword-bearer."

He looked at Aidan. "Training a Gairden is a duty undertaken by our bloodline. But Tyrnen, as the Eternal Flame of Crotaria and your mother's friend, was given the opportunity to participate in your training and tutelage."

Aidan felt numb. "He must have been quite disappointed when the sword rejected me. But why now after eight hundred years? He could have wormed his way into the lives of any of our bloodline and manipulated them."

Charles cleared his throat. "You are the strongest Touched in our line yet, Aidan. But you are also pliable. I love you, so please don't take offense at my words, but you have never had an affinity for responsibility. Of course, that might not be entirely your fault. Mathias likely preyed on your feelings to ensure that when the time came to put his plan into motion, you would act as he wished, do as he wished."

Aidan's thoughts darkened. Sixteen years of being raised by a man who had been like a grandfather to him, and all Tyrnen had wanted was to use Aidan as a tool, just as Luria used him.

"I'm going to kill him," Aidan said flatly.

"Killing Destruction's Champion will not assure victory," Ambrose said to him. "Hundreds of thousands of Sallnerians, Torelians, Darinians, and Leastonians have died these last eight hundred years. Tyrnen could draft any one of them into his army of the dead."

Aidan felt a twinge of panic. "That doesn't matter. I can—"

"You are strong," Charles interrupted, "but the harbingers can band together. We do not know how many of them walk Crotaria, nor the guises they assume."

Aidan's shoulders sagged. They were right. Tyrnen had him vastly outnumbered. "What can I do?"

His grandfather gave him a level look. "You must return to Sunfall and take back the Crown of the North—and you must repair the damage done between Torel and Darinia."

"We believe the war is a vital component in Tyrnen's plan," Ambrose said. "Torel and Darinia go to war. One of them destroys the other. The nation left standing will surely be vulnerable. Tyrnen and his vagrants sweep in and decimate the survivors—with Dimitri Thalamahn, as likely as not."

"But the Prophet still guards the Serpent's Fang," Aidan began. Then he remembered Ambrose saying Tyrnen had confronted the old woman. "She's dead, isn't she?" he said quietly.

Anastasia nodded. "I'm afraid so. Without her to guard it, Tyrnen has likely recovered Dimitri's blade."

Aidan ran a shaky hand through his hair. "This is all my fault."

Charles gripped Aidan's shoulders. "Remember what the Prophet said, Aidan. You have no time to attribute blame or feel sorry for yourself. What's done is done. Do not dwell on mistakes. Instead, concentrate on fixing them. What will you do?"

Aidan scratched at his cheek. "I will go to Nichel and explain what has happened. I will tell her that Torel and Darinia must stand together against Tyrnen and the Thalamahns. I will need to approach the merchants' guild, also. Tyrnen has manipulated the north and west. I doubt he has left Leaston alone."

Ambrose shook his head. "You must reclaim the Crown of the North first, Aidan. As long as the harbingers act as rulers, they control Torel's Ward."

Aidan grimaced. "Isn't there a way I can show people what those impostors really are?"

"If there is," Anastasia said, "we do not know of it." She sounded apologetic. Aidan understood why. The magic that flowed through his veins and through the veins of so many Gairdens before him carried Anastasia's gift. If she, perhaps the most powerful Touched Crotaria had ever known, did not know of a magic, it probably did not exist.

"It is time for you to depart Sanctuary," Ambrose said to him. He pointed at the sky. Aidan saw a red dot hanging stationary among the clouds like a floating ember. "To leave, simply focus on the star, and—"

"Wait," Charles said. "There is the other matter. The one concerning his friends."

"My friends?" Aidan asked, his voice tense with worry. "Are they all right?"

Ambrose scratched at his chin before grumbling, "No easy way to say it, I suppose. That Sallnerian girl and her brother have betrayed you."

"Garrett and Christine? That's impossible. Christine and I..." He shook his head. "Why would they do that?" A thought occurred to him. "Is Daniel all right?"

"He will live," Charles assured him. "As for why..." He shrugged as a sad smile settled onto his face. "The same reason humans can be persuaded to do nearly anything. Tyrnen paid them a large sum of money."

Aidan felt his face heat. Was there any facet of his life Tyrnen had not corrupted?

"The Sallnerian girl seems to have some good in her," Ambrose said, though he sounded as if the words had been pried from him. "She tried to stand against Tyrnen and her brother. Even so, keep your guard up."

Aidan nodded and clasped the man's extended hand. "There are many more who are eager to meet you, though it will wait until another time," Ambrose said. His eyes hardened. "Be wary, Crown of the North. You must—"

Aidan gasped. His life had changed so quickly that he had forgotten what being the sword-bearer meant. Heritage was more than a blade at his waist and a contact with his family. It was a crown, albeit one worn at his waist. From the moment he had accepted Heritage, he had been king. *From the moment Tyrnen killed my parents.*

Charles gripped his grandson's shoulder. "Do not fear, Aidan. Your family is with you, now and always. Call to us, and we will answer."

"Thank you."

The trio faded away, leaving Aidan alone with his thoughts.

For the first time since he had entered Sanctuary, Aidan was alone. He looked up at the sky and focused on the red star. His feet left the stone platform, and he rose like a bubble in water. The star seemed to shine brighter and grow larger as he rose. The sky changed color, blue fading to red before sudden darkness consumed him.

Wind rushed over him. A puddle of light appeared beneath his feet, and another faded into view before him. He stepped into it, and the next, and the next. Growls and heavy footsteps crunching over dead leaves and branches echoed around him. Briefly he wondered how he'd come to be in the Duskwood before realizing that the Prophet must have taken him here when Tyrnen had attacked.

Tyrnen.

The darkness around him matched his mood. He gritted his teeth as he remembered the look on his father's face as he was forced to watch his wife die, and the look that had come over Annalyn when she had seen Edmund's battered body. Aidan Gairden felt betrayed. He also felt used, as though a sacred part of his life had been nothing more than a lie.

More than anything, Aidan Gairden felt angry.

Chapter 28

Friends and Foes

CHRISTINE HAD TRIED TO slip past the harbinger one time and one time only. It stood outside the cabin, never moving, never speaking, barely seeming to breathe. She had slipped a dagger from a vagrant and crept up behind the harbinger, thinking to stab it and make a run for the trees that bordered this mysterious place painted in flowers and birdsong when the rest of Sallner, her homeland, sat in perpetual rot. She had been perhaps two steps from the harbinger's back when it had spun and rooted her to the spot, fear forming in her belly like a block of ice.

The face staring back at her had been her own. It had grinned as she dropped the dagger and slowly backed away. It changed its appearance as she went, bones snapping like dry twigs as its skin shifted: Daniel, then Garrett, then Tyrnen, and herself—again and again it cycled through those faces. It smiled through all the changes, and through the beating Garrett had inflicted on Daniel as punishment for her attempt at flight.

She thinned her lips. Thinking of the problem had never been a productive way of looking at things. It was time to find a solution. Cautiously, she rose to her feet and crept toward the back of the cabin. As she moved, she kept an eye on Garrett, who slept in a bedroll by the door. Finally she reached Daniel, who lay curled in a ball in one corner. His face was puffy and bruised. Dry blood speckled his cracked lips.

"Daniel?" she whispered.

He stirred, groaning as his body shifted. She clamped a hand over his mouth and tensed, glanced over at Garrett. He snored but gave no sign of movement. Christine let out a silent breath and turned back to Daniel. She would shake him awake if she had to—but gently. Just as she opened her mouth, Daniel's teeth clamped down on her fingers.

"Please," she hissed as softly as she could. "I'm trying to get you out of here." She bit down on her lip as the pain increased. "*Please*!"

Daniel narrowed his eyes and spat her hand away. She cradled it to her chest and glared at him.

"You'll forgive me for not biting more tenderly," Daniel whispered hotly.

Christine opted to grimace in pain instead of snapping back. He had every right to hate her. "I'm sorry for betraying you."

"Oh, well, if you're *sorry*."

"We were supposed to turn Aidan in for a reward. I never wanted either of you to get hurt." She liked Daniel, she truly did. And where Aidan was concerned... No, not now. She could not afford to worry about what Aidan would think of her. She did not *want* to.

"What my brother did was—" she began.

Daniel's cracked lips twisted into a scowl. "He had help."

She nodded. "I'm truly sorry." What else could she say?

"Prove it."

She gestured to the dying embers of the fire in the hearth. "One of the vagrants will be in soon to renew the fire. We eliminate him, and—"

"With what? Your brother took all my weapons."

Christine pulled a dagger from her boot. "Always be prepared. So, we deal with the vagrant and make our way to the woods."

Daniel twisted to glare at her brother's sleeping form. "And Garrett?"

"What about him?"

"He'll raise an alarm if he's able to speak. We'll need to make sure that doesn't happen."

Christine hesitated. "He's asleep. If we just slip by him, we—"

"Second-guessing your allegiance, again?"

"No, it's just... he's my brother. I don't want to kill him. I can't."

Daniel's eyes went flat. "I'll do it."

"No." She took a breath. "If he wakes up—*if*—then we do what needs to be done. Otherwise I will not let harm come to him."

Daniel grunted. "Fine. Where will we go?"

"Somewhere Aidan can easily find us."

"We'll figure it out on the way, I guess," Daniel said. "But we can't leave without Heritage."

Christine suppressed an impatient growl. "Don't you think Aidan would rather us escape with our lives than his sword?"

"It comes with us." His tone left no room for argument.

She looked back to her brother. His arms were curled tightly around his chest. Firelight glinted from the steel he cuddled in his arms like a child's night toy. "He sleeps with it," she mumbled.

Daniel's face became incredulous. "What?"

"He *sleeps. With. It.* He's so afraid of anyone stealing it that he holds it while he sleeps."

"I don't care how we do it, but if you really care about Aidan, you'll understand how important Heritage is to him, and to his family," Daniel said. "We are *not* leaving it behind."

She sighed. "Fine. Work the kinks out of your joints then wait for me by the doorway. Stay out of sight. I'll get the sword." She extended her dagger to him, then pulled back when he reached for her. "Do not use it on my brother."

"All right, all right," Daniel said, pocketing the blade. He pushed himself up slowly from the floor, breathing hard through swollen lips.

Crouching, Christine made her way across the room to Garrett. Thinning her lips, she reached for Heritage, intending to slide it slowly from his grasp, when he snorted and rolled onto his back. His arms fell open, leaving the sword in the crook of one arm. *This will be easier than I thought.* Carefully, she eased her hands under blade and hilt, and lifted it up. She closed her eyes, expelled the breath she had been holding, and opened them.

Garrett, eyes bulging, a maniacal grin twisting his face, stared back at her. His foot shot out and caught her in the chest, sending her tumbling away. Heritage clattered to the floor. For a moment, no air would enter her lungs, and she panicked. Then breath returned, squeezing through a hot tightness in her ribs.

"Thinking to cut my throat while I sleep?" Garrett asked. He leered over her, bouncing the flat of Heritage against one palm. "Going to run off and find your hero? I won't let you ruin this for us, Christine. We've been promised more riches than you can even imagine, and I—"

Daniel barreled into him, shouting and hammering at Garrett with his fists. Heritage skittered from Garrett's grasp and stopped at Christine's boots. She scooped it up with trembling hands and pulled herself to her feet. Across from her, Garrett rolled over to mount Daniel, pinned his hands to the floor, stood, and dropped one knee squarely into Daniel's exposed ribs. Daniel wheezed and turned purple.

"Garrett," Christine said in a calm voice. Her brother whirled on her, snarling. He saw the shaking sword in her trembling hands.

"You can't do it," Garrett whispered, advancing. "Give me the sword, Christine. You don't want to hurt me; you *can't* hurt me, but I'll hurt you, Christine, I'll hurt you bad if you don't *give me the damn sword!"*

She winced and stepped back. She took another step back and bumped into the wall. Garrett came on, smiling now as he stalked her. She raised the sword and swallowed. She didn't know anything about swordplay, but one didn't have to be a master swordsman to swing and hit something.

Noises from outside stole their attention: shouts, roars, a flash of light, silence. Then the back wall of the cabin exploded, vomiting dust, dead grass, dirt, and wood over the floor and walls.

Coughing and sputtering, Christine looked up. Aidan stood in the splintered hole. She would have shouted with joy had another cough not reared up from her throat. He reached to her, and she almost slipped her hand in his before following his eyes. They rested on Heritage, not on her. She gave it to him. The sword-bearer's hands wrapped around the hilt. Instantly his eyes lit up, blazing like fire.

Garrett swallowed and quickly stepped forward. "Aidan, you've come at last! Thank goodness you're here, my friend. We were ambushed by—"

Aidan pointed a finger at him. Garrett stared at it, curious. Aidan kindled. Garrett shot through the doorway, hands wrapped around his stomach as if he'd been kicked by a horse. There was a loud thud and muffled cry as his body landed somewhere outside.

The sword-bearer turned, locking Christine in his white-eyed gaze. She swallowed but did not back away. He was here, right in front of her, alive and—from the looks of it—unhurt. She could confess everything, and perhaps he would spare her and maybe, just maybe, still care for her.

"Aidan, I—"

The whole cabin burst into flames, as bright as the Lady's light reflected on a field of snow. Aidan's eyes flared. "Get Daniel out," he yelled before shifting away.

Aidan reappeared outside. Behind him, the cabin vomited flames. Smoke poured through every opening. He barely noticed. Standing across from him was Aidan Gairden. The face changed, becoming his mother, his father—Tyrnen.

Aidan blinked. *Ordine'kel* soaked through him and he charged forward, Heritage cleaving and swinging. His strikes were not timed and measured, not carried about by the precise and tactical hand of an expert warrior like Ambrose or his father. He did not want to dissect the harbinger standing calmly across the Vale. He wanted to *butcher* it, to rend and tear it into slabs of meat, to—

The harbinger shifted behind him and threw thin bolts of lightning. Aidan kindled, slicing the light in half for a shift and a return blast of his own. All across the Vale they jumped, magic cutting and burning the air and mixing with the pure-fire that reduced the cabin to a smoldering ruin. Aidan chopped and stabbed with Heritage when he appeared near the harbinger, but the undead was always one heartbeat ahead of him.

Suddenly the pure-fire vanished, leaving a pile of charred remains where the cabin had stood. Hefting Heritage, Aidan spun around, but like the magical flames, his enemy was gone.

"Aidan!"

Christine scrabbled out from beneath the rubble. Her face and hair were black with ash. One arm was wrapped around her chest.

"Where's Daniel?" Aidan asked, tensely, sweeping his gaze around.

Christine gestured helplessly at the cabin's remains. "Probably under there," she said from between fits of coughing.

"Why didn't you shift him away?"

"I can't! Tyrnen tied me. I—"

A torrent of choking coughs broke out from behind them. Aidan turned and saw a hand claw through smoldering wood, clutching at the air. He leaped forward, gripped it, and pulled. Daniel crawled out, covered head to toe in ash.

"Are you all right?" Aidan asked, swatting aside charred debris and pulling Daniel to his feet. Daniel nodded, hacking and spitting. He took a step and fell. Aidan caught him.

"Thanks," Daniel said, looping an arm around Aidan's neck as Aidan tugged him free from the ruins. Suddenly he grinned and wrapped his hands around Aidan's throat. The sword-bearer gagged, dropping the huge and useless Heritage to beat and claw at the hands digging into his throat. Daniel's hands began to glow. Heat seared Aidan's skin—then the tip of Heritage erupted from Daniel's forehead, splashing Aidan with green gore.

The harbinger went limp and crumpled to the ground. Rubbing gingerly at his neck, Aidan watched, bewildered, as another Daniel Shirey tossed Heritage at his feet.

"This is becoming a dangerous habit of ours, good prince," Daniel said, his voice raspy from smoke. Christine stumbled to his side and threw one of his arms across her shoulders.

"It was the harbinger," Christine said, staggering under Daniel's weight. "They can change their appearance. The vagrants, too. They—"

"I know what they're capable of," Aidan snapped, still

massaging his neck. He still felt as if he wore a necklace made of fire. He scooped up Heritage and hurried to Daniel's other side. "Are you all right?" he asked, slinging his friend's other arm over his shoulder.

"Never better."

"Is there any sign of Garrett?" Christine asked.

"Are you concerned about him?" Aidan asked her.

"No, I just—"

"No sign," Aidan said. He eased Daniel over to Christine. "Stay with him. There's something I have to do."

Aidan moved briskly to the rubble of the cabin. *Would the Fang have been inside?*

His family didn't respond for several moments.

—We do not feel its presence, Anastasia said. *If Tyrnen would have found it, surely he would have severed the mask we placed over its compulsion magic. And yet...*

What?

—Look around you.

Raising his eyes from the charred debris, Aidan started in shock and disgust. The leaves of the trees bordering the vale withered before his eyes, fading to autumn-orange then charcoal black. Others crumbled, sprinkling to the ground like ashes. Bark rotted and peeled from trees. Flowers shriveled and died. The water in the stream ceased its cheerful burbling and became a greenish-black, as though vagrant blood ran through it.

What's happening?

—The Thalamahns tainted everything they touched, Anastasia said. *Their corruption lay at the very core of their souls. With the Prophet dead and the shield removed, the Serpent's Fang would spread that corruption like mold on fruit.*

—The same way the Serpent King corrupted his kingdom eight centuries before, Ambrose added.

Aidan nodded, thinking. *I don't think Tyrnen found it, though. Given the state of the vale, wouldn't we see a trail of corruption leading out of the Duskwood?*

Heritage was silent. Then: *—Excellent reasoning, Aidan,* his grandfather said. *See if you can find it. Do not touch it if you do, though. Use the lines. Keep a steady hand, just like waiting for a bite from Lake Carrean.*

Aidan smiled in spite of his bleak situation. Rising, he went to where the ground was blackest. *The corruption spreads outward from here.* Like a pebble cast into a pond, the corruption spread out in ripples—black at its core, then brown, yellow, and green through the Vale where the corruption had not touched. Drawing light, Aidan muttered a prayer to the Lady and cupped his hands over the dead earth. Dead grass and dirt came apart with dry rips that sounded like tearing leather. The hole gradually widened until Aidan saw a flash of blue approximately six feet down.

I see something. Refocusing, he closed his hand into a fist, kindled, and prayed to the Lady, throwing open his hand as he did. The blue light shuddered. Aidan beckoned with his fingers, reeling in his catch. The pulsing blue light wriggled toward him, crawling up the side of the hole. When it finally crested the lip of the hole, Aidan hissed and stepped back. He had expected to find Dimitri's weapon, but it was the blade's resemblance to Heritage—black instead of white, a blue jewel in the guard where the Eye of Heritage was red, and encased in a black guard covered in glowing green swirls—that sickened and shocked him.

I have it.

—How do you feel? Charles asked.

Pondering, Aidan shrugged. *I don't hear any voice coaxing me to trade my soul for eternal agony, if that's what you mean.*

—I hope you would decline.

I am rather attached to my soul. It's flawed, but it's the only one I've got.

—The shielding must still be mostly intact, Charles said.

—Is it safely covered? Anastasia asked.

All but the hilt.

Aidan felt a surge of exultation from the sword. *—We've got him,* Anastasia said. *Do something about that hilt, will you?*

Looking around, Aidan went to the dead harbinger, cut off its shirt, and wrapped the bloody article around the hilt. *I'll be safe so long as I don't touch it, correct?*

—Correct, his grandfather said, *but make sure your cover does not slip away. If your skin so much as grazes the sword, Dimitri could pounce.*

—Your grandfather is correct, Aidan, Anastasia said. *We will need to summon Disciples of Dawn to forge a new shielding once you return home and tidy up after Tyrnen and his creatures. In the meantime, tell us immediately if you hear or feel anything out of sorts. It could be that Dimitri's soul has not awakened yet and detected your presence. The moment he does, he will want to add your power to his own.*

Fear rippled through his anger. He forced it down and started to rise when something gold caught his eye from between brown blades of grass. His Cinder Band, hidden in a pocket of charred flowers and earth. He plucked it up and cocked his arm back, ready to hurl it into the endless night and unseen horrors of the Duskwood. Then he reconsidered.

Tyrnen had given him the ring, and that had meant more to him than receiving the ring itself. Now that memory, like all the times he had spent sitting in front of Tyrnen's hearth drinking tea and listening in rapt attention as the old man regaled him with myths and legends, was like a poison in his system. A disease that had lain dormant only to suddenly reawaken and eat away at him from the inside.

The gesture was poison, but the Band was not. Tyrnen had been as much a friend as a mentor, but neither he nor his mother had made lessons easy just to coddle their prince. The Band was his by right, if for nothing else than as a testament to all he had survived over the past month. He shook his head, amazed. His life seemed to have divided in two: before his sixteenth birthday, and after. The latter period felt like another lifetime spent in a different place among different people, lived by another prince.

He pocketed the ring and went back to Christine, slinging one of Daniel's arms over his shoulder without a word.

Chapter 29

Roadside Talks

AIDAN STEPPED FROM THE darkness of the shanty out into the sickly green glow of the haze that hung over Sallner. Daniel limped between them, one arm slung over each pair of shoulders and dragging his feet behind him.

"Down," Daniel gasped.

Aidan and Christine eased him to the ground. Christine immediately folded her arms and stepped away, gazing around at the ruins of the southern kingdom. That was good. Aidan did not want to see her face. One look at those almond eyes, or the way her hair framed her face and spilled over her shoulders, or the way her boots hugged her—

His lips thinned. He kept his gaze fixed on Daniel, on the way he clutched at his ribs and hissed in each breath through his teeth. Christine was partially responsible for this. She didn't deserve his forgiveness.

"We need to get you to a healer," Aidan said. "If I can get us to the tunnels, can you find us a key back home?"

Daniel nodded and took Aidan's offered hand. Christine reappeared as suddenly as she had vanished, ducking under one of Daniel's arms.

"How far to the tunnels?" Daniel asked as they started off.

"The ones we used to get here?" Christine asked. "They should be just—"

"A few hours north," Aidan said over her. He squinted up at the sky. "I'd rather shift us there to save you walking, but the Lady's light is..." He shook his head.

"The screen blocks it," Christine said.

"The screen?" Daniel asked.

Christine nodded at the clouds overhead. "When Anastasia Gairden and the Disciples of Dawn exiled Sallner from the rest of Crotaria, they created an artificial cloud cover to block Sallner from the Lady's sight. They didn't want any Touched—any *Sallnerian* Touched—sneaking back home to cast spells, I assume."

Aidan glared at her. She was not wrong, exactly, but he did not care for the insinuation behind her words. His ancestors had had no choice but to exile Sallner, especially with the Serpent's Fang and Terror's Hand hidden in the remains of the south. Perhaps if the Sallnerians had not fallen under Dimitri and Luria's influence, they could have kept their realm.

"So this green light," Daniel began.

"Magic," Christine said, nodding. "An artificial twilight that lasts for eternity."

"You sure know a lot about Sallner," Daniel said.

"I've read the texts, that's all."

"And you're Sallnerian," Daniel pointed out.

"You noticed." She was smiling.

"What's this like for you?" Daniel asked. "Walking through these ruins? Is it... I don't know. Do you feel anything?"

Despite his desire to keep his anger at Christine stoked nice and hot, Aidan found himself looking over at her, curious. He had never interacted much with Sallnerians. They made their way to court infrequently, preferring, he supposed, to stick to their camps on the Territory Bridge and the isolated homes they made among the other three realms.

Christine was silent for several minutes. "It's like..." She twisted her head to look this way and that, taking in the gutted structures, the shards of glass that threw glints of the false light back at them, the piles of charred white stone. "Like walking through someone else's memories. Or like walking through pages of history texts. I have read accounts of Sallner, and have learned about their—my, I should say—architecture, habits, and so forth. But those are just words, the same words you, Aidan, and anyone else who didn't live here eight hundred years ago would read."

Her mouth twisted. "Also, most of the accounts dwell on the Serpent's War, and reveal little of what the south did before that."

"Attempting to overthrow neighboring realms tends to stick with a people," Aidan said.

"Eight-hundred-year-old history," Christine shot back. "The Sallnerians alive today took no part in the Thalamahns' dark experiments."

Daniel glanced nervously between them.

"Torel's Ward is always putting down insurrections at the Territory Bridge," Aidan said. "For all we know, you snakes are getting ready for another revolt."

Aidan regretted the slur the moment it left his lips. Christine went pale. She threw Daniel's arm away and spun on Aidan, inches from his face.

"Garrett and I were born and raised on the Bridge," Christine said, her voice quiet and shaky. "My father is Torelian, and a Touched. He dreamed of doing great things, as men do, but my mother was plain and sickly, and Sallnerian. He couldn't possibly take a *snake* out into the world, could he? So we stayed there, a family of four crammed into a little Torelian hut, one in a neat line of huts bunched shoulder to shoulder along dirt roads. Those insurrections you speak of were not insurrections. Fights broke out over food because large families such as mine received small rations along with any food adults able to find work could bring home.

"My father could have left us, but he didn't. He wanted to, I think. But he didn't. He found what work he could as a scholar before he moved on to... to better things. He took us away from the Bridge, but not before my mother died. She was sick, but the healers don't visit the Bridge very often. Did you know that, Aidan Gairden, Guardian Light of Crotaria? Your people to the south deserve equal treatment, but you have more important people to save."

"I... We didn't..." Aidan swallowed. For some reason he found himself at a loss for words.

"The Gairdens are supposed to protect all of Crotaria's people—north, east, west, *and* south. And that is what we are, Aidan. Sallnerians are not snakes, just as Darinians are not the wild animals drawn on their bodies. We are people. And we are *your* people. Anastasia *Thalamahn* is your matriarch. The blood of *snakes* slithers through your veins, too. Or had you forgotten? But you think what you want. Do what you want. That is your way."

Wiping away tears, she ducked back underneath Daniel's arm and pressed on, practically dragging the two men in her wake.

Chapter 30

Ralda's Inn

SILENCE WRAPPED AROUND THEM, cold and uncomfortable. Three hours later, Aidan led Daniel and Christine through the curtain of dead vines and through the mouth of the cave to the tunnel below. Daniel pointed out the V-in-a-V, the key that would take them to the cave where they had taken shelter what seemed like years ago. He pointed out others even closer, several within Calewind and on Sunfall's grounds. Aidan heard the whispers that formed the words to the Language of Light, but he remembered the prayer he needed. Reaching across Daniel's back to touch Christine, Aidan darkened using the inky night flowing through the veins in the walls and fast-traveled to the waypoint where they would have emerged had they followed the passage beneath Sunfall's east courtyard to a hub. The tunnel was plugged with rocks.

"Can you blast through it?" Daniel asked. They were the first words spoken since Christine's outburst.

"I could, but that would give us away, I think," Aidan said.

Daniel stepped away from Aidan and Christine to lean against the wall. "All the tunnels in and around Calewind are probably blocked off," he said, knuckling his back. "Our best bet besides returning to that inn in Tarion—"

"Which we should assume Tyrnen also blocked," Aidan said.

"—is a little village that sits on the border between Leaston and Torel. It's not ideal, I know," he said over Aidan's objection, "but at least it will get us out of this light-forsaken darkness so you can get back to shifting us across the continent."

Aidan glanced at Christine. She stood with her back to him, making a careful inspection of the threads of shadow running along the walls.

"That will do fine," Aidan said.

Silently, Christine ducked under Daniel's arm and stared straight ahead. Aidan went to Daniel's other side and hesitated. Words arranged in pleasantly humble configurations—pleasant to Christine—danced on his tongue, but he couldn't get them to take the plunge. *Apologies rarely set sail from the lips of Leastonian traders*, the saying went--a saying fashioned by Leastonians, so he didn't think they would mind.

The long walk down to the tunnels had given him plenty of time to reflect on his exchange with Christine, and to realize, begrudgingly at first, that she had been right. People were people, be they from Torel, or Sallner, or far beyond Crotaria's borders. Calling a Sallnerian a snake was not viewed as severely as labeling a Darinian a wildlander, even though it should be.

But the slur itself was not even the worst part. He had been angry with her, with Garrett, with Tyrnen, with so many people. With himself. So he had fashioned a whip from words and raw emotion and lashed out, not looking to engage in any intelligent, adult discourse, but to cut her, and cut her deep. It was a regression, he admitted, a return to the childish, petulant brat of a boy that had punched a window and stung his mother with hurtful words the night a talking sword had embarrassed him in front of thousands of people. That Aidan seemed a different person, one who had no place in this Aidan's life.

"Should we go ahead without you?" Christine asked, slouching under Daniel's long arm.

Aidan swallowed the apology. This was not the right time.

They returned to the waypoint and turned around and around until they found the key Daniel was looking for, an inverted "Y" between two lines, about halfway up one wall. By the time Daniel reached the tunnel opening, his clothes were soaked in sweat. Aidan gave him some time to catch his breath then gathered Daniel and Christine to him, bracing for the icy touch of Kahltan's shadows. To his surprise, they did not freeze his bones this time. He had found light magic stifling at first, too. Perhaps he was simply getting used to the feel of shade in his veins.

Following the tunnel dropped them at the mouth of a cave deep in a copse of birches. Aidan tipped his head back and smiled, letting the Lady caress his face. He had been too long without daylight. They eased Daniel down onto a patch of dirt and leaves, one of many holes in the carpet of snow. Aidan gripped Heritage with one hand and placed the other on Daniel's chest.

Grandfather?

—Yes, Aidan?

I need some healing magic. Could one of you...?

—I can help, Aidan, Anastasia said. *Draw in light and pray. I will take care of the rest.*

Aidan soaked up the Lady's rays and passed them to the

sword. Heritage held them for a moment before pushing the light back to Aidan. As before, the light felt changed, like how his father could take slabs of steel and shape them into weapons and tools. *Had been* able to. Aidan spoke a prayer and felt the light flush out through his fingers. Daniel gasped and stiffened, then sighed and slumped back in relief as his cuts knit closed and his bruises faded away.

Standing, Aidan pulled Daniel to his feet. Daniel stretched, danced a quick jig.

"That's something, all right," he said, running his hands along his face and chest, cautiously at first, then prodding harder and grinning. "Thank you, Your Princeliness."

—He'll need to take it easy, Anastasia said. *He may feel fine, but healing works much like herbs and salves, just a little faster: he still needs plenty of bed rest and fluids to make a full recovery.*

Aidan repeated her words. Daniel gave one last spin and bowed deeply. "As His Princeliness requests."

Christine looked at Aidan in amazement. "You studied healing?"

"No. My grandmother did." When she frowned in confusion, he said, "Anastasia. She supplies the spell, I supply the light."

"Tell her I appreciate it," Daniel said.

Aidan glanced at the sword for several moments, then raised an eyebrow. "Grandfather Charles says he'd like to know what happened to the flagon of Leastonian Red he kept in his cabinet around the time we were eleven years old."

"I don't know anything about that," Daniel said quickly. He turned, getting his bearings, and pointed through the screen of trees. "The border into Torel is about a day's walk that way. The village I mentioned, Sordia, is the closest to the border. I presume you'd like to let the Lady's light whisk us away?"

"Actually, I thought we'd walk for a bit," Aidan said, stealing a glance at Christine. "You could use some fresh air."

Daniel followed Aidan's gaze. "You know, I think a bit of walking would do me good," he said loudly, throwing Aidan an obvious wink. Aidan resisted the urge to groan.

"I'll just lead the way, shall I?" Daniel went on. He walked up to a tree, snapped off a branch, poked at the ground, then nodded, satisfied, and leaned on his new-found walking stick.

"Let's stay off the main road," Aidan said.

They started off, Daniel walking a good distance ahead. Christine started after him and Aidan hustled to walk beside her. Silence stretched out for several long minutes as Aidan considered and summarily dismissed elaborate, heartfelt apologies. Finally he scrapped them all and let the right words tumble out.

"I'm sorry," he said. Christine looked over at him. "I shouldn't have called you... what I called you," he pressed on. "It was childish and cruel. A lot has happened to me since my birthday, and I like to think those experiences have made me a better person." He wanted to explain, to share those experiences with her, but thought she might interpret them as rationalizations. He swallowed the words. "I'm sorry," he said again.

He kept his eyes on the road before daring to look up at her. Slowly, like the Lady breaking through clouds after a rainstorm, her face grew warmer.

"Forgiven," she said simply. They walked on, standing a little closer. When Christine tentatively reached for his hand, Aidan pulled away.

"I'm still very angry with you," he said.

She nodded. "I know. And I understand." She tucked a wisp of hair behind her ear. Ahead, Daniel whistled an old Torelian tavern song. Birds flitted through branches and sang their pleasure at returning home after the long winter. Aidan blinked. Around him, dirt and grass popped through snow like holes in a white blanket. Winter was over, and spring was settling over the lower regions of the north. He thought back to the snow and ice that had covered Calewind's streets and rooftops like icing on a birthday cake. Had so much time really passed?

"Is there anything I can do?" Christine asked. "To make amends," she explained when he looked at her with a puzzled frown.

He stuffed his hands into his pockets. "How much of what you've told me, of who you are, is the truth?"

"Most," she said. "I trained at the Lion's Den. The Spectacle is real, but it is a cover. We are bounty hunters. Chasing thieves and brigands across Crotaria paid for most of my education."

"I was an assignment, then?"

"At first," she said, and her voice sounded pained. "We were summoned to Sunfall to speak with the Eternal Flame. Tyrnen asked us to bring you home. He said that you were guilty of treason."

"So you work for him?"

"I did. We followed you and Daniel north. When we met up with you at the Hornet's Nest, it was fortunate that we were able to save you from getting attacked."

Aidan thought back to his and Daniel's desperate flight from the vagrants and whispers that had attacked the Nest, and the fortuitous appearance of Christine and her brother. "The Sallnerians and the whispers. Were they with you?"

"No."

He nodded, waiting for her to continue.

"The night you left, Tyrnen came to the Fisherman's Pond. We followed your trail into Sallner and stopped at the Duskwood. Going through was..." She shivered. "Once we left that dreadful darkness, we emerged in the vale. Tyrnen told us to wait outside with Daniel. He went inside the cabin, and for a short time, everything was quiet. Then these terrible sounds came from inside the cabin. They sounded like... like meat being torn apart."

She shuddered and closed her eyes. When she opened them, Aidan was looking at her, his face horrified.

"What is it?" she asked.

"An old woman lived there, in the cabin," he finally said.

"In the vale?"

"Yes. Tyrnen killed her. She was... my friend."

"I'm sorry about your friend."

Neither said anything for a time. Earth and rocks poked through slushy snow. Small buildings in the distance squatted at the foot of a hill.

"Why didn't Tyrnen take Heritage with him?" he asked.

"He gave it to Garrett to look after because he knew you would come for it. It was bait." She shook her head angrily. "Garrett did not take much convincing, I'm afraid."

"He is your brother. Don't you care what becomes of him?"

"Yes," she said quietly. "And... no. He has always had a cruel streak, though never toward me. I still care for Garrett—he *is* my brother—but I don't believe Garrett feels much affection for me. Forming Spectacle and chasing after bounties was his idea; I went along with it because I had no one else, no other plans. My magic provided him a life of warm beds, good food, and some small renown. Now he has Tyrnen, and his dependence on me has ended."

They drew near the tall wooden walls of the village. To their surprise, the gate stood open. Daniel leaned on the wall to one side, arms crossed, one foot back against the wall. Aidan pulled the hood of his cloak over his head. Tugging at either corner of his cloak, he covered the sheathed weapons at his waist.

"This is Sordia," Daniel said, jutting his thumb over his shoulder when they joined him. "I've paid our way in." He leaned closer. "If they ask, we're road-weary travelers in need of a good bed and a warm meal." At that, his stomach gave a mewling growl. "Which is true," he added.

"What is your plan?" Christine asked Aidan.

"We're going to stop here so Daniel can recuperate. I've done what I can, but he needs rest." He paused. "You can go wherever you wish from here, I guess."

Before she could answer, he started through the gate. They passed small but sturdy buildings topped with slanted black roofs. Clumps of dirty snow clung to the sides of the roads like wisps of hair on a balding head.

"I'll pay for Daniel's room," Christine said, coming to walk beside Aidan.

"Thank you," Daniel said from Aidan's other side. "My purse has shed almost as much extra skin as I have."

"And I would like to talk to you before you leave," Christine said to Aidan. "There are matters between us that need settling."

He started to object, but her mouth was set. Her eyes dared him to argue.

"Fine," he said. They stopped before a large, two-level building built from oak. The walls bore deep, rippled circles. A sign proclaiming *Ralda's Inn* hung over the entrance. Inside, a fire crackled in a stone hearth along the far wall. The oak's dark coloring made Aidan feel as if he had just stepped into a cozy tree. A slight, short-haired woman served drinks to a group of men sitting around the fire before she bustled over to them.

"I'm Ralda," she said with a pleasant smile that dipped into a frown as she looked Daniel up and down. "I'll dispense with the pleasantries, sir. You look like you could do with a week's worth of sleep."

"We need two rooms, please," Christine said.

Daniel whispered something in Christine's ear. She gave him a steady look and sighed. "And a tankard of your finest drink."

"Ale on the tongue soothes like the sounds of the sea," Ralda said, winking at Daniel.

"I think I love her," he whispered to Aidan.

"You can have two rooms at the end of the hall," Ralda continued.

"Those will be fine," Christine assured her. "I'll be back to pay you once we're settled."

"Very good," Ralda said, squinting at Aidan's face hidden in the shadows of his cloak. He bowed his head lower, nearly touching his chin to his chest.

"Come on," he mumbled.

They moved quickly down the hall and settled Daniel in one of the open rooms.

"Your ale is on the way," Aidan told him. "Can I get you anything else?"

"Only your fine company and finer wit, my fair prince."

Ralda entered with a soft knock, setting a tankard and three mugs on the nightstand near the bed before fixing Aidan with another scrutinizing look. Christine opened her purse and placed half a dozen Torelian crowns in the innkeeper's hands. Ralda stared wide-eyed at the coins, suddenly no longer interested in Aidan at all. She bobbed her head and closed the door behind her.

Daniel stretched out on the bed and watched her go. "I think I'm feeling better."

"Not well enough to chase a skirt," Aidan said. "You need rest." He turned to Christine. "I need some time with my friend."

She stiffened. "All right. I will wait for you in the other room."

"You should go easy on her," Daniel said after the door closed.

"She betrayed us. If it wasn't for her—"

"I'm not denying that," Daniel interrupted. "But she also tried to help me escape. She has some good in her, unlike her brother." Daniel scowled. "By the way, if Garrett's still alive, I'd really like a few words with him."

"He escaped."

Smiling, Daniel leaned back. "Good."

Aidan sat at the foot of the bed. "A lot has happened."

Daniel folded his arms as he listened. After Aidan finished, Daniel cleared his throat. "I'm sorry about your parents. They were good people, and they didn't deserve to die like that."

Aidan nodded.

"What will you do now?" Daniel asked.

"I'm going to take my throne."

"Good plan. And then?"

"Repair the alliance with Darinia."

"And then?"

"I'm going to find Tyrnen. And I'm going to kill him."

"Now *that* is definitely a good idea."

The two friends shared a wide grin, and for a few brief moments, the pressures of the challenges that lay ahead lightened.

"You can't do this alone," Daniel said, sitting up. "What do you need me to do?"

"I need you to get healthy," Aidan said. "I know you want to help, but if you're to be any use to me—"

"Already shuffling your loyal subjects around like toy soldiers,

I see."

"Only the impertinent ones."

Daniel winked. "And after I've gotten plenty of care from the fair Ralda?"

Aidan stared at the ceiling. Avenge his parents, retake the Crown of the North. That was as far as his thinking had extended. "At dawn I leave for Calewind. Rest here for two days, then start home."

"Two days!"

Aidan nodded firmly. "That's non-negotiable. You need to heal, and you won't miss anything exciting. I've got to mend matters with Nichel as soon as possible. Tyrnen tricked her as easily as he tricked me, and my parents. We've got a war to think about, just not against each other."

He hesitated. "There's something else." He unbuckled the Serpent's Fang and set it on the bed between them. "This is Dimitri Thalamahn's sword."

Daniel's mouth dropped opened. "Where did you...?"

"Underneath the cabin. I need to watch over it, but I can't take it back with me. There's a chance Tyrnen could get his hands on it, so I need you to carry it back home."

—This is not a good idea, Charles said.

Yes it is. We can trust him. If not for Daniel, I'd never have made it to the Prophet. He paused. *He's the only friend I have left, Grandfather.*

He heard Charles sigh. *—Very well. I just hope he handles blades more carefully than he handles toy wagons.*

Daniel was leaning forward to inspect the Fang. He reached toward it. Aidan caught his hand.

"There is something you need to understand," Aidan said. "If you touch the sword—"

"—I'll lose my soul and suffer until the end of time, if not longer?"

"Actually, yes."

Daniel pulled back his hand and laced his fingers together, as if to keep them leashed. "What can I do with it, then?"

"Leave it sheathed. Don't remove the cover from the hilt."

Nodding, Daniel reached for it, paused, then grabbed it and shoved it under the bed as if handling a hot coal.

"I'll see it safely to Calewind. I promise," he said, wiping his hands on his trousers. He leaned back on the bed, yawned, and crossed his legs. "What will you do about Christine?"

Aidan tensed. "What do you mean?"

Daniel shrugged. “I meant what I said. She tried to make up for what she did, even tried to stop a bunch of those smelly corpses from pounding on me when Tyrnen showed up. That’s what got her—what do you magical folks call it? Tied? Just give her a chance. Hear her out.”

“I will,” Aidan said, a little too quickly. “Since you think I should, I mean.”

Daniel fixed Aidan with a solemn gaze. “Go forth and conquer, Prince of Passion.”

Aidan left the room in a huff.

Chapter 31

Trust

CHRISTINE WAS SITTING ON her bed when Aidan entered, wincing as she gingerly ran a hand across her chest. She didn't look up. Aidan leaned against the door after it closed, unsure how to proceed.

"You don't need to say anything," she said. She didn't look at him.

"Yes, I do. I just don't know where to begin."

"Then let me start," she said, rising to face him. "I know my betrayal was wrong, and if I could take it back, I would."

Her words stunned him. "You would... take it *back*? Well, I appreciate the sentiment, but that's not possible, is it? Your actions nearly cost Daniel his life. I trusted you."

"I know, and that is important to me. Tell me how I can re-earn it."

All of the sudden, Aidan felt very tired. He had traveled from near the northern peak of Crotaria deep into Sallner, had lost his parents—whom he still hadn't had time to mourn—and been betrayed by his friend and mentor. Now he needed to return home and fight for a birthright he hadn't even wanted.

"Should we even bother with this?" he asked, running a hand over his face. "I'm so tired of fighting, Christine, and I still have so much more fighting to do."

"We *should* bother with this, yes."

"Why?"

She took a step toward him. "Because of what you mean to me, and because of what I think I mean to you."

He stepped away, raising his arms. "I don't know what to say to that. For all I know, you made advances toward me to keep me in one place long enough for Tyrnen to—"

Her face nearly burst into flames. "First you call me a snake. Now you call me a—"

"Well, what would *you* think? You confessed to being hired to track me down. Your brother insisted that Daniel and I stay one more night in Tarion. I almost thought he would tie me to a chair if I refused."

She nodded. "I suppose I can understand your doubt. I can only tell you that I do care, Aidan." She took a breath to continue then winced, holding her ribs.

"What's wrong?" Aidan asked.

Sitting on the bed, she managed a thin smile. "Do you think I decided to bruise my own ribs?"

"I don't understand."

"When Daniel and I tried to escape, Garrett caught us. He nearly beat Daniel to death. It wouldn't have taken much to finish your friend off. He had suffered much already at my brother's hands. I tried to stop him, but without magic..." She shrugged.

His eyes softened. "I didn't know."

She rubbed gingerly at her ribs. "Maybe you're right. Maybe we've been through too much. If you don't believe that I care for you, maybe we should—"

"I care, too, Christine. Kahltan help me, but I do."

He sat down beside her and took a few moments to put his words together. "I was running from my family. Well, I thought they were my family." He shook his head. "Tyrnen and my *parents* wanted me to help orchestrate a war I didn't believe in. I chose the path of least resistance. You know the rest. What I did at Sharem was... It was horrible. *I* was horrible."

"You were tricked. It wasn't your fault."

Shaking his head, Aidan stood and walked to the window. "No. I mean, he did, but that doesn't matter. I should have known better. It's like you said: the Torelians are just one group of people under my care. What I did at Sharem can never be forgiven."

He heard the bed creak as she stood. A moment later, her hand rested on his back. Her touch was tentative, as if afraid he might turn around and bite her. When he didn't tense or shrug her away, the hand moved up to settle on his shoulder.

"Then what will returning home prove?" she asked.

He turned to her. She did not remove her hand. "I must return because the creature sitting on the Crown of the North is not my mother."

He told her everything. "I need to take back my family's kingdom and slay the creatures impersonating the two people I loved most in the world," he finished. His eyes went flat. "And I need to confront Tyrnen."

"For vengeance, or because the realms depend on your victory?"

"Both," he admitted.

She looked away and withdrew her hand. "I am so sorry for my part in all of this, Aidan." She folded her arms and tried to step away, but Aidan caught her hand.

"Did you suspect Tyrnen of any duplicity?"

"No. Retrieving you was a job." She poked him and barked a humorless laugh. "And a fine-paying one, too."

"Exactly," Aidan said. "You did not know he intended to use you, just as I never suspected him of using me."

"But I made my own choices, just like you."

"Yes. And like me, you recognized your mistakes and tried to make up for them."

She looked at his hand holding hers, back up to him. "That is why you are a good man. I care for you, Aidan Gairden. And I intend to see you alive through this."

Aidan nodded, then put one hand on the flat of her chest above her breasts, mumbling under his breath. His other hand gripped Heritage. She blinked at his boldness—though she did nothing to remove his hand—then gasped as icy relief seeped into her battered chest. Aidan prayed again, and again Christine shuddered. The chill turned to warmth as it leaked into the pit of her stomach. It dwindled away after a few seconds, and as she opened her eyes, it was as though a world she had known and loved for so long was no longer separated from her by a vast ocean.

"Did you...?" she began.

Aidan nodded and dropped onto the bed. "I trust you, Christine."

Kindling, she gave an excited giggle as a small ring of flames danced between her hands. "Thank you," she whispered. The flames blinked out of existence, and she walked to the bed to stand over him. "Do you trust me?" she asked.

"I already said I—"

"I need to hear it again," she said, her tone insistent. "It's important, Aidan. Please."

"I trust you, Christine."

She lowered herself onto his lap, kissing him softly at first, then harder as he returned her kiss.

Heritage buzzed at Aidan's waist.

—I think this might be an appropriate time for us to leave you in peace, Charles said.

"Wonderful," he murmured.

Aidan untangled his body from Christine's as dawn lit the window. He slipped from the bed, then tugged the blankets over her. Dressing, Aidan crossed to the door then turned back to look at her. Her breathing was slow and steady. One bare leg stuck out from the covers. He stared at it, his heartbeat accelerating as he remembered her touch, how she had—

—She will return with Daniel, I'm sure, Charles said. *Right now your focus must be on retaking Sunfall.*

He slipped into the hall and closed the door, cutting her off from view. He resisted the urge to bolt back in and be with her again. Striding down the hall toward the common room, Aidan donned his hood, slowing at the sound of voice in the corridor.

"... come to say goodbye?" Ralda was saying. Aidan paused near the room's entryway, listening.

"Aye," a man said in return. "Orders came last night by messenger."

"I saw him," Ralda said bitterly. "He came in for a drink. Almost had him thrown out."

"Now, Ralda," another man said in a soothing tone. "It's not his fault. He looked just as sour about it as I did."

"I know," she admitted. "It isn't fair, that's all I'm saying."

"General Calderon and the Crown of the North need more men," a third voice said. "And with the pay they're offering, we'd be fools to pass up the opportunity."

"A purse full of gold's worth more than your life, is it, Harold?" Ralda's tone had taken a scolding edge. "This war's foolish. You said so yourself not even a week ago."

"And I still believe it," Harold answered. "But the farm's not doing well, and I'm not a sailor. I need the money, Ralda, plain and simple."

"You make it seem as if going to war is our choice, Ralda," one man said softly.

"The fighting's getting serious, that's what he told me," she said. "You know there's a chance none of you will come home."

"That it is. We're supposed to invade Darinia by the week's end," Harold said.

Silence answered him, broken only by the sounds of shuffling feet and mugs scraping against the counter top.

"Excuse me," Aidan said, stepping into view. Everyone turned to look at him. His face was concealed within his cloak.

"What can we do for you?" one spoke up at last.

"I couldn't help but overhear that you were joining Torel's Ward."

"We are indeed," one said. "And I reckon you are yourself."

"Of course. We invade Darinia by week's end, then?"

“That’s what we heard,” another said. “Right through Sharem, we’ll go. Others’ll be taking ships across the Avivan.”

“Torelian ships?” Aidan asked.

The man called Harold snorted. “Not unless you fancy walking along the bottom of the river. No, these are Leastonian ships,” the man finished, a mark of pride in his voice.

“The merchants’ guild sided with the Crown?” Aidan asked, amazed.

Another man shrugged. “Seems that’s way. Call to arms came just last night.”

“That’s why we’re leaving immediately,” another put in.

“Aye,” Harold said with a nod. “The threat of treason is as compelling as the Torelian coin.”

“Like what happened to Aidan.”

“*Prince* Aidan,” one corrected, drawing a deep harrumph from his friend.

“Not a prince anymore, is he?”

“Maybe not, but you still need to show respect toward—”

Aidan appreciated the man sticking up for him but didn’t wait around to offer his thanks. He crossed the common room in three long strides, bursting through the door and into the Lady’s light.

Chapter 32

Homecoming

AIDAN PLUNGED ACROSS THE continent, shifting from village to hilltop to city to plains like a stone skipping across water. He alternated between kindling from his lamp and the Lady's warm, springtime light. He rested at night, but never inside walls where anyone might recognize his face and bring Wardsmen or worse down on him. Heat bubbles stitched from the light of his lamp were his blanket, the hollows of tree trunks his bed. Each night he forced his eyes shut and tried to push away thoughts of what awaited him at Sunfall, and to keep a quick but reasonable pace. He felt fully rejuvenated from his mad jump from Sharem to Sunfall, and he knew he would need every scrap of strength he could muster to confront Tyrnen and the harbingers.

Closing his eyes did him no good. The anxiousness that plagued his every step took root deep in the back of his mind and grew into monolithic fear that chased him through his dreams. He saw Tyrnen blast away his mother's legs, and her look of fear as she scrabbled away from him on her hands. He saw the harbingers peel away the faces of his parents to reveal their puckered eye sockets and fleshy bars over their mouths.

On the morning of the fourth day, Aidan no longer needed to look out over the horizon and pick a spot to land from his shift. He knew where he was. He popped into existence in the woods a league south of Calewind, the very trees he had considered fleeing to on the morning of his birthday. Squinting, he saw forms in snow-white armor patrolling the walls and manning the pylons tucked into each corner of the city. He sipped light from his lamp and shifted just outside the tower he had crossed through on that fateful morning so many weeks ago, appearing in the lee of a stack of crates piled against the wall. A vendor's stand stood in front of him. The wiry merchant himself juggled his wares in front of his booth, shouting prices to tempt passersby.

Aidan took a breath, pulled his hood low, and slid from the shadows and around the stand to slip into the traffic flowing through the south district. Feet and carriages churned away the last traces of snow and mush along the smoothly paved cobblestone. Vendors held up their wares from storefronts, proclaiming springtime sales and promising more goods once Leastonian merchants took to the roads again.

Frowning, Aidan glanced around. At first, winding through the capital city's boulevards had helped him to relax. Calewind's maze of shops and homes were as familiar to him as Sunfall's dustiest rear passageways. Despite the dangers lying in wait for him, he was home. Now, though, something did not feel quite right. Unease settled over him like a too-heavy cloak. He heard shouts of vendors, the steady clomp of horse hooves, the creak of wagons rolling down roads. He did not hear the babble of voices that always filled the marketplace like the constant chatter of a stream running over rocks.

He looked around. The people scuttled more than walked, hustling to where they needed to go, and practically tripped from their haste to get inside. They kept their eyes to the ground, ignoring the calls of vendors and never stopping to talk to friends from far off who had not made the trip to the capital since the wind had grown chill. The few who did stop exchanged only a few words and spoke under their breath as if afraid of being overheard.

Aidan rounded a corner and collided with a man coming from the opposite direction. Out of habit he looked up to apologize, only to drop his eyes and hurry on. It was a Wardsman. Nine other Wardsmen fanned out around him. Frowning, Aidan stepped behind a shop and examined the group. Passersby edged around them like water cutting around a large rock. Each man carried a shield emblazoned with a family crest; the other fist gripped spear or sword. They strode through the crowd, eyes set straight ahead.

"Don't even watch where they're walking," came a growl at his side. Aidan turned to find the shopkeeper whose establishment he'd ducked into standing beside him and staring after the departing party with a baleful expression.

"Why are they out in such large numbers?" Aidan asked, adjusting his hood.

"Are you a fool?" The man spit as he flicked away a tuft of hair. "The war, man. Orders direct from the Crown. She says the streets are dangerous, though I ain't seen nothin' to account for harassing people the way some of them do." He snorted and huffed back into his shop.

The merchant didn't seem to be the only one unhappy with the armed Wardsmen. All around him furtive glares stabbed at armored backs. Those who looked up to where Sunfall sat narrowed their eyes and quickly looked away, as if the palace might suddenly pounce on them.

Aidan's stride quickened. His stomach churned. He was home. The reality of what that meant sank in like a stone. He had to confront Tyrnen and the impostors, but how? He could not just walk up to Sunfall and ask for an audience. He—

"... have to pay for that like everyone else."

Aidan turned toward the voice. His eyes found a rotund man standing in front of an apple cart. The vendor's face was bright red. Across from him was a Wardsman. He leaned against the cart, smirking as he bounced an apple on his palm.

"Surely an exception can be made for a loyal member of Torel's Ward," he said. Some of the Wardsmen with him looked a bit uncomfortable. Some wore amused or excited smiles, like wolves watching prey that had not yet realized it was cornered.

"I'm as loyal as the next man," the merchant replied, "but I've also got a family to feed."

"And one apple will put your family on the streets, will it?"

"It might, 'specially during these times," the man replied. "I preserved those apples through the whole winter. They—"

"Perhaps you should join up," the Wardsman said. "The sooner we rub all those wildlanders into the ground, the sooner your worm-ridden fruit may turn a profit."

The vendor went pale. "I wouldn't fight in the Crown's foolish war if it would save my own mother."

The Wardsman straightened as if struck. "Foolish?" he repeated, tossing the apple aside. His fellows tensed; the ones who had been watching in amusement looked eager.

"That's right," the vendor replied. "And I wouldn't serve in the Ward for all the gold in—"

The Wardsman's sharp backhand sent the man staggering. He gaped at them, one quivering hand touching his cheek.

"You'd better watch what you say, friend," the Wardsman said. "One might think you were speaking treason. We know what happens to those who speak out against the Crown."

Aidan heard his name sweep through the crowd in nervous whispers.

Suddenly the merchant spit in the Wardsman's face. The nervous whispering ceased.

"Kahltan take you," the vendor croaked, "and Annalyn, and her damn war, too."

The Wardsman's face darkened. He lunged and grabbed two

fistfuls of the man's collar. A few men in the assemblage raised their voices in protest, but fell silent when other Wardsmen drew steel.

Aidan was not so easily cowed. He pushed his way through the crowd and shoved the Wardsman away from the trembling vendor.

"Don't touch him," he said. Instantly he was aware of every gaze in the growing crowd locking on to him. What he did not realize was that his brisk march forward had pulled his hood from his head.

"An accomplice to treason, are you?" the Wardsman asked, then cut off with a strangled gasp.

"This man was being bullied," Aidan said. "Everyone here saw it."

"You," the Wardsman whispered. The crowd inched away, murmuring. Aidan again heard his name pass through dozens of lips in tones of fear—and another tone, one he didn't recognize.

"Well, well, well," the Wardsman said, confidence replacing his initial shock. "Aidan Gairden. Welcome home. Things have changed since you ran off, boy. The biggest change of all being the price on your head."

"I am here to settle things with my... parents," Aidan replied. "You will take me to them. Now."

For the first time the Wardsman appeared unsure. Glancing around, he straightened. "You will come with us," he said loudly. "As our prisoner." He stepped forward.

"Do not lay a hand on me." Aidan's hand rested easily on the hilt of Heritage.

—Don't hurt him, Charles said. *He is an ass, but he is also a man of the Crown.*

I want *to hurt him,* Aidan sent back. *But I won't.*

The Wardsman drew back, hesitant. The crowd watched in silence. "Very well," he said, not as assertively as before. "If you would please—"

At that moment all heads turned toward a ruckus from up the street. Columns of Wardsmen mounted on armored horses draped with caparisons of striking colors marched ten abreast down the street toward Calewind's southern gate. The crowd parted like a curtain, hugging storefronts and dropping back into alleyways to make room for the force. *This must be the force leaving for Darinia,* Aidan thought. Then he noticed the figure at the head of the procession, and his mind went blank.

Tyrnen led the sinuous column that wrapped through Calewind's streets and up the mountain pass that led to Sunfall.

Aidan's mouth went dry. He was unable to move, barely able to breathe. A flurry of emotions whipped through him. Part of him wanted to cry out in rage, to ask why the old man he had loved had betrayed him so viciously and completely. Another part of him loved the old man still, and wanted nothing more than to shut himself away in Tyrnen's tower and drink hot cocoa while Tyrnen told stories.

He watched Tyrnen lean over to speak to the man riding beside him. No, not a man, Aidan realized as his father nodded and straightened, sweeping a cold gaze over the people huddled along the street. The harbinger wore Edmund Calderon's face, but that *thing* was not Edmund the Valorous, General of Torel's Ward. It was *not* his father.

Aidan remained standing in the center of the road, lips drawn together, one hand gripping the hilt of Heritage hard enough to stamp imprints of jewels and grooves into his palm. At first the Eternal Flame seemed not to recognize Aidan.

"Get out of the way," the old man shouted at him. Then he drew his horse up and gaped. Noticing Aidan, Edmund's face went hard. He shouted the command to halt. The order echoed down the columns behind them. Horses snorted into the silence.

"So you've come home," the impostor said. His voice carried down the still, silent street. Aidan said nothing, glaring at the creature seated atop his father's horse, wearing his father's armor and face.

"Have you had a change of heart, son?"

"You are not my father."

The harbinger's eyes narrowed. "No, I am not. Not anymore. Aidan Gairden, you are under arrest for treason. You will surrender yourself to—"

Aidan's hands burst from beneath his cloak. He kindled and whispered a prayer for pure-fire, wanting nothing more than to see the impostor burning and screaming until he became a pile of melted flesh and bones.

—*Watch out!* Charles cried.

Tyrnen's hands had appeared, too. Aidan turned to the Eternal Flame, swallowing his first prayer and forming a new one. Too late. A sharp pain gripped his chest, spread down into his gut. He winced as tears formed in his eyes. It felt as if claws were rending his stomach. Desperately he tried to draw light again, but the Lady's light did not soak through his skin to heat his blood. He had been tied.

The sword, he remembered. His ripped Heritage from his

scabbard just as something crashed into his side and drove him to the street. Air left his lungs in a great whoosh. Heritage flew from his hands and skittered to a stop in front of the Eternal Flame. Aidan struggled in the arms of his attacker—the Wardsman who had bullied the apple vendor, he saw—as hard as he could, but the other man was bigger, stronger. The Wardsman wrenched his arms behind his back, strung thick cords between his hands, and hauled him to his feet.

The Edmund-harbinger stepped down from its horse and came to stand before the sword-bearer. Aidan's eyes radiated hatred. The harbinger smiled and slapped Aidan across the face. At Sharem, the harbinger had slapped him with a bare palm. Now it wore a gauntlet. Pain exploded across Aidan's face. Tears filled his vision. He felt warm blood run down his nose, over his lips, dribble down his chin.

The harbinger turned back to Tyrnen. It was clear to Aidan—and everyone else, judging by the uneasy muttering that had broken out—that the king and general of the north was waiting for the Eternal Flame to tell him what to do next. The old man gave a barely perceptible nod, his eyes seeming to hover on Aidan's chest. Reaching below Aidan's collar, the harbinger grabbed the chain that held his lamp and tore, shattering the chain and raining links to the street. It pocketed the lamp then climbed back onto its mount.

"A lesson," it said, its voice ringing through the assemblage, "to any who would speak out against the war or my wife." It looked down into Aidan's eyes as it continued. "You have committed treason for the last time, boy. Aidan Gairden's trial shall be carried out when the Lady takes her leave this evening, in the west courtyard of Sunfall. Let it be known that the punishment for those found guilty of treason is death."

"Your Majesty," the Wardsman holding Aidan said. He straightened as the harbinger's gaze fell upon him. "That man," he gestured with his head to the terrified apple merchant who was attempting to melt into the crowd, "also spoke out against the war with Darinia."

"Did he?" the harbinger said coolly.

The Wardsman bobbed his head.

"Arrest him," the harbinger said. A Wardsman detached himself from the throng and tied the vendor's arms behind his back. The vendor gibbered, his face ashen and covered in sweat.

The harbinger turned and signaled. After a few moments, Brendon Greagor emerged and steered his horse to a stop beside his commander. “Continue the march to Sharem,” the creature commanded. “The Eternal Flame and I will join you after matters here have been settled.”

Brendon nodded, casting a quick glance at Aidan. A fleeting look of regret flashed across the man’s face. Then it was gone. He returned to the head of the column, barking orders as he went.

“You!” the harbinger bellowed at a Wardsman standing near the mouth of an alleyway. The man stiffened and bowed low, fastening his gaze to the ground.

“Your Majesty?” he asked.

The harbinger pointed at Heritage. “Pick up the sword.”

The man did as commanded.

“My son stole that blade from his mother. I am certain she will be most pleased to see it returned. You, and you, and you,” the harbinger continued, thrusting his finger at three other Wardsmen. “Go with him. Do not stop until the sword reaches the throne room.”

The Wardsman holding Heritage nodded, head still bowed, and fell in with the three other men heading toward Sunfall. The harbinger turned back to Aidan and the vendor. A humorless smile split his face.

“Take them to the depths.”

As the troop holding Heritage disappeared around a bend, Aidan watched his last hope vanish with them.

Chapter 33

Choices

THE DEPTHS WERE LESS a dungeon and more a pit, a hole in the ground dug six hundred years ago while construction of a proper prison in Calewind was finished. No Crown of the North had used it since then. Aidan, it appeared, warranted special treatment. Torches hanging high above the cells that ran along either wall lit a dim, flickering path down the center of the aisle. Water dripped from the mossy ceiling into puddles. The stench of mold permeated the air, seeping into the stained walls and broken, uneven floor. Mold, and worse. Bodies. Waste. Death.

The Wardsman fumbled with a large set of iron keys and finally threw open a cell door. The rusted bars squeaked open.

"Get in," the Wardsman said, shoving the apple vendor inside. He slammed the door and pulled Aidan further down the passage. When he stopped, Aidan peered into the cell across from the one his captor was unlocking. Aidan barely recognized the man huddled in one corner.

"Cotak?" Aidan breathed. The clan chief who had been captured on the day his parents—on the day the *harbingers*—declared war looked as wasted as the ruins Aidan had passed on his trek through Sallner. Cotak's eyes were glassy and vacant, like a vagrant's. His skin drooped from his bones like loose clothing. Flies buzzed over the waste heaped around Cotak. Others swarmed over still forms shoved into the corners of adjacent cells. The clansmen that had accompanied Cotak.

"In you go," the Wardsman said cheerfully, steering Aidan to the cell across from the clan chief's. Aidan entered wordlessly, turning when he reached the far wall to slide to the ground with a soft thud. The Wardsman slammed the door closed and strode from the room. The single door in and out of the depths boomed shut, leaving Aidan with the crackling torches and the steady drip of water plopping into puddles for company.

Aidan squeezed his eyes shut. Every Wardsman up above knew of his capture by now. Even if he made it out of the depths, there was no way he could possibly get to the throne room. He leaned his head back against the wall. *I've failed them. I've failed them all.*

"You're a hero, you know."

Aidan raised his head. The voice came from the merchant's cell down the passage.

"A lot of us common folk support what you did, leaving Torel in protest," the merchant went on. "Wish I'd had the courage to do the same."

Aidan smiled sadly. "It didn't do me any good."

The merchant snorted. "People remember how a man died. You stood against this war, said out loud what everyone else is thinking."

"You stood against it, too. I heard what you said."

"I shouldn't have said anything."

"Why not? You just said you respected me for—"

"Who's going to care for my family? I should've kept my mouth shut."

Aidan sat forward, hugging his knees to his chest. "Neither of us should have to die for this."

"True enough." The merchant fell silent.

Aidan's head thudded back against the wall. *I'm sorry, Grandfather.*

—You can't give up yet, Charles replied. *We can't see what's happening; the Wardsman draped something over the Eye. It's up to you. You must keep trying to—*

The entrance door banged open. Footsteps entered and stopped in front of Cotak's cell.

"Out you go, wildlander."

Cotak did not put up a struggle. He let the Wardsman haul him to his feet and drag him down the passage to the merchant's cell.

"Not too late to give me that apple," the Wardsman said. The merchant did not reply.

Keys jangled and the cell door creaked open. After a few moments, three pairs of footsteps made their way to the exit. Aidan heard the Wardsman mumble something. A moment later, the door closed, but lighter footfalls made their way slowly back to Aidan's cell. A small flame hovering above an old, wizened palm floated into view. Tyrnen stopped in front of Aidan's cell and folded his arms behind his back. The flame continued to dance in the air, sending shadows flitting along the walls.

The Eternal Flame chuckled as he shook his head. "I spend

over a month looking for you, chasing you, and what do you do? You just... come back home. Your mother and I thought you were smarter than that, boy."

"That *thing* is not my mother."

"Maybe not. But as far as everyone else is concerned, that thing *is* your mother, and that is enough." Tyrnen pursed his lips. "It didn't have to be like this, you know. You could have followed orders, did as you were told. But you decided you knew better." His eyes trembled inside their sockets. "You could have had it all, Aidan! But you chose to go against me."

"I chose to take control."

"And look at what that brought you." Tyrnen's beard rustled as he shook his head. "We could have ruled Crotaria together."

"I don't want to rule Crotaria."

"And what is it you do want, now that you're a big boy who can think for himself?"

"I want my kingdom back—the kingdom you stole from me. More than anything, I'd fancy your head on the tip of my sword."

Tyrnen's jaw quivered. "And what sword would that be, boy? Heritage? I think not. My faith in you was misplaced, it would seem. That blade is of no more use to you than it is to me, or anyone else on Crotaria. I waited so long for you to become the sword-bearer, convinced myself that—"

"I *am* the sword-bearer, Tyrnen."

"Oh?" the old man said, sounding amused. "Says who, boy? You?"

"The Prophet," Aidan replied.

Tyrnen's eyes narrowed.

"The Prophet," Aidan said again, pronouncing each syllable clearly as if the old man were deaf. "I am your opposite, Mathias. I am the Champion of Peace."

Tyrnen drew back with a hiss. "That can't be."

"Why do you think I took Heritage with me?"

"You're lying!"

"Bring me my sword," Aidan said flatly, "and I'll prove it to you."

Tyrnen's lips worked soundlessly for a moment. Abruptly his eyes glazed over. Then he reached into his robe and withdrew Terror's Hand. Aidan stared at the scepter, transfixed. Everything in his periphery disappeared. His grandfather's voice, asking him why he'd suddenly gone silent, disappeared like water swirling down a drain.

"Touch it, boy," Tyrnen said softly. Hesitantly, Aidan

extended his hand. The scepter shook in Tyrnen's grasp. "Touch it, and—"

He cut off with a grunt as Aidan's hand suddenly snatched his robes and pulled him forward, slamming his face into the bars. With a strangled curse, Tyrnen clawed at Aidan's grip, digging long, yellow nails into his flesh. Aidan flung him away and Tyrnen stumbled back, smoothing his robes.

"We could have had everything," the Eternal Flame said. Aidan was surprised to see tears in the old man's eyes. Terror's Hand dangled in limp fingers. "But you fought me. You railed against what was best for you."

"At least I fought," Aidan wheezed, straightening painfully, one hand wrapped around his aching middle. "I saw your eyes, Tyrnen." He gestured to the scepter. "You weren't intending for me to touch that. It was *her* idea."

Tyrnen looked at the scepter and blinked as if surprised he held it. It disappeared within his robe.

Aidan began to laugh softly.

Tyrnen's visage darkened. "What is so amusing, boy?"

"You, Tyrnen. You condemn the choice I made that day at Sharem, and the choices I've made since then. But do you know something? *I* made them. For better or worse, no matter the consequences, I made them. They were mine. When was the last time you made a choice? Eight hundred years ago, I suspect. It's sad, really. I resisted, my mother resisted. Did you show that golden rod to Christine, too? I bet you did. You seem to be the only person in eight hundred years who was stupid enough to actually touch that thing."

A growl rose from deep in Tyrnen's throat. He took a step forward, then hesitated.

Aidan's eyes widened. "You're afraid of me." It wasn't a question.

"Afraid of you?" Tyrnen laughed, but the sound was hollow. "You don't have that damned sword, and I've tied you. I could kill you right here."

"So go ahead," Aidan said. "There's nothing stopping you. I don't have my sword, and I can't draw light." He smiled. "Or are you going to give me another scary dream instead? How did you do that, anyway? Shift away, I mean. You know about the wards set to prevent anyone from shifting in or out of Sunfall. Luria must be powerful indeed. That's good. At least selling your soul gained you something."

Tyrnen bared his teeth in a smile. "The shadows hold many

secrets. Not that your Lady would permit you to so much as glimpse them."

Aidan blinked. Tyrnen laughed, obviously mistaking his former pupil's dawning realization for confusion, but Aidan ignored him. *Of course*, Aidan thought. *He rode the shadows away, just like I rode them through the tunnels.* All at once, the power of dark magic awed and terrified him. The tunnels were only a formality, a way for thieves and spies to move around unseen. A man could, conceivably, step into one shadow and emerge from any other, like a doorway that opened anywhere.

"I gave you every opportunity," Tyrnen said. Aidan saw triumph in the old man's eyes. "But you've failed me time and time again. She—*I* have decided that there is no further use for you. You will be made an example of to all who would defy Lur—who would stand against this war. You will die today, boy."

Tyrnen strode from the depths and slammed the door behind him. The flame he'd created winked out.

Aidan let out a breath, relieved that Tyrnen had finally left. An idea had come to him. He looked toward the darkest corner of his cell—and knew immediately that it wouldn't work. The glow of torchlight from across the aisle lapped the bars of his cell like a low tide. It was faint, yet strong enough to push back the gloom and reveal a hint of grimy stone walls everywhere he looked. He intuited that he needed unfiltered darkness to ride the shadows far enough to escape, just as he needed a moderate source of light to shift a respectable distance. And wouldn't he also need to select a pocket of shadows as his destination? He assumed that was so.

He straightened, resolved. *I tried,* he told himself. But he hadn't. His mind recalled the prayer he had shared with Kahltan. The idea of wrapping his tongue around those words, of twisting the Language of Light into something terrible, sent a chill through him.

Shoving the thought away, Aidan went to the bars and peered out.

I need to get out of here.

—*Yes*, Charles agreed.

"But how?" he said into the silence.

Suddenly a grinding sound came from his left. Aidan stood and peered between the bars to see two large stones parting. Daylight filtered through, lifting some of the gloom from the depths. A Wardsman crawled through, a lantern held in one hand, his face hidden by his helmet and the gloom. Aidan squinted, straining to make out the newcomer's face as the moving chunks in the wall slid back into place.

"You're the Wardsman from the street," he said, surprised. "The one who retrieved my sword." *For a moment, he looked almost exactly like...*

The Wardsman removed his helmet before raising his head. Now Aidan could see his face clearly. Contempt bubbled inside him. It was the harbinger who wore his father's life like a mask.

To Aidan's utter amazement, the man raised his head to face him. His eyes shimmered behind a blurry veil of tears.

"My son," Edmund Calderon finally said. His voice broke, and he wept.

Chapter 34

A Visitor

THE HARBINGER LOOKED AWAY and pulled itself under control. Aidan took a step back from the cell door, frowning. *He's a fake*, he reminded himself, caught off-guard by the uncharacteristic display of affection. His father—his *real* father—had been a solemn man in public, but had never hesitated to show his emotions in private. What sort of play was the harbinger attempting, breaking down in front of him now? And why had he changed into Wardsman's armor?

—*What's happening?* Charles asked.

'Father' stopped by for a visit.

"I know what this looks like," the harbinger began, running a hand over his face. "But I swear to you—"

"Your word means nothing. Do what you came to do, or be gone."

Edmund's left hand clenched around the hilt of the sword at his waist. Aidan studied the movement. It was familiar; Edmund habitually clutched Valor's hilt, and always with his left hand.

"I should have known Tyrnen intended my trial to be a farce," Aidan said. "Are you here to kill me, then?"

Edmund tugged on his sword, the blade hissing against the sheath as it retracted, and held it up for Aidan's inspection. His eyes were immediately drawn to the word etched into the flat of the blade, a word carved by his father's own hand. *Valor*.

Aidan went numb. He remembered his reaction when his grandfather had said that Edmund's soul had not entered Heritage. Could it be...? Then he stiffened at a sudden thought.

"That doesn't prove anything," he said. "You stole it. You stole every aspect of his life. You're nothing but a—"

Edmund nodded, and that surprised Aidan most of all. This impersonator seemed willing to accept his doubt, and accept it calmly. A far cry from the hostility and disgust the creature had displayed toward him since Tyrnen had set this whole farce into motion.

Edmund slid Valor back into its sheath and absently fingered the hilt. "On your birthday," he began. His voice was scratchy, an instrument only just removed from its dusty case after years of neglect. "On your birthday, I was so proud as I watched you walk toward me, and when you reached the throne, I whispered something in your ear as I pulled you close. I said, 'Happy birthday.' Do you remember what I said next?"

Aidan stayed silent. He remembered. What was important was that his *father* remembered.

"I said, 'I am so proud of the man you are, and the man I know you will become.'" He smiled. "Does that sound about right, Prince of Mischief?"

A lump welled in Aidan's throat. He scrubbed at his eyes, blinking as if waking from a long, deep sleep. His father was still there, slumped against the cell door, travel-stained, scarred, bruised, and looking exhausted—but it *was* his father. The harbinger would not have bothered sneaking in through some secret entrance to see him. But that was not how he knew for certain. Edmund's eyes told the truth. The eyes of harbingers and vagrants were glassy, devoid of life. Edmund's eyes shone with emotion and vitality. With life.

—What's happening? Charles asked.

My father is alive, Aidan sent back, reeling from a battery of emotions. Elation. Confusion. Amazement. Hope.

—Aidan, you cannot allow yourself to be fooled by these impostors.

Aidan reached through the cell door to touch his father's face. Carefully he pinched at the skin, tugged at it. It did not pull away like a veil. *It's him, Grandfather,* he thought, joy warming him in a way the Lady's light never could and burning away the last of his doubts. *It's really him!*

Edmund did not seem to mind being prodded. He let his hands settle on the younger man's shoulders.

"How did you survive?" Aidan asked. "I saw what happened at Lake Carrean. The vagrants—"

"Vagrants?" Edmund interrupted. "That's what those creatures are called?"

"I saw them overwhelm you. I used a spell to review a memory Mother extracted from your mind before Tyrnen... Before he..."

Edmund's eyes grew stony. "You remember the night of your birthday? The conversation we had?"

Aidan nodded, though he wished he could forget.

"Tyrnen was waiting for me when I left the sword chamber,"

Edmund said. "I didn't know it was him, at first. Someone leaped out from behind a corner and grabbed me before I could react. The next thing I knew, I was on Lake Carrean's shore. I fought off those... vagrants. Then your mother..." He looked away, shaking his head. "The next thing I knew, I was being dragged by my arms through the woods. The man dragging me... it was me. Or at least, it *looked* like me."

"A harbinger," Aidan said. "Like a vagrant, but a Touched."

Edmund's brow rose. "That explains what happened next. I didn't want the... the harbinger to know I'd regained consciousness. Not that I could see much, anyway. My eyes were almost swelled shut, and my entire body was a mass of pain. It stabbed me, the harbinger. I guess I passed out from blood loss. I don't know how far we walked. I stayed quiet and still. I had little strength and knew I had to bide my time. Finally we stopped. The harbinger pulled me to my knees and said... dreadful things. While it talked, it slowly drew its sword. I lunged for it and swung. The harbinger disappeared into thin air, but I felt my weapon connect with something solid just before it vanished, like a practice dummy that I couldn't see."

Edmund smiled grimly. "The harbinger reappeared almost instantly. Its mouth hung open, and its head slid off its body. And it rotted right there in front of me, like it had been dead for months."

He cleared his throat. "I staggered back to the cabin, and when I got there, I saw your mother." His voice shook as he continued. "They'd just left her there, like discarded firewood. I wanted to come for you right then. I didn't know if you were still at Sunfall—I prayed to the Lady that you weren't—but I knew I had to find you. I went into the cabin and patched myself up, but it was days before I could travel. I got to Calewind as quickly as I was able, but talk was that you'd denounced the war and left. So, I stayed out of sight, figuring you'd come back eventually.

"I'm sorry, son," he said, unable to look at Aidan. "I wish I could have prevented all this." He swallowed hard. "I wish I could have saved her." His voice broke, and he looked away.

"It's all right, Father."

Suddenly the door flew open and the leering Wardsman who had arrested Aidan strode into the room. He jerked to a halt when he noticed the visitor standing before Aidan's cell.

"Who are you?" the Wardsman said, squinting in the room's dim light.

"Just wanted to pay my last respects to the prince," Edmund

said gruffly, keeping his face in the shadows.

The Wardsman's eyes narrowed further. "I didn't see you come by the desk."

"That's probably because you're usually not there when you're supposed to be, Lew."

"What are you—"

"Do you want me to tell the general that you're always leaving your post to get a bit of necking time with your Samantha?"

Lew paled. "There's no need—"

"There'll *be* need, unless you mind your own affairs. I'll be back out in a bit. Why don't you try to stay at a post for more than fifteen minutes at a time, eh?"

Lew stiffened and strode from the room, slamming the door behind him.

Determination lit Edmund's eyes. "We haven't much time, son. I couldn't help your mother, but I'll kneel at the feet of Kahltan himself if I fail you."

"Wait," Aidan said. "Much has happened." He gave his father a condensed version of events since Tyrnen had lured Edmund and Annalyn from Sunfall.

"What's our plan?" Edmund asked when Aidan finished. The question took Aidan by surprise. His father was looking to him to lead. Could he do that?

Keys jangled in the door.

Aidan bit off a curse. "I need Heritage."

"I had to take it to the throne room," Edmund said as he quickly rose and made his way toward the wall through which he had entered. "Long story. But I'll get it back."

"Good. Make your way to the west courtyard once you've retrieved it."

"Do you have a plan?"

"Of course," Aidan lied.

The stones began to slide open again, the grinding covered by the creak of the opening door. His father rose and moved stiffly through the opening. The limp was slight, but it made Aidan sad—and angry. His father had defeated every vagrant that had stood against him, but at high cost. His wounds had not been properly treated and would likely have permanent effects. Edmund the Valorous, whose fighting prowess and dexterity had been compared to Ambrose Gairden's, would never move the same way again.

Tyrnen was as responsible for Edmund's injuries as he was for Annalyn's death. One more debt the old man would pay.

The stones slid closed, safely hiding Edmund from view. Filled with hope, the sword-bearer turned his attention to his newest visitor. The face of Edmund Calderon leered at him from the other side of the bars, his lips peeled back to bare his teeth.

"We've time yet before your trial begins, Prince of Tears," the Edmund-harbinger said. Reaching to its waist, it withdrew a set of keys, turned one in Aidan's door, and stalked in, tossing the keys up and catching them. "I thought we might talk for a bit. Just the two of us."

Chapter 35

Trial

EDMUND WOUND HIS WAY through the sneak tunnels that crisscrossed beneath Crotaria. He smiled as he went along. The labyrinth, and the band of thieves who maintained it, were two of Leaston's best-kept secrets. He remembered telling Aidan bedtime stories about gangs of thieves that could pop up anywhere at any time. His son had lit up with wonder and curiosity. Edmund could not wait to see his son's face when he revealed that the tunnels were quite real, and quite useful.

Normally, marks on the wall guided travelers from one hub to another. But there were a few secret passages among the secret passages, unmarked tunnels that led to places of great convenience across Crotaria. Like Sunfall's throne room, for example. Only Gairdens and high-ranking officers in the Ward knew of that particular tunnel. Edmund had considered informing Tyrnen some years back—the Eternal Flame would surely find such information useful—but Annalyn had convinced him that some secrets should stay in the family.

Like Heritage, now as good as in the hands of the beast impersonating his wife. He had wanted to hide away and give Heritage to Aidan in the depths, but he hadn't been able to do that while in a party of other Wardsmen. He had considered shaking them off his trail, and roughly. But that would have attracted the worst kind of attention. Besides, those men were *his* men. They had no part in what Tyrnen and his undead were doing.

At that, black thoughts swept through him. He pushed them away. Revenge would come later. Right now, his son needed his blade.

—Aidan.

Yes, Grandfather?

—Will you please tell us what's happening?

The Edmund-harbinger is leading me to my trial, from what I can tell.

—From what you can tell?

He put a hood over my head. I can't see anything.

—You seem rather calm about all of this.

Aidan was glad his grandfather thought so. The truth was he was having a great deal of trouble thinking of anything besides the stabs of pain flaring up along his body. The harbinger's discussion in the depths involved few words but lots of fists raining hammer-like blows on his chest and torso. But Charles and the others didn't need to know that. They had enough to worry about, what with the end of all life on Crotaria only days away.

Where are you, Grandfather?

—The throne room.

Is there anyone with you?

Charles was silent for a few moments before answering.

—No. It's empty. Wait a moment... Someone just came through the doors.

Is it a Wardsman?

—Yes. Should we be expecting someone?

Aidan smiled, calm the stench of sweat and blood soaked into the hood. *My father.*

Charles listened as Aidan paraphrased Edmund's tale of survival. When he finished, Aidan was surprised to hear Charles swallow a choked sob.

—I am grateful your father is alive, boy. He is a good man, has been since the day he enlisted in Torel's Ward. It just makes me wish there was a chance your mother could have survived. I hope that doesn't sound unkind.

I understand, Grandfather.

Charles took a deep breath. *—What's your plan?* he asked, voice steady again.

Aidan heard other footsteps fall in with his and the harbinger's. A cool breeze caressed his skin and ruffled his clothing. They were outside. Ahead, he heard the drone of murmuring voices. He stumbled slightly, catching against what felt like a step. The harbinger pulled him along, practically dragging him. He fell back into step and heard his boots clomp over wood. A stage of some kind? Yes, he decided. Likely the one his mother used to address assemblages out-of-doors. The hum of voices grew louder.

I need Heritage in my hands, he sent to his grandfather.

—So you have a plan?

Sort of. Mostly.

Charles sighed. *—Very well. I will help your father retrieve*

Heritage and reach you.

Suddenly a hand tore away his hood. More than a few hairs went with it. He blinked in the harshness of the Lady's light until his eyes focused. In front of him stood a man nearly a head taller than Romen of the Wolf. His thick, muscular arms were folded across his chest. His pants were the color of dried blood and hugged legs as big around as tree stumps. A black hood masked all of his face except his eyes, eerie yellow orbs narrowed into slits.

Hundreds of onlookers filled the courtyard below the platform. Turning to follow their gaze, Aidan saw a large wooden block at the far side of the platform. Its top and sides were stained crimson. An axe nearly as long as Aidan was tall was buried in its top. The heads of Cotak of the Spirit and the apple vendor from the market rested at its base, their wide eyes gazing up at a Lady who had not answered their pleas. Their bodies had been shoved to one side like dirty clothing.

Aidan turned away, his lips a thin, white line. *Grandfather?*

—Yes?

Please hurry.

Edmund looked around as the stone panel slid closed behind him. The throne room was empty. He moved toward the twin thrones at the far end. Between them sat a small oak stand. Curved arms rose from either side like antlers, ending in claws. Heritage lay between them, one claw gripping the blade and the other holding tight to the hilt.

Edmund frowned. This stand had been present when he had delivered the sword to the monster wearing his wife's face, after the monster wearing his had taken notice of him in the alleyway during Aidan's arrest. He'd never seen it before. When the sword wasn't at Annalyn's side, she kept it in the sword chamber where no one but she or their boy could get to it. The stand was a new addition to the throne room, like the creatures that occupied the thrones.

He grabbed the hilt of Heritage and pulled. The sword did not release. He twisted and tugged, trying to snap the wooden claws from the stand or cut through them with the sword's razor-sharp edge, but the sword held fast. He crouched down and examined the stand. A gem was set at the base of each arm. Magic. No surprise, there. He ran a hand through his hair. He had come up against more than his fair share of magic as the General of Torel's Ward, but Annalyn was usually on hand to help with those matters.

Edmund rose and placed a hand on Valor, sheathed at his

side. The stand *looked* like wood. Maybe he could cut Heritage free. If not, Aidan would have to—

The stand trembled. Edmund took a cautious step back. The table trembled again. No, he realized. The table was not moving. Heritage was shuddering, nearly convulsing. The clawed arms abruptly snapped away and clattered to the floor. Heritage followed right behind it, thudding against the carpeted walkway.

Across the room, the door began to open.

Instinct took over. Edmund ducked behind his wife's throne and held his breath. The doors boomed shut, and footsteps came forward, leisurely at first then breaking into a run.

"What is this?"

He stiffened. Her voice was more familiar to him than any other. Annalyn. Or rather, the *thing* that looked like her. He stepped out to face her.

"What are you...?" Her lips curled in a smile. "There you are, *dear*." She gestured to the shattered stand. "Tyrnen sent me for the sword. I see it gave you trouble. Better you than me. Our master says he's running out of bodies for these souls." She laughed. Edmund tried to suppress a shudder and failed. The laughter and the words were issued in Annalyn's voice, but there was a flatness to them that flew in the face of his memories of his wife. Even in the worst of times, Annalyn's voice sounded like chimes in a spring breeze, at least to his ears.

"I thought you would be with our son," she continued, her grin twisting cruelly, "in his final moments."

Edmund pushed away a surge of anger that mixed with cold fear for Aidan. He did not trust himself to speak. *How dare you look like her! How dare you speak of our son using her voice!*

The Annalyn-harbinger's face contorted into a wicked expression. "Gather it up, then, though be wary. I am all too familiar with how the sword reacts when touched by someone it dislikes." She chuckled; it was a dry, vindictive sound. "I'm looking forward to this. It is a pity Aidan Gairden's death will be a quick one." She turned and began to cross to the doors. "His soul will make a fine addition to our ranks, though," she continued, "alongside his mother's. It gave me great pleasure to watch as our master broke Annalyn Gairden's soul as easily as he broke her body. Her screams made me quiver. I still dream of them, of—"

She gasped as Heritage appeared at her throat, cold and razor sharp.

"Open the doors," Edmund said.

"What are you—?"

"Open them."

The harbinger lifted shaking hands to do as he commanded. Two Wardsmen bowed their heads as the doors swung open. "Your Majesty," one, a young man named Ein, began, "is everything all—" His face went pale as he noticed the blade at the Crown's throat.

The other man, Barth, wasted no time with words. He leveled his spear at Edmund. At first, he was surprised they did not recognize him. He supposed his mask of weeks-old beard and abrasions made a fine disguise.

"If you so much as touch me," Edmund said, "I will hand you her head."

The two Wardsmen fell in behind him as he passed. Other Wardsmen took notice and moved from their posts to surround him, drawing steel and looking between the Crown of the North and the man who would surely die for taking her hostage.

"Where is Aidan?" Edmund whispered.

"You have no chance of—"

The blade dug in, drawing a thin line of blood. He almost recoiled. It was dark, but not red. Green. A few of the Wardsmen gasped and looked around uncertainly, but did not lower their weapons.

"Back," the harbinger gasped, waving away the closest men. "Stay back."

"Where?" Edmund said again.

"The northern courtyard," she said, voice not as steady.

He grabbed a fistful of hair and pushed her forward. The blade at her throat did not waver. As he moved, a line of terrified Wardsmen trailed behind.

Tyrnen led a group of Wardsmen onto the platform. They fanned out in front of Aidan, blocking his view of the assemblage. The harbinger stepped from the line and leaned in close to Aidan.

"Remain silent," it hissed, "or I will continue the discussion we began in the depths."

Aidan's calm wavered like a candle flame in a breeze. The harbinger had bottled up a good deal of frustration with the unruly prince, it had explained down in the depths while it had pummeled Aidan's ribs and gut—areas the gathered crowd could not see.

Its snarl transformed into a solemn frown as it turned back around. "The Crown of the North will join us momentarily," he said, voice booming over the crowd. "My wife had to compose herself. She is still grief-stricken over the path her son has chosen."

The harbinger ran his eyes over the large gathering. "The sense of peace we have enjoyed for so long was shattered by Darinia's betrayal. Our realm stands united against the savagery the west prepares to unleash against our kingdom. At the end of the long war we face, Torel *will* stand triumphant!" A few cheers sprang up, but most glanced around uneasily.

"Darinia's treachery means more than the termination of a long-standing alliance," the harbinger continued. "It means the end of centuries of friendship."

Hurry, Grandfather.

The harbinger turned to regard Aidan. It shook its head, and a look of sadness ghosted over its face like a stray cloud. "To be betrayed by friends and allies is terrible enough, but to be betrayed by family is far worse. Aidan Gairden has committed treason. As much as it saddens me, I have no choice but to silence this voice of disunity, for the needs of a people must come before the love of a father. I must allow you to see Aidan Gairden for who he truly is."

Aidan blinked. His heart began to race. *Grandfather, I know what to do. How close are you?*

—There has been a development. Stall.

The harbinger stood before him. "Aidan Gairden, you are guilty of treason."

"I was under the impression that this was a trial," Aidan said, hoping he at least *sounded* calm.

"And you have been found guilty. Your sentence is death."

Digging his hand into his blue robe, Tyrnen moved to stand before Aidan.

"Not only is Prince Aidan guilty of treason," the old man said, slowly withdrawing his hand, "but he is a Touched. As the Eternal Flame, it is my duty to take a hand in deciding his fate. I will not allow my people to wantonly disregard the Crown's—"

"I did not know the Eternal Flame kowtowed to any monarch," Aidan said.

"They do not," Tyrnen said. "I simply agree with Annalyn's findings. Your actions affect your fellow Touched as much as they do Torel." He withdrew his hand from his robe. Clutched in his fist was a small orb filled with a thick, fog-like substance. The spirit stone. Suddenly a face appeared from the roiling storm clouds within the orb. Her face was gaunt and drawn. Hands, wispy and ethereal, pressed against the glass, and her mouth opened in a silent scream. The fog-like cloud billowed over her, sucking her back in, and she was gone.

Rage consumed Aidan.

"You will not be executed like a common man," Tyrnen continued. "You are guilty of—"

"The only thing I am guilty of is taking the lives of innocent men."

The harbinger grabbed at his arm as Tyrnen reached for him with the orb. Shouts from the crowd caused them both to pause.

"He has a right to speak!"

"Let us hear what he has to say!"

Tyrnen took a step toward Aidan, ambivalent to the crowd's cries.

"If you kill me right now," Aidan said evenly, not looking the old man in the eyes, "none of the seeds of deception you planted will bear fruit."

His face twisting in rage, Tyrnen stepped back. The shouting continued until the harbinger bowed, then moved to stand beside Tyrnen. The old man's arms—and his spirit stone— disappeared within his robe. He watched his former pupil with narrowed, burning eyes.

Aidan continued. "I, like all of you, have friends in Darinia. Romen of the Wolf and Cynthia Alston, may the Lady warm them for eternity, were my friends. The men whose lives I stole at Sharem—they were my friends. I am a Gairden. I am charged with the protection of all Crotaria, not just this realm. I believe that the war between Torel and Darinia is wrong, and I chose to stand against it. For that, I stand before you today, preparing to part ways with my head."

—We're almost there, Aidan.

"As I have walked these streets," he went on, "I have listened to the whispers of those who walked beside me. I am not the only person who believes this war is wrong. No one can take away your choice. I have made mine: to never again take the life of an innocent. Do not let fear keep you from doing the same."

The harbinger's face had gone crimson. "You dare encourage my people to participate in treason? You are a disgrace to your people and to your family. You are not my son!"

"That much is true," a voice rang out from the back of the assemblage.

Shocked cries sprang up from the rear of the crowd, and from the Wardsmen fanned out across the platform. The crowd parted, allowing two forms to pass to where Aidan stood. Every pair of eyes flitted between Edmund Calderon who stood on the platform, and the two new arrivals—one of whom was Edmund Calderon.

Chapter 36

Eyes Opened

CONFUSION AND PANIC SWEPT through the crowd. A second Edmund the Valorous had appeared, but more alarming was the sight of Annalyn Gairden, one arm twisted behind her back, her own blade pressed to her throat and held by her husband. The string of Wardsmen followed, shouting at onlookers to stay back and fanning out to cut a larger path through the crowd. Only Aidan and the executioner stood unfazed. The big man remained just as he had been: feet spread, corded arms folded across his chest.

This must be done carefully, Aidan thought as he scanned the crowd. Most of the staring faces fell somewhere between utterly perplexed and terrified.

—What will you do? Charles asked.

I will show them the truth. Be ready.

"You're powerful, perhaps even more so than I gave you credit for."

Tyrnen stood next to Aidan, his face impassive, lips barely moving as he spoke. "I've seen power in you since you were an infant. You are the reason I came to this land, Aidan. With my help, you can have anything—you can have *everything*. I offer you one final chance. Together, we could—"

"Thank you, Tyrnen."

The Eternal Flame smiled. "You're welcome, boy. I—"

"If not for your unusual form of guidance, I would not have grown into the man I am today. Now get away from me. You smell like mothballs and death."

Tyrnen's gaze became murderous.

Slowly, his father came up the platform, wrangling the Annalyn-harbinger. The harbinger went willingly, eyes flitting between Tyrnen and the edge of the blade at her throat. The line of Wardsmen came with them, spreading out around the platform and glancing nervously between each other and the two kings.

"Deception was used to describe Darinia," Aidan said to the crowd. "Everything you have been told by that man," he pointed at the Edmund-harbinger standing by Tyrnen, "and that woman," he pointed at Annalyn, "has been a lie. Deception comes from within Torel, not from without. The day after my Rite of Heritage, my parents departed with the Eternal Flame on a short retreat. I was invited to accompany them, but I chose to stay behind. I doubted myself and my capabilities, but stronger than doubt was an overwhelming sense of negligence. I didn't want responsibility. While I remained here, pouting, an attack on my parents did indeed take place, but it was not at the hands of Romen of the Wolf. It was at the hands of the Eternal Flame."

The crowd broke into a new round of murmurs. Tyrnen stood still, seemingly unperturbed.

"Tyrnen lured them away from their home so he could kill them and replace them with creatures that would more easily succumb to his will."

The uneasy muttering grew louder. For most, magic was uncharted land: unable to be felt or heard, only seen—all too often—as a destructive force. They would need proof of his claim, like men who needed to see the sky to believe it was blue.

"That is a serious charge," Tyrnen said, nodding. "But I ask you to look at each Edmund Calderon closely. Who can see any difference between them? I, for one, cannot." He pointed at Aidan. "Who's to say that this deception is not Aidan's creation?"

At this, many onlookers regarded Aidan uncertainly. He knew right then that targeting his false father would not work. That there were two Edmunds was the most obvious abnormality, but Tyrnen made a valid point. There was no easy way to prove the harbinger's false claim. He needed to target his mother. The Crown of the North. The sword-bearer.

Get ready, he sent to his grandfather.

"The time for words has passed," Aidan said. Mouths fell silent as Aidan turned to Annalyn's impostor. "My mother has yet to share with us which story she believes. Surely the Crown of the North can point out her own husband."

Aidan nodded to his father, and Edmund looked at him hesitantly before lowering Heritage and stepping away from the harbinger. She turned to Aidan, her face heated yet uneasy.

"Mother," Aidan said, dipping into a low bow. "Your people and your family need guidance only a sword-bearer can provide." He gestured to Edmund. "The sword my father—my *true* father—holds is Heritage, sacred to the Gairden family. Any man can hold the sword, but only the sword-bearer, can tap into its full potential. Mother," he continued, his voice sweet, "please take your sword.

Help us solve this mystery so that our people may rest easy once again, safe in the knowledge that the Gairdens watch over and protect them."

—*That was dramatic,* Charles said.

It's a natural talent.

—*No arguments there.*

Aidan ignored that. "Father, would you please present the sword-bearer with her blade?"

Edmund knelt stiffly at the Annalyn-harbinger's feet and held out Heritage. The creature's hands fidgeted, clenching and unclenching.

"Mother," Aidan said, sounding utterly perplexed, "why don't you take Heritage?"

Annalyn glared at him. Then she slowly, slowly raised shaking hands and wrapped her fingers around the hilt. She flinched, as if expecting the sword to drive back into her belly. Nothing happened. A grin spread across her face. She gave a triumphant yell and lifted the sword high above her head. Tyrnen looked nonplussed.

Drop, Aidan commanded.

The blade dropped with a crash. A look of confusion splashed across the harbinger's face. Her hands remained fastened around the sword's hilt. She strained to lift it, grunting, but the point of the blade rested on the ground, immovable, as if fitted with a giant weight. Suddenly the Eye flashed, and a clap like thunder rang through the air. Red sparks hissed and spit from the Eye, which pulsed a low, angry red. As one, every voice in the crowd cried out in fear.

Calmly, Aidan crossed the dais to Heritage and picked it up. *Grandfather, could you...?*

The bonds around his magic fell away. Aidan raised Heritage and blinked. The people appeared as black outlines on a pure white canvas, their eyes wide as they stared up at him and pointed at his ivory-colored eyes. The masks worn by the harbingers vanished; they appeared to him in their true forms: hollow eye sockets, fleshy bars spread across their gaping maws.

"I am Aidan Gairden," his voice rang out. "I am the Crown of the North. I am the sword-bearer." He leveled Heritage at the Annalyn-harbinger. "And that is not my mother."

"This has gone on far enough!" his mother's impostor cried. "Wardsmen! Obey the Crown. Seize my son!"

The Wardsmen spread across the platform took a hesitant step forward, then regarded Aidan's glowing eyes warily. Shrieking in rage, the Annalyn-harbinger charged. Aidan drew light and snapped off a prayer. Two beams shot from the Eye of Heritage and lanced the platform at her feet. The Edmund-harbinger lunged at him from the side. Aidan raised Heritage to strike but his father got there first, swinging Valor up to crash against his impostor's blade, forcing him back.

Cries rang out from every direction. Many in the crowd shoved their way toward the gate. They needed to see what he saw, or Aidan would lose them.

Anastasia. Can you reverse transfiguration?

—I... could try, she sent back. *I need light. Lots of it.*

Aidan opened every pore of his body, drinking in the Lady's warmth. He had only been tied for a few hours, but gorging on the sweet warmth was like diving into the clearest, coolest lake after crossing the Plains of Dust. The Annalyn-harbinger drew light and prayed, throwing a ball of fire at him. Aidan raised Heritage, deflecting it, then shifted behind her and grabbed her around the throat.

—Now! Anastasia cried.

The light drained from his body and into the sword. The Eye flared red, then the energy poured forth, baking the harbinger in a red glow. The skin beneath Aidan's fist shifted like loose fabric. Ripples spread over her body, her face, her legs. Sounds like snapping twigs filled the air. Her skin became moldy and cadaverous.

—It's done!

Aidan reeled back and stumbled, falling to his knees. He felt light-headed and feverish, drained. The fever was not as debilitating as it had been after Sharem, but he felt far from spry and alert. He was so faint that the first few cries of alarm did not register. Then he saw trembling fingers pointing at the platform behind him. Aidan looked. His Sight had fallen away, but his mother's impostor stood revealed. Fleshy bars covered her mouth and vacant eye sockets stared sightlessly. His father's impostor stared at her in horror and compulsively reached up to pat at his face.

"What in Dawn's name...?" his father breathed.

The courtyard exploded in pandemonium. Several of the Wardsmen turned on their fellows, rushing them with flat, dead eyes. Several men died before they could grasp what was happening, blood spilling from torn necks and bellies. Those who did get a hold of their wits could do no more than raise their blades and deflect blows, gaping in confusion and horror as the fleshy masks of their adversaries faded to reveal skulls spotted with dirt and rot. Shrieking, the crowd boiled over, spilling out into the mountain trail, shoving and trampling in their terror.

And there, far in the back near the gate opening on to the mountain pass, was the massive head cook herself, striding toward the platform against the current of terrified witnesses. Vagrants threw themselves at her, their blades glinting in the Lady's light. Helda never so much as glanced at them. She swung a stout log in cleaving strokes, batting them aside and roaring like an angry bear.

The sight of Helda cutting a wide path toward him left Aidan amazed and deeply comforted. But he had only an instant to register Helda's inexorable advance. Behind him, Tyrnen growled a prayer. Aidan whirled but the old man vanished, kicking up a gust of wind. Howling in rage, the exposed harbingers rushed them. Behind them, the executioner stalked in, clenching and unclenching hands as large as Helda's biggest plates. Edmund tore Valor from its sheath and adopted a defensive stance. Raising Heritage, Aidan stepped beside him.

Another gust of wind tugged at his clothes. Before he could turn, a hand gripped his neck. Nails dug into his skin, pinching hard enough to make him gasp.

"You have ruined my plans for the last time," Tyrnen whispered.

Blackness swept over him.

Chapter 37

Night Terrors

THE PINCHING SENSATION DISAPPEARED and Aidan whirled, spinning Heritage in a wide arc. The sword bit through the air—nothing else—and not the fresh air that announced the arrival of spring. He was in the center of the throne room. All the windows along the walls that normally flooded the room with the Lady's light were blank, as if the panes of glass had been removed and replaced with slabs of wall painted black. The flicker of torches between the balconies lit the room with a dusky glow. Shadows stretched out from corners and the gaps between balconies like cobwebs. Behind him, the Crown of the North and its smaller companion throne sat empty.

—*What's happened?* Charles asked, sounding uncertain.

Aidan was not quite sure how to answer. His thoughts were hazy, as if he had been woken suddenly from a deep sleep.

—*Night Terror*, Ambrose said tensely. *He's pulled you in.*

Aidan felt panic creep in. He raised Heritage and asked his family to illuminate the Eye. The jewel flickered, bathing the room in deep red light for an instant. Then it faded.

—*We cannot see, Aidan,* Anastasia said. *The Eye is blind.*

Fear washed over him, prickling his skin. He forced himself to take a few deep breaths and think the problem through. *I can't see normally*, he thought, then felt a rush of triumph as an idea came to him. Tightening his grip on Heritage, he summoned the Sight. Black on white greeted him as the *Ordine'kel* swept through him, mating with *Ordine'cin* to flood every fiber of his being. Every mark on the floor, every contour of the walls, stood out as if an artist had sketched the room using charcoal.

—*Excellent thinking, boy*, Charles said, sounding proud.

Behind him, Aidan heard a gasp. He turned smoothly, his terror buried under the calm discipline of *Ordine'kel.* A form huddled between the thrones.

—*What's wrong?* his grandfather asked.

"Someone else is here," he whispered.

He took a few cautious steps forward, Heritage raised and ready to turn away blows using precise parries that Aidan did not, would not understand. The man wore the mail and colors of a Wardsman. He looked up, and Aidan saw scraggly beard that barely covered cuts and bruises.

—*Who is it?* Charles said.

"Father," Aidan said, releasing Sight and kneeling in front of Edmund.

Edmund looked up at him, teeth gritted in pain. "What happened?"

"Tyrnen pulled us into a..." Aidan frowned, wondering how to explain. "It's like a dream, this place, except what happens is real. If we die here..."

His father nodded. His teeth began to chatter. Aidan removed his cloak and wrapped it around his father's shoulders. "Are you all right? Father?"

The general's eyes rose to take in the dancing shadows that began to slide down the high walls behind Aidan. The wispy shapes crawled toward any torches in their path, wriggling around flames as they descended.

Edmund had spun without thinking the moment he had felt the pincer-like grip on his neck, thrusting Valor out. He drove the blade into a tree bare of leaves, rattling its branches and calling down a shower of snow and ice. He yanked his blade free and took in his surroundings. Snow covered the ground and fell thickly from gray clouds. Bare trees covered in snow and ice stretched around him in every direction.

He started to sheathe Valor then thought better of it. He crept forward, eyes flitting front trunk to trunk. The unbroken snow glittered under the Lady's glare as he moved along. That pulled him up short. The Lady had been settling over the far horizon as he had entered the courtyard minutes before. Had Tyrnen used some trick to send him to the far reaches of Crotaria where the Lady had not yet turned the sky over to the Lord of Midnight? Perhaps that was it.

He resumed his slow, cautious pace. Minutes later he emerged from the grove to find a small cabin sitting near the frozen bowl of a lake. He was at Lake Carrean. Terrible memories came rushing back, burying years of fonder ones.

"Kahltan damn you, old man," he growled. He glanced near the cabin. Annalyn's body was gone, or perhaps hidden under the snow. He told himself that he could not dig for it right now, not with their son in danger. Annalyn always wanted him to tend to their boy first, him second, herself last. Emotion welled up in his throat. He swallowed it and stalked toward the cabin. If Tyrnen was inside, he had better be prepared for a fight.

Movement at the edge of his vision. He went to the shore and scanned the horizon, but saw nothing amiss. Then he detected motion again, this time at his feet. Looking down, Edmund gasped and fell to his knees. The bloated face of his wife stared back at him from beneath the surface of the frozen lake. Her hands pressed against the ice as if trying to lift it away. Her eyes were wide with sadness; questions and accusations swam out of her glassy eyes and stabbed him in the heart.

Edmund pulled himself to his feet. "I'll get you out of there," he mumbled. Gripping Valor like a dagger, he stabbed the blade into the ice. The jolt from the impact almost brought him to his knees. He stabbed again and again, chipping at the ice but making no real progress. He was so involved in his labor that he didn't notice the shadow sliding along the ground beneath him, swallowing up his own silhouette.

—Something doesn't feel right, Charles whispered.

What do you—? Aidan began. Something cold, like a rag dipped in ice water, touched his foot, seeping through his boot. He grabbed his father and dove to the side. They landed in a mass of tangled arms and legs. Sitting up, Aidan pulled Edmund to his feet.

"Father, are you—"

The cadaverous face of the harbinger stared back at him. Aidan kicked free of the creature's grasp, rolled to his feet, fell into a run—and slammed face-first into a column of stone. Pain exploded across his face and his eyes filled with tears. Aidan ignored them. The torches had been snuffed out, leaving him in darkness.

"Your end is near , boy."

The words were close. Aidan felt his way around the column and stumbled forward, fingers fumbling for his sword. They brushed an empty sheath. Heritage was gone, he realized, probably near the thrones where he'd dropped it when he'd thrown himself and the Edmund-harbinger out of harm's way. He turned around—at least he hoped he had turned completely around—and hunched over, groping his way back to the throne. Hoarse laughter from afar reached his ears and abruptly rolled closer, rising in pitch.

Aidan threw himself forward and collided with one of the thrones. The chair crashed to the ground, and Aidan tumbled along with it. He groped about and decided he had found the sword when his finger nicked the edge of something sharp. Patting the blade, he seized the hilt and blinked, calling forth Sight. Whiteness descended over his vision like a curtain. He saw the harbinger halfway across the room, its true face open in a silent scream. It stood calmly, a sword in its hands, its shoulders shaking with... laughter?

A mass of darkness crashed into him like a wave of liquid ice. Laughter filled his ears, drowning out his scream. The whisper filled him, pouring down his throat, seizing his legs, pinning his arms. He wanted to retch but could not. His chest was unable to rise or fall, and the inability to draw breath sent waves of panic through him, freezing rational thought. Sight slipped away, plunging the room back into darkness. The creature's murmuring increased, growing frenzied at the taste of his flesh, of his fear.

Valor flashed as Edmund weaved around the executioner. Cuts and stab wounds crisscrossed the big man's chest, belly, arms, legs, back—but he never seemed to slow, ignoring the wounds as if they were the probing teeth of the smallest, peskiest insects.

Edmund grimaced as he continued to move. This was his first battle since surviving Tyrnen's ambush, and he felt like a man twice his age. The executioner's surprising agility didn't help matters. The size of the man was in stark contrast to his dexterity. Edmund rolled and slid around the behemoth's club-like fists, thrusting and cutting with movements as precise as his footing in the ankle-deep snow allowed.

The giant lunged and Edmund saw his chance. He started to dive forward, intending to hamstring his opponent, but his left leg—the one bludgeoned by several of the vagrants that had ambushed him near this very spot—gave out. He collapsed, but did not give in to the disadvantage. Instead he threw his weight to one side, falling into a roll. The giant's foot clipped him, sending him tumbling. He rose smoothly, shifting weight to his good leg and taking a moment to find his balance.

A moment was all his opponent gave him. The big man had sensed his advantage and charged, swinging those tree-trunk limbs. Edmund gave ground, slashing and cutting and thrusting, barely avoiding the other man's reach. His foot caught in the snow again and he fell backwards. His warrior's mind ran through options as his body fell. He could roll and regain his feet, or he could lie prone, feigning weakness. *Wouldn't be much feigning involved*, he told himself, deciding on option two. He let himself crash onto his back, hoping the executioner took the bait.

The Lady's own luck was with him. The big man moved in, lacing his hands and driving them down like a sledgehammer. Edmund rolled to one side, threw all his weight on his good leg, and sprang up to drive Valor through the man's skull. He grunted as the blade chipped off but recovered quickly, stabbing between the man's shoulder blades. The executioner threw his head back and howled. Edmund scrabbled back, his breath puffing out in the cold air as he prepared to wade in. What happened next left him frozen to the spot.

Roaring, the executioner ripped away his hood. His head was covered in bright red scales, each as tough and thick as plates of steel. His eyes were yellow slits. Scaly lips peeled away in a snarl to reveal sharp, pointed fangs. Crimson stained each jagged yellow tooth.

It roared again and advanced, corded arms flexing as it pounded forward.

Aidan couldn't move, helpless against the heavy force that pinned his body to the wall. His outstretched hand was all that remained viewable, the rest lost beneath layers of shadow. He wanted to close his eyes and let the darkness have him, let his burning lungs expire so he could drift away...

—Do not give up!

The cry within his head brought him back to full alertness. He still couldn't breathe, and without air, what chance did he have? His fingers fluttered, and steel grazed their tips.

The sword!

His hands. His fingers still gripped the hilt. He blinked, returning Sight, but could not move his body to strike.

Fire! he sent desperately.

A thin jet of flame shot out of the ruby, lighting the room in a brilliant scarlet glow. The congealed mass of whispers screamed as the fire cut through the bulk like a hot knife, and the whisper shrieked again and fell away, peeling like strips of paper that shriveled into nothingness. Pulling himself to his feet, he gasped in enormous gulps of air. It tasted sweeter than any pie or cake he had ever filched from Helda's kitchens.

—You are still in danger, Aidan, his grandfather reminded him.

Aidan froze. *The harbinger.*

As if his thought had summoned the creature, he turned and caught the flat of its sword full in the face.

Edmund fought for breath as he worked against the creature's relentless attacks. Cutting its face did no good. Valor had drawn no blood, only sparks. He stuck to body attacks after that failed attempt, carving the humanoid body with slashes and stabs. Not that the creature seemed to notice. He slid forward, feigning a dive and bracing his legs to launch himself at the beast's legs. *Stupid!* he cursed just as he began to push off. Abruptly his bad leg shuddered, and what began as an upward spring became a clumsy stumble as pain shot through him.

A fist slammed into his chest like a battering ram. The world became a whirlwind of white and blue before he crashed in the center of the hard, ice-covered pond. Edmund sat up, the world around him still spiraling. He heard the heavy steps of the creature coming for him, but he did not look up. He was fixated on a spider web pattern that had formed where he landed. He smiled, then watched the beast approach. One fist was clenched and held in the other, and both were upraised like a hammer waiting to fall.

Edmund rolled as the beast leaped and brought his hands crashing down. Its fists smashed through the surface as if it were glass. It teetered, but kept its footing. Screaming in pain and fury, Edmund slid forward and threw his bulk against the creature. It toppled into the icy depths, hands shooting up to grip at the edge of the covering sheet. Struggling against dizziness and nausea, Edmund ignored the rapidly spreading web of cracks and hacked and stabbed at the beast's hands, chest, shoulders—any flesh he could see. Finally its fingers slipped from the edge. Then it sank, disappearing in the blue depths.

Fatigue careened into him. Fumbling, Edmund sheathed Valor as he began crawling back to the shore. His pain, the giant creature—everything but his original mission, to pull Annalyn from the frozen depths, was forgotten. When he reached her, his breath caught. She was smiling. Her hands smashed through the icy surface and dragged him down.

Aidan no longer wielded Heritage. He *was* Heritage. The pure whiteness of Sight painted an onyx outline around his enemy, the sword a blur in his hands. Ambrose whispered words in his ear, guiding his every movement, helping him stay two steps ahead. The harbinger came at him in relentless assaults, its sword spinning and slicing. Heritage met it again and again. Sight cast away the creature's disguise, bringing its true form to bear. Its eyeless holes remained narrowed during their struggle. Its mouth was set in a similar position, though occasionally a cockroach would scuttle through the fleshy bars that stretched over the maw.

Ordine'kel carried Aidan forward, giving him the understanding behind each stab, slice and parry. Their counters and strikes flowed seamlessly, each intercepting and playing off from the other, forming a chain of delicacy and death. Aidan stiffened his arm to catch a downward swing from his opponent, spinning the sword out of his way. He had thought to push the opposing weapon to the ground, but to his surprise the harbinger pressed his way into the spin, forcing Aidan to press Heritage against the blade to hold the creature at bay.

The harbinger snarled, narrowing its eyes again before leaping forward. The blades crashed and came apart multiple times in a blur of motion.

—Press him, Ambrose said, and Aidan smiled. His ancestor's voice was tight, but tinged with excitement. The strategy of swordplay, the ability to outthink an opponent and land a winning stroke. Ambrose had lived for this, had never felt more alive than when he was in the thick of battle. Now Aidan had become a vessel that thrummed with his ancestor's ability, and his passion for the fight.

The harbinger proved a worthy opponent. The creature pressed forward then, suddenly, fell back, stepped into a shadow near one of the columns—and vanished.

Where...?

—Behind you! Ambrose said.

Aidan turned to see the harbinger leap from another band of shadows. He raised Heritage and deflected two quick blows, stepped forward in a thrust. But the harbinger had jumped into another pool of darkness. This time Aidan heard it mutter a clipped phrase. Dark magic. He recognized the Language of Light. He pivoted, eyes darting around to anticipate where the beast might reappear.

—Bide your time, Ambrose said tensely. *He will slip up. And when he does—*

But Aidan had another idea. He had been the prey for weeks, always waiting for hunters who wore darkness like a cloak to make the first move, expecting him to react. That, and his body could not keep up this pace much longer, not even with Ambrose guiding him like a mother holding a babe's hands while he took his first steps. Unlike *Ordine'cin*, overuse of *Ordine'kel* came with no fever. Physical exertion inevitably pushed the body to exhaustion, and Aidan's body had already been fed through a grinder. His ribs flared with pain, bruised or worse from the harbinger's beating in the depths. His arms burned; the sword felt unbearably heavy in his hands.

Aidan stopped pivoting and lowered his guard, panting.

—*What are you doing?* Ambrose said in a strangled tone.

Footsteps sounded behind him, rushing from a bank of shadows behind the thrones. Aidan stepped to one side and heard the harbinger's blade whistle as it cut the air. Not daring to think, he plunged into the shadows and drew them in around them, embracing cold and darkness. The prayer the harbinger had used passed through his lips.

Then he sped across the room to another cluster of shadows. He looked around frantically, trying to get his bearings. His eyes caught sight of a balcony far above. He darkened and prayed again and suddenly he was soaring toward it, like an arrow taking flight. He looked down to the shadows between the thrones and flowed there, rushing in. The sensation was exhilarating, not quite as instantaneous as shifting or fast-traveling the tunnels, but smoother, like water streaming over a fall. He enjoyed the movement, and marveled in speeding from spot to spot.

He looked below and saw the harbinger twisting around as he had, spitting curses and trying to pinpoint where Aidan might reappear. Aidan waited until he stepped near one of the side walls. Abruptly he was there, lunging at the harbinger. The Edmund impostor had just enough time to raise his blade, but Aidan's stupendous momentum sent him sprawling. His blade skittered away, lost in darkness.

Aidan wasted little time. He hit the ground running, called Sight, and leaped atop the harbinger, pinning it on his back.

"You've lost," Aidan said.

It would have smiled, had it been able. "Not quite." Its hands shot forward, palms open. Strands of darkness shot forth, wriggling like worms and straining for Aidan's throat. Aidan grunted and felt his arms quiver like chords. A chill had settled over him from the darkening.

"Fire!" Aidan cried in desperation, raising the Eye to point at the harbinger. A fresh jet of flame leaped from the jewel, carved through the strands of shadow and poured over the harbinger's face. It screamed and thrashed. The flame cut off as Aidan rolled free, sword raised, ready to continue the fight.

But the fight was over. The harbinger's cries died away and it fell still. Tendrils of smoke rose from its face. The last sense Aidan had of coherence was the smell of burnt flesh, and with it, the memory of what he had done at Sharem.

Cold stabbed every inch of Edmund as the creature who wore his wife's face dragged him deeper beneath the surface. He beat at her unyielding arm with one hand as the other stretched forward, gripping her face, gouging her eyes in a desperate attempt to be released. She jerked away from his grip, and to his horror her face slipped off easily in his hand. The true face of the harbinger stared back at him. Cockroaches and maggots floated to the surface, kicking and struggling before the water's icy clutches stilled their tiny legs.

Edmund released the mask. His wife's face stared blankly at him as the disguise floated to the surface. His free arm returned to squeeze at the creature's hand still clutching his neck. He kicked at it, but the water slowed his kick, muting it. His lungs burned. Her grip tightened as spots wavered across his vision. He kicked out again with one leg. From the boot on the other he tugged free a dagger and drove it through the back of its fleshy head. The thin strips of flesh covering the orifice trembled and went still. Its grip slackened, and the creature drifted toward the dark, icy depths, its empty eye sockets bulging and its mouth frozen in an endless scream.

Edmund felt his lungs burst into flame. The last sight he saw before blackness took him was his wife's face, floating up to the surface.

Chapter 38

Flight of an Arrow

AIDAN GASPED AND SAT upright, sweat rolling down his bare chest like a tepid, sticky waterfall. The dream, again. Tyrnen. Chasing him. Catching him. Killing him.

He looked around the room and let out a long, slow sigh, expelling his terror like steamy breath in winter air. He was back in his bed in Sunfall, and Tyrnen was gone. Not locked up in the depths beneath the palace, but safely away from his home. At least he hoped so. He settled back and closed his eyes. Within moments he felt his eyelids grow pleasantly heavy.

—There's no more time for sleep, I'm afraid, his grandfather said.

Aidan covered his face with his blankets.

"There's always time for sleep," he mumbled.

—Not for you. We gave you two full days to recuperate.

His eyes flew open. "Two days?"

—You were in and out, and I suppose you did need the rest. You pushed yourself hard again, Aidan. He paused. *Darkening saps the body of even more strength than kindling, as I understand it.*

Aidan ran his hands over his face. His mad flight from Sordia to Calewind, the energy he had given to Anastasia to reverse his false mother's transfiguration, the bone-chilling cold of the dark magic used to swim the shadows in his battle against the Edmund-harbinger... His grandfather was right. He did not feel as weakened as he had after the battle at Sharem, but he certainly wasn't ready to race Daniel through Sunfall's corridors.

Frowning, Aidan looked around again. *How did I get back to my own bed?*

—You were found in the throne room, barely cognizant and delirious from fever. Wardsmen found you, and Christine—

His face warmed at the mention of her name, and the memory of the night they had spent together. And, his grandfather hadn't referred to her as "that Sallnerian girl." It was a start.

—put you to bed and gave you healing. How do you feel?

"Tired," Aidan said.

—Do you remember much of what happened?

"Yes." He remembered all of it: the trial, the fight for his life in the Night Terror. But what he remembered more clearly than anything else was his mother's tortured face peering at him from within the spirit stone.

"I saw her, Grandfather. I saw my mother."

Charles said nothing.

"I will free her. She will not suffer another night as Tyrnen's prisoner."

—Once a soul is captured, it cannot be released unless the stone is broken, or unless the stone's master grants it release, Charles said. His voice was firm, practical, but Aidan knew his grandfather well enough to see past his gruffness. There was an underlying despair in his tone, not much, but enough to shake the old man's confidence like a wind pulling leaves from a tree.

—The harbinger you killed in Night Terror is, for all intents and purposes, still alive, Anastasia interjected. *You only destroyed a temporary vessel. As long as Tyrnen controls their souls, he can resurrect his slaves again and again. All he needs are bodies.*

"But destroying Tyrnen's spirit stone would free those souls, *and* prevent him from creating more harbingers."

—Yes, Anastasia said.

"Then that's what I'll do."

—It isn't that simple, Charles said. *Getting to the stone means getting close to Tyrnen.*

"That's fine with me," Aidan said grimly.

—It shouldn't be. Remember, your soul is vulnerable to him.

I thought you would want her set free as badly as I do, Aidan thought angrily. A wave of shame settled over him as Charles inhaled sharply. *I'm sorry, Grandfather. I really need to learn to keep a hold on my temper. I just felt so helpless seeing her that way.*

—I understand. And I do want her with us. But remember that Heritage cannot protect you from a spirit stone. It did not protect your mother. You must be careful. If you fail, every soul on Crotaria will be lost to Tyrnen, not just your mother's.

Aidan nodded and swung his legs to the floor. "I'd better get moving. We can—"

—There's something else we need to discuss, his grandfather said, voice prickly.

Aidan sighed again. He should have known this was coming. "Dark magic."

—*We know you used it to run the tunnels*, Anastasia said. *We understand.*

You do?

—*You needed to reach the Prophet quickly, and she... did not dissuade its use, exactly. But dark magic is still forbidden. Remember what it did to my parents.*

Aidan's eyes widened. Aside from the legend relayed during every Gairden's Rite of Heritage, little mention was made of the fact that Anastasia was Dimitri and Luria Thalamahn's daughter. In a very, very distant way, the Thalamahns were family. And he thought *his* parents had been strict.

—*It leads to corruption in all who use it*, Anastasia went on. *Darkening is dangerous.*

"I haven't sprouted a second head, nor do I feel any inclination to take over the world."

—*Do you ever listen to yourself talk?* Charles muttered.

Aidan ran a hand through his hair. "I'm sorry, Anastasia" he said. "Please forgive me."

—*You have been through a lot*, she said after a moment. *You are a remarkably strong young man. But I will not let the matter drop so easily, Aidan. This is important to me. I need your word that you will not darken again.*

Aidan folded his hands. "No." He braced himself for a tirade, but received only silence. Anastasia drew in a large breath. It was like the creak of a catapult drawing back.

—*Perhaps we should ask Aidan about his reasoning,* Ambrose interjected in a soft tone.

—*Husband!* Anastasia sounded shocked. *You saw firsthand what my mother and father became. You agreed that—*

—*I did then, and I do now*, Ambrose said. *But Aidan has given you your say. I think we deserve to hear him out.*

—*I agree, Anastasia,* Charles said. *Aidan can be impetuous, yes. Emotional, very much so. A bit slow at times, I'll concede that. A procrastinator, no doubt. And he tends to—*

"Where exactly are you going with this?" Aidan said tensely.

—*My grandson is an intelligent young man,* Charles said. *I say we hear his reasoning.*

The three Gairdens muttered for several moments. —*Very well*, Anastasia said. *You may speak, Aidan.*

Aidan took time to wrestle with his thoughts. His feelings on the subject of dark magic, and its brighter counterpart, had been jumbled and slippery since his first time darkening in the tunnels. He had not had time to sort through them in all the excitement since then. Now, he knew, was the time. Not only to share his thoughts with his family, but to finally take firm hold of a concept that had been dancing just out of his reach for days.

"When I darkened in the tunnels, I was not sure what to expect, what I might feel. What I felt was... well, I felt cold, like I had decided to go hiking through a blizzard wearing only my skin. The sensation was the opposite of what I feel when I kindle the Lady's light. Other than that, everything felt the same. I used the Language of Light—which seems an inappropriate name for what appears to be a universal language of magic—and Kahltan answered my prayer.

"That surprised me, at first. Why would the Lord of Midnight answer the call of a servant to the Lady of Dawn? But he did." Aidan hesitated, his heart beating faster. "And then, in the recall spell, I watched as the Lady gave Tyrnen spells to kill my mother."

—That is blasphemy, Aidan, Anastasia said sharply.

—Let him finish, please, Charles said. The old man also spoke tightly, but he also sounded curious.

"Thank you, Grandfather. And Anastasia, you know my thoughts. You must know I love the Lady of Dawn, as I loved her Prophet. But I saw what I saw, and I heard what I heard. Tyrnen prayed to the Lady. She answered. I'm not so sure that's how it works, now."

—How what works, Aidan? his grandfather asked.

He fell silent again, try to shape his thoughts. "When a man fires an arrow, he chooses the target. Magic, to me, seems to function the same way. We draw in the resource we need, speak the words, and create a result. We use the word *prayer*, but that doesn't seem quite right. We set the arrow, take aim, and release. I mean, it makes sense, doesn't it? Why would the Lady answer Tyrnen's request for magic to destroy a Gairden, a member of the bloodline she chose to protect her people? Because he didn't *ask* her."

His voice grew quieter. "Why would the Lady grant me the power I needed to cause such destruction and bloodshed at Sharem? What I did was terrible—and it was my choice. Not hers. That's how the Prophet described it to me in the Duskwood. She said the Lady's light can be used to destroy, or to protect peace. It seems to me that dark magic works the same way. Your parents, Anastasia, used it to destroy. I used it again to battle the harbinger, a force of destruction, who used it to battle me, an agent of peace.

We selected the same tool and used it to achieve different ends.

"Why would the Lord of Midnight help us both? Well, I don't think he did. Maybe... maybe he doesn't have anything to do with what we do. Maybe the Lady doesn't, either." Realizing what he had just said, he rushed on: "Or maybe not as much as we think."

He sat back, took a deep breath, and waited for someone to break the silence. Not surprisingly, Anastasia spoke up first. What did surprise him were her words, and tone.

—You have given us much to think about, she said thoughtfully. *I... am sorry for being so harsh before. You have indeed put a great deal of thought into this.*

Aidan shrugged, smiling a little. "Just a little here and there, in between running for my life and battling the walking dead."

She laughed, full and rich. Then she grew quiet again. *—I would like to talk more of this. For now, we need to concentrate on your immediate concern,* Anastasia went on.

"Tyrnen," he said.

—Nichel, Charles corrected. *You have a war to stop, first.*

Chapter 39

Promises from the Past

AIDAN GROANED. "THE CLANS. I almost forgot."

—There wasn't any 'almost' involved, boy, Charles said, though his voice was light. *Now then, find your father, and—*

"My fa..." His eyes widened. "Is he...?"

"Alive," said a voice from the doorway.

The door swung open to admit Edmund. He limped into the room on a sturdy pair of crutches. His breeches and green shirt seemed odd to Aidan's eyes; he was so accustomed to seeing his father in armor that Edmund had convinced him that he wore it to bed until his mother had rolled her eyes and intervened. Weeks' worth of stubble had been shaved away, revealing a smooth face covered in faint scars.

Aidan rose from the bed and embraced his father. Edmund said nothing, only patting Aidan's back.

"I haven't seen this much of you since we went swimming in Lake Carrean when we were twelve," said a voice from behind Edmund. Daniel, his face covered in sweat and his clothes stained with dirt, grinned as he entered. Christine flowed in behind him, her eyes bright. Looking down, Aidan blushed and leaped back under his covers. Christine sat next to him and scooted close. Edmund frowned disapprovingly between them, but neither noticed.

"How did you get here so quickly?" Aidan asked Daniel.

"Christine learned how to travel the tunnels," Daniel said, shrugging.

"What tunnels?" Edmund asked.

"The sneaks move underground to get from place to place," Aidan explained, glossing over the method of fast-travel. He was not ready for another discussion on dark magic just yet.

Edmund looked crestfallen. "You already know about those?"

"How are you feeling?" Christine asked, placing a hand on his forehead. The other was curled protectively around her belly.

"Better than I was, thanks to you," he said.

Christine blushed. He was once again struck by how beautiful she looked when he managed to catch her off guard. He would have to get better at that.

"You look awful," Aidan said to Daniel as he took in his friend's haggard appearance.

"Not as bad as you," Daniel said back.

"I mean you're filthy. Did you run here all the way from Sordia?"

Daniel's smile was not quite genuine. "I just returned from an errand," he said, glancing at Edmund.

"An errand?" Aidan repeated. He looked questioningly at his father.

Lowering himself beside Aidan with a weary sigh, Edmund said, "We'll discuss that in a bit. What did Tyrnen do to us, Aidan? One moment we were in the courtyard. The next, I was back at Lake Carrean with..." He swallowed and looked away.

"A spell called Night Terror. It is like a nightmare, but what happens there is real."

"They pulled me in with you," Edmund said. "Probably wanted to get rid of both of us in one fell swoop." Aidan's eyes widened as his father's story unfolded. When Edmund reached the point where the beast unmasked itself, Edmund stopped, swallowing hard.

"I don't know what manner of creature it was," he said. "It had a curved head with red scales that turned away Valor like a rock turns away wind."

—Did it have sharp, pointed teeth? Ambrose asked.

Aidan relayed the question, then his father's affirmative answer.

—A leviathan, the Gairden patriarch said. *During the Great War, the world saw all types of aberrations created by dark magic. The leviathan was one of them. No one except Luria—and now Tyrnen, of course—knows how they are created. They have the bodies of men, but their heads are impenetrable, made from the thick, scaly hide of creatures rumored to exist many, many eons ago.*

"What happened next, Father?" Aidan finally said.

Edmund blinked, then narrowed his eyes in thought. "I finally tricked the beast into shattering a weak part of the ice. With its enormous weight—and my sword stabbing it anywhere I found an opening—it didn't have a chance for survival. I began to crawl back toward the shore, when suddenly one of harbingers pulled me into the water. I struggled with it when suddenly everything started to shimmer. Next thing I knew, I was in the throne room, and the harbinger was right there with me. There were Wardsmen surrounding our sleeping bodies, and—you won't believe this—Helda was there, too. She pounced on the harbinger and bludgeoned her to death with a log."

Despite the seriousness of the situation, Aidan broke into a wide grin. "I can believe that."

"You were there as well, though we didn't know that at first," Edmund said. "As I was being helped to my feet, we heard you cry out from the uppermost balcony across the room. You were thrashing about on the floor. The other harbinger's body was with you."

Shaking his head, Aidan said, "Why would Tyrnen take us to the throne room?"

—Night Terror draws in one's consciousness from one's body, just as your consciousness entered Heritage and left your body behind, Anastasia explained. *In both scenarios, the body is still vulnerable, as is the caster. Tyrnen likely wanted to take you somewhere where he thought he wouldn't be disturbed. If someone had come upon him, Tyrnen would have been just as vulnerable as you.*

Aidan relayed the information. Edmund's mouth tightened. "To think we could have stopped him right then and there..." He shook his head. "What else have you learned, son?"

Thinking back to the short time he'd spent with the Prophet, Aidan grimly told them about Dimitri and Luria Thalamahn's attempts at resurrection, and how Luria controlled Tyrnen through Terror's Hand.

"The weapons themselves are cursed," he finished. "From within them, the Thalamahns call to those they deem worthy of providing host bodies and blood for their souls."

"And if you answer their call, your own soul is sacrificed?" Christine asked.

Aidan began to explain that one must willingly touch one of the weapons when the sibilant whisper of steel being drawn from a scabbard caught his attention. Turning toward the sound, Aidan's words died in his throat. Daniel stood at the foot of his bed, the enchanted scabbard for Serpent's Fang at his waist. The sword was in his hands. Daniel stood staring at it, utterly spellbound.

Growing aware of their stares, Daniel blinked and looked up. "An utterly dark blade seems fitting for the king of all evil, I suppose." He swung the Fang, then slipped it into its sheath. Folding his arms across his chest, he looked between his friends and noticed their horrified stares. "What?"

"Are you all right?" Aidan said, shrinking back slightly.

Daniel shrugged. "Tired, but I feel better than you look. I even look better than you look, but that's always been the case." He tried to smile, but the grin faltered. "What's wrong?"

Is he...? Aidan thought.

—I sense nothing amiss, Anastasia sent back.

—He's not cursed, but there's definitely something amiss with that one, Charles muttered.

Aidan ignored his grandfather's jab. "Did you touch the sword of your own accord, Daniel?"

"Yes. I know you told me not too, but the sheath slipped off when Christine and I were leaving Sordia."

"Did you hear a voice telling you to touch it?"

"A voice?"

"Yes. In your head."

Daniel's eyebrows rose. "I believe you're the only one who hears voices in his head."

"I touched it as well," Christine said. "I volunteered to carry it for Daniel. He was still weary on the ride back. I heard no voice," she said as Aidan opened his mouth to speak, "and I feel no different than before I touched the blade."

Chewing his lip, Aidan lifted Heritage from his nightstand. He held out his other hand. "May I have it?"

—Aidan! Charles said.

Can you examine the sword for enchantments through Heritage, Grandfather?

—Anastasia can, but I would rather her not do so at the expense of my grandson's soul.

I feel no compulsion to touch it. This is of my own volition.

Daniel handed the Fang to Aidan. Rubbing sweaty fingers together, Aidan took a breath, then gripped the Serpent Fang's hilt. He tensed, expecting... exactly what, he was not sure. But nothing happened. He drew in light and fed it to the sword. The Eye of Heritage flashed, faded.

— This cannot be the true Serpent's Fang. It seems Tyrnen has tricked us.

Aidan cursed silently. *Do you think he has the genuine blade?*

—We must assume he does, and going further, that he has found a suitable host for Dimitri. Be wary, Aidan. In all probability, you now face the might of Tyrnen and the Thalamahns.

Cold fear clenched his stomach. When Christine touched his

arm out of concern, he gave her a small smile and quickly relayed to them what he had discovered. Even Daniel went ashen.

"Half-men-half-monsters, eerie old men controlled by golden rods, and the return of the worst tyrants in Crotaria's history," Daniel muttered, scrubbing a hand through his hair. "I wish I could go to sleep and have someone wake me when this is all over."

Christine's smile was tight. "If only our dreams were safe."

"What do we do, son?" Edmund asked. Aidan relayed the question to his family.

—Be vigilant, Charles said. *If Tyrnen has the Fang, then he has it. Focus on what can be changed. Your priority must be Darinia.*

Aidan nodded, and, tossing the ersatz relic aside, told his friends the rest of what he had learned during his visit to Sanctuary. After he finished explaining the spirit stone, he turned to his father. "Mother's soul is trapped within the spirit stone. If I can destroy the stone, she will be freed, along with the other souls Tyrnen has imprisoned."

The color had drained from Edmund's face. "That must be our first priority, then."

Aidan faced his father in silence. "I'm sorry, but it must be my second priority. I've got to get to Nichel and persuade her to re-forge Darinia's alliance with Torel, and bring Leaston into the fold. Alone, any of the three realms will fall to Tyrnen's forces." He reached forward and gripped Edmund's hand. "I will free her. You have my word."

Tears rolled down Edmund's cheeks. He took a breath and wiped them away. "Whatever must be done, will be done."

A knock interrupted their conversation. Christine gestured to Edmund to remain seated and crossed to the door. A purple-robed attendant entered carrying a golden crown inlaid with gems. Eight tiny spires rose from the base of the circlet. Another scurried in behind him carrying a tray topped with four crystalline goblets filled halfway with a rich, red drink. The attendants paused in front of Aidan, issuing a deep bow.

"Your Majesty's Crown," the first one said.

Aidan glanced at his father, his eyes widening.

Rising, his face tightened in pain, Edmund reverently took the crown from the cushion and placed it atop Aidan's head. "It's your time, son."

At that, everyone fell to one knee. Aidan felt his face catch fire. He had knelt before that crown his entire life, but this was the first time anyone had ever knelt to *him.*

After several moments, the servant carrying the drinks looked up at the Crown of the North, dropped his eyes hastily, and held the tray toward Aidan. Edmund took it and dismissed the servants, who bobbed their heads and avoided looking Aidan in the eyes on their way out. As the door clicked shut behind them, Edmund passed around the drinks.

"To my son," Edmund said, his face aglow with pride, and... was that *amusement?* "Long live the Crown of the North."

"Long live the Crown of the North," Daniel and Christine echoed. Edmund and Daniel tossed their drinks back. Aidan, still stunned, took a sip, then swallowed the berry-tasting liquid in two gulps.

"Leastonian red," he said to Christine as he wiped his lips. She smiled at him, and he noticed she had left her drink untouched. Just then, Daniel spoke up.

"If His Majesty permits, his loyal servant has a suggestion."

"Sure," Aidan mumbled, his face burning from the drink more than shock and embarrassment at his father—the General of the Ward!—kneeling before him.

The corners of Daniel's mouth twitched. "You might not look as silly if you wear clothes while that thing sits on your head."

Aidan made a strangled sound. He looked to his father. Edmund wore a wide grin. Aidan's eyes drifted to Christine. Not surprisingly, she did not blush at all. Summoning what little dignity he could muster, Aidan set the crown and his empty goblet on the bed beside him.

"If you'll excuse me," he said evenly, "I'm going to get dressed."

"I'll help," Christine offered.

Daniel got up from the bed, nudging Aidan with his elbow as he rose. Edmund did not rise

"Word of what happened during your trial has spread, as has the truth behind our war against Darinia," his father said. "Torel knows you are the sword-bearer, Aidan, and its king. Before we depart, your people must hear from you."

Aidan's stomach churned. "I'll address them," he said faintly.

Edmund nodded and stood, brushing aside all three of them when they moved to help. "Away, away. I can do this myself." He took to his feet and worked the crutches under his arms. "Would you two mind if I had a word alone with my son?"

Aidan tore his gaze away from Christine. "I'll see you in a bit."

"All right," she said, giving his hand a squeeze. Her fingers left his reluctantly.

Edmund waited until the door had closed behind them then faced Aidan.

"She seems like a lovely girl, son, but—"

"I know what you're going to say. She's Sallnerian. Well, I don't care. I—"

"Is she?" Edmund said, feigning surprise. "I hadn't noticed." His face grew serious. "That doesn't concern me. She saved my son's life; that's all I need to know about her. What does concern me is a prior obligation that seems to have slipped your mind."

Aidan stared blankly.

"Nichel, son. You are still promised to her."

Aidan's face had been twisting in dawning horror from the moment his father had said the wolf daughter's name. "Dawn's light, I... I forgot."

Edmund chuckled. "As I suspected."

Aidan flopped back against his pillows. The arrangement between the Crown of the North and the war chief had been made moments after Nichel was born. Aidan had had no part in it. Surely Nichel wouldn't want to keep to the agreement after all that had happened. And...

"I think I love her, Father," he said softly.

Edmund sighed and eased himself down onto the bed. He was silent for several moments.

"The agreement might not even be valid," he said at last. "This war has changed everything. My advice, if you want it—"

Aidan sat up. "I do."

"—is to put this situation out of your mind for now. You must repair the alliance between Torel and Darinia." Edmund smiled. "After all, a man's got to be alive to marry."

Aidan nodded, feeling a little better. Edmund patted his leg and stood.

"Meet us out in the hall. *After* you get dressed, please. Let's not get your people *too* excited."

Chapter 40

Different Directions

AIDAN BUTTONED HIS SLEEVES as the party of four strode toward the western courtyard. His left hand moved to his waist to clutch at the hilt of Heritage, the gesture a perfect mimic of his father's, whose hand gripped Valor's hilt. Christine slipped an arm through his as they walked. Daniel led the way, clearing a path as they hurried toward the southern courtyard. A sound like muted thunder reached his ears.

Aidan tried to let his mind wander. How things had changed since his birthday. He had grown, and despite fearing that growth and the duty it entailed since he was old enough to comprehend it, he could not fathom returning to the carefree days of his boyhood.

They finally reached the antechamber. Swallowing hard, he stepped forward, then looked back. Daniel and Edmund smiled; Christine offered a playful wink. After another deep breath, he nodded to the Wardsmen to pull open the large front doors.

The sudden roar of the assemblage almost knocked him back. A sea of cheering faces stared at him, their eyes wide with awe and excitement—and hope. He mounted a small set of stairs that led to the wide dais where he'd stood days before—now devoid, he was pleased to note, of chopping blocks and harbingers. Moving to its center, Aidan looked out over his people. They filled the courtyard to surfeit and flowed down the mountain pass.

He raised his hands for silence, a wish granted after several minutes. When he next spoke, he drew in light and amplified his voice to reach the far corners of the courtyard.

"I stand before you today a different man from the Aidan Gairden many of you saw two months ago. It took the death of my mother, as well as a war instigated by a false friend, to mold me into the man you see standing here today."

He paused. "Our war against Darinia is over."

He waited for the renewed cheering to fade, though it took considerably longer. "The war was an act of deception. Together, we cast out the deceivers. But only for now. I will depart in an effort to repair our bond with Darinia." He roamed his eyes across the crowd. "Our time is short. The main force of our army has already been sent to the borders at Sharem. They are not aware of our victory here over the traitorous Eternal Flame, and if I do not act quickly, the bloodshed will continue. Tyrnen has fled, but he has not been defeated. Many of you were present at what was almost my execution, where the true nature of Tyrnen and his followers was revealed. He is more than a traitor and a murderer." Aidan had to pause to wet his lips. "Aiding him are the souls of Dimitri and Luria Thalamahn."

The whispers became cries of fright, but Aidan raised his hands, asking for quiet so that he could continue. "Our enemies are as ancient as the Thalamahns: vagrants, rotting corpses disguised as men and women, walk Crotaria under Tyrnen's control. The coming months will bring more horrors. But we will be strong. We *must* be strong. The true war is just beginning, and many adversities lie ahead. But we have survived hardship before, and we will persevere."

The eruption of cheers was louder than any that had come before. He let them bask in their own fervor, their determination. They would need both to survive the times that swiftly approached. He was about to duck back into Sunfall when the deafening roar coalesced into words.

"Aidan! The Guardian!" came from one pocket of the crowd. From another: "Crown of the North!" More and more cheers rose up, each draping him with a new title. One that caught on quickly was "Corpse-slayer." A chill swept through him. As a boy, Aidan had envied his father's designation of Valorous. He had not spent nearly as much time thinking over what his father had done to earn the title.

Re-entering Sunfall, he saw Edmund and Daniel whispering intently in one corner.

"What is it?" Aidan asked as he joined them.

Edmund carefully appraised his son. "Vagrants."

Aidan tensed. "Where?"

"Stragglers have been caught and killed over the last few days," Daniel said. "Two nights ago, one was spotted near Calewind's southern gate. They're out in the open, Aidan—no disguises. Their faces..." He fell silent.

Aidan nodded. Tyrnen must feel the need for stealth and disguises had passed. "What happened when you spotted the vagrant?"

"I killed it," Edmund said. "But the next day, two more came.

The position was fortified, of course, but... Aidan, they came during the night and caught one of the Wardsmen unaware. The man must have fallen asleep, or was lured away from the others. We're not sure. The body was dragged away and the next day, two more vagrants came back. The Wardsman was with them. Was *one* of them."

"We destroyed them, then ordered the bodies to be burned," Daniel picked up. "I followed it south for about four leagues. Aidan, it joined a massing of thousands. They were forging weapons and they faced Calewind."

"So you believe they're readying an attack?"

Daniel nodded. "Your father and I expect them within a fortnight." He hesitated, glancing at Edmund. "We've quarantined the city. No one comes or goes without your father's permission. And yours, of course."

Aidan took a deep breath. "A good move. We can't have vagrants walking the streets. Even so, with thousands of them outside... How many Wardsmen stayed behind from the march to Darinia?"

"Approximately fifteen hundred," Daniel replied.

Aidan's eyes went hard. "I need to see Nichel. She must hear about what's happened from me. Stay behind and help fortify Calewind. Organize evacuations of all neighboring villages and cities and bring their people here. Anyone who is able will need to be ready to fight."

"I will stay behind to fortify the city," Edmund said, already glancing around as if making mental sketches of where and how Sunfall could be reinforced.

"Actually, I need you elsewhere," Aidan said. "We do not know where Leaston stands in all this, or if they even know about Tyrnen's threat. They will need to hear from one of us, and I need to get to Darinia."

"I'll go, son," Edmund said. He hesitated. "But Brendon marched with Torel's Ward. With the Crown of the North, the general, and the colonel absent from Sunfall..."

"I will speak to the lieutenants," Aidan said. "The chain of command will take over. Just get to Ironsail as quickly as you can. The merchants' guild must stand with Torel and Darinia." He turned to Daniel. "Can you get me a key into Darinia?"

His friend nodded slowly, his tongue darting over his lips. "I know a place."

"Good. I'll be in Tyrnen's tower. There are some things I need to gather, there. Please bring me the key as soon as you retrieve it.

I will return home as quickly as I can after I speak with Nichel. After I leave, relay my orders to the lieutenants." He held his friend's gaze. "You understand the horror we face. You've seen it. Please help here where you can."

Daniel straightened. "Calewind will be ready." After saluting to Edmund and bowing to Aidan, he dashed off toward the southern courtyard.

Aidan turned back to his father. Edmund was watching him with an odd smile. Suddenly, Aidan felt his cheeks warm. "I'm sorry," he mumbled. "I didn't mean to order you around."

Edmund laid a hand on his son's shoulder. "Don't apologize. You took charge, and made decisions that I would have made."

Aidan's eyes widened. "Truly?"

"Truly." Edmund's grip tightened. "I'm proud of you, son. You will make a fine king."

Aidan nodded. "I'll see you soon, Father. "

Edmund smiled and began to walk away.

"Father?"

Edmund turned back.

"You will see Mother again. I promise."

Edmund stiffened. His eyes grew moist. After a few moments, he turned and walked away.

Footsteps from behind took Aidan's attention from his father's retreating form. The men and women of Torel's Dawn seemed to glide down the hallway, their emerald-colored robes covering their boots. Christine stepped out from behind them and came beside Aidan.

"I've made some new friends," she said.

A chiseled man with a dark goatee inclined his head. "Your Majesty," he said.

Aidan returned the gesture. "Well met, Cinder Coren Landswill."

Coren straightened. "You are aware that it is not the custom of the Touched to swear fealty to any crown." He paused. "Yet in this matter, the Dawn feels there is no alternative. We have come to pledge our allegiance to you, Crown of the North. We did not know of the Eternal Flame's... We are yours, Your Majesty. We will help you in the coming struggle."

"I welcome your allegiance. Thank you."

A tall woman with curly red hair stepped forward. "We will journey with Christine Lorden to the Lion's Den guildhall," she stated.

Aidan looked at Christine inquisitively.

"We go to convince the First that the Touched must align with you," she explained. She gestured to the other woman. "Cinder Keelian Faltan feels that Torel's Dawn alone will not be enough, so—"

"Ernest Lorden must know of what the Eternal has done," Keelian interrupted. "Once he hears of Tyrnen's crimes, he will most assuredly grant you the use of Crotaria's Touched in the coming struggle."

Aidan's mouth fell open. "Of course," he said, turning to Christine. "Your father is the First."

"Yes," she said.

"But that means that, now that Tyrnen has been stripped of his title..." He turned to Torel's Dawn. "He has been stripped of the title of Eternal Flame, I presume?"

Keelian nodded. "He has, whether he knows it or not."

"Will Ernest Lorden ascend to Eternal Flame, then?"

Christine's eyebrows rose. She looked questioningly at Keelian.

"It's likely," Keelian said.

Aidan turned back to Christine. "I can't believe I didn't realize this until just now."

"As I recall, you were busy sitting alone in a tavern talking to your sword when we first met."

Aidan ignored that. "The plan is a good one," he said to the waiting Cinders, "and will benefit Crotaria greatly. Will you leave now?"

"Yes," Keelian answered. "We must make haste. It is doubtful that word of all that has happened has reached the First's ears. He must be informed."

"We will return here with the Cinders once the First has granted permission for the Mages to aid Torel and Darinia," Coren said. "If that is your wish, Crown of the North."

Aidan nodded. "Thank you, all." He turned to Christine after the Dawn had shuffled off to the side. They leaned forward, whispering among themselves, but he paid them no heed.

"Thank you for doing this," he said. "I never would have even thought of it."

She laughed softly. "You've got a lot on your mind, Aidan Gairden." She cocked her head. "I wonder if there is anything I can do for His Majesty to take His Majesty's mind away from all these serious matters."

He grinned. "There certainly is. But unfortunately, that will have to wait."

Christine gave a mock pout. "Very well." Then her tone grew sober. "You'll be careful?"

"I promise. Tell your father I said hello."

She rolled her eyes. "You have no idea how delighted he'll be. You wouldn't believe the expectations I had to live up to because of the 'phenomenal abilities' of Torel's crown prince."

They laughed softly and fell silent. Aidan tried to look away but found he couldn't. Her eyes were so bright. He hesitated a moment longer before drawing her into his arms. Christine was ready for him. She wrapped her arms around his neck and stepped into his kiss. Vaguely, Aidan was aware of a servant rounding the corner, squeaking in surprise and embarrassment, and scuttling back the way he had come.

Slowly, lingeringly, Aidan pulled his lips from hers. She rested her head on his chest.

"When this is over," he began.

"The sooner, the better," she said. She straightened and cupped his hands in hers. "Come back to me, Aidan."

He bent down to kiss her hair and broke away, turning and moving quickly down a far corridor, his eyes locked ahead so he could not look back.

Continued in
Point of Fate: Book Two of the Gairden Chronicles

Coming in 2016

Glossary

A

Alston, Cynthia:. Wife of Romen of the Wolf and mother to Nichel of the Wolf.

Alston, Nichel: Daughter of Romen of the Wolf and Cynthia Alston. Before birth, she was promised to Aidan Gairden, next in line to become Crown of the North.

Apprentice: Third rank of a trained and educated Touched. Apprentices wear an orange band.

Architect: A Touched who applies his or her magical abilities to architecture.

Avivian River: River that runs north to east through Crotaria.

B

Band: See "Cinder band."

C

Calderon, Edmund: General of Torel. Father of Aidan Gairden and wife of Annalyn Gairden.

Calewind: Capital city of Torel and the site of Sunfall, home to the Gairden family.

'cin: See "*Ordine'cin*".

Clan Chief: The leader of a Darinian clan.

Cinder: Fifth and final rank attained by a Touched over the course of their formal education.

Cinder Band: Golden band with an embedded amethyst signifying the rank of Cinder. Worn on right forefinger.

Clan: A tribe of Darinians united under the leadership of a clan chief.

Creed: A professional pursuit or occupation selected by a Touched following his or her graduation.

Crotaria: Main continent divided into four realms: Torel in the north, Darinia in the west, Sallner in the south, and Leaston in the east.

D

Darinia: Western realm of Crotaria made up of hot, dusty deserts. Home to the clans of Darinia.

Darinia's Fist: The combined warriors of all Darinian clans, united under the leadership of the war chief.

Dark Magic: Rooted in death and practiced by those who

worship Kahltan, the Lord of Midnight. Dark magic is forbidden and punishable by death.
Disciple (of Dawn): A Touched devoted to serving the Lady and spreading her word.

E

East Road: The main road between Ironsail, Leaston's capital city, and Sharem.
Eternal Flame: Leader of all Touched on Crotaria. The Eternal Flame swears no fealty to any ruler or realm, but is expected to act according to the laws of the realms.
Eye (of Heritage): A magical ruby embedded within the hilt of Heritage. Through the Eye, Gairden ancestors can guide their descendants and pass along knowledge.

F

Fever, the: Kindling saps the strength of the Touched as they cast spells. As they grow weaker, tiredness sets in, recognizable by the onset of a fever that worsens until they rest.
First, the: Second in command of the Touched after the Eternal Flame of Crotaria.

G

Gairden, Aidan: Son of Annalyn Gairden and Edmund Calderon. Prince of Torel and next in line to become Crown of the North.
Gairden, Ambrose: Patriarch of the Gairden line. Husband of Anastasia Thalamahn Gairden. *Ordine'kel* comes from Ambrose's exemplary skill in combat.
Gairden, Anastasia Thalamahn: Matriarch of the Gairden family and daughter of Dimitri Thalamahn and Luria Thalamahn. *Ordine'cin* comes from Anastasia's potent magical abilities.
Gairden, Charles: Father of Annalyn Gairden and grandfather of Aidan Gairden.
Gairden, Annalyn: Crown of the North, wife to Edmund Calderon, and mother to Aidan Gairden.
Goddess of Light: See "Lady of Dawn".
Gotik: A small village in Torel, a few miles south of Calewind.
Greagor, Brendon: Colonel of Torel's Ward.

H

Hands of Torel: Nobles hand-picked by the Gairdens to govern cities, towns, and villages in the name of the Crown of the North.
Healer: A Touched specializing in the art of healing.
Heritage: Magical sword passed down from generation to generation in the Gairden family.

Hillstreem, Jonathan: Advisor to Romen of the Wolf and a Touched.

I

Ihlkin Mountains: Mountain range that borders Crotaria.
Inventor: A Touched who specializes in researching and executing breakthroughs in magic.
Ironsail: The capital of Leaston and the largest port city in all of Crotaria.

J

Janleah: Janleah of the Eagle, clan chief of the Eagle clan and the first war chief of Darinia.
Janleah Keep: The largest city in the west named in honor of Janleah of the Eagle, the first war chief of Darinia.

K

Kahltan: Known as the Lord of Midnight by Torelians and Leastonians.
'kel: See "*Ordine'kel*".
Kietel, Lotren: General of Torel's Ward killed by invading barbarians.
Kindle/Kindling: The process by which a Touched casts magical spells granted to them by the will of the Lady of Light.

L

Lady of Dawn: Goddess of Light. Also referred to as the Lady. Individuals "Touched" by the Lady can wield magic by praying to her.
Lamp: An object capable of storing light that a Touched can use to kindle at any time, much like a water skin from which one can drink when one needs water.
Language (of Light), The: An ancient, universal language used in spell casting. The Touched draw in light and release it as a spell by praying in the Language of Light.
Learner: First rank of a trained and educated Touched. All learners wear a dark blue band.
Leaston: Eastern realm of Crotaria ruled by the merchants' guild.
Light Magic: Magic drawn from a source of natural or manmade light and heat.
Lion's Den, The: The most prestigious magical university in all Crotaria, located in Sharem.
Lord of Midnight: See "Kahltan."
Lorden, Christine: A powerful Touched at only 17 years of age. Sibling of Garrett Lorden and daughter of Ernest Lorden. Half-Torelian, half-Sallnerian.
Lorden, Garrett: Sibling of Christine Lorden and son of Ernest Lorden. Unlike his twin sister, Christine, Garrett exhibits Torelian features.

Also unlike his twin sister, he is not a Touched.

Lorden, Ernest: First of Crotaria. Father to Garrett and Christine Lorden, and a Torelian.

M

Merchants' Guild: A ruling council made up of men and women who govern Leaston.

Meshia: a large, horned creature that roams the deserts in the west. A favorite meal among Darinians, especially cooked over an open flame.

N

North Road: A main road running up from Sharem into Calewind, the capital of Torel.

O

Ordine: "Guardian" in the language of the Darinians. A gift bestowed on the Gairden bloodline by the Lady of Dawn. *Ordine* manifests itself in every Gairden in one of two ways: *Ordine'kel,* or *Ordine'cin.*

Ordine'cin: "Guardian Light" in the language of the Darinians. Bestows a Gairden with the gift of magic. A Gairden gifted with *Ordine'cin* is stronger by far than the strongest Touched outside of the Gairden bloodline.

Ordine'kel: "Guardian Blade" in the language of the Darinians. Bestows a Gairden with Ambrose Gairden's skill in combat.

P

Philosopher: A Touched who spends his or her days studying and pondering magic, Crotaria, and the mysteries of the world beyond the home continent.

Plains of Dust: A desert in Darinia that stretches on for hundreds of miles.

Q

Queen of Terror: See "Thalamahn, Luria".

R

Rite of Heritage: Ceremony that culminates in the official anointment of a Gairden king or queen.

Romen of the Wolf: War Chief of Darinia. Husband of Cynthia Alston and father to Nichel of the Wolf.

S

Sallner: Southern kingdom of Crotaria.

Sanctuary: A resting place for Gairden souls located within the Eye of Heritage.

Serpent King, The: See "Thalamahn, Dimitri".

Serpent's War, The: A devastating war waged by King Dimitri Thalamahn and Queen Luria Thalamahn of Sallner.

Sharem: A trade city located at the heart of Crotaria where all four realms meet.

Shift: Magical method of transportation dependent on the Lady's light.
Shirey, Daniel: Wardsman. Best friend of Aidan Gairden and a Leastonian.
Snake: a racial slur that refers to Sallnerians. They have slanted eyes, but the slur also references their corruption under the reign of Dimitri Thalamahn, the Serpent King.
Soldier: A Touched devoted to defending Crotaria in times of war.
South Road: A main road running down from Sharem to the Territory Bridge, which leads into Sallner.
Sunfall: The ancestral home of the Gairdens, rulers of Crotaria's eastern kingdom of Torel.
Sword Chamber: A magical chamber where Heritage rests when not in use. Only Gairdens may access the chamber.
Symorne, Tyrnen: Eternal Flame of Crotaria. Mentor to Aidan Gairden. Traveled to Torel shortly after Aidan Gairden's birth in order to petition Queen Annalyn Gairden for permission to assist in the mentorship of her magically gifted son.

T

Tarion: The second largest city in Torel.
Territory Bridge: A strip of land leading into the main body of Sallner, the dead realm of Crotaria. What remains of Sallner's population lives on the bridge in communities closely guarded by Wardsmen from Torel's Ward.
Thalamahn, Dimitri: The Serpent King. Co-ruler of southern kingdom of Sallner and a confessed Disciple of Kahltan.
Thalamahn, Luria: Queen of Terror. Co-ruler of Sallner before she was executed at the end of the Serpent's War and a confessed Disciple of Kahltan.
Tied: The process of severing a Touched's connection to their magic. A tie can only be performed and removed by a Touched.
Torel: Northern kingdom of Crotaria ruled by the Gairden bloodline.
Torel's Dawn: Elite group of Cinders under the direct command of the Eternal Flame. Torel's Dawn serves and protects Torel and the Gairden family, though they still answer to the Eternal Flame, like all Touched.
Torel's Ward: Army of the kingdom of Torel.
Touched: One blessed with the gift of magic.

V

Valor: Sword wielded by Edmund Calderon.

W

War Chief: A Darinian clan chief who holds the power to lead all Darinian clans during times of war.

Ward, The: See "Torel's Ward".

Wardsman / Wardsmen: A fighting man in Torel's Ward.

West Road: A main road running across Darinia and into Sharem.

Wielder: Second rank of a trained and educated Touched. All Wielders wear a purple band.

Wildlander: A pejorative term for Darinian.

Z

Zellibar: Darinian city renowned for the work of its metal smiths.

Author's Notes

HERITAGE IS MY FIRST novel. Not just the first novel I published. The first novel I wrote. Which is not to say I sold the first draft still hot off the presses of my college computer lab's printer and became an overnight success. Oh, no. That first draft was good for little more than firewood (*kindling*, if you get the joke), and the flames might very well have spat it out in disgust. Most writers chalk up their first novel as a harsh learning experience and banish it to the proverbial trunk before cracking their knuckles and starting something new. Something better (and believe me, after the first draft of a first novel, the only way to go is up).

Heritage was better than that. I would not banish Aidan, his magical sword, and eight generations of his family members to the pits of literary hell where first novels go to suffer eternal agony. Every story has a genesis. Fix yourself a hot drink, curl up, and get comfortable. I'd like to share the story behind the story with you.

The idea for Heritage—not the book, but the sword—came to me in early 2004. When I wasn't attending college courses or ringing a cash register at my local Waldenbooks, I read a lot of fantasy novels. A steady diet of Robert Jordan, David Eddings, Sara Douglass, R. A. Salvatore, and Terry Goodkind gave rise to an idea to which I'm sure those writers and others can relate: *I should write my own fantasy novel!* But what would it be about? Well, it would be about a sword. Of course it would.

I loved swords, and the fantasy authors I read certainly favored them. Rand al'Thor of *Wheel of Time* fame wielded *Callandor*, a crystal sword through which he could channel great quantities of magic. In *The Sword of Truth*, Richard Rahl used (wait for it) the Sword of Truth to arbitrate matters and root out fact from falsehood. Drizzt Do'Urden from R. A. Salvatore's *The Legend of Drizzt* brandished his magical scimitars, Twinkle and Icingdeath, and cut a path through prejudice and injustice across the Forgotten Realms.

My close examination of the Fantasy Novel Recipe picked out two key ingredients: a protagonist with a catchy name, and a sword. Aidan Gairden didn't come along until a year or so later, but I hit on the defining element for his sword right away: family.

I lost my father in 2002, when I was 19. I knew my dad as any boy knows his dad: cool guy, sense of humor, loved me, was proud of me, hooked up my video-game consoles to the TV before I was old enough to know how to set them up without electrocuting myself, and took us kids out for a night on the town every weekend we visited. My favorite memory of my dad is of Christmas morning in... I want to say 1989, but it might have been 1990. I was seven, maybe eight. That year (whichever it was), I asked for a Game Boy, and I got it. I knew I got it before I opened the package. I'd spent enough hours with my nose and fingertips pressed up against the glass display case at Toys R Us to recognize the Game Boy-shaped box (which included *Tetris*!) disguised in wrapping paper on Christmas morning. But Dad didn't know I knew, and I decided to string him along a bit.

We went through the usual routine: the kids went to the tree and sorted gifts, passing them around in orderly fashion until everyone had a sizable pile by their chair or spot on the sofa. Then we dug in. The sounds of little hands shredding wrapping paper followed swiftly by squeals of glee filled the living room. I saved the Game Boy (plus *Tetris*!) for last. I held it in my lap and turned it over, as if there was anything to see besides a wrapping-paper patchwork of Santa and his reindeers, and a tag: *To: David, From: Dad and Teresa,* my step-mom. Holding it close, I peered around, feigning curiosity in what curios had been deposited down the chimney for my kid sisters and brother. *Oooh, a* Little Mermaid *doll? Nail polish? Fisher-Price toys (Daniel was only one or two that year)? How wonderful for you!*

All the while, I watched my dad out of the corner of my eye. He had taken my grandpa's recliner (a bold move) and had unwrapped the prerequisite cologne set and tie, the usual knick-knacks kids get their dads for Christmas. Now he was watching me, appearing at ease. He folded his hands. Then he leaned over the arm of the chair. He looked like... well, like a kid on Christmas morning, waiting for the alarm clock to tick over from 5:57 to 5:58, look away, doze off, look back and *oh finally THANK GOD*—wait, no, *it's still 5:58 ARE YOU KIDDING ME RIGHT NOW.*

"David," he said finally, and not a little impatiently. "You've still got one more present, there."

Oh? Do I? Why, I plumb forgot!

I peeled off the wrapping paper slowly, carefully, like one of those people crazy enough to attempt to save the paper for next year. I glanced up. Dad's eyes were popping out of his skull. I ended his torment, and mine: I shredded, I saw the purple Game Boy logo, the gold-and-white Official Nintendo Seal of Quality, and man, I flipped out. I whooped, letting out all that pent-up excitement, and paraded my prize around the living room like it was the Stanley Cup. Dad watched, laughed, and clapped, absolutely delighted that he had made my day.

Fifteen (maybe sixteen) years later, Dad was gone.

When I think of him, I see the man whose smile outshone mine on the Christmas morning I opened my Game Boy. That's how I remember him because that's how I knew him, and that's bittersweet. There's a difference between knowing your parents as a kid, and knowing them on an adult-to-adult level. Commiserating with them over taxes, long hours, bills, and relationship problems. Meeting them for lunch, and picking up the check for them for a change. Watching their eyes light up when you're old enough to know them, *really* know them, and place something more thoughtful than a stupid tie under the Christmas tree.

That wound will never close, but in 2004, it was still fresh. Leaky. Dad was gone, and I missed him terribly. *I wish I would have said all the things I never said, or said only in passing*, I found myself thinking at least 76 times a day. Let me give you an example: "Love you, too." It sounds so perfunctory during a goodnight kiss. You mean it, but it's ritualistic, just like, "How are you?" to which you reply, "Good, and you?" I wish I could have sat him down, looked him in the eye, and said, with no presents or Saturday night dinners and trips to the arcade and the bookstore acting as a motivator: "I love you."

But it was too late. Dad was gone—but he had thoughtfully germinated my fictitious sword with the idea I needed to set it apart from the likes of *Callandor* and Icingdeath. Heritage. My sword would be called Heritage. At any time, a king or queen could pick it up and talk with their parents, their grandparents—about guidance in matters of monarchy, for access to magic spells lost to time, and, more than anything else, for the opportunity to say the things they didn't think to say when their loved ones were alive.

I'm proud and grateful that I've been able to get to know my mom, my biggest supporter, as an adult over these last several years. (I won't kid myself and believe I'm her equal, because no one is or ever will be.) But one day, she'll be gone, too. Wouldn't it be nice to be able to talk to her, and to dad, and so many other loved ones, when that day comes?

I spent all of 2004 and the first nine months of 2005 fleshing out my Great American Fantasy Novel. When my legion of fans (Mom, Gramma, and later, my wife-to-be) asked what the book was about, I put on my poker face. "It's about a sword," I replied. It became an inside joke, but as the years went by, I realized my inside joke was kinda true. Heritage had a purpose, but what about Aidan Gairden, the boy who wielded it? A protagonist without a soul is like Pinocchio: he looks like a real boy, talks like a real boy, and walks like a real boy, but he's a puppet, make no mistake about it.

It wasn't until 2012, *eight years* and I don't even remember how many drafts of *Heritage* later, that I hit on the reason I wanted to tell Aidan's story. The reason I *needed* to tell his story. We've all faced peer pressure. Some of us have even stood our ground against it, and good for you! But most of us haven't. Most of us know that it's easier to keep our mouths shut and do as we're told. No questions. No thinking. Just follow. Aidan knows that, and he suffers unending consequences for it.

Whew. Okay, that's enough with the drama, don't you think? The third and final reason for the existence of *Heritage* is less sobering. There's a certain spirit—a certain magic, if you will—about a party of adventurers gathered around a campfire, sharpening their swords and preparing to catch some shuteye rolled in a sleeping bag in a ditch before rising at dawn to get back on the road toward the black tower off in the distance. Of battling fantastical creatures over sprawling, empty countryside. Of sitting in a study, the smell of old books overpowering the scent of stew roasting over open flames, and listening to wizened sorcerers talk of ages past. Of sucking in our breath when the heroes get knocked down by some ancient evil force, and cheering them on when they get up, dust themselves off, and give as good as they got. Of turning pages late into the night because fantasy worlds are so much fun to visit when the chaos of work, school, and family responsibilities press in a little too tightly.

I wrote *Heritage* because I had something I wanted to say, and because, as a writer, I let my characters do the talking for me. But I also wrote it because I wanted to pay tribute to the magical, mysterious, and wonderful stories I grew up reading.

In January 2013, with snow piling up outside and my apartment good and toasty, I doped Aidan with anesthetic, picked up my scalpel, and commenced surgery on what would be the second-to-final draft of *Heritage*. Two months later, Aidan came to, groggy, but so much stronger than before he'd gone under the knife. *Heritage* was done-ish. I sent it off to Margaret Curelas at Tyche Books. Four months later, I uncrossed my fingers long enough to open the email I'd been waiting for: Margaret read *Heritage*, and she loved it.

We had a little more work to do, but not much, to my delight and hers. Margaret is a fantastic editor because she helps her writers smooth out edges rather than ask them to build an entirely new piece. She helped me hit on the right word when I was almost-but-not-quite near it, pointed out inconsistencies, and offered suggestions designed to help me tell the story I'd set out to tell.

Three rounds of edits later, completed over roughly two months, and *Heritage* is done. Not done-ish. Done. Finished. THE END. And that's weird. It's weird to think—to *know*—that Aidan will never again pop into my head for a late-night chat about *Heritage*. I stick to a writing schedule, as some writers do, because it's the only way I know to stay disciplined. There were nights when a flurry of ideas would batter at my brain. I'd type furiously in the book's journal and go to bed, as excited to wake up refreshed and ready to write with Aidan as that nine- or ten-year-old boy was to open his Game Boy so many Christmases ago. That's something Aidan and I have done for 10 years, and I'm proud to say that each draft of his first adventure turned out so much better than the one before it.

Yes, *our* book. Aidan is real to me. That's how it works. Writers aren't drivers. When the writing is going well, *really* well, we're in the passenger seat, giving out directions when needed, but also knowing when to switch off the GPS and let our crazy drivers call the shots. Aidan took me places I never imagined back in 2004. I enjoyed the journey, and I hope you do (or did), too.

And we're not done yet. *Heritage* is only the first leg of our journey together—you, me, Margaret, and Aidan "It's about a sword" Gairden. I hope you'll stick with us. We've got more to say, and more fun to have together.

David L. Craddock - 12 January 2014, Canton, OH

Author Biography

DAVID L. CRADDOCK LIVES with his wife in Canton, Ohio. He writes short and long fiction, nonfiction, and grocery lists. His nonfiction publication, *Stay Awhile and Listen: Book I*, chronicles the history of *World of WarCraft* developer Blizzard Entertainment and became a bestseller on Amazon.com less than 24 hours after its release. Tag along with him online at davidlcraddock.com, facebook.com/davidlcraddock, and @davidlcraddock on Twitter.